The Spheres of Heaven

METAMORPHOSIS

D.C. Johnson

authorHOUSE

AuthorHouse™ UK
1663 Liberty Drive
Bloomington, IN 47403 USA
www.authorhouse.co.uk
Phone: 0800.197.4150

Published by AuthorHouse 07/25/2015

ISBN: 978-1-5049-8759-2 (sc)
ISBN: 978-1-5049-8760-8 (e)

Print information available on the last page.

Any people depicted in stock imagery provided by Thinkstock are models, and such images are being used for illustrative purposes only.
Certain stock imagery © Thinkstock.

This book is printed on acid-free paper.

Because of the dynamic nature of the Internet, any web addresses or links contained in this book may have changed since publication and may no longer be valid. The views expressed in this work are solely those of the author and do not necessarily reflect the views of the publisher, and the publisher hereby disclaims any responsibility for them.

Scripture quotations are taken from the Holy Bible, New International Version®. NIV®. Copyright © 1973, 1978, 1984 by International Bible Society. Used by permission of Zondervan. All rights reserved. [Biblica]

Chapter 1

MARTA 1942

Marta Salomonovich and her youngest son fled Germany and landed on the Suffolk coast during the turbulent spring of 1942. It was the day of her son's fourteenth birthday. She and Joel were the only members of their family to survive the Nazis' terror.

Marta's husband, Simon, and elder sons Reuben and Benjamin, were marched from the University of Hamburg and put against a wall. Simon was an intellectual; his sons were intellectuals; they were Jews; the fatuous edict was Himmler's; the decision had been taken by the Third Reich at Wannsee, Berlin. They were shot.

A crowd gathered late that freezing March afternoon; a hoard reminiscent of those accompanying the tumbrels of aristocrats brought through the boulevards of Paris for their gruesome appointments with Madame Guillotine during 'the terror' some one hundred and fifty years earlier. But this was not an animated convocation of passionate enthusiasts crying Liberté, égalité, fraternité at the Place de la Concorde. This miserable, melancholic band had gathered out of morbid curiosity; scenting the blood of scapegoats among the detritus of their bombed city. Someone had to pay for their grinding poverty, their loss of dignity and the hopelessness that had festered since the tragedy of Versailles. They viewed the macabre slaughter with dispassionate fascination. Many had children by their sides, as previously had the French. This was a mob, uneasy with its conscience, reinforcing a self-delusional solution to its intractable problems.

Joel still flinched at the memory, burning with a hatred that had festered and burned for sixty years. His mother had held him back, preventing him from running to his father. He had watched the soldiers take aim and fire. The salvo rang out and the man and his sons dropped to the ground, shirts drenched crimson; innocent leaves falling from the verdant trees of summer and of spring. Joel turned into his mother's arms hiding his head in her bosom.

Joel's sister, Rebecca, an auburn beauty of eighteen years, joined them in that embrace. Almost immediately the depraved officer, who had ordered the executions of the innocents, screamed a manic order and two soldiers ran towards the huddled figures. They wrenched Rebecca from her kin and began to drag her away. Rebecca screamed as she struggled to reach her loved ones. Marta ran towards her daughter, put her arms around her waist and tugged in a desperate attempt to release her. Her reward was a downward blow from the butt of a Maschinenenkarebinen rifle, a kick to the side of her face from a huge leather boot and a snigger of psychotic insanity that seeped from the sneer of SS Obersturmführer Reinhardt Bühler's salivating mouth.

The violence had whetted the tyrant's appetite and he scrutinised the crowd for further victims, eager to gratify his lust for destruction and yearning to wield yet more gratuitous brutality under the aegis of law and order.

Bühler caught Joel's eyes resting upon him. The piercing, ice blue, fanatical stare of the officer was met with the white heat of brooding hatred and contempt of the boy. A paroxysm of pleasure gave rise to a malign smile. An erotic charge shuddered through Bühler's body and Joel noted the pleasure, pain and fevered anguish of the depraved sadist.

'Ah, the puppy stares', shrieked Bühler, enthralled by his own chimerical gravitas. 'Is this defiance? Good.' Shaking violently he lurched forward and grabbed Joel's hair, holding his head as if it had been plucked fresh from Madam Guillotine's decapitation basket. He paused, looked at the crowd in magisterial triumph, and with vicious intent threw Joel's head against the remains of a stone gable end. He rebounded into the adjacent gutter. 'That is where you and your kind belong, swine', ranted Bühler with savage, fevered fanaticism. He reached down taking Joel's face between his vice like leather-gloved hands as his tirade continued. 'I am polluting my hands by touching you. Look at me. Look me in the face. Remember this face. Let this face haunt you. Let it haunt you for the remainder of your miserable existence.'

Joel did exactly as he was asked. He remembered Bühler's face. He remembered it for the remainder of his existence.

The despot grabbed Joel by the hair pulling him to his feet. Joel continued to stare at his nemesis, fearless and uncomplaining. Mercilessly Bühler began to slap him with a sickening rhythm; his right arm swinging from side to side, time and time again like a pendulum before releasing his grip on the mutilated child. With considerable measure he pulled back his right arm, smiled a sickening smile, and delivered a fearsome punch to the boy's midriff causing him first to vomit and then to splutter for air. Repulsed he pushed Joel away violently, sending him reeling backwards towards his murdered kinsfolk. Joel struggled to his knees and crawled towards his mother, blood pouring from the side of his mouth. Marta lifted Joel's face from the charred ground, and then collapsed.

The bloodletting was over. Joel kneeled over his mother's unconscious body and stared in mute disbelief at the corpses of his father and brothers. Not a tear fell to gratify The Third Reich.

It was several seconds before Marta regained consciousness. Joel had remained kneeling by her side. She groaned, blood oozing from a purple abrasion at her temple.

'Rebecca. Joel' she screamed. 'Thank God Joel', she sobbed, recognising her son's face as the mist cleared from her eyes. She placed a hand on either side of her surviving son's head and begged of him. 'Where is Rebecca? Where is Rebecca?' She wailed further, incoherently and inconsolably, as she and her son knelt holding onto one another in the grisly amphitheatre of their horrific nightmare.

Joel stared at her unspeaking. The appalling magnitude of events had taken away his voice or his will to use it. He stood in pain, conscious of no other sensation. Marta struggled from her knees and reached for Joel to help her gain her feet. She staggered as she rose.

'Oh Joel, Joel, Joel', she cried, as she took him in her arms. For the remainder of his life Joel would feel that same ethereal embrace: At his mother's funeral, his son's birth, ever in times of trial and always when others tolerated discrimination and injustice. Seminal!

The corpses of the men folk lay like unstrung marionettes amongst the rubble and smouldering embers of the half demolished buildings as Marta and Joel turned towards Bühler as he barked his marching orders.

An old man remonstrated with the soldiers as they left. They heard another psychotic laugh followed by a barked order, then a further salvo of gunfire. The man's chest burst open and he too dropped to the floor amongst the endless detritus.

The pitiless officer marched his men a little distance before turning on his heels, his face contorted with rage. Clearly, his voracious appetite had yet to be satiated. Further victims would be required before the day was out.

Punctuating each syllable with a sinister slap of a leather glove into the palm of his left hand and with a frenzied scream the madman raged. 'This will serve as an example to you all.' Joel's eyes landed on Bühler's again.

The victims had been clearly identified. The example was less transparent. What had his family done? What were the fabricated absurdities masquerading as facts that had led to their slaughter? Why were they shot? What was the example? It was of no matter to a despotic regime! Order had been vehemently and violently maintained. The ends would justify the means. Joel considered that this was to be a reciprocal arrangement and one that he would seek the opportunity to deploy for the remainder of his life.

The SS officer had commanded a solitary soldier to remain as a sentinel to guard the execution site. The implausibly young and unimpressive young man stood to attention until the murderous squad had marched from the square. The sound of goose-stepping leather boots marching on the damp cobbled street receded and the crowd dispersed as mysteriously as it had assembled; inactive but silent participants in the macabre spectacle.

The sentinel stood by the disposed of quarry, all duty and purpose, his rifle slung low across his body. He was no more than a boy.

Bent double in pain and with a numbing horror gnawing at her soul, Marta shuffled to each of the unseeing corpses in turn, ignoring the soldier, who now approached her waving a pistol in her face. He shouted nervous obscenities, as if to echo his leader's example, but his words were uncertain and rang with the hollow lack of conviction as he sought to assert his authority.

There, amid the debris, Marta and Joel took leave of their loved ones. Marta kissed each one on the lips in turn and closed their unseeing eyes. She muttered an indecipherable litany. She offered a prayer; perhaps a last farewell? Most certainly she had made a solemn promise.

Marta's hitherto indomitable heart was broken and the tears poured down her cheeks running onto the hands supporting her head. Straightening she looked back one more time and shuffled Joel away. She knew that she must. She acknowledged and comprehended the cultural familiarity of an ancient refrain echoing through the millennia. Resolutely she gathered herself. 'From this moment...' she muttered, as she looked down at her youngest child. 'Come Joel. Come.'

Now all that she had was Joel and Rebecca. But what had happened to Rebecca? Where had they taken her?

During the following two weeks Marta and Joel searched the streets of Hamburg carrying a photograph of Rebecca and showing it to anyone who would do them the courtesy of looking at it. Few did. Marta begged for information that might help them to trace Rebecca's whereabouts. They were treated like lepers. Some shunned her, being too afraid to be seen talking to her. Others were openly hostile.

'Go about your business foolish woman, scorned the baker's wife. 'It is always trouble with you and your kind. Don't come here again.'

'Even now you dig deeper', chided the bank clerk, refusing her wish to withdraw money. 'Go away, and stop pestering honest folk.'

'Questions! Always the questions', said an old woman scathingly as she stopped sweeping the pavement in front of her newspaper stand. She pointed her brush at Marta and Joel menacingly. 'Go away and don't come back. You are not wanted. Don't you understand? Your daughter was a whore. She's probably plying her trade in the back streets even now. You are not wanted here.'

Joel ached for the tenderness of his father's voice and the hugs that only Rebecca could give. He missed Reuben and Benjamin and his daily wrestling bouts with them. He missed too the exciting academic lessons that his father gave him after his school had ceased to accept him as a student. Still he did not speak. The trauma had anaesthetised his brain and he continued to stare into a remote future.

As he walked the streets with his mother, further warming memories helped to insulate him from the harsh reality of his horrific trauma. He had loved to spend so many precious hours with his father in his study. His father had marvelled at the precocious boy. He had asked astute questions from an early age and Joel regularly surveyed his father's desk picking up manuscripts, essays and documents and asking what they were and what they meant. At first the answers were concise but soon, of necessity, they became more detailed and expansive as the boy posed evermore complex and perceptive questions of his father and brothers.

He recalled his father saying, 'One day you will join Reuben, Benjamin and me at the university my son.' This thrilled the boy who doted on his father's praise. 'Not only will you join us, I believe that one day you will lead us', said Reuben. 'Yes and of course then there will be no more… tickling,' said Reuben, suddenly leaping towards Joel. Joel had screamed with joy and had run around the desk only to be caught and held by Benjamin until Reuben's arrival.

Now Joel's little heart was heavy. Two weeks had passed since the appalling murders. Two weeks of grief, mourning and searching the streets of Hamburg for Rebecca. 'Perhaps she wasn't even in the city. Perhaps she wasn't in the country. Perhaps she…' The distraught mother shook herself determined not to be negative. Two long weeks and they hadn't discovered a scrap of information regarding Rebecca's whereabouts. The toll was etched in their faces.

Early one morning the Gestapo returned. They kicked down the door of the small family apartment and dragged Marta and Joel into the middle of the street placing them in line with thirty or so other frightened women and children. Not one of the children looked older than Joel. They were put into rows of five and force-marched out of the city.

The sorry troupe walked alongside the railway line that went southwest and would eventually lead to Bremen. It began to rain heavily. Twenty soldiers marched with them and this lent a growing credence to Marta's belief that they would be shot once out of sight of the citizens of Hamburg. In the light of her recent experience these murders could be considered sanitised for god's sake. There had been many rumours of such cases and little evidence to contradict them in recent weeks. The women held their children ever closer.

On the outskirts of the city a huge black locomotive let off steam as if impatient to be on the move. Twenty or so cattle wagons were coupled to it.

Joel noted the steam billowing from the huge, black cylindrical body of the engine. The cold driving rain struck its warm iron shell and poured onto the track below. Plumes of steam rose from the huge beast.

'Like a canvas of the English painter Turner', thought Joel. 'Yes, as amorphous as a Turner landscape.'

Joel, like his father and brothers, being intellectually gifted and highly knowledgeable in a number of disciplines, was able to synthesise the scene even at this distressing time. This was as inevitable as it was sagacious and discerning.

The ragged gathering was herded into an adjacent field where they joined by almost five hundred similar souls. The forward wagons were opened and still more wretches, who looked to have already travelled far, were ordered to join the Hamburg contingent. All were made to stand in rank and file and obliged to lower their heads. An officer began counting the gaunt creatures.

They stood for more than an hour in the driving rain. Some children cried and mothers did the best that they could to protect their offspring from the elements. Many were up to their ankles in mud by the time that they were ordered to board the train.

When the wagons were crammed full the soldiers pointed their rifles at the women as if to fire. This caused panic and the women recoiled leaving a small vacant space at the doorway. An additional five petrified souls, some parted from their kin, were added to the wagons and the huge wooden doors were secured with a five-foot steel bar.

Some of the women and children had vomited. Others had defecated in fear. The stench was appalling and the journey had yet to begin. They were soaking wet, had muddy feet and were frightened speechless as they attempted to breath in the dark damp confine of the cattle wagons.

Marta and Joel were fortunate enough to be loaded onto the same wagon. The line had been halted and a wagon door bolted when they were to the fore of the line. Marta felt sure that she and Joel would go together into the next wagon. She breathed a sigh of relief when they did. They boarded and walked to the rear of the wooden box and waited for the inevitable crush to come.

When the doors closed there was silence. Marta peered through the gloom and took stock of their predicament. She knew that if the journey was to be long that not all of the children would survive the journey. Many looked to have travelled far already and had the appearance of those well used to forced labour. Many were weak or ill from the trek that they had made to Hamburg. Some had running sores and clearly did not have access to medical treatment. It was unlikely that they would in the foreseeable future. Their belief in salvation had been extinguished and the premonition of death lingered among the petrified innocents, like the morning mist which pervaded the surrounding forest.

Marta noticed that the women were young. Almost all were under forty. Where were they going and why were their children being taken with them? Not all could sit; there wasn't room, so the women and older children took it in turns to stand. Amongst them silence hung heavily.

The train rattled through the flat countryside and gradually Marta's eyes became accustomed to the meagre light. There was a small window high on the damp wooden wall of the wagon and one of the taller women began to describe what she could see from it. She stood on tiptoe and gave intermittent reports.

'Water! The river runs with us here.' Then: 'A convoy of trucks moving in the opposite direction. And later: 'Soldiers on a motorcycle and side car.'

Joel considered the information. If the land was flat they must be travelling west. That was certainly the direction the train had been facing when they boarded. If he could have seen the sun he would have known for certain whether the train had changed direction, but the heavy, murky weather seemed to have set in. 'The river runs with us', the woman had said. This too indicated that they were travelling west. Joel remained silent.

After several hours the train stopped and the wagon doors were slid aside. The women and children disembarked upon the uncompromising command of the officer in charge. Marta recoiled in horror. It was none other than SS Obersturmführer Reinhardt Bühler. She shuffled Joel behind her, bowed her head and adjusted the headscarf she wore to conceal her face. Bühler made for the carriage engaged immediately behind the locomotive's tender.

It was early evening and the unfortunate wretches shielded their eyes from the setting sun as the evening gloom relented. Bereaved mothers were reluctant to leave their lifeless loved ones in the wagons but knew that the survival of their other children depended on sustenance. They left the wagons and their dead.

Several tables had been set in rows and soup was served to the queue from iron ladles into small dirty earthenware bowls. Each of the captives was given one full ladle. Water was provided too and, within fifteen minutes, the bedraggled party was made to board the train again.

Marta noticed the guards. One sat atop each wagon perched uncomfortably behind machine guns mounted on fixed tripods. 'One sits above us as we travel,' she thought. 'This is not a time to attempt an escape. Perhaps the chance will present itself later. Better not to…'

Suddenly there was the sound of several screeching women. It came from those whose children had died on the journey. They had been forced to leave the corpses behind when they had joined the ration line. On returning to the wagons they now discovered that their loved ones had been taken away. It was too much for one woman who ran away from the party. A single shot rang out and she dropped to the muddy ground. She writhed in her death throes, which was ended swiftly by a single pistol shot to the brain delivered courtesy of Obersturmführer Reinhardt Bühler's luger, the barrel of which he had placed dispassionately behind her right ear. Her suffering was over. The officer stood astride the corpse and waved the pistol angrily in the direction of the train. The gathering responded.

Again Marta felt the danger of being separated from Joel. She tarried, just a little, which brought them to the back of the line. Both boarded the last wagon. The women ushered their children to it and helped them to board. There was a little more space now.

The engine chugged along for a short time and the tall woman's reports became more frequent and animated. They had travelled alongside a canal for at least a quarter of an hour.

'Zwolle', shouted the commentator. 'Does anyone know of a place called Zwolle?'

'Are you sure', asked the woman sat next to Marta and Joel. 'But Zwolle is in the Netherlands. Why? What are we to do there? The rumour is that our kin have all been taken east before – not west.'

'We are travelling in the direction of Amsterdam', replied the commentator.

'No, we are going to the munitions factories in Utrecht. I know it,' said another.

Within an hour, at dusk, three RAF Wellington bombers spotted the train. They were returning from a failed mission and still carried some of their ordinance. It was an unexpected opportunity for them to relieve their payloads profitably before returning to Kent. Clearly the contents of the wagons were unknown to the airmen or, presumably, they would not have attacked.

An officer barked orders and the guards responded quickly swinging their MG 42 machine guns upwards unfolding their anti-aircraft sights as they did so. The planes screamed as they dived towards the train and machine gun fire. Delivering one thousand eight hundred rounds per minute, the machine guns matched the deafening scream of the planes.

The first seven wagons took direct hits as did the second and third to last. Joel and his mother were in the twentieth and last wagon but the impact of the shell blew away part of the wooden floor of their prison, killing or maiming half of the poor wretches inside. The train had been stopped. Annihilation would surely follow swiftly.

Several of the women took hold of the wooden floorboards and began to pull them aside frantically, others removed the dead blocking their way and stacked them to the far side of the wagon swinging them by their arms and legs onto a grotesque pile. 'At times of adversity the human condition is as resourceful and it is dispassionate' thought Marta. Joel took note.

Soon the aperture was wide enough for a body to drop through it. At first there was hesitation. Who would go? Then there was pandemonium as the twenty or so remaining souls rushed forward dropping through the splintered opening. Reason and sense were in short supply. Marta held Joel close to her in a corner of the wagon. There they stayed until the wagon was empty save for the pile of mutilated corpses. Instinct told her to stay.

The planes became a distant hum and were gone; their lethal alternative mission ended and their arsenals relieved. The timing of their departure was as tragic as the timing of their arrival and proved fatal for the escapees. One guard sensed movement below and turning, spotted women and children making for the embankment to the rear. The machine guns swung from the sky towards them. The unsympathetic moon lit up the fleeing figures as they swarmed the embankment and rushed towards the adjacent wheat fields.

The machine guns began to rattle again, this time accompanied by the horrific screams of women and children which pierced the evening mist. The guns harvested the fields and Marta guessed that many had perished on the wretched track and beyond. The remainder would be hunted down. Intermittently a solitary shot of a pistol was heard and Marta knew only too well what that meant.

She looked down into Joel's terrified face wondering frantically what her next move should be. The wagon had taken a huge blast and the mangled wreck would be of no further use to the soldiers. Amazingly it had remained upright and had clearly stayed on track. Once again she heard the rattle of a machine gun in the distance. Then all was quiet save for the heavy beating of her heart.

Presently she heard the sound of marching soldiers. Then machine gun fire yet again. Now the soldiers were close by. Intuitively she pulled Joel down behind the stacked corpses. Almost immediately machine gun fire ripped through the wooden sides of the wagon. Marta protected Joel by putting her body between him and the corpses as an addition barrier for the safety of her child. Both would remember the sound of the bullets pounding into the protecting dead carcasses for the remainder of their lives. The screaming nightmare lasted for twenty seconds or so. Then more marching and finally silence.

One bullet had grazed the side of Marta's neck, and another had fractured her left collarbone. A third had grazed her temple. Her blood was now just one more confluence flowing into the red river seeping between the wooden boards and onto the rails below.

She and Joel looked at one another as they heard the steam engine approach. There was much activity outside the wagon now. Was the line damaged? Were the other wagons derailed? She could only guess. Their wagon began to move. Firstly forwards, then backwards a little. They were being shunted. This continued for some minutes. The locomotive hissed. It was very close. It was moving towards them. The wagon jerked backwards as the huge engine engaged it. They moved slowly at first. Soon they were gathering pace.

The noise of the engine became more distant but they continued to rattle along the lines faster and faster. Fear tore through them once again as the wagon left the lines. A shrill scream of grinding steel pierced the night air as it ploughed a path of destruction. Reaching the embankment it catapulted one hundred and eighty degrees before landing on its roof into the lake below. The screaming and grinding stopped as a deluge entered the wagon half filling it within seconds.

Marta had not let go of Joel even as they were thrown about the wagon along with the twenty or so corpses. She panicked as the water level rose rapidly but it stopped rising as quickly as it had begun. There was a chilling calm and only the soft ebbing of the water lapping against the walls of the wagon disturbed the silence.

Marta waited. She didn't hesitate. She waited. It was a judgement; her call. The water was cold but still she resisted the urge to move.

It was impossible to know where the window or the hole in the floor was by sight such was the impenetrable darkness. The angle that the wagon had come to rest in the water didn't help either. Marta felt the freezing night air entering what had been either the window or the hole that the RAF had grievously bequeathed. She led Joel towards the breeze.

'Wait', she whispered as she moved the arm of a dead child from her face

'Take their hands and feet. First five, then four, then three. Do you see?

Marta and Joel made the cadaverous pyramid with considerable industry and resolve. Supported by Joel, Marta climbed out of the wagon. She dropped waist deep into the water and sank ankle-deep into the muddy bed. The clouds parted for a moment and the moon shone across an expanse of water.

'Joel. Come quickly.' Joel's expressionless face appeared, lit by the moonlight.

'Jump, I will catch you', whispered Marta.

She held her arms towards her son and he dropped into the water beside her. The freezing dark water swilled over his chest as they waded towards the grassy distant bank. Intermittently they stopped to listen.

They were at the edge of a long stretch of water hidden from the railway by tall reeds. The moonlight trembled on the surface of the lake as they waded in silence. 'The water is not salty', thought Marta 'nor is it deep.' Safety would be on the far bank and she made for it. The Germans had, perhaps, thought the water to be deep enough to sink the wagon. Perhaps they didn't care whether the wagon sank or not. Whatever, it appeared that they had not stayed behind to find out.

'The bastards', she swore, finding little comfort in her words.

Joel stood transfixed. He had never heard his mother swear before and he never would again. There was no recognition of the fact that she had but it registered with a harsh resonance. He continued to stare into the distance as if in a trance.

They crouched, listening again. Marta pointed to a spot on the bank near a brace of willow trees, which she thought might afford them some cover. They waded towards them, the water reddening with her blood. They rested for a few moments, listening again. She peered into the night. Nothing! It was scarcely credible. They had been left behind.

They lay on the bank, taking refuge by the reeds for a short while before making for the railway lines and heading in the opposite direction to the engine. Marta did not know where she was going or why but, instinctively, she felt it right to go in the opposite direction to that damned train. Joel's body was hardly functioning but his mind was active and he did not object to the direction that his mother had chosen. It was east.

Dripping muddy water, they walked along the side of the railway surmising that it must eventually lead to a town or village. What they hoped to find there was unclear but putting distance between the train and them seemed to be the imperative and what else was there to do?

Every fifty yards or so they stopped and listened, then moved on prepared to bound into the undergrowth if they heard the slightest sound.

Where were they? How long could Marta last without seeing a doctor or losing consciousness? If they found people, whom could they trust? Their pace slowed until Marta knew that she could go no further. She made a tourniquet from filthy strips torn from her underskirt and Joel tightened it according to her instructions. The bleeding stopped but she knew that she was weak and could not continue for much longer. She bathed the wound with water that she had wrung from her clothing and they lay down to rest on a mossy patch in a copse of silver birch, the chill night air adding to her discomfort.

Joel lay with his eyes closed. Marta fought the dreadful fatigue that threatened to swamp her; the pain in her neck was excruciating. 'Soon, very soon this must be treated', she said to herself. She grimaced as a wave of pain washed over her and she turned to the sleeping Joel.

'Joel', she whispered to her unhearing son, 'With every fibre of my being I will protect you. I solemnly promise, as there is a God in Heaven, you will survive. You will survive and live a full life. You will survive to see justice for your family. You will survive and return to find Rebecca. I know that you will. God will provide for you even if he cannot provide for me.'

After an hour Marta and Joel moved on with nothing more than the hope of finding divine providence or intervention before the dawn. Soon after they had resumed their way they heard a train in the distance. They climbed down the embankment and lay out of sight. Presently the goods train passed.

Marta considered it advised to leave the railway behind and they began to walk what Joel imagined to be north. Within a few minutes they were walking along the bank of a wide canal. A distant road sign indicated that Harderwijk was two kilometres away. 'It's all well and good if you know where Harderwijk is', Marta mumbled.

But a name like that! Dutch, it must be Dutch. The train had travelled southwest from Hamburg. Holland would be logical. But why had they travelled to Holland? It didn't make sense, but then, none of this war was making any sense. Neighbours that they had once talked to and done business with had disowned her family. Her husband had been spat on and she and her daughter had been called whores. Her husband and sons had been shot. Why? What drove people to...? This was getting her nowhere and, rapidly collecting herself, she resolved to concentrate on the immediate future.

Pragmatic! Marta had always been pragmatic. A Hausfrau; a mother; a woman of self-deprecating charm, humour and self-confidence. In her younger days she had been elegant and intelligent. In a later age she would have flourished in academia. As it was she had worked as a seamstress and had met Simon at a family gathering. She was betrothed and had five children, her first being stillborn. She had accepted her lot and was a dutiful wife and loving mother. She taught her children well. All had been highly articulate and literate and all had been destined for academic success. As Marta saw it the money she earned was to provide funds for her children's university education. She had not had the opportunity – her children would have.

Marta had many qualities. Steadfastness, resolve, determination and a dogged refusal to accept defeat were seminal. It was these qualities that enabled her to refocus her energies; what was left of them; that and the sustenance she drew from the well of anticipated retribution. The fascist assassins and their lethal ideology, the complicit, supportive, supine and sycophantic spectators, the whereabouts of Rebecca and the fatuous pretext for their evacuation all concentrated her mind and increased her growing resolve. She reflected for a moment, between paroxysms of pain and anguish.

She recognised the corrosive nature of negative thought and likewise understood that wallowing in self-pity would prove counterproductive. What had her own mother said to her so many years ago? 'You can't travel far with the devil on your back.' How true. Now it was time for her to clear her mind and take decisive action. She must be positive. Once again she must be pragmatic.

The canal narrowed. At first it had run roughly north but as they completed the first kilometre a long bend swept to the west. When, the canal eventually straightened they saw a light in the distance and then, as the moon emerged from the clouds, lock gates reflected in the still canal water. Soon Marta and Joel saw the source of the light. It came from the window of a small stone cottage standing adjacent to the lock. They approached the ancient grey stone building with trepidation, moving cautiously and silently.

Marta looked through the window and saw an elderly buxom woman gently swaying backwards and forwards in an old chestnut rocking chair. She was knitting and toasting her legs beside a fire glowing in a big open hearth. A small gaslight hung from a roof beam. It was the lighting of 'The Night Watch', by Rembrandt thought Joel behind his impassive face. 'Probably painted not so far from here', he rationalised.

It was dark and quiet but for the groaning of the rocking chair. The woman appeared to be alone, save for a small black and white cat that lay contentedly at her feet in the glow of the fire.

A large hand descended onto Marta's injured shoulder. She screamed in pain as she turned towards her assailant. A booming voice demanded to know something in a language that Marta recognised but did not understand. It was Dutch.

'Bitte', she begged.

'Deutch?'

'Yes, I am German.'

The old man looked deeply into her face. He spoke to her in German.

'What are you about?' he bellowed suspiciously.

Marta's eyes began to lose focus. She could not stand still. She swayed more than the old woman in the rocking chair. She was spent and reaching for Joel, half as a prop and half in a last ditch effort to protect him, collapsed.

Chapter 2

EXODUS

Marta neither lost consciousness, nor slept. It was, perhaps, thought her traumatised but still inevitably analytical son, that she resided in that indefinite state between sleep and unconsciousness inconveniently left without a name.

She relived flashes of the horrors of her recent experiences and the subsequent terror of her flight. A crimson and purple collage of images and distant faces moved frighteningly towards her, passing through her body and imbuing her soul with unwanted spirits; a legacy of her appalling nightmare; a stark unforgiving relentless trauma. Delirium followed and it was some time before she regained her senses.

She was lying on a well-worn floral couch in the lockkeeper's cottage. Her shoulder had been dressed. Turning to look for Joel she was checked by the pain.

'Joel', she whispered. Joel was sitting nearby. His face was clean and his clothes changed. She smiled. Joel had not seen that recently.

Marta looked into the stern censorious face of the lockkeeper's wife wishing to indicate her gratitude. The old woman scowled fiercely as she wiped Marta's forehead with a damp cloth. It was not the action of a dedicated nurse mopping a casualty's fevered brow. No, there was an expedient motive. She wanted Marta and Joel out of the cottage and back on the road as soon as she could manage it and she clearly wanted them to know as much.

The ruddy complexion and rounded features of the voluminously clad woman added to the intensity of her demeanour. She was highly animated and peppered the lockkeeper with a stream of vitriol. Neither Marta nor Joel understood what she said but it was clear that she was acting against her better judgement in helping the two of them and that she was letting her husband know just that.

The old lockkeeper, recognising Marta's perception, spoke, puffing at his old white clay pipe. 'You are correct. My wife doesn't want you here. She says no good will come of it. We are in danger if you are on the run from the Germans. You are on the run from the Germans are you not?'

Marta looked up into the huge face half lit by the flames of the small fire. The lockkeeper had a benevolent smile even though it emanated from below his thick nicotine stained moustache and between his yellow tobacco stained teeth. Marta felt reassured and returned a smile to the old man gaining comfort from his reciprocated gesture.

'What do you know sir? And what are you going to do now? What of us?' She beseeched him.

'Do not concern yourself with my wife. She is a good woman but we have come close.' To what, Marta noted, they had come close to, he didn't say. She refrained from pursuing the matter.

'We have been in great danger over many months now and can trust no one. My wife has done much, perhaps too much', he sighed reflectively. 'She is a good woman'. Enough.' He stiffened embarrassed by his self-indulgence.

We must concentrate on what is at hand,' he said, recapturing the resoluteness, which had initially defined him to both Marta and Joel. 'I have heard of the train. You were on that train, yes? It is remarkable. No? 'And that you are here and have not been caught... that too is remarkable. There is no talk of survivors. All were killed, that is the news. Perhaps we should lend credence to that, yes? But God has spared you.'

Clearly the stern censorious woman understood her husband's German. She stared out of the little round black eyes, set deeply into her fat mottled face, and scowled further caution.

Unperturbed the lockkeeper continued with his duty. 'I have asked the boy many questions but he does not answer. I have seen this before when... no matter. I will do what I can. It is no more than my duty. There are many dangers and you cannot stay here. Please to wait here until I return. Yes?'

Marta asked, 'How long have we been here?'

'Let me see', he said, taking an English half-hunter from his waistcoat pocket.

'It was at eight-thirty in the evening when I, shall we say, 'met you?' You have slept the clock around and a bit more. He noted her concern. 'Ah yes, it is so long. It is almost nine o'clock, no? Do not worry. My wife will do her duty. She has been with you while I have been away for many hours already. I must go.' Marta made as if to beg him not to leave. 'Do not worry. I will return. So far you have had nothing but tragedy. Tonight ... well tonight, perhaps, could be your salvation. Perhaps you are lucky? Perhaps. Sleep.' He smiled at Joel. 'Both of you. Sleep; you will need it.'

Another hour passed before the nauseous sickness began to abate. A very long tedious hour. Marta had not been able to sleep. She looked at the woman rocking backwards and forwards in the old creaking chair, her face resolute and unchanging. She had clearly decided to remain detached. Marta lay there holding Joel's hand as he sat beside her. She looked at his little pinched face as he slept. Were they to be betrayed? Would the lockkeeper return with the Gestapo? Was this all a sham? A canard delivered to delay the fugitives.

'He seemed to be genuine', she thought, 'but then hadn't so many other people had seemed genuine in the recent past?' She felt the dressing on her shoulder rationalising that it was quite likely that it was the seemingly intractable woman who had dressed the wound. She touched it again smiling at her as if to acknowledge her help. The woman bristled, shrugged her shoulders and was having none of it, lowering her eyes to her knitting and recommencing her rocking.

There was nothing else for it. To flee would precipitate a search and she and Joel were in no position to run. Perhaps the woman would stop them? She was robust but it was unlikely that she could move quickly enough to stop them. Her corpulent body was not designed for speed and the many layers of clothing hardly added to Marta's perception of her agility. It was hypothetical, she thought. She would put their faith in God and hope that the lockkeeper was as good as his word. Her recent experiences only fuelled the speculation of conspiracy but she resolved to dismiss the notion. A rigorous sift through the evidence of betrayal was, she considered, to be counterproductive. The decision to stay had been made. Now it was time to turn her mind to practicalities beyond their immediate needs.

She watched the clock on the mantelpiece. Ten o'clock, eleven o'clock, midnight. Each hour felt like an eternity. 'Be positive. So far, so good. I am recovering', she thought as she raised her wounded arm. She grimaced. 'But slowly.'

A further twenty minutes later the door creaked open and the cold night air rushed in. The silhouette of the lockkeeper bridged the doorway. He whispered melodramatically, 'All is well. Come, quietly, come', as he motioned them to follow.

Marta had been sitting for some time and had begun to recover her strength but she swayed as she rose and Joel, who had stirred only a few moments earlier, helped the lockkeeper support her as she made her way to the doorway. She turned to thank the lockkeeper's wife but the old chair now rocked silently its burden having being relieved. The woman's duty had been done. Her part fulfilled - she had washed her hands, as Pilate had.

Clouds hid the moon as the unlikely party left the cottage and the darkness comforted Marta. The three made their way along the narrow towpath and after few minutes they came to another lock.

'Stay here', said the lockkeeper as he scanned the canal banks and fields.

He motioned with one finger to his lips.

'One moment.' Joel looked back along the towpath they had travelled then turned to where the lockkeeper had been. He had disappeared.

The moon emerged between the huge dark cloudbanks and Marta could now see that the canal was adjacent to a large lake. 'Surely', she thought, 'we cannot be far from the coast.' Joel instinctively put a reassuring arm on her good shoulder. Still he had not spoken but he was clearly alert and sensitive to his mother's fears and their perilous predicament.

Joel shivered and his mother held him close as she considered the question of God's will and justice. 'If there is justice it is not dispensed during our time on earth. No, it must be at a later time. On the dreadful day of judgement. That is when justice will be meted out.' It was not at all Joel's perspective.

Marta's pragmatism was waning as the pain in her shoulder welled once again. She knew that the dressing ought to be changed every six hours or so. How could she...

The lockkeeper appeared as mysteriously as he had disappeared causing both Marta and Joel to jump. 'Come', he whispered.

They walked onwards for another hundred yards or so, on past a small tributary that fed the canal until they reached a small stone bridge. They walked under it and halted, listening. After a few moments reconnaissance they moved on a few yards further, then crouched down behind bushes. Hidden from the towpath, they waited in silence.

'Listen very carefully', said the lockkeeper in a conspiratorial whisper, 'I have a friend who is, shall we say, going fishing this night. He will take you to the coast and from there...well from there it's up to you. He is a good man and you can trust him. Do as he says. I can do no more.'

He put his arms around Marta. 'Be strong and good luck.' He bent down and looked into Joel's face. 'Look after your mother young man. It is your duty.' With that he ruffled Joel's hair and rose to go. 'Good bye.' He glanced over Marta's shoulder and smiled causing her to turn to see what had taken his attention. Less than fifty yards away, moving slowly towards them, was a barge. Marta had not heard the gentle phutt, phutt, phutt of the engine until now.

Standing at the bow of the boat was a giant of a man with a full-untrimmed raven black beard. His enormous head was complimented with commensurate facial features. He wore a navy blue tea shirt and dark corduroy trousers. A wide black belt wound its way around his huge belly and restrained his bursting corpulence. He looked as if he might explode at any moment, like a breached dam. It was impossible to tear one's eyes from him. It wasn't a disagreeable sight. He was somewhat avuncular, a Father Christmas character, a Falstaff in seafaring garb. Marta imagined him to be in his forties but at first glance he had looked much older.

The mariner laughed in a deep rich voice as he threw a mooring rope to the lockkeeper. The laugh was slow, deliberate and muted. It was clear that there was great warmth and affection between the two men. Joel noted their gestures and the sparkle in their eyes as they addressed one another. He also noted that they continually scanned the water and the towpath as they spoke.

Joel also observed that the portly mariner had a habit of leaning towards the lockkeeper when he spoke to him and imagined discourse with him it to be quite intimidating.

Marta envisaged that he would be excellent company on more auspicious occasions. An entertainer; a man with a good yarn to spin, a joke to tell or a rhyme to recite. Unfortunately she knew that the accuracy of her appraisal was unlikely to be tested. He was bursting with life but was containing his natural exuberance recognising the gravity of the situation and the terrible risks that lay ahead. He turned to Marta who held Joel ever closer.

'Welcome, I am the captain of this heap of junk', said the mariner in a serviceable German.

Marta caught the sight of a figure, hitherto unseen, moving at the rear of the boat. The lockkeeper nodded in the direction of the figure. 'Jol', he said. The man barely acknowledged the greeting.

The shadowed figure was tall and slim and he looked to be in his mid-thirties, thought Marta. He sat next to a bucket, which was half full of wood chippings and a pile of sticks. He had a large knife in one hand, which he employed in whittling the stick. The chippings shot across the deck and into the bucket. He didn't raise his eyes but Marta was aware that he was listening intently and would miss little of the conversation.

'This is the mate', said the captain. The man's eyes began to lift towards recognition but lowered truculently before they reached their target; the need for warmth seemingly a distant memory. He threw what remained of his stick into the bucket and reached for another. Marta reflected that he would be a good man to have on your side if things got tough. She would rather have him with her than against her. 'A lot of pain has accompanied this man's life. He's not a man to cross.'

'Arne', the captain greeted the lockkeeper, 'Is it as you said?'

'Yes', he replied.

Marta and Joel listened attentively.

'Then it is decided. We go tonight. I will see you when the war is over. Do you have the papers?'

'Just the two. They won't believe you about the others. You know that don't you? You do know that?'

'I know. I know. What else shall we do?'

'Be careful', take great care', the lockkeeper offered. 'They don't take kindly to their officers being killed or maimed. Keep your wits about you.'

'I'm always careful', he replied.

'Good luck. Stay safe.'

The two shook hands and put their arms around one another. 'I will see you again one day soon my friend. God speed,' croaked the lockkeeper, attempting to keep the emotional quiver in his voice under control. Joel saw that the two men had looked into each other's eyes with mutual respect and admiration and wondered about the extent of their previous conspiracies.

The lockkeeper stepped out of the boat and was about to throw the mooring rope to the mariner when Marta stepped back onto the towpath and reached for his arm. She bent down on one knee and kissed his hand.

'I thank you for my son and for myself. I will never forget your kindness.'

Embarrassed, the lockkeeper abruptly retorted, 'Go', then softly and warmly repeated, 'Go.' Marta stepped back onto the boat and it slid away into the night.

Marta turned but there was nothing but the phosphorescent ribbon reflecting in the water stretching out behind them. He had disappeared just as quickly as his wife had when her duty had been completed.

'Go on. There you go. Be careful of the steps. There are three of them', the captain said. Joel led and Marta followed him, holding onto what remained of her skirts. The cabin was dark and damp but the stench of the sluice was infinitely preferable to the fetid atmosphere of the cattle wagons.

Joel couldn't see. He hit his head on the bulkhead and tripped over someone's legs as he entered. Marta followed and recognised three sitting figures. Joel got to his feet embarrassed by his fall. Marta apologised on Joel's behalf as she peered into the dark cabin. She could barely make out the fellow travellers that were huddled together sitting on a bench behind the small galley table. There was a couple in their mid-thirties and a girl in her early teens sitting between them. The girl slept. No one spoke.

The Spartan cabin was small. The decor consisted of the table, two benches, a small narrow cupboard and a small sink.

After an hour the silence was broken. 'Spackenburg', said the terse younger mariner from the deck above.

'Aye', registered the captain.

Then later 'Huizen', and later still, 'Volendem.'

Clearly these were the names of the places that they were slipping past in the night but they meant nothing to Marta or Joel. The still night had given way to a gentle off shore breeze. The weather was changing.

As morning broke the male passenger spoke to his wife. He spoke in Dutch and was clearly explaining something to her. He then turned to Marta and said, in German, 'I have just told my wife that we have rounded Den Helder and are soon travelling along the coast. The captain looks that he is going fishing, but in a barge? I don't think so. No, he is preparing for something a little more than that. He does have some fishing equipment on board but... well; I don't know how sea worthy this vessel is. It is far too small for the open sea. I'm afraid we are in his hands. I don't want to cause you distress but I thought that you should know these things. Yes'

'Allow me to introduce myself. My name is Vincent Haan, this is my wife Ruth and here is my daughter Rachael.'

Marta and Joel could see their fellow passengers quite well now that dawn was breaking. Vincent was a stocky fellow. He had thick sandy hair and a trim smart red beard and moustache. He looked as much a mariner as the captain and his mate did. Marta thought that he must have been a handsome chap before stress and strain had etched recent ordeals into his face. He clearly adored his 'two girls', as he referred to his wife and daughter and regularly touched them affectionately, encouraging them to stay positive. Marta estimated that he would be tall but it was difficult to be precise within the confines of the cabin.

Ruth was beautiful. Marta had thought, with measured vanity, that she had been attractive too, but though she could make out little more than Ruth's nose, mouth and dark hair in the gloomy cabin, knew that she was quite beautiful. Though now dirty Ruth was attired in clothes of good quality. She wore a heavy woollen suit with a long pleated skirt. This would have cost more money than Marta could ever have afforded for herself even if she had not had her children's university costs to meet. It was clear that the woman had taste and had had the money to indulge it.

The two women smiled at each other warmly each lifting the other's spirits a little.

Joel glanced at his mother. She had smiled again. That was the second time in two days that he had observed as much. He looked across at Vincent and Ruth and they smiled at him too. He looked away before they caught his eye. His gaze settled on Rachael. Like her mother she too was going to be a fine looking woman. Joel was too shy to smile at her but couldn't resist the occasional glance when he believed himself to be unobserved.

The passengers fell silent as the barge murmured slowly through the dark water. All were thinking desperately but making little sense of their predicament, suppressing their fears in order to boost their fellow traveller's spirits. The pernicious effects of fatigue had deprived them of their mental agility. They had little chance of resolution. Fortunately, for now, their stupor would not be held up to scrutiny.

'I believe that I can hear the sea', said Vincent, after dozing for a short while. 'Yes, it is near.'

'Perhaps our luck will change?' whispered Marta.

'I always believed that fate of my family was in the hands of God. Now... now I believe that you are right too. Luck may have a part to play too', replied Vincent.

Marta spoke her thoughts out loud. 'There must be a heaven because there is no justice here on earth and there must be justice. If it is not here then it must be elsewhere. It is the place where the dreadful day of judgement will take place. I now know it,' she offered, reprising her earlier thoughts and strengthening her resolve.

There was a long pause before Vincent took a deep breath and replied, dolefully echoing Marta's sentiments. 'Our fate is in God's hands.'

'That is true', said the captain who had descended the first of the three cabin steps. He stooped as he spoke into the dark cabin. 'You are also in my hands and it is that which now concerns us.'

He looked at Vincent and continued to speak in German.

'We will be polite my friend. We must speak German so that our fellow travellers can understand us. Am I correct when I say that you must not be identified?' he said, speaking to Vincent. 'Forgive my rude assumption but you must escape or lay low for a very long time? Yes? And that is impossible? Yes?'

'You have it', said Vincent.

'I will not ask why... Perhaps later.' Then to himself. 'Perhaps there is no reason. Perhaps there is every reason. No matter. Later,' he reflected.

The giant rubbed his beard as if it itched a little then, smoothing it with a downward swish, turned back towards Vincent. 'You will have to remain out of sight for the remainder of our journey?'

Vincent looked at his 'two girls'. With a resigned sigh he nodded.

He turned to Marta. 'And the same for you?'

She nodded.

'We too', Marta sobbed as Joel moved to comfort her.

Marta had had no aim, no long term plan or strategy other than to put distance between that appalling train and Joel. But where would he be safe until this senseless war was over? And what of Rebecca? She had not considered what was beyond their immediate needs. She had completed the immediate pragmatic requirement. Now she recognised the need for a medium term strategy. But where and what next?

The three adults turned towards the huge silhouetted figure filling the hatchway.

'Where are we exactly'? Vincent enquired.

'Don't ask. It is enough for you to know that I am following a tributary of the canal parallel to the coast for a few more miles. This will take us to a bay I have used since I was a child. I have a boat there and I will be going fishing tonight. However, God willing, it is my intention to land my empty nets in England. The weather tonight is fine but it may change tomorrow and I don't know if we can get there by then or not. The journey will be perilous. The boat we will take is small but strong. I am convinced that we can make it. However, the sea is not our only enemy. The Germans are everywhere. On the water, under the water and in the air. It is very dangerous but the mate and I have no alternative. We are definitely going. We must. Perhaps like us you have no further options. Perhaps you want to take your chances and remain here. I have outlined what is possible and also what is probable. Shortly you will make your choice. I hope that we all make the right decisions. I can take you or I can leave you. It is up to you.'

'There is no going back', said Vincent to his wife.

The truth was rapidly overwhelming Marta but instinctively she railed against it. 'But my family, my Rebecca, my daughter. I have nothing. I have lost everything. Only my darling Joel remains.' The enormity of the situation struck her. She heard what Vincent had said and turned to beseech the captain.

'But Rebecca. Have I lost Rebecca? No, it is too much. I cannot go to England. I cannot.'

'But can you go back to Germany?' asked the captain. 'Can you return to your home? Your town? Your country? What will they do to someone such as you who have escaped from their grasp once already? What do you think they will do? Perhaps you will remain here on the coastline or in Amsterdam. Yes?

Where are your papers? Trust me they will want to see your papers.' He turned, shrugged his shoulders at the mate on the deck above and waited for her response. The two looked at each other for a few moments before he lowered his eyes and turned away.

Marta perceived that the captain and his mate were rationalising and consolidating their own thoughts. She was being used as a sounding board. He was doing a pretty good job of convincing himself that his plan of action was the correct one. Joel observed the same.

'What will I do if I go? How will I survive in a country where I don't even speak the language? In England I have nothing. Nothing!' She broke down and Joel, putting his arm around his mother's good shoulder, attempted to comfort her once again.

'What do you have in Germany? What will you do if you don't come with us?' asked the captain, in as an avuncular fashion as he could muster. 'The boy has a life to live. Agh! I leave it to you. It is your choice. Perhaps you are right. Perhaps you are wrong. Who knows?'

It was the first and last time that Marta was to hear Ruth speak. Her voice was soft yet decisive. She spoke clearly and with quiet conviction. The words conveyed were no more than had been uttered by others.

'There is no going back.'

The impact of this one line ended the conversation. It was a brutal reality; the delivery of a simple and obvious truth uttered at a seminal moment. Ruth's dulcet yet unequivocal evocation betrayed not a jot of ambivalence. She had said little; but she had said all.

It was decided. Marta knew it. Vincent knew it. God help them, they all knew it.

The giant seaman must have known it too. He hadn't waited for the verdict.

Chapter 3

GEORGE MERRICK

George Merrick was observing seagulls through the lenses of a particularly fine pair of field glasses that his father had bought for him on the occasion of his ninth birthday a little more than four years earlier. What a present! They had rivalled the microscope that he had received at seven and the telescope at eight.

George's passion was the observation and documentation of birds, bacteria and planets, indeed, almost any intriguing scientific phenomenon. And most scientific phenomena were intriguing to George.

It being spring, and the weather being favourable, he had rationalised that the logical option for today's scrutiny was to be ornithological in nature.

One of his favourite places to observe birds was along the Suffolk coast and, when he had completed all of his school homework thoroughly, he enjoyed cycling the half mile cross country trek from his village to a small secluded bay.

Here, amid the sand dunes, he would meticulously catalogue the native species of birds and animals and make copious notes regarding their habits and habitats. The scientific accuracy of his log had been commended by no less an authority than Sir William Wyatt, president of the Royal Ornithological Society.

George had won a national bird watching competition run by 'The Times' four years earlier and he and his parents had attended a presentation evening at The Grange Hotel near Colchester. After the presentation the nine year old had been introduced to Sir William in the foyer of the hotel.

'And how do you intend to build on this work?' teased the ancient Wyatt.

George pushed his glasses back from the end of his sharp nose, a habit he enacted at the beginning of any serious discourse he was about to embark upon.

'I may not sir.' replied the precocious child. 'Indeed, I have yet to decide upon the precise direction of my vocation let alone the parameters of my studies. I have the requisite proclivity and passion for scientific research, that is true, and it is therefore a rational assumption, that, at this juncture, I dedicate my life to science. However, it is not my intention to disassociate myself from other academic disciplines, research and study. We shall see. I am of the profound opinion, however, that it is within the field of science that I shall realise my ambitions and, further, that it is within one of noble disciplines that I shall be able to render myself most serviceable to society'.

'Of course', he went on, 'it is of paramount importance that I discern the university course appropriate to and commensurate with my development. I can't over stress the turbulent ingenuity of youth. It is imperative that the product of a fertile mind is cultivated effectively with an early, sharp focus and is harvested efficiently and comprehensively. Clearly I have a considerable responsibility to make a sound judgement in this regard.'

The answer astonished Wyatt who responded with a wide-eyed inspection of the bespectacled prodigy followed by a silent appeal towards the attendant parents.

Professor Sir George Percival Merrick and his wife, Doctor Emily Sarah Merrick looked back at Wyatt enquiringly. Wyatt had smiled at the boy's precocious response. He had thought that this would elicit a reciprocal smile from the elderly couple. It had not. As far as the Merricks were concerned the boy had spoken as accurately and as precisely as they would have expected him to; neither more nor less. The question had been asked and, to all intents and purposes, it had been answered quite adequately.

Wyatt shrugged his shoulders, rather like Doctor Watson confounded once more by the arcane Holmes. Hesitantly he took his leave shuffling off and mumbling as he left.

'A remarkable young fellow. An inordinately remarkable young fellow. Mark him down Gregson', said Sir William to his chauffer, 'Mark him down. Extraordinary! A remarkable young fellow. Remarkable indeed.'

Great things were expected of George. His sharp intellect and unquenchable thirst for knowledge augured well for the future of science. At seven his interests, other than science, had included, philately, playing the violin, identifying and acquiring antiques and cycling through the Suffolk countryside. He had a compendium of railway steam locomotives, which he regularly and punctiliously updated, and a library many a postgraduate would have found both challenging and exacting. These latter passions, however, were subordinate to the former scientific data collecting. George's prodigious knowledge was widely recognised, as was his impatience with the less gifted members of the human race, which often led to difficulties.

Unsurprisingly he was a loner. A loner but not lonely. He didn't seek his own company; it was more likely the case that boys of his own age rapidly lost their appetite for companionship when George's enquiring mind obstructed their natural propensity to have fun.

George would cycle along with a classmate and, on spotting a rare butterfly, pursue it, jar it and talk endlessly about its classification and habitat. This was not at all what the classmate, who had probably been dragooned into meeting George in the first place, had envisaged to be his afternoons entertainment. The boys, even though chosen for their pedantic qualities, enquiring minds and scientific bent, would eventually lose interest and beg their parents not to be sacrificed at the altar of George's intellect ever again; or at least not to do more than was to be his turn on the dreaded rota. The 'volunteers' were getting thin on the ground as George recognised their hostile recognition of his intellect and became disaffected by their presence.

Consequently George was all too often to be found on his own. He was conscious of this but considering the alternatives was satisfied that internal reflection would be ultimately more rewarding than prosaic interaction and that more of his time was likely to be spent productively and profitably in his own company than with some nincompoop, no matter how affable he was considered to be by others. Listening to the tedious, inane and banal remarks of 'some chap', that was quite likely to be as vacuous as the subject of his incessant chatter, did not fill him with enthusiasm.

Some boys had risible academic pretensions. These misguided few he considered to be deserving of his derision and he patronised them before impatience drove him to pour scorn on their postulations, premises and assertions before exposing faults in their rationale. He did not believe that these sacrificial lambs would ever shift the tectonic plates of science as he would do and it was, ergo, most unlikely that their contributions to any discourse would be of interest to him. Anyway, he reasoned, soon he would go to Cambridge and there he would, perhaps, meet souls who may benefit from his hypotheses and some of whom may well even be deserving of his time, consideration and largesse.

George was a genius and he knew it. He did not suffer fools gladly. Indeed he didn't suffer them at all.

None of this was at all surprising. His father and mother were elderly when George was born. He was one of their very few miscalculations. The two academic parents certainly did not intend to have a child and their bi-annual lovemaking had always been brief and unrewarding. Amazingly George's mother had become pregnant and there was nothing for it but to rear the child.

This the academics did with good will and considerable dedication. They never resented George's intrusion into their lives; it was just that he had not been accounted for in their matrimonial vision. Now that he was included in the equation he became the third adult in the family as a matter of course.

It would have been difficult for a stranger to discern the fact that his parents loved George. Indeed, it is doubtful that they had ever have mentioned the fact to him. It was clear that there was a mutual respect and correctness about their relationship. It had ever been so. Hadn't his father given him a dictionary for his fourth birthday and spent many a fascinating evening showing him the finer points of its use?

George was given time with the broadsheets after his father had devoured them and conversations were held at the dining room table where his opinions were sought on subjects ranging from fine art, opera, porcelain, theology and political reform to scientific invention and critiques of operatic opus.

He was always impeccably well dressed, had sufficient spending money for his conservative needs, a bicycle and a well-stocked library. Indeed, George believed that he had everything that any young man could ever want.

Sir George Merrick was an emeritus professor in his early seventies, his wife a retired doctor just sixty. Both were from ascetic academic stock and neither had a least concept of what a sense of humour was, nor did they aspire to discover the purpose of any such a notion or phenomena. George's father was born in the 1870s and was a Cambridge student in the 1890s. 'Things had moved on and not much for the better since those halcyon conservative days', he believed. He was often heard to say that the nineteen twenties and thirties had heralded a new age of lethal ideologies that passed for liberal radicalism and that this had led to denigrating self-gratification and shallowness. He was not bitter about the fact nor did he resent it. He observed the manifestation and was displeased with its possible ramifications for the future. As always logic was his master and emotions considered gratuitous.

The academically gifted George junior was destined for great things. His career would be his life. He was self-assured, confident and his prospects excited him. He deferred to his parents but tolerated his teacher's shortcomings and understanding with decreasing patience. He was a young man, never a child, who, as the years went by, would, inevitably, draw more and more into himself. This detachment would be born of self-imposed isolation and his relentless thirst for knowledge. His impenetrable intellect both isolated and insulated his soul.

George picked up the field glasses again following two gulls that were having a contretemps regarding the ownership of a tasty morsel of sardine. The glasses swung up, then down swooping after the birds. Then up again and rapidly to the right. An image registered in his mind. He thought that he had seen something in the distance as the birds had dived down and out across the bay. He took the glasses from his eyes and looked out to sea scanning the horizon but he had lost his focus and direction. He scanned the scene again and, on his search being unsuccessful, went back to following the gulls. Now he had lost those too.

'Gosh. What bad judgement. I fell between two stools. That will teach me. A bird in the hand and all that sort of thing', he thought, satisfied that the lesson was well learned and that he had suitably chastised himself for the blunder. He considered the incident clinically, formulated an opinion with respect to his actions and delivered the important diagnosis. 'It really wasn't bad luck at all. It was lack of concentration', he said out loud. 'It really isn't good enough.' A mental note was made and the mistake would not occur again.

The clouds were gathering after a glorious day that early March. He sensed a change in the weather and made a note in his well-worn pocket book, to check the barometer that his parents had bought him for Christmas the previous year when he returned home.

A stiff breeze came in from the sea and the soft mist that had lingered throughout the day began to disperse. 'How quickly the scene changes', he mused. He put on the waterproof coat that he had carefully placed in his saddlebag, picked up his bicycle and, preparing to leave, glanced out to sea one last time.

There floundering some half a mile out in the bay was a small boat. Clearly it was listing badly. He lifted the field glasses, which hung around his neck. This time he took careful note of the boat's exact location. 'The result of another lesson well learned', he praised himself. Someone on board the boat was waving what looked to be clothing or, perhaps, towels. Another was shouting into a loud hailer. The remainder were attempting to paddle holding something in their hands.

George knew what to do. 'First fix the boat's coordinates. If I stand on this bank the boat is between the distant headland and me, give or take a few feet. Secondly inform the coast guard. There is a telephone box down the pathway in the village. I have the number in my pocket book. Next, return to the scene and be ready to point out the boat's position or, at least, the position where it was last seen.'

He deliberated over his plan of action and, on deciding that it was appropriate, cycled quickly to the telephone box. The antiquated red box was a little less than half a mile from the bay. He gave his name, age, and location to the operator. When he had ascertained that she had recorded his initial information correctly he determined that he would then outline the details of the emergency. This he did clearly, explicitly, succinctly and without panic. He had read that this was how it should be done in the government's leaflets on the subject.

Returning, he peddled as quickly as he could along the pathway to the coast. He travelled faster than he would normally do and recognising the fact slowed a little. 'Better to get there safely than not at all', he rationalised.

As he cycled he gathered his thoughts. 'Better take care when I get there too', he conjectured. 'It could be a German boat. No; unlikely; too small. Anyway, clearly the craft was unsuitable for the open seas.'

George's assessed the situation in light of the risks now to be taken by the lifeboat men. 'There is a propensity for some folk to sail without checking the forecast for the area. Now men's lives have to be put at risk. It really isn't good enough. It is as intrepid as it is foolhardy.'

He hardly noticed the return journey to the beach such was the depth of his analysis and his growing indignation at the peril that the lifeboat men faced due to the lack of foresight and planning of others. He was pleased with his rationalisation of the situation and resolved to note down his logic at a more opportune time.

The small boat was still afloat when he arrived back on the beach. Now it was very low in the water. The paddling had ceased. The crew had accepted the hopelessness of that. 'The prevailing wind should help', thought George.

'If only they can keep afloat for a little longer. They are six hundred yards or so from shore but they will sink very shortly. They ought not to have gone out; it really is quite absurd not to plan these things meticulously. It isn't at all sensible', reprised George. 'The regulations clearly state that' … The reprise of rule four, which was to be found in the aforementioned coastguard leaflet that he had read the previous summer, was interrupted by the arrival of five lifeboat men.

It was unnecessary for George to point out the boat to them. It was there in the middle of the bay, still a little less than five hundred yards from the shore. It was being battered by the foaming waves, which showered its small deck. It didn't look at all like it was going to come any closer now. It was going down. A few more minutes and it would be gone.

The white foaming surf smashed back into the sea as the wind lifted the ferocious waves which constantly pounded the small vessel. Six hundred yards in that sea would challenge the strongest of swimmers. It looked to George that there were children on board too.

The lifeboat men ran down the cove as the heavy rain pounded the beach. George had been observing the white gulls against a blue sky barely twenty minutes before. Now the horizon had disappeared. The sky and sea were shades of grey and white. Spray, rain, waves and clouds merged into one diaphanous, amorphous hostile scene.

'A Typical Turner canvas', thought George. 'Very much a Turner seascape.' The boat groaned and began to sink beneath the waves. The frantic passengers and crew were preparing to abandon the vessel having left the inevitable until the very last moment.

Four of the lifeboat men had now reached the boathouse. The lifeboat was launched almost immediately. George noted the well-rehearsed drill as the crew ran to their stations. The little craft bounced on the crest of each wave, barely touching the sea. A bolt of lightning lit the sky and George waited for the thunder to follow. It did so almost immediately. He left the beach to gain some cover from the driving rain; his exposed position at the water's edge having rendered his limbs almost numb. There was an outcrop of rocks to his right and he made for the refuge it would afford.

By the time George raised the field glasses again the fishing boat had sunk. He peered through the wind and rain attempting to decipher what was happening. He watched the lifeboat manoeuvre around the area where the boat had gone down and he saw a body being pulled from the foaming water. The weather was deteriorating rapidly and lives were being lost. The breaking waves pounded into the beach and the deafening sound made it impossible to hear the shouting and screaming mayhem that would inevitably accompany the tragic scene being played out before him.

George put his wet hand into his pocket and brought out a pencil. He wrote in his notebook. 'Check the barometer and record the pressure.' The pencil would hardly write on the damp paper. 'Never mind', he thought. 'The paper itself will be sufficient to remind me of the task to be done.'

The lifeboat crew continued circling searching for bodies but after fifteen minutes or so, they returned to the beach. George had predicted a point on the beach where the boat would bring any survivors. He was pleased with his prediction.

'The boat must come here. This is the nearest point to the road. The boat will then be returned to the boathouse', he had surmised.

Three of the lifeboat men helped the four survivors out of the boat and were greeted by villagers equipped with blankets. Two adults and two children had been saved. A stocky bearded male survivor wrapped a young girl in a blanket and lifted her into his arms. George noted their anguished faces. A small boy walked by the side of a woman who was being carried on a stretcher. He was holding the woman's hand. It was clearly his mother. It was frustrating to George that he was unable to make out the survivor's profiles in the dark violent tempest that had developed so rapidly. He would have enjoyed the dispassionate challenge of assessing their characters based on their features and their demeanour.

Several more villagers arrived, as always happened when the lifeboat was called out. Some were curious observers. Some anxious for their kin and others attended in the hope of being able to render a service. George considered the former's attendance as gratuitous as it was unnecessary.

Mr. Stephenson, the local garage proprietor, beckoned the skipper of the lifeboat to bring the survivors to his delivery van, which was waiting for them on the narrow muddy cart track. He would convey them from the beach to the village.

George pressed forward inquisitively. 'Where are you taking them?' he asked, feeling that he had some investment in proceedings. 'To the village', replied PC Holdsworth of the local constabulary.

'Are you the fellow what raised the alarm?' the constable enquired, preening his huge white handlebar moustache as he spoke.

'It was I who informed the authorities', affirmed George.

'Good lad', he said, ruffling George's hair as if he was a Labrador that had just retrieved a stick. 'I'm sure that you can come along. You deserve a piece of chocolate cake and a drink of pop I'm sure.'

George was not amused. 'Sir', he retorted. 'I am sure that the chocolate cake is excellent and I am equally sure that you can recommend it', he added, looking at PC Holdsworth's expansive girth. 'However, though not necessarily within my remit I would, never-the-less, ask that I be present when those rescued are questioned, given that this falls within the correct protocol. Might my contribution not be of value to your enquiry?'

29

PC Holdsworth appeared to be in urgent and immediate need of an interpreter.

George saw the perplexed frown on the PC's forehead and recognised the need for translation. He announced very slowly and deliberately, fixing PC Holdsworth with a withering stare. 'I am an eye witness?'

PC Holdsworth thought for a moment. The safe thing was to pontificate then concur. In all cases, when one didn't understand the finer points of an argument, he had found that the best course of action was to feign deep thought, then agree.

'Of course young laddie', he said. The 'young laddie' always made PC Holdsworth feel that bit superior and in control of situations. 'I was about to suggest the very same myself. I don't want you running off just now', he commanded. 'I will need you as a witness and no mistake.'

George bit his tongue and acquiesced deducing the expediency of such a strategy at this juncture. This caused him to make a mental note to reassess his debating strategies and not to converse with PC Holdsworth any more than was absolutely necessary should that unfortunate need occur.

The PC turned to go, preening his moustache with his right hand; a habit that he had acquired since he first grew it on joining the police force some thirty five years earlier.

'Just one small point.' George raised his eyebrows enquiringly as if to offer PC Holdsworth the opportunity to fill in a missing word. 'Just a very small point', he pressed.

Clearly the venerable policeman had not understood the nature of the enquiry. 'Yes laddie?'

'The venue?'

'The what?' enquired the bemused officer of the law.

'The ... where in the village are you going to take the survivors?' said George restraining his inclination to ask the chap if he was either deaf or stupid. 'If I'm to meet you later, perhaps I ought, do you not think? To know the whereabouts of their destination?

An awkward silence ensued before comprehension registered across PC Holdsworth's face. He smiled contentedly at his undoubted acumen. 'The village hall of course. Dear, dear dear. I don't know, I really don't. That's where we always takes folk. Well, that or the police station anyway. You'll never make a policeman unless you start thinking about things you know. The village hall's where we will take the unlucky survivors. That's the place laddie. That's the place, and no mistake. Now you make sure you get there, I'll be needing a statement from you, you see.'

George avoided the highly improbable topic of 'unlucky survivors', and, deciding that discretion was the better part of valour, adopted expediency once again. Exasperated by his ordeal with the bucolic law officer he turned away slowly and walked pensively towards his bicycle. There was much to be assessed.

Chapter 4

THE VILLAGE HALL

The rain had set in for the evening and the temperature had dropped. George cleaned his glasses and put on his cycling cape to protect his legs from the driving rain. He cycled along the treacherously rutted, muddy path towards the village hall. The wind blew him along swiftly and he arrived there barely a couple of minutes after the survivors and their entourage had.

George's parents would have expected him to be home by now. Confirming that the survivors, rescuers and villagers had indeed entered the aforementioned village hall he returned to the telephone box and called his parents. It was his father who answered.

'Father', George began, 'I am sorry that I will be home late. Please convey my apologies to mother. There has been a shipwreck in the bay and I am a key witness to the event. I believe that the authorities will require my assistance with regard to the matter. It is possible, therefore, that I may be delayed a little while longer.'

George's father agreed with his son. 'Apprise me of developments as soon as you are able. I will speak to you at that time. I will let your mother know that she is to delay your meal.'

George and his father were as astute as they were academically gifted. Both understood the value of George returning to the village hall immediately. George junior had not proffered unnecessary details of the incident at this point and George senior had not asked for any. They had recognised and understood the need for brevity.

It was dusk as George looked across the street. The warm glow of the village hall's gaslights reflected on the wet pavement. George anticipated that the blackout curtains would soon be drawn and said, 'I must go. I shan't be able to see very shortly, it is dropping dark quite quickly I fear.'

George put the telephone down and concentrated in silence for a moment almost distracted by three species of moth trapped in the box. It

31

was a transient aberration. Quickly he rationalised his approach, prioritised his objectives, considered the viable options, and then walked his bicycle to the village hall. As he entered the porch the blackout curtains were being drawn. Almost feeling his way into the porch he leaned his bicycle against the ancient grey stone wall.

As George entered the hall he noted the dreadful atmosphere. There was a terrible sadness and he felt it likely that there had been a tragic loss of life. PC Holdsworth had asked the perfunctory questions that he was obliged to ask and had had little success. Now Dr. Owen, the local GP, was making further enquiries.

He asked both adults to ascertain the wellbeing of their children. 'Mrs. Madam er, Frau? Yes Frau? er. Your name please?' The woman spoke as George entered the room and walked towards the four-blanketed survivors.

'Meine name ist Marta Salomonovich und', she said putting her arm around the young boy. 'Mein sohn ist Joel. We are of Hamburg.' She sat up on the stretcher. 'Mein sohn ist sehr kalt. Very cold, yes?' she whispered 'aber alles gut', she said in pigeon German, hoping that the English people would better comprehend her meaning.

Doctor Owen looked at the poor woman's bandaged shoulder, the scarlet graze on her temple and the bruises on her legs.

'You don't look good to me if you don't mind me saying so Frau Salomonovich,' he tried in his best school German.

She waived his comment aside. 'Alles gut, aber...' She pointed at the man holding the young girl. He was sobbing, holding her to his breast. He kissed her forehead and held her close as if to protect her.

The good doctor attempted to elicit how many had been on board the boat. He turned to the sobbing man.

'Ruth. Ruth', wailed the man who followed that with what PC Holdsworth later announced to be 'one long word.'

'They're foreigners', revealed the constable. 'Can anybody talk French?' he asked.

Doctor Owen informed PC Holdsworth that he himself spoke French fluently but that it would be of little value as the language spoken by the man was Dutch.

'But the lady spoke German', said George, 'it is logical that we begin by speaking with her. 'We can make more headway and the chap can fill in the blanks afterwards. My German is quite fluent', he added without a trace of arrogance.

This approach seemed eminently reasonable to Doctor Owen who acceded promptly. PC Holdsworth then agreed with the doctor and nodded his assent sagely.

George proceeded to ask the woman how she and her son were but she was more concerned about the man and his daughter. She revealed that the man holding the girl could also speak German. George relayed this information to the gathered company.

'Ask her how many were on board', said PC Holdsworth mystified that anyone could make head or tail of foreigners.

'Please constable, let us first establish the state of health of our patients', urged the doctor.

'Of course, of course', agreed PC Holdsworth. 'I was just looking at it from another angle you see sir.'

George didn't agree with either approach and suggested that they ought to let the folk say what they felt was imperative and thus asked open questions.

The doctor saw the sense of George's remark and nodded 'To be sure, quite right.'

'Of course', said the constable in a matter of fact sort of way, changing his opinion in favour of what he judged to be the common wisdom.

George crouched down to speak to the survivors and turned his attention to the woman once again. He smiled in an attempt to reassure her. 'Bitte erzahalen und langsam', he said in the pedantic fashion that he believed would best elicit the required information.

George listened patiently as the woman began. Firstly she named the passengers and crew and continued with an account of the sinking of the vessel and the tragedy of the three who had lost their lives. George had hoped that she would have begun by relating why they were on the boat in the first place but recognised the woman's need to relate more recent events. He relented and allowed her to speak without interruption.

The narrative seemed to last an eternity to those not conversant with the German language. An incomprehensible stream of vocabulary flowed from the woman. It was as illuminating to George as it was frustrating for the others present.

There had been seven on board including the captain and mate. Both crewmen had gone down with the boat. The two had stayed on board until the boat sank in an attempt to get the passengers into a small rowing boat located at the stern of the boat. The captain, fighting the elements at the wheel, had commanded that the man who had survived to get into the dingy first so that he could receive the others. The man's daughter went next and then the boy had followed. The girl's mother screamed that she could not make it to the boat.

'Go. For the sake of God go', the captain had screamed at her. The boat began to sink and the captain and mate threw her towards the rowing boat. Her head had struck the side of the craft and she disappeared beneath the foaming water. The captain, his mate, and the surviving woman were the last three remaining on board the boat. They were standing up to their knees in the freezing waters of the North Sea. There were but a few vital seconds remaining.

The narrator was next. She had launched herself towards the violently pitching rowing boat. She landed in the water within grasping distance of the boat. She reached forward and suddenly her son was holding her arm screaming into her face at the top of his voice. 'Hold on Mutter. Hold on.' The man and boy hauled her into the tiny boat and she collapsed into its keel. The boat was being buffeted up, down, backwards, and forwards and all seemed hopeless. The rowing boat was taking in water and they were fearful that soon it too would sink.

The woman saw the captain and mate on board the boat as it went down. They had no need to jump; they were up to their waists in the water before they left the deck. They swam away from the vessel looking for the woman who had struck her head. The man in the rowing boat jumped into the foaming sea and joined them in the search. He surfaced only long enough to scream 'Ruth. Ruth. Ruth', then he dived again.

'We saw the lifeboat for the first time but it was too late and she had gone and the two sailors could not be found either', she said.

The girl's father surfaced under the sinking rowing boat striking and cutting his head quite badly. He was unconscious. Luckily the waves threw him up and towards the side of the rowing boat once more and the boy had held him there. The man was heavy and the boy held on for all that he was worth. The lifeboat arrived not a moment too soon for him. He was hauled on board and the rowing boat was pulled alongside.

Four of the seven were rescued; a man and his daughter and a woman and her son. Three had perished; the man's wife and the captain and his mate. The woman almost collapsed with the effort of relating their ordeal and turned her attention to her son.

PC Holdsworth sat listening to the narrative with the deep intensity as was befitting his station. The fact was that it was totally incomprehensible to him did not blunt his professional demeanour and he synchronised his nodding with young George Merrick.

When the woman appeared to have finished the officer looked grave and full of understanding, then added what he would call, was his 'own two ha'porth'.

'So where have you come from then?'

'That really is crassly insensitive I must say', rebuked the doctor. 'We have just established the fact that these good folk have been traumatised. I insist that there is nothing more to be done at the present. I really do feel that these unfortunates should be allowed to rest and sleep. Sufficient unto the day and all that.'

Feeling chastised the policeman contrived, 'Quite right. Well said. That is precisely what I was about to say. So I will leave them in your good hands doctor and I thank you. That will be all for this evening folks and that's a fact', he commanded as he ushered the villagers away from the survivors.

The father of the girl moved the blanket, which hitherto had partially covered her face, and he kissed her forehead. He offered her more of the soup that had been prepared in the small kitchen by two fussing elderly spinsters of the parish.

George caught a glimpse of the young girl. She was quite beautiful he thought. The village hall's gas lamplights reflected in her eyes and he could not account for his embarrassment as he found her looking back at him. He blushed and turned towards the doctor who was now bending over a boy of his own age. George was able to engage the boy's eyes more confidently than he had the girl's.

'I have not heard this chap speak', said George looking at Joel.

'He doesn't appear to speak at all', said the doctor. 'We shall find out more in the morning. They all need rest. We all need rest. As I said, sufficient unto the day. We must let them rest before they collapse.'

George has assimilated enough information to warrant another phone call to his father and he left the village hall. He returned to the telephone box in the drizzle that heralded the end of the storm and rang home. He began by outlining the extraordinary events that had taken place during the preceding hours.

His father was most pleased with the précis. Factual, succinct, structured and chronologically sequential the account was ample as an appraisal of the facts. He was quite sure that a meticulously comprehensive account and detailed analysis would follow at the appropriate time.

George explained the necessity of following up proceedings. 'Clearly there is much to be explained. Why were Frau and Joel Salomonovich on the boat in the first place? And what of the Haan's? Where had they come from? Who were the crew?'

'George', said the professor, quite suddenly interrupting his son's flow. 'Salomonovich, you said Salomonovich? Are you quite sure? Do you know from whence they originated?'

'Quite sure', replied George courteously but a little offended that his recollections were being questioned. 'And from Hamburg is the answer to your second question.'

'I will come along and collect you', said George's father rather stridently, which George thought to be most odd. He added, 'I'm sure that the bicycle will be safe in the hall for the night. Mr. Atkinson, the verger, will look after it for you. He is a sensible fellow. I will leave immediately.' George returned to the hall perplexed by his father's obvious increased fervour at the name Salomonovich.

The lights of the village hall had been dimmed and most of the folk had left for their homes. George stood in the vestibule for a moment pondering why on earth his father had felt it necessary to come to the hall at all when he could quite easily have cycled home.

The verger was appraising Reverend Pugh of recent developments, the vicar having being out of the parish at the time of the incident. He spotted George as he entered. 'Oh there you are George', said the cassocked pair in unison. 'I trust your parents are well', added the bespectacled cleric, the question being rhetorical. 'I go away for two minutes and all this - pandemonium', he said prattling on in the vacuous manner which his flock had learned to endure.

George discerned the verger's widening eyes at the Reverend Pugh's comment. He imagined that this was an indication that the vicar was often missing for more than two minutes and that he found it difficult to believe that pandemonium broke out every time that he left his parish. George nodded, smiled, begged their pardon politely and walked over to the survivors.

The four lay silent. It was impossible to tell if they were asleep or not. He left them to rest and turned to talk to the doctor.

It was fifteen minutes later when George's father entered the village hall shaking the rainwater from his raincoat and umbrella.

'Not a clever night sir', offered PC Holdsworth.

'No, quite', said Professor Merrick, wondering how on earth a night could be clever. People who could not speak the King's English often exasperated him. The only clever night would be a clever knight, he might have offered, had he thought that an English lesson could possibly have profited the constable. Summarily dismissing PC Holdsworth he moved across the room.

He greeted George. 'I believe that you are to be congratulated but I am sure you recognise that this is not an imperative and may be done somewhat later. I would appreciate it if you could now give me a comprehensive appraisal of the situation.'

'Well sir', began PC Holdsworth, who had followed the professor across the hall.

'Thank you, thank you constable. I am sure that you are very busy and I must not keep you from your duty. My son's account of the evening's events will suffice. Thank you once again.' If the dismissive manner of the professor's retort did not convey the impression that father wished to speak with son and son alone, then the dismissive waive of the hand certainly did.

PC Holdsworth blustered, 'Of course. I only thought... But then I really don't have the time. Pressing matters. Pressing matters you know sir', he said, full of self-importance.

'Quite', was Professor Merrick's terse response recalling George's earlier telephone counsel that 'any coherence in the fabric of PC Holdsworth's conversation will be purely accidental or coincidental?' Professor Merrick turned abruptly on his heels and engaged George. 'Please begin.'

George gave a detailed report of the incident. He did not offer thoughts or opinion. This was an account, a description and clinical exposition; in short, a list of chronicled pertinent facts. It was not a version, a rendition or an erudite treatise. Neither was it interpretive. It was a meticulous and definitive account. George dealt in evidence, nothing more and nothing less.

'I have but two questions', said his father at the conclusion of the George's account. 'What, would you estimate to be the age of the surviving mother?'

George had anticipated further questions but this was quite unexpected. 'What on earth?' He looked at his father questioningly. His look went oddly unobserved. His father was acting most strangely; something that George had not encountered before. He paused for a moment then, undeterred, but not unconcerned, answered his father's question.

George began, hesitatingly, and looking enquiringly at his father said. 'She has clearly had much sorrow and hardship and her recent harrowing past has etched additional years into her face, but I imagine her to be in her early fifties. She is injured and bears the pain exceedingly bravely. The boy, like the girl, is probably my own age. He has quite an exceptional aura about him. He has, I believe, yet to speak.

George noted that his father had been almost inattentive and impatient when he had spoken of Joel and the girl but had paid great attention to the description of Martha Salomonovich. His father became aware of George's observation and lifted heavy eyes towards his son.

'Oh, oh yes. You're right. There is, perhaps a little more to this.' He rubbed his chin with his index finger, as he often did when making calculations.

'George, I am unable to enlighten you at the moment. Suffice it to say that you have apprised me of surprising information. I do not wish to sound mysterious and I may, I say may, reciprocate shortly.'

George was astonished. How could his father have 'surprising information?' He had only walked into the hall five minutes ago! He considered the position and shot back, 'Your second question father?'

'What are the arrangements for tonight and the morrow?' Sir George enquired.

'Now there I can help you sir', interrupted PC Holdsworth who had hovered nearby determined to show that he was still in command of the proceedings and very important to the resultant procedures. 'PC Watts and me are going to watch over them tonight. The doctor will return arter his rounds at about eleven-thirty. I should think that they will need 'til then to turn around', he said nodding in the direction of the survivors.

George and Professor Merrick nodded in acknowledgement of that communication though neither believed that it was one with its origin based in the English language.

'Come George. By allowing them to sleep we serve the survivor's best interests. We will return in the morning. I suspect that we shall be required then and that there is little further to be gained this evening. There are sizeable gaps in our information and we are, perhaps, wise to contemplate what we have ascertained at this juncture.'

George and his father remained silent as the old black Austin Seven meandered its way home along the elm-lined lanes. Both were deep in thought. Both too were analysing the evening's events and considering the logical plan of action for the following morning.

'As you will be aware my boy, we must not linger after supper. I believe that I shall set the alarm for six o'clock. We shall breakfast and arrive at the hall at six forty-five. The authorities will arrive early I'm sure.'

'Precisely', George replied. 'Excellent. That is the correct time and plan of action.' This was stated with the concurred certainty that only Sherlock and Mycroft Holmes might have expressed at their zenith.

The rain had eased and the wind abated as they parked the car in the driveway of the old stone cottage that had served as George's home since his birth. Deep in thought the two walked up the path, through the small orchard and through the portals of the homestead in silence.

Had the survivors asked George, he could have pointed out, in precise detail, and in equally precise meteorological terminology, how it was that a deep depression had led to their horrific ordeal. Indeed, he would have been delighted to have done so.

Lives had been irreparably ruined yet George thought only of the mechanics and practicalities of the coming days and of his father's mysterious behaviour. What was the significance of the name Salomonovich and the city of Hamburg? His unquenchable ego and unshakable self-belief left no time for sympathy and compassion for the survivors. The incident was clearly about George Merrick.

George lay in bed as the wind abated. He was disturbed. Not by what he had seen or reasoned. This was different. Very different! Three unheralded unfathomables, (he had previously doubted the existence of such phenomena), had challenged his consciousness within a single day. His father's perplexing behaviour, the girl's considerable magnetism and the profoundly disturbing boy with the piercing ice blue eyes. A formidable aura surrounded the boy. His intensity was tangible and his charisma unassailable, even in his silence.

The portents hung heavily. George reluctantly accepted that he had not yet comprehended all manifestations of life and that there was an urgent need for review.

Chapter 5

REVELATION

The scarlet morning sky heralded a clear day that was particularly cold for the time of year. George Merrick and his father had risen early and had breakfasted while listening to the news on the wireless. George senior cranked up the Austin wearing the leather gloves he kept in the glove compartment specifically for that purpose. He drove along the pathway that led to the old lane. Neither he nor George spoke as they travelled; both were deep in thought. He turned right at the fork in the road and drove along the main road towards the village. George knew that the village hall was exactly half a mile from that particular spot; indeed he knew the exact distances between most places in the locale. The familiar village hall came into view and Professor Merrick pulled in by the roadside noting the gathering villagers by the gateway.

'Idle curiosity I shouldn't wonder', remarked the professor indicating distaste for his observation. 'I suppose that it is to be expected.' He pulled out his half-hunter pocket watch and smiled with satisfaction. 'Punctual, as everyone ought to be', he reflected. Father and son walked towards the portals of the village hall at six-forty five precisely.

They were prevented from entering by two uniformed members of the home guard, one an elderly man and the other a youth. The latter held his rifle across his body and demanded to know who the Merricks were.

'Don't you never mind', said the elderly chap to the boy, 'this here's Sir Professor Merrick. How do you do sir?'

'I'm quite well….and you, er?'

'Warren sir. Alfred Warren sir. I once spent some time painting your house if you do remember sir.'

'Oh yes. Of course. Do forgive me. I trust you are protecting and detaining the unfortunate shipwrecked four?' said Sir George offering the obvious rhetorical question but receiving an answer never the less.

'Yes sir. Just until the authorities arrives sir', beamed the old chap proudly grateful that a former patron had remembered him.

'Very good, a job well done; but I do not think that you will be requiring the rifle Mr. Warren. I do beg your pardon, Corporal Warren', said the professor noting the two stripes on the old chaps arm. The two men of the Home Guard parted and Professor Merrick and George passed between them.

As they entered the hall they spotted PC Holdsworth's burly figure rise and head towards them. George hailed Doctor Owen in an attempt to pre-empt his move. The adroit move caused the policeman to abort his intended engagement. He feigned sudden recollection, snapped his fingers and turned away to attend to more important matters. The law proceeded across the hall to the elderly spinsters making endless pots of tea in the kitchen and informed them of the gravity of the situation and the considerable responsibility the incident had placed upon him. The spinsters sympathised with him offering a second cup of tea. The great officer of the law cast away their concerns with considerable pomposity and the ladies were reassured that he was well and truly on top of his latest case and that the village was under safe stewardship. Even so PC Holdsworth scanned the hall nervously.

The professor and George met at the far corner of the hall. 'Oh, there you are doctor. A very good morning to you', said George.

'I do hope that you have been able to get a little rest old chap?' George's father enquired.

'Good morning', replied the rather tired and dishevelled doctor. 'I thank you for your concern. I am quite well and am confident that the physical health of our surprise visitors does not warrant the further presence of a doctor. However, I will remain for a little while. Trauma is a common result of such incidents and often manifests itself well after the cause.'

George was keen to know of any further developments regarding the shipwrecked four.

'Nothing really', said the good doctor as he wiped his brow with his white monogrammed handkerchief. 'The man is clearly grief stricken having lost his wife. He won't let go of his daughter. The girl has not spoken. The boy hasn't either. The only one that has given us anything to go on is the woman. Her first name, I gather, is Marta. Her surname is, and I hope I pronounce this correctly, Salomonovich. She says that she is from Hamburg.'

The doctor pronounced each syllable of the name Salomonovich separately and distinctly. 'It sounds eastern European to me, Russian or possibly Polish? I don't know.'

'Polish', pronounced the professor instantly. 'Of course. Salomonovich may well not indicate *their* country of origin, it may indicate the country of origin of their progenitors, but they have certainly not arrived directly from Poland.'

George added. 'And the bearded Rufus', indicating the shipwrecked man, 'is most certainly not eastern European.'

'Indeed he is not', said the doctor.

'Dutch is my assessment and, unless I miss my guess the woman speaks the truth and is indeed from Hamburg', said Sir George. 'Continue with your rationale George', said father to son.

Looking somewhat puzzled by the certainty of his father's pronouncement with regard to the woman's origins, George continued with his deductions.

'The inescapable conclusion is that they set sail from either Belgium or Holland; that they drifted from their course in the prevailing wind; and, that only expert seamanship saw them as far as the English coast. But the intriguing question is not where they came from but why? Why would anyone take such a risk with one's family?' George turned to look at his father.

'Cos they was escaping', announced the conspiratorial voice of the crouching policeman, who had been eavesdropping, behind George and his father.

'Precisely', said George, irritated at the interruption.

'I knew I would get to the bottom of it. It's just a question of working it out you knows; just a little knowhow and experience. I'm sure you'll find that that's correct', hailed the resplendent Holmes.

'Quite', said George's irritated father. 'Now if you wouldn't mind, with the permission of the doctor', they nodded to one another, 'we should question the survivors further.'

'Exactly right', said Holdsworth. 'Now's the time.'

The three men and the boy walked across the hall to the four forlorn souls. Both of the surviving parents held their offspring in their arms. Both had lost so much and clung on tightly to what remained of their family.

The doctor smiled as he arrived at the four mattresses on the floor of the hall that had been used as makeshift beds.

'You all look to have a little more colour', he suggested in the stilted, pigeon English that many appear to believe makes comprehension more affordable.

'Perhaps you feel a little better now?' Looking for assistance he turned to the Merricks.

'My school German is more than rusty', said the doctor apologising unnecessarily. 'The folk are much improved physically if not emotionally. Please ascertain what you feel to be pertinent but do try not to over extend them.'

'Go ahead George', urged Professor Merrick, perhaps viewing this as yet another learning experience for the young protégé.

George had addressed the woman on the previous evening. It was logical now to speak with the man. The man saw that he was about to be spoken to and tightened his grip on the bundle of blankets that cloaked his daughter.

'Please', began George in his faultless German. 'You are quite safe here. Do you understand German?' Vincent Haan nodded slowly. 'I believe that you are Dutch. Am I correct?'

The bearded Dutchman, to the surprise of all present, replied in English. 'Ja. My daughter and I are Dutch. The other ones, they are mother and son, they are German.'

'German?' said a shocked PC. Holdsworth with all the rhetorical clumsiness that an affable buffoon such as he could muster, 'German?'

'If you are quite ready I will continue', chided George.

'I know but, well, shouldn't we inform the authorities or something?' Holdsworth blustered, tweaking his moustache.

'It would be a little late now. I believe that the coastguard has complied with the correct procedures and that all such matters are in hand. It may be later on in the morning before the military arrive. There is a war on you know', said George impatiently.

PC Holdsworth was about to retort that he knew there was a war on and that he would have willingly enlisted had it not been for the 'state of his feet' but fortuitously the doctor interrupted him.

An almost imperceptible conspiratorial nod passed between Professor Merrick to Dr. Owen. The doctor rose.

'Constable, I wonder if I might have a moment. I think the matter to be very important.'

'Of course sir', said a very pleased Holdsworth. 'Now laddie', he said to George. 'You find out what you can and I will be back before you can say Jack Robinson. The doctor and I have a few important matters to attend to.'

'Of course, of course', the Merricks concurred in unison.

George turned back to Vincent Haan. He noted a resolve within the man that had not been evident on the previous evening. He viewed the large figure with renewed respect. He was a proud man. The brown eyes that had been dimmed by the tragedy were now alert and intelligent. The red beard was newly trimmed. The man was making a stoic effort.

'And so', began George. 'Where were we? Oh yes. Now sir, perhaps you are able to answer a few questions? Good.'

George was in his element. This was the time for forensic analysis. This was a moment when revelation would be the result of his astute deduction.

The blanket enveloping Rachael Haan dropped from her shoulders revealing her features for the second time. George's deductive powers dissipated. He froze. The girl was the most beautiful creature that he had ever seen. He swallowed before speaking. He looked at the father now, reluctant to take more than a glance at his daughter.

Shyly he glanced again and fought for his equilibrium. The sensation was unknown. His precise, well-ordered, intellectual capacity was momentarily impaired.

'George', enquired his father. 'George?'

It took a few moments for George to collect himself.

'I'm sorry father. You were saying?' he floundered.

'I wasn't saying anything actually. Really! You were enquiring of the gentleman about his recent history', he pronounced, clearly disconcerted at his son's lapse. 'Would you rather I continue', he enquired.

George's father never thought that he would hear the words, 'If you wouldn't mind,' from his son and looked somewhat bemused and perplexed.

George always sought to solve riddles. An enigma merely represented a challenge. His father generally watched and evaluated his son's performance ever mindful of the feedback that he would relay later.

Professor Merrick took the view that something was amiss. George had cycled in the wind and the rain on the previous evening and had risen early on the morning. Perhaps this was fatigue. Neither father nor son knew the meaning of the word but...

There were more pressing matters. That debate could wait.

'Mr...?' Merrick senior enquired.

'My name is Vincent Haan', said the Dutchman in a very acceptable English. 'This is my daughter Rachael. We are from The Netherlands. Maastricht actually.'

Professor Merrick caught George staring at the girl.

'George?' he said, perturbed.

George turned to his father abruptly.

I'm sorry sir. I was er'

'No matter. Please go on Mr. Haan', he said looking uncomprehendingly at his son.

He looked back at Vincent Haan and repeated, 'Please go on.'

'There is no beginning, or should I say there are several beginnings. All I know about the lady; and she is a lady I must say; is that she and her son too were escaping the Nazis. The lady is called Marta. The boy is Joel. He has not spoken since I met him two, or is it three days ago. I forget all the days...'

'Yes, I don't mean to press you but please do go on', said Merrick senior anxious for the tale to be relayed before the military arrived.

'I don't know the details of Marta and Joel. I believe that they are the only survivors of their family although Marta speaks of her daughter Rebecca in her sleep. Always she is saying, 'Rebecca, Rebecca, my Rebecca. I only know that she seeks her daughter and that by coming to England she feels that she has abandoned her. Guilt is a heavy burden sir. I know this very well.'

'She told me that they were taken from their home and put on a train along with many others. They did not know, how do you say it, oh yes, their destination. I do not know the details of the story but again they were fortunate, if it can be called that when one has lost so much', he added reflectively. 'They escaped from a train and believe that they were the only ones to have done so. Somehow they came to Harderwijk and it was there on a barge on a canal that we met them.

'As for my beautiful wife Ruth, beautiful daughter, Rachael, and I, there is another story to tell.'

Chapter 6

VINCENT HAAN'S STORY

Vincent Haan smiled at his daughter. It was a wounded smile of love and pride, his stoical façade belying the gnawing anguish of his loss. His mouth turned upwards and his head tilted affectionately towards her. His eyes still bore the pain of bereavement. Ruth had gone. Gone forever! Ruth, his beautiful wife, gone forever. How could he live on? He stroked his daughter's hair and looked into her beautiful face and knew the answer. Rachael.

Unspeaking he promised Ruth that he would love and care for their daughter, praying for her spiritual aide and she confirmed his supplication from within his pounding breast. Out loud he whispered his amen. 'The three of us will always be together and we will be with you every day. This I promise.'

He wondered what Rachael had understood of the conversation with the Englishman. She was just fourteen years old but was exceptionally bright and had an aptitude for languages. She spoke her native Dutch as an educated adult might, had a comprehensive understanding of English, French, and German vocabulary and a smattering of Flemish. It wasn't her ability to comprehend the conversation that Vincent questioned; it was the state of her traumatised young mind.

He fixed his attention on Sir George and began: My brother, Rudi, worked against the Nazi occupiers. He has committed many acts. Do you understand? Sabotage. Yes? He blows up railway lines, docks and the place where you keep weapons and explosives. I don't know your name for it.'

'They cannot find him. They shoot against a wall six of the men folk of my town and the seventh gives our home as a place to go. Perhaps we will know? No? Yes? I don't know. Perhaps they think but… The Gestapo appear at my neighbours door, by mistake, and ask where my brother lives. They knock down the door. They say that they don't know whom, whom yes? They are asking for us and say but that we live in the next house.'

44

'We hear all of this. I take my two girls and we leave by a window at the back of my house just minutes before they come. We hide in our barge by the canal and contact my brother. Rudi has heard. Do you understand all of this?' He searched Sir George's eyes for understanding.

Sir George nodded. 'Yes please do go on', he said absorbing every detail of the tale.

Rudi knows everyone. Yes? We were to board another barge on the canal and put our trust in the captain. After many hours the woman and the boy, Marta and Joel, joined us near Harderwijk. How we travelled down the canal and into open sea without being stopped I will never know. Perhaps', he said, with tears welling. 'Perhaps...' He stopped to reflect, 'Perhaps my Ruth would be...' The rest was incoherent.

It took several moments for Vincent to compose himself again during which he hugged his daughter with great tenderness.

Rachael Haan put her arms around her father. Vincent looked down at her as he wiped his eyes with the white monogrammed handkerchief he had accepted from Dr. Owen. He saw Ruth's face shining through his daughter's and he smiled a smile, which moved the Merricks, who were not accustomed to their emotions being aroused so intensely. George, who was unaccustomed to being stirred by anything other than scientific revelation and fine art, lost his mental equilibrium for the first time in his life. He felt hot and a little giddy and wished that he had not worn his thick roll neck sweater.

Vincent gathered himself again.

'The decision to cross to England was that all of us agreed. My wife insisted. She insisted,' he sobbed and took a deep breath. 'To begin with we could not believe our luck. The sea was calm and we avoided the Germans. The captain was an expert and very cunning I think; he had, perhaps, what you call 'inside knowledge', yes? Perhaps we had luck too', he reflected. 'Perhaps it was both – a combination yes? I don't know. All I do know is that the captain said that we were ten kilometres from the English coast and it was very dark. The engine was making bad sounds now and the captain and his mate looked concerned. The captain reduced the power and we began to drift. The engine would not take more he said. For many hours we travelled north. The dawn came, and still we drifted - but not to land. We drifted all through the day. The captain says that every hour is a good hour and that we are improving our position. But I know that this is for our moral.'

'Morale', corrected Sir George, immediately wishing that he hadn't. 'Please continue,' he urged, chiding his folly.

'The weather began to turn very bad. The sky turned grey, the wind blew and the water became high. We saw land and, as we did so, the engines stopped for the last time. The captain told us to paddle with whatever we could find and that land was very near.'

Vincent came to an abrupt end and stared into space.

Sir George understood that the next part of the narration would include the death of the poor man's wife.

Vincent Haan was holding back his tears. He held the bridge of his nose between fingers and thumb of his free right hand and took another deep breath.

'Steady old chap', comforted Merrick senior. 'Mr. Haan. You are amongst friends now. You and your daughter are safe. Please take your time. Shall we take a break? Would you like a cup of tea perhaps?'

Vincent indicated that he would and, seeing Rachael's look of concern, gave her a reassuring hug and smile in an unsuccessful attempt at showing her that he was in control of his emotions.

The girl had comprehended the English words that her father had spoken but was indeed too traumatised to concentrate on the account being related. However she understood, from her father's demeanour, that he was nearing the end of his rendition. She put her arms around him and put her head into his chest.

George saw the side of the girl's face. It was a beautiful and intelligent face, he believed. She was immaculately groomed, even after the shipwreck and a night on the mattress in the village hall. She had beautiful large dark brown eyes, long black hair tied back in a ponytail, a petite nose and full red lips. 'Elegant and intelligent', though George. 'That's the sum of it. A girl well worth engaging in conversation.' It was the first girl that he had considered worthy of that honour. 'Beautiful and intelligent', he mused.

George had had little contact with females. Indeed, it was certainly true to say that his mother was the one female that he had ever engaged in conversation, other than those with whom he had exchanged pleasantries or those in the guise of customer or passenger.

Vincent took yet another deep breath, preparing for a final burst. He continued. The mate of the boat had spotted land as the passengers continued to bail out the boat frantically using a bucket and several kitchen utensils. The captain encouraged them to work harder saying that they were no more than a kilometre from the coast.

The weather was deteriorating rapidly. The boat was getting lower in the water and Vincent, Ruth and Marta left Rachael and Joel to bail out the boat. They joined the mate and captain in paddling with pieces of what had been the wooden cabin table. 'It's time', the captain shouted, as a huge wave broke over the boat knocking Ruth to the deck. Blood spread into the fabric of her drenched pleated skirt as she attempted to get to her feet. Vincent staggered towards her across the pitching deck and supported her. She was clearly in pain but this was not the time for first aid. Rachael saw Joel raise her mother's head from the deck before her father took her in his arms.

The captain stopped, looking at the mate. They nodded to each other.

'Time to abandon ship and take our chances in the rowing boat', shouted the captain. 'It is only small but we have no choice.'

Vincent paused to blow his nose more frequently as the story progressed.

He related how the captain and mate had lowered the rowing boat and the mayhem that followed as the fishing boat went down.

The sea was a white foaming torrent and the crashing of the waves had been deafening. The boat was awash when the rowing boat was lowered. The captain ordered Vincent to jump into the little boat first. He had objected. The captain screamed at him that this was necessary. He looked at his two girls with his eyes wide open. He assured them that all would be well and jumped. He landed awkwardly and fell. He was up in an instant, arms held out to catch his daughter but it was Joel that the captain had designated to jump next. Joel put one foot on the side of the vessel and leapt into the rowing boat adroitly and without visible fear.

Vincent saw the fear in his daughter's eyes as he urged her to jump. She turned to her mother. Her mother smiled and mouthed the word 'Go.'

As Rachael jumped the small boat lurched sideways. Rachael landed on the deck and would have fallen backwards into the sea had it not been for Joel's quick reactions. He grabbed her arms and pulled her towards him. He held her for a brief moment before her father took her from his arms. Joel recovered his senses and looked to lend assistance, turning back to the fishing boat. Vincent and Joel beckoned the dazed Ruth to jump. She attempted the same manoeuvre as Joel but missed her footing. The rowing boat lurched away from the larger vessel and Ruth vanished beneath the raging sea.

Vincent dived into the sea after his wife. 'While I was in the water the boy's mother had launched herself from the partly submerged vessel and took no more than three strokes of her arms to reach the relative safety of the rowing boat. Joel found the strength to pull her into the boat, ignoring his mother's screams of agony as he pulled on her injured shoulder to haul her on board. She collapsed from exhaustion and pain onto the wooden deck. This is what she told me during the night. Yes?'

Rachael shivered and Vincent lowered her to the mattress and pulled a sheet to her chin. The Merricks noted that he had never let go of her hand.

The fishing boat had almost sunk. There was no need for the captain or mate to jump. They were up to their waists in water and swam from the submerged deck. The sinking boat was rolling in the surf, being tossed back and forth in the shallow waters.

Vincent surfaced screaming 'Ruth, Ruth, Ruth', his voice chillingly frenzied.

The captain and mate joined Vincent and they dived together.

The sinking boat lifted from the sea in a last agonising roll and crashed over the three men. The last thing that Vincent remembered was seeing the large grey hull bearing down on him. He screamed in the water and all went black.

He had no memory of his rescue. He remembered briefly regaining consciousness at one time in the lifeboat. He saw his beloved daughter and lost consciousness again.

'I believe that I have that young man to thank for my life', he said, pointing at Joel. His mother told me that it was he who saw me drifting by the rowing boat. He dived into the water and pulled me to the boat. A brave boy. He grabbed me and held my head above water at the side of the boat. It must have taken everything the young boy had inside of him. As you can see I am not a small man.'

Vincent paused and smiled at Joel. Joel looked through him. Rachael lifted her head from her father's chest then looked at Joel comprehending and empathising with his grief.

George noted the look of gratitude on Rachael's face and felt unaccountably jealous that he had not been able to help in a more direct manner. Sir George turned to see the boy still gazing at her.

'Quite', mused the professor, somewhat disturbed by his son's inability to concentrate and articulate. 'Do continue.'

'Well sir, I believe that you know everything else. The lifeboat was so close. If only…if only…' Vincent raised his head and collecting himself yet again in a painful attempt to conclude his story.

'The mast of the fishing boat was still above the water as the hull was thrown about on the sandbank below. The lifeboat pulled alongside and was tied to the rowing boat. That too was sinking. There was no sign of Ruth, the captain or his mate.'

Both Merrick senior and junior noted that Vincent's rendition of events had closely mirrored Marta Salomonovich's recollections. The recounting of the story had clearly been an ordeal for Vincent Haan too but it had been a cathartic experience and perhaps all the more valuable for that, thought George. He noted that this would be the beginning of the healing process.

Sir George thanking Vincent for his narrative smiled then beckoned George to follow him. He begged Vincent Haan's pardon as they moved to a niche of the village hall that afforded him some degree of privacy.

'George', he said impatient with a son that had clearly not been himself. 'Well', he pursued more urgently.

'Oh, er. Yes, well, I mean', he stuttered.

'Really George! Do pay attention. In short what do you deduce of the veracity of the story?'

'Well father', began George, regaining his legs, 'it is as genuine as it is tragic.'

'I concur', was the father's reply. 'And now?

Chapter 7

RACHAEL HAAN

Rachael Haan, like her mother Ruth was an only child. She was born to grateful and loving parents and was cherished by both.

Vincent and Ruth Haan had first met at The University of Maastricht. He studied architecture and she classics. Vincent was best described as jovial, though how he got to be so was a mystery. Both of his parents were killed during The Great War in 1916, when he was just nine years old. He was brought up in an orphanage and prospered there. Ruth's father was a banker and her mother of aristocratic lineage. Her mother became a wealthy dowager by the time her only child was twelve.

Vincent and Ruth fell in love in the summer of 1925 and married two years later. Ruth's mother was apprehensive at the haste of their marriage and had not taken to Vincent at first. It hadn't taken long for Vincent to win her over. He was a caring son-in-law and his easy manner disarmed the old lady. She could also see the sparkle of love in her daughter's eyes whenever she turned to look at her husband and this, in these uncertain times, was reason enough for her to change her attitude. Vincent had made her daughter as happy as she had once been and she was grateful for that. Never the less protocol was protocol and she always retained an element of temperance and moderation in her dealings with him; the pervasive influence of her genes, station and eminence demanding self-control, discipline and restraint.

Vincent and Ruth's modest matrimonial home was located less than a mile from the dowager's mansion and, while the lady visited infrequently, her daughter and son-in-law were most dutiful in that respect.

Ruth was young, beautiful and in love. She and Vincent had bright futures ahead of them and they prospered. Their one remaining wish was to have children. Ruth miscarried twice, both times after six months, and the doctors assessed that it was better to accept the situation and not take further risks. At that appointment Ruth was one day pregnant.

Rachael was born on the fourth of July 1928. Now Vincent and Ruth felt that they had it all. She grew up pampered but unspoilt by her parents and her sole surviving grandparent. Ruth did not pursue her career after Rachael's birth. Vincent was 'happy for her to care for Ruth and Rachael.' The two became Vincent's 'girls.'

The family prospered for the next ten years as the 'storm clouds gathered over Europe' and the Nazis malign influence and power began to take an iron grip on the affairs of the continent. When the Netherlands was invaded, on the tenth of May 1940, Vincent continued to work at his business and kept himself to himself as much as he was able. His brother, Rudi, joined the resistance movement and inevitably sought help from Vincent, as an architect, with regard to the layout of building occupied by the Gestapo and other Nazis. Vincent was careful. Rudi was reckless and he worried Vincent greatly.

Rachael's grandmother insisted on sending Rachael to private school. 'The girl is clearly very bright and really ought to follow in the family tradition.' Vincent was not at all convinced but understood the look that Ruth gave him when confronted with his mother-in-law's logic and his wife's subsequent demure, wide-eyed request. Was it rationally or irrationally that he acquiesced on grounds of love and harmony?

Rachael excelled and by the age of twelve would quite easily have been accepted by universities had her parents insisted that this was not at all what they wanted. Ruth stood firm against her mother and she and Vincent decided that fifteen was to be quite early enough.

Rachael's days were filled with love and knowledge. She was well liked and several close friends happily thought of her as their best friend. This did not present a problem to her. She had an excellent understanding of human nature and was mature beyond her years balancing her time and affections with equanimity.

She read extensively having a penchant for reading French literature in the native language; everything from Moliere to Zola. Flaubert's 'Madam Bovary' and his protégé Guy de Maupassant's short stories were particular favourites. Stendhal's Rouge en Noir with the driven Julien Sorel, who harboured romantic illusions, yet fell under the powerful machinations of the influential, fascinated and intrigued her and nurtured her understanding of the human condition.

She loved evenings in her grandmother's reassuring arms listening to her mother play Chopin and Liszt on the piano or singing excerpts from Schubert lieder.

When the Gestapo came her idyllic world came to an end. It was evening. Firstly they heard the goose-stepping marching of leather boots on cobbled stones. Her father went to the sitting room sideboard and took his wallet and papers. Then they heard the smashing of a window at the house next door. Her mother gathered their coats. Next there came shouting and confusion at the realisation that the Gestapo had entered the wrong premises.

Her father put a finger over his mouth to indicate to Rachael that she must be quiet and then assisted his 'two girls' out of the kitchen window at the rear of the house.

They ran towards a copse of silver birch some sixty metres beyond their small garden. As they approached the tree line Vincent turned to see torchlight in the vacated kitchen. It had been a close run thing and there wasn't a moment to lose. He and Ruth took Rachael by the hand and ran through the trees. Soon they came to the old towpath running alongside the canal.

There on a capstan sat an old man smoking a white clay pipe. He had neglected to shave and his unkempt appearance matched his slovenly demeanour. His yellow whiskers and teeth gleamed in the moonlight and the reek of tobacco drifted through the cold evening air. He turned his head acknowledging Vincent's presence with a laconic wave of his pipe.

Vincent began. 'The spring is late this year.'

The old man took his pocket watch from his waistcoat, took note of the time and nodded, 'Yes, but the tulips will still bloom.'

'Where is Rudi? We are in urgent need of help.'

'Get on board. It is not far.'

The old man's gait changed. He was deceptively agile. He untied the rope, helped the three fugitives on board and was underway within moments.

After a short time they pulled in to the far canal bank. Dark figures approached the barge. Vincent immediately recognised the rolling walk of his brother and jumped from the barge onto the towpath. He and Rudi put their arms around one another.

'Are you well?' Rudi enquired as they pulled back.

'For the moment but they are on to you Rudi. We must all get away from here.' Rudi reached forward and swept his niece from the barge. 'And how is my favourite niece? He asked the beaming girl.

'Your only niece is quite well Uncle Rudi. But I am a little afraid.'

Rudi Haan crouched and put his arms around Rachael. 'Do not worry princess. All will be well. Soon the war will be over and we shall all remember these difficult times. But they will pass. All will be well.' He saw Ruth and rose to greet her. They held each other for a brief moment.

'It's time to go. Follow me.' The small group made their way into the woodlands and presently came to a small farm. They entered the barn and climbed the ladder to the loft.

'This is where you will stay. It will take a day or so to organise. I have contacts.'

Vincent took Rudi by the arm and looked him in the eye. 'And you Rudi? What of you?'

'I do not have a wife and child. However I do have many friends. It won't be for long. I am quite safe.'

'No one is safe', insisted Vincent knowing only too well that when Rudi had made up his mind the devil himself could not alter it. He relented.

'For God's sake be careful', he sighed.

'I will. I will.'

Vincent knew that Rudi could be a lot of things but careful was not one of them. Reckless? Perhaps. Careful? Never.

It was the following evening when Rudi returned. He whispered, 'There is no going back,' Vincent stared into Rudi's eyes and knew that it was time to go. 'They have confiscated your house and are looking everywhere for us. You must go and go now.'

The three were given a small bag of food each and three small bottles of water and taken to the edge of the wood. Rudi bid them farewell and they turned towards the canal. When they turned around he has disappeared.

Rachael heard a noise close behind her and jumped in fear. There stood a giant of a man. He had a huge black beard fixed to a huge round head. His piercing blue eyes shone from his fresh red face. A belt was fastened tight around his corduroy trousers below supporting the expansive girth above it. Rachael froze and could not take her eyes from him.

He spoke. 'There are three of you, yes? Come.' He invited them on board a barge moored close by.

They entered the small cabin and sat at a table that had a bench seat at either side. The three huddled together for warmth. Rachael ached for her warm bed and for the evening talk that she and her mother usually had before going to sleep.

The huge man poked his head down into the hatchway. 'We are heading for the coast. It is dangerous. If you wish to leave us you only have to say so. I do not want your capture on my conscience. We have papers and are not particularly conspicuous but we will need luck.'

'The coast? said Vincent, 'but...'

'Yes there are many dangers there. But I have spent my life in these waters. Before we get to the coast there is a river. A small tributary runs to the north of the canal and into a secluded bay. There we have a boat. There are Germans there but they are used to seeing this boat. We fish offshore two, sometimes three times a week. Unless they know of our exploits and connect them with this boat all will be well. If not...' his voice petered away as he lifted his head to scan the banks. His head appeared again. 'If you have better ideas then you will let me know?' He didn't hesitate. 'Good. We go.'

Rachael heard a voice call out to the man. 'Captain. The light.'

The passengers had not seen the first and only mate of the two-man crew until he appeared on deck. They could barely make out his shape let alone his features but it was clear that he did not share the same appetite for hospitality as the captain.

It was later on the same evening that further passengers were taken on board. A woman and her son.

Rachael had sat in the dark with her parents for several hours. She heard an exchange of voices and soon the bustle of two figures descending the steps into the cabin.

The smaller figure tripped over her father's leg and fell to the floor. She heard a woman speak in German ascertaining his well-being. The intruders sat on the bench at the opposite side of the table. There was an absurd silence.

Rachael tried hard to stay awake but was unable to and when she awoke it was morning. The cabin was still quite dark but she was able to make out the features of the two strangers opposite. The woman opposite was clearly in agony and she could see the anxiety and hurt in her son's eyes. Such languid eyes; such intelligent eyes. Her own plight was momentarily forgotten as the distressing sight of her fellow passengers moved her.

Clearly her father had communicated with the woman while she had slept. The ice had been broken. She recognised the rapport that had already formed and developed.

She turned to see the boy looking at her. Before she could avert her eyes he quickly turned to look at his mother. Rachael saw the love and affection that he had for his mother. She also noted the boy's handsome profile and considerable stature. There was something about him that she could not place. A disturbing gravitas; a presence; a charismatic aura, though, as yet, she had not heard him speak a word. She reflected on this for a short time then turned to catch him glancing at her again. It was difficult to tell in that light but she believed that he had blushed. She noted that he resolved not to look again.

The barge left the canal for the tributary which in turn led to a small cove. The captain and his mate moored alongside a small boat. They scanned the bay while preparing the boat for sea. When they were satisfied with their work they sat for a short time observing the cliffs. All seemed well. Quickly the passengers were transferred to the boat and the boat began forging its way out to sea.

The boat began to pitch as it left the protection of the cove and Rachael began to feel ill. Vincent found a small pail and Ruth held it for her as she wretched over it. She had hardly eaten for the past two days and had little to throw up and this worsened her condition. After a while Joel reached forward and took the bucket on deck. He returned the pail which smelled of seawater and it was clear that he had washed it out. Rachael was somewhat surprised by Joel's action. She was grateful to him and wanted to show her appreciation but he did not appear to be at all attentive beyond his duty.

After a short while the engine slowed causing the boat to lurch and toss beyond its previous parameters. The swell was considerable now and Rachael was not alone in feeling ill. None of this affected Joel's constitution and he left the cabin to offer silent assistance to the captain and his mate.

They sailed for more than five hours before the engine began to splutter. The captain set sail and consulted his charts. They drifted north in the currents for several hours before the cooled engine was engaged again. Within the hour the pistons capitulated and all fell silent. Again the captain set the small sail; the grim expression on his face far from comforting his anxious passengers. They sailed for several more hours. The captain sighted shore and asked for all those who were able to come on board. Rachael remained with her mother in the cabin and it was only as the boat began to flounder that they climbed onto the deck to face the storm.

Rachael saw the small rowing boat being lowered into the sea and her father and Joel leap into it. The captain brought her and her mother to the edge of the boat and urged her to jump. She looked in terror at her mother and then at her father screaming at her from the rowing boat. She jumped.

At that moment the rowing boat lurched sideward and it was Joel's arms that caught her as she landed on the deck and began to fall backwards into the sea. He held her firmly until she had regained her equilibrium. Her father took her from him and placed her on a seat in the boat. He and Joel turned back to the boat. She glanced up to see her mother jump for the rowing boat but lost sight of her as she missed her footing and fell into the white surging sea.

Her father dived into the water and disappeared. Rachael screamed then fainted. Joel caught her again.

When she opened her eyes it was Marta who held her in her arms. She turned to look for her parents and saw Joel, manfully holding onto a figure in the water. He was struggling hard and using every nerve and sinew. It was her father and Joel would not be able to hold on for much longer.

The tiny boat was thrown in all directions as the fishing boat disappeared into the surf.

'Mother, where is my mother', she cried. She tried to get to her father and fell, striking her head on the hull of the boat. The next thing that she would remember was being carried into the village hall by her father.

Grief overtook her and she disintegrated. She was there in the hall but it was as though she viewed the scene from beyond the grave. She was not a participant. It was a play and she sat in the audience transfixed by the tragic plot. She stared into the distance as the boy Joel had done, unchallenged. Her mind was numb and she did not feel the intense cold of her body. Her father held her tight and she was grateful for that. She glanced at the adjacent mattress again aware of Joel's gaze. He turned away from her embarrassed at being caught again.

Another boy had entered the hall and was approaching them. The boy was clearly proficient in German but she did not pay much attention to him as her heart was heavy with the loss of her mother. She wished that he would go away and leave her father and herself alone to grieve but she remained silent.

The bespectacled boy was small and wiry. His large sharp nose contrasted acutely with his small round face. It was as if a jigsaw had been made from two different boxes. The parts fitted but didn't appear to match. Rachael turned to her father supplicating much needed reassurance.

Her mind was in turmoil as the reality of the loss of her mother overcame her. Much of the following hours were lost to her. There were questions and the movements of persons unknown before her but her mind had transcended reality and slipped into that fortunate state that inures the mind from overload and puts the body into automatic override.

The horrors of the night fought with her extreme fatigue. Her eyes would not stay open yet she could not sleep. She lay on her allotted mattress in that twilight area twixt consciousness and sleep. She saw her mother at the side of the boat and recalled the terror etched into her face. She tossed and turned as she ached to see her beautiful mother and be taken into her arms once again.

How would her grandmother survive the knowledge that her only child had drowned? Who would tell her? She would know that the family were on the run but she would not know of their present circumstances or of the loss of her daughter.

She opened her eyes, incomprehensively startled. She did not know whether she had been asleep or not and looked to see her father. He was sat at her side. He reached down and touched her forehead. He leaned forward and kissed her cheek.

It was a few moments before he spoke. 'Rachael', he said heavily. 'Rachael we have survived the Nazis and the sea. Tell me, what do you think that your mother would want for us now?'

She answered immediately. 'To remember her forever father.'

Her father had thought that he would elicit the idea that Ruth would have wanted her daughter to live a happy and healthy life. He was unprepared for the answer she gave and it was he who began to cry. Rachael put her arms around her father and said. 'I will always love you father. Always. I promise.'

It was several moments before Vincent was able to pull himself together.

He began again, 'We must always remember your mother. How can we forget her goodness and her love? It is not possible. Rachael, she would also wish for you to be happy. I do not know what tomorrow brings let alone anything of our future here in England. All I know is that we must do what we can and, using your mother as an example, try to remain positive. 'What', she would say, 'is the alternative? There is no turning back. Remember?'

The bespectacled boy returned with two civilians and one uniformed man. The boy and civilians appeared to find the uniformed man tiresome. She did not know what the uniform represented. It didn't look like a military one. She guessed that it would be a policeman's uniform

The uniformed character was larger than life. If he were indeed a policeman any thief with a turn of heel would make an easy living. He had a huge belly and a huge moustache to match and stepped from foot to foot as if anticipating a particular stimulus for him to respond to. He didn't give the impression that he was in charge of matters at all.

Rachael looked at the old man who sat with the boy and recognised that they were from the same mould. The same round heads and pointed noses indicated father and son.

Her eyes were heavy and she fell asleep in her father's arms, a collage of Turner's amorphous world inhabiting her dreams.

When she awoke she was laying on her mattress covered by a blanket. At long last she felt warm. Her father lay asleep beside her. The unwelcome images of the shipwreck pervaded her thoughts and she relived the terror of her recent young life.

Chapter 8

JOEL SALOMONOVICH

Marta Salomonovich had listened to Vincent Haan's rendition of the tragedy with frequent nods of assent. She sat on her makeshift bed nursing yet another cup of tea proffered by the ever smiling spinsterhood of the parish. She had listened attentively, occasionally stroking Joel's forehead as Vincent's harrowing narrative chronicled his misery. Joel sat expressionless at his mother's side throughout, his impassive, enigmatic countenance well recorded by two particularly keen but frustrated observers. Recognition of the talk of his bravery; the death of Ruth and the rescue of Vincent had not registered on his face. Recognition that he was being observed hadn't either.

Vincent's English had been a little stilted and Marta's own English was severely limited but she had understood the content of his conversation. She noted the change in Vincent's face. The optimist she had seen in him only a few short days ago had been replaced by defeat and, in turn, defeat into hardened realism and a pragmatism born of despair. Now, as he related his account of the tragedy, she saw the inner strength and resolve that George had noted earlier.

The intensity of his loss and his grief and pain echoed like a refrain throughout his discourse. The air was charged with unfettered emotion as his poignant narrative ended in a thundering silence. George and his father remained seated for some time before rising in order to give Vincent a little time to recover himself. Merrick senior had reached forward and placed his hand on Vincent's shoulder in an awkward and rare overt display of tenderness. The Merrick's moved away a little and engaged in conversation.

It was then that a solemn yet demanding voice sliced through the febrile atmosphere like a samurai's sword. Joel Salomonovich stood in the centre of the hall arms outstretched to the heavens.

'Culpe poenae par esto', came forth the incontrovertible and unambiguous curse. The vituperative bold and measured delivery of Joel's

words sent a chill through the ether. The Merricks, the Haans, Dr. Owen and PC Holdsworth stared at the boy in disbelief.

'He can talk', revealed PC Holdsworth, sotto voce and rather predictably. 'I still am 'aving a little trouble with his Dutch though you know. Sounds double Dutch if you ask me. I'm flummoxed and no mistake.'

Dr. Owen raised an eyebrow as he glanced first at George and his father before addressing PC Holdsworth in the same whisper. 'That double Dutch is Latin constable.'

'Oh that's why', said a wary PC Holdsworth as if understanding the explanation. Then, 'But you said he was Dutch not Latin.'

Dr. Owen shook his head in despair before turning to the apparition caught in the shaft of sultry dawn sunlight filtering through the leaded east window of the hall.

The passionate intensity, heart-rending anguish and virulent acrimony of Joel's few words, invoked evil retribution and sent a shiver through the small group remaining in the hall, regardless of PC Holdsworth's banality and the incomprehensibility of its content. The menace of Joel's uncompromising words shot down the spines of the onlookers. Joel wore a new mantel. The young boy portrayed a dark and ominous character and the tangible magnetism and charisma he exuded bode the coming of a sinister evil. This was a returned Heathcliff: Dark, brooding and menacing.

There was silence.

The boy stared ahead like a saint witnessing a sacred vision; his eyes wide open; transfixed by something not visible to the common man.

PC Holdsworth broke the silence once again, unable to rest his tongue.

'Don't know what he said sir but I knows enough to know that he said it with some nastiness. I trust it warn't against us sir. I won't 'ave it you know.' PC Holdsworth was floundering now. He often began on a theme and, losing the thread, failed to extricate himself from the delivery of it. He muttered a few more words to himself before Dr. Owen, mercifully, ended his ramblings.

'Extraordinary', proclaimed the doctor looking for confirmation from Sir George.

The professor was also stunned by the intensity and bile of Joel's words. The malice had been awe inspiring from one so young.

George stared at Joel. He had known many boys at school. Never had he met one with such charisma, gravitas and dark intensity.

Joel's words left George's mouth slowly. 'Culpae poenae par esto. Let the punishment fit the crime.'

On hearing George repeat his words, Joel turned to him, engaged his eyes and invoked another coruscating invective, his top lip curling with hate. *'Sic vis pacem para bellum.'* The ethereal energy left Joel and he collapsed with the effort of his exhortations.

'My God he's going to get revenge', declared the doctor. 'My word he invoked a blessing to carry out the task.'

'All well and good sir', said Holdsworth uncertainly, 'but I don't think old Hitler's going to lose too much sleep. He's only a lad you know. What was that Latin thing that he said anyhow?'

Marta had remained quiet. She had always known Joel possessed a rare and special quality and that, one day, he would have his say in the world. It was the timing of his graduation and his strident malice that had surprised her.

George translated. 'Sic vis pacem para bellum. To prepare for peace, prepare for war.'

PC Holdsworth could not explain his sense of foreboding and the uncomfortable aura that had settled over the hall so he stroked his moustache and nodded his head sagely.

George was staring at Rachael who, in turn, had been staring at Joel. An unaccountable pang of jealousy pierced his heart. He felt blood rushing to his cheeks as he stole another glance at her. Her face was fine and delicate, her lips moved as she leaned towards her father who responded by putting his arm around her slender waist. He noted her grace and squirmed at his own awkwardness. Leonardo had said that wisdom was the daughter of experience. He understood the truth of that now. He lacked reference points and the uncomfortable outcome, which he readily recognised and acknowledged, was the loss of his emotional equilibrium. He considered the point and believed it just conceivable that not all emotions could be harnessed and reined in at will, as he had previously believed. Had he considered the trials of Julien Sorrel, Madam Bovary, et al, worthy of his time, as both Joel and Rachael had, he may well have had an insight into the emotional turmoil torturing his soul.

Sir George took the gold half-hunter from his waistcoat pocket. 'It is half past eight and I see that the army has arrived', he said, noting a young captain and his burly sergeant walking purposefully towards them.

The professor whispered a few words to Dr. Owen and beckoned George to follow him. They left the hall quickly and quietly as PC Holdsworth welcomed the army to the village and made it known that he was in charge and at their disposal.

At last the wind had dropped.

Chapter 9

BILLETING

The fresh-faced young captain and his seasoned sergeant approached Dr. Owen and PC Holdsworth. He began by addressing the law.

'I take it that you are in charge here sergeant.'

'I am indeed sir. Indeed I am', replied PC Holdsworth self-importantly.

'Good', the captain went on, 'I should like to be made au fait with the facts if you please.'

'Er, Oh', began Holdsworth. 'You see, well it's not that... It's er... It's best if it comes from one as I've delegated sir. Now where's my professor? Er.'

Holdsworth looked around for Sir George and his son.

'Really constable', began the captain before being interrupted by the policeman.

'You see sir', he said, recovering himself, 'they was foreign and my languages being a little bit rusty and that, like the doctor's sir, I asked for assistance. There was a chap and his son who must have just left as you arrived', he squirmed, scanning the room for the Merricks. 'You see sir, they are the ones you want sir. You must have seen them sir? They were the ones who questioned the foreigners sir. I didn't realise that they was leaving sir. They never said that they woz. I'd 'ave put my foot down if they ad said they woz and no mistake.'

'Where do they live?' demanded the captain, restraining his impatience.

Dr. Owen sat in the far corner of the hall near the survivors smiling at the adept movement of the Merricks. It was with some surprise that he noted Sir George's ancient perambulation change to a rapid cha cha as he had weaved his way between the clerics and parishioners, parting the waters for his son and heir. He stepped forward smiling. 'I will take you to Sir George Merrick's home if you wish captain. Perhaps our survivors can remain here for the time being. I can vouch for them to be sure.'

'Merrick you say? Merrick? Not Professor Sir George Merrick by any quirk of fate?

'The very same', was the quizzical reply. His reciprocal puzzlement, thought the doctor, was assiduously ignored.

'Forgive me', began the captain, clearly mulling over his recently acquired information. 'Mr er?'

'Doctor Owen. GP hereabouts don't you know. If you have finished here' said the doctor, glancing at PC Holdsworth, 'please follow me.'

The physician turned on his heels, put on his old trilby and left the hall with the captain in tow, precisely as the professor had said that he would. What had Merrick said to him? 'There are things to be discussed with the captain. Things that it was necessary to discuss sub Rosa. Now what on earth?'

The army jeep followed Doctor Owen's prized Daimler up the Merrick's drive and the two vehicles stopped beside an old oak tree that shaded the frontage of the cottage during the summer months.

Sir George was at the threshold as the captain approached the cottage and offered his hand as he entered the portico.

'Please do come in. The weather improves but it really is still quite damp.'

The captain, his sergeant and Dr. Owen followed the old academic into the front parlour where they were acquainted with his wife. Dr. Merrick was not a domesticated woman. Tea was not offered.

George was as intrigued as Dr Owen. Why had his father planned for the captain to visit his home? It had been done with such certainty and aplomb? The manoeuvre had been as effective as it had been simple. He had wanted to speak with the captain, away from the hall, the village folk and PC Holdsworth, and had achieved this feat with the consummate ease of a diplomat. George entered the parlour and sat on the floor beside the burnished brass fender half expecting to be asked to leave the room.

'So captain', Sir George began, 'what do you want of me?'

'That was the question I was about to ask you professor', returned the captain.

'You are most astute if I may say so. Refreshingly so in this modern age I might add. You are right. I did leave the village hall ahead of you intentionally. I knew that our affable policeman would not be able to relate the information you would require and that shaking off the said 'arm of the law', within the confines of the village hall, would be nigh on impossible. Now - to business. I trust that you have been briefed? Good. I have many contacts captain. Information is passed to me quite regularly. My wife, son and Doctor Owen may be taken into our confidence. I am sure that each has a part to play.'

Now George knew many things about his father but what on earth did he mean when he spoke of 'many contacts', 'trusting that the captain had been briefed' and of 'all having a part to play?' He listened intently.

Have you ever heard of Simon Salomonovich?' The professor enquired over his pince-nez.

'Go on', answered the captain, ignoring the question and catching his sergeant's eye, then glancing at the doorway.

The professor waved his hand towards the old couch. 'Please captain, do take a seat.' The captain sank further into the ivy patterned sofa than he had imagined that he would and his feet stretched out before him. He leaned forward to indicate his interest, to gain a footing and to avoid losing his Brylcream to the crocheted antimacassar.

'Simon Salomonovich was a Pole' began the captain. 'His field was genetics. He worked at Tubingen University near Stuttgart. You will know of it I am sure?' Sir George waived his hand dismissively to indicate that he did and the captain understood that he was to continue. 'Salomonovich then moved to Cambridge University and, finally back to the town that his parents had brought him to as a child. Hamburg. He worked at Hamburg University for more than twenty years. He was, as you will have gathered, of Jewish descent. He was not a practicing Jew and he did not visit the synagogue.'

The captain paused. 'Professor, it appears that I am doing the talking. Would you like to continue?' Sir George smiled to himself, a fact that did not go unnoticed by his bemused son. Still perambulating the parlour, index fingers and thumbs in waistcoat pockets, the professor took up the story of Simon Salomonovich.

'When the Nazis came to power Simon knew that they would find him. They seized his papers and dragooned him into working for them. He knew that he lived only because of his genius. What was he to do? He waited for an opportunity to escape. It never came. They watched Simon and his family like hawks. He knew that it was impossible for them all to disappear and that he would not leave any one of them behind. He had to work. But he did not have to be productive; indeed, red herrings were rapidly becoming his speciality. His eldest two sons, Benjamin and Reuben, were his postgraduate assistants and confidents. He demanded that he work with his sons, and they alone, and he was granted that concession. Three weeks ago our contacts in Hamburg were betrayed to the Gestapo. Simon had been passing information, the real stuff, to our boys for some time. He and his two elder sons were marched out of the university and his wife, daughter and youngest son were brought to watch them being shot. It was not known what happened to Simon's surviving family until now. Indeed we still do not know of the whereabouts of his daughter.'

'How did you know that he had ...' the captain began.

'Been killed?' Interjected the professor, taking his faded but favoured armchair by the window. I told you that I have many contacts.'

George was astounded by this revelation and listened, fascinated by his father's rendition, another fracture wounding his belief structure.

'Do not worry. I will verify that I have a right to that particular piece of information. I'm sure that you know that it is now de-classified. I am sure too that you have been well briefed after my telephone call of yesterday evening. It was I who discovered the significance of our survivors. My wife, son and the good doctor are present but I assure you that nothing resembling a state secret will pass my lips. You can close the clip on your revolver, which I noted you undid upon my first disclosure. Incidentally, there is no reason for the good sergeant to inch closer to the doorway either. I don't believe that I am in a fit enough condition to make the quick getaway that he is perhaps anticipating.'

Wide eyed, George glanced at his mother who, much to his further astonishment listened intently to the remarkable revelations, seemingly undisturbed and unsurprised. Perplexed, his analytical mind racing ahead, he returned his attention to his father.

'When I heard the name Salomonovich in connection with Hamburg University I immediately knew there to be a connection with Simon. Who else could it be? When the boy Joel spoke with such authority this morning and with such piercing certainty, I recalled a lecture I attended in Berne in 1934. Simon Salomonovich denounced the Nazi party as the party of anti-intellectualism with a fervour I have not seen until today. I have only heard the boy speak two sentences, and both were in Latin, but I tell you; Joel Salomonovich is the son of Simon Salomonovich. Of that there is no doubt.'

'But how did you know to go to the village hall,' asked the captain who was clearly fascinated by the story.

'It was my son George who first spotted the boat in the bay', replied the professor. 'That is the most extraordinary coincidence. I am a man of science but if you will have it, you may call it fate.'

Professor Sir George Merrick rose arthritically from the deep seat. He stopped by the window and appeared to reflect on the recent past for several moments before proceeding further.

'It is unlikely that the boy or his mother will have academic knowledge of Simon's work but you will understand that they may have information with regard to his recent focus. That may be too much to ask. However, they may possess information that would be of strategic importance to the military. The others were on board the fishing boat as it passed down the canals too. What have they seen? They too must be debriefed.'

The captain asked pointedly, 'Is there any more Sir George? I feel that I am missing something. You tell me about the importance of these particular refugees and then offer me no more than that some may only have seen something that might be helpful to us. That hardly seems to be an adequate reason for the cloak and dagger theatricals used to procure this clandestine meeting'

'There is a possibility', said the professor as he moved towards the door. He caught a quick glance of the captain and an almost imperceptible affirmative nod of his sergeant. The sergeant moved away from the door towards the centre of the room. 'It is as I have said. There is the possibility of Simon's wife or son having knowledge of his recent work.'

The captain stood and pondered for a moment recognising that his question had been parried. 'What is it that you want of me professor?' not at all convinced.

'Good man', replied the professor, 'a man of thought and action. There is an old hunting cottage hereabouts called 'The Pheasantry' just behind the copse in the distance', he said pointing out of the bay window. It is small but would house the father and daughter adequately. There is also the Old Bothey cottage, by the mill, on the way into the village. A little restoration work by some of your chaps would certainly make it habitable for the mother and son.

'To what purpose professor? I understand the point in your desire to debrief the personnel but we would do that very thoroughly ourselves. Why should we provide a safe haven for them?'

Professor Sir George Merrick stood looking through the bay window surveying the distant Suffolk landscape. He turned to the assembled group and said. 'Because Simon Salomonovich was a genius. Yes, he studied genetics. Yes he studied micro–biology but he also studied physics until 1934. He saw which way the wind was blowing in his adopted land and by the time of the Berne conference was moving from a discipline which the Nazis could have used with deadly effect to one he felt would benefit mankind. How could he know that both disciplines would be abused?' He paused for a moment. 'In any case this country will be in need of such folk when the war is over. Helping the Salomonovichs will not harm us, will it?'

Conceding the fact that it was unlikely that he was going to get a straight answer and rationalising that Sir George was a safe bet, the captain walked towards the door. He turned as he held the handle. 'I'll see what I can do professor', he said slowly as a question sprung to mind. 'Professor, what branch of physics was Simon Salomonovich's original calling?'

'We all shared the same calling, as you put it, my dear captain. Nuclear physics.' An almost imperceptible tick flicked across the captain's face but all three Merricks caught the impact of Sir George's words on him. Sir George continued. 'When Simon Salomonovich left Berne he flew to Cambridge and there spoke of the curtailment of his nuclear research. He talked at length about his long cherished principles; condemning the misuse of nuclear physics in all its manifestations, without qualification. He believed that it heralded Armageddon and that the next war would end with a single explosion.

Simon Salomonovich would be proved wrong. It took two.

The captain left. His sergeant parked his jeep amongst a nearby copse and began a lonely vigil.

Chapter 10

SIR GEORGE MERRICK

Sir George Merrick was not a man given to posturing. Indeed he had devoted his life to science and, ultimately, to the good of mankind. He was not a kindly soul. Many believed him to be cold and dispassionate. He was, however, clearly of the belief that Nazism, Communism; indeed all totalitarian regimes were intrinsically evil and flawed. He could not understand those who believed that the ends justify the means. 'What on earth does that mean for heaven's sake?' Neither did he accept that systems, which were in themselves laudable and even equitable, were acceptable if their application was not possible. 'What', he would say, 'is the point of designing a ship that meets the requirements of the crew and passengers if it sinks when launched? It is not good enough to say – Yes, but that is how things should be; they were not.'

Intellectuals always feel the rage of totalitarianism. Books were burned and thoughts were erased and debate stifled. The learned were often murdered. From ancient Greece and Rome to Spain and Berlin the story remained the same. The concept of left and right annoyed him intensely. Extremists were extremists and stood side by side and apart from civilised society. The extreme left and right were kin or at the very least kindred spirits.

Sir George knew too that the threat of invasion, in the early years of the war, had been real and that he must to do his part. He had written to the War Office and offered his services. They were delighted with his patriotism and politely requested that he continue with his scientific work as his part of the 'war effort.'

Dismissing Sir George was never likely to be a formality and so it proved. He left Cambridge railway station for London King's Cross having secured an appointment with a diplomat; the son of an old boy of his venerable school. It had taken guile and not a little persuasion to arrange the meeting.

Sir George outlined his value to the government, convinced those present and was provided with a contact. As he left the building a clerk, who wished to avail him of expenses and claim forms, approached him. For the first time in the young man's career he was rebuffed. Sir George considered that duty did not have a price. He formally accepted his office without pay. He was given a number of clandestine tasks and produced profiles of academics and their supposed whereabouts. He sought the company of those he believed may be guilty of collusion with the enemy and did so while continuing with his day-to-day tasks and lectures at the university.

Over the previous three years Sir George had proved himself to be a valuable asset to the War Office. Now he was charged with the task of debriefing the refugees. He began the task immediately and with some relish.

Chapter 11

THE NEIGHBOURS

Two days after the captain had left the Merrick's cottage, trucks arrived at The Pheasantry and The Old Bothey. The soldiers worked for several days from early morning until late into the evening on the old stone buildings, which had stood semi-derelict for almost ten years.

The Pheasantry had been the old gamekeepers lodge. Lord Allenby had died a drunken bachelor at the wheel of his Rolls Royce. He hit the wall of the bridge spanning the river bisecting his land when returning from one of his late night drinking sessions. Both wall and car plunged into the shallow water below. He was trapped beneath his car and drowned in sixteen inches of water. The noble lord was in up to his neck in debt too and the death duties due heralded the end of a six hundred year dynasty.

The Manor House was put on the market but the war had not proved an auspicious background for the purchasing of buildings in need of repair and the sale had stalled and died. Professor Sir George Merrick was not as wealthy as the gentry had been. However, he and his wife had made a good living over many years and they had had very limited outgoings. The 1933 Austin seven-box saloon was the one purchase that could be considered to be frivolous. The couple were not thrifty. They simply did not need more than they had.

Their money had accumulated and a major patron of the physics faculty of the university had suggested to them that buying land and property was always a good investment in the long term. The professor had taken the patron at his word and bought the Allenby land that encompassed his cottage, the Pheasantry and The Old Bothey. An architect had bought the old manor house and the larger tract of land to the other side of the river and thus the ancient estate was divided, if unequally, between the two.

Sir George agreed to pay the costs of the materials required to make the Pheasantry and Bothey habitable and the army, in turn, agreed to provide the manpower that was in such short supply. The renovations were not intended as an investment. They were there to provide homes for the refugees. Never the less the sale of either property would reap huge rewards had the professor the slightest inclination to sell them. When the buildings had been completed they were, indeed, very desirable properties and worth considerably more than the purchase price.

It was a further week before smoke rose from the chimneys of the two properties. The Pheasantry housed the Dutch father and daughter, the Bothey, the German mother and son. The three buildings were some five hundred yards apart and formed an almost perfect equilateral triangle through the woods of the estate.

Work had to be found for the adults and school for the youngsters. Vincent Haan was adamant that he would do anything he could to do his part for the war effort and to raise money for Rachael's education. He had been an architect before the war and prior to the Nazis commandeering his offices. He had been denied access to his records and belongings and consequently had no option but to declare himself bankrupt. His indomitable spirit had carried him through the dark days of occupation. The important thing in his life had been his 'two girls' and he soon found employment working as a draughtsman's clerk. The pay was sufficient for the time being.

Ruth's wealthy widowed mother offered the little money she retained after her home was commandeered by the Gestapo. The little she had was offered during the closing hours of her grief at the loss of her ancestral home but Vincent was proud and independent and was adamant that he and he alone, would provide for his family.

Now, in England, it was not surprising that Vincent had found immediate employment working as an architect's assistant, translating for the army and helping with the harvest in the evenings. Saturdays and Sundays were special days however; days to be spent with his beloved daughter Rachael.

Marta was a revelation to the Merricks. She was given secretarial work at a local solicitors firm and after a few weeks was, in the words of Mr. Alec Hanson of Hanson and Hanson, 'running the place.'

She worked long hours. She had been brought up to believe in the work ethic. If a job was worth doing it was not only worth doing well but worth doing to the highest standard that one was capable of attaining.

When Simon Salomonovich met Marta he knew her to be self-educated and lacking the structure of the formal education that he had had the good fortune to have been exposed to and nourished by. As an academic he recognised that there were many gaps in her knowledge and understanding. He also acknowledged her intellect. Perhaps this was the quality that had drawn him to her. When they met she was an uneducated highly intelligent woman. Five years later she was an unqualified academic.

Marta Salomonovich was not unique. It was a story with a recurring theme throughout the world and the ages and Simon had often wondered about the latent talent that was still lost to the world, the triumph of qualifications over intelligence and the importance of the ability to apply and enhance knowledge and understanding.

Marta's heart ached for knowledge of Rebecca. She cried throughout her restless nights, praying constantly.

Joel's trauma was seminal. The bright playful, loving child had been replaced by a driven youth. He was never morose; never lethargic. Passion and drive spurred on his malign hunger for revenge. A spectacular eruption burned on a slow fuse. His day would come. Each day he remembered the German officer who had had his father and brothers shot. He felt the painful vice-like Nazi's grip on his face and he remembered the crazed eyes and manic words of Obersturmführer Reinhardt Bühler. 'I am polluting my hands by touching you. Look at me. Look me in the face. Remember this face. Let this face haunt you. Let it haunt you for the remainder of your miserable existence.'

It was doing so.

Chapter 12

REBECCA

Rebecca Salomonovich had been dragged away from her mother and brother screaming and kicking. It was the first time in her life that she had resorted to such measures. It was also the first time that she had felt the need to.

Obersturmführer Reinhardt Bühler had been preoccupied with the executions and was in raptures with the effect that they had had on the crowd. He was a man possessed. His actions demonstrated the chilling response he felt commensurate to his displeasure. His lust for destruction, torture and death imbued his body with acrid paranoia. Malevolence seeped from every pore. His fanatical piercing ice blue eyes offered a window into his unhinged mind and the neuroses that had long festered within it. As always with people of Bühler's ilk, ferocity erupted without warning and with little, if any, justifiable provocation. Trivialities unleashed the firestorms of pent-up hatred and rancour. Regardless of substantiating evidence of innocence there was no refuge from the madman's paranoia.

An old man had remonstrated with the Obersturmführer as he had left the square. Bühler had taken the pistol from his holster and shot him without a second thought. The man questioned his authority. He was shot. The legality was unquestionable, his rationale unanswerable.

The platoon marched towards its barracks. Bühler's trance was interrupted and, calling, 'Halt', he had turned on his heel to identify the cause of the disturbing screams. He marched towards Rebecca. Two of the soldiers held her by the arms. Without notice Bühler punched the girl in the stomach. The sickening blow took the air out of her lungs and she sank like a badly stuffed marionette.

'I see we have decided to be quiet now', fumed Bühler. 'Let me hear no more of your whining you little slut. Whores like you have lost the right to live amongst decent folk. Even in death your family and the likes of you, pollute our streets. You will not pollute them much longer.' He grabbed her hair and yanked her to her feet then, raising the back of his gloved hand made as if to strike Rebecca again. He refrained seeing the terror in her eyes. He pushed his leering face into Rebecca's and whispered, 'Have you had enough?'

Rebecca nodded submission but this was not acceptable to Bühler. He slapped her across the face leaving a tooth loose in her jaw. 'I repeat. Have you had enough? On your knees and beg me.

'Please, please', begged Rebecca. 'I have had enough. I will be quiet - please.'

'And you will do what I say?' screamed Bühler.

'Yes, yes', cried the piteous puppet.

'Oh after I have finished with you, you will do anything I ask – believe me. Anything! You will beg me to shoot you if you do not immediately obey every detail of my commands. But', Bühler hesitated as he considered Rebecca's fate,

'I will not shoot you. No, that would be too easy. You will serve the Reich well. Of that I am sure. Enough.' The Obersturmführer turned crisply on his heels again and marched to the front of his men. The sergeant issued the command to follow and shortly afterwards the platoon marched into the Hamburg barracks.

Rebecca was taken to a cell and left alone for the evening. She relived the horrors of the executions and the parting from her mother and Joel many times over. Now she was alone. Terrified of every sound and expecting further punishment from the demented officer, she did not sleep. She curled into a ball on the little wooden bed that constituted the furniture of the room and prayed.

It was a little more than five hours later when seven soldiers entered the small cell. Rebecca lost her virginity to the first soldier and her sanity to the last. The ordeal lasted no more than an hour. They released her arms and she slumped onto the bed, deranged.

The soldiers visited Rebecca during the early hours of each morning for three months. She wasn't beaten but the men were rough and took pleasure from their prey without compassion. Rebecca initially resisted the men's attacks but recognising the futility of her actions, eventually submitted meekly. Her capitulation lessened the pleasure of the men and she rationalised why it had.

She did not want to live and looked for a way to end her misery. The opportunity did not present itself and she continued to endure the sordid practices of the despicable soldiers as the weeks passed by during which time she was as broken as Obersturmführer Reinhardt Bühler had said she would be. He had been right. She would beg to be shot.

Early one morning the cell doors opened and Rebecca braced herself for more degradation. She turned from the wall to meet her assailants. How many would it be tonight? How drunk would they be? What was to be their pleasure? There stood Bühler. She had imagined that he would have visited her many times before now, but he had not appeared. Why now?

'Come here', he commanded. 'On your knees whore.'

Rebecca dropped to her knees 'Take off your clothes' Rebecca moved quickly to accommodate the officer. She wore only a short dress and she dropped it to the ground. 'Kiss by boots slut', he snarled. Rebecca knew that the penalty for disobedience would be horrific and played out her role at Bühler's leisure. She bent her knees, lowered her head and kissed his boots, first one, and then the other. Bühler seemed satisfied.

'Good, you have learned to be obedient. It is time for you to leave.' He caught the hope of relief in her eyes. 'You are going to serve the Reich well by opening your legs for the gallant men who fight for the fatherland. This is your purpose. I am told that you are good at it and have learned well. Now you can put your learning into practice. It is a job well suited to your kind.'

Rebecca had waited for Bühler to approach her. She looked for the lust that she had seen in the eyes of so many of the soldiers that had visited her so regularly. It was not there. Bühler stood in front of the naked Rebecca and was unmoved by her body. There was a dawning understanding. Bühler's orientation did not involve females. She felt both relief and fear of the unknown.

An hour later six soldiers arrived. All took their pleasure with Rebecca before making her dress and escorting her to a small truck. The tailgate was lowered and she was lifted roughly into the back of the vehicle. The soldiers mocked her by thanking her for her services and pointing out, what they opined to be, her shortcomings as a whore. For all her resolve Rebecca could not hold back the tears and she began to sob uncontrollably.

Arms were wrapped around her and she instinctively knew that this was compassionate contact. She looked into the dim truck. There were several other young women in it. She passed out.

It was several minutes before Rebecca regained consciousness. The truck had travelled to the railway station. The rear tarpaulin cover was raised and the tailgate lowered. Soldier offered their arms to the women in order to assist them getting down from the truck. They were liberal with their hands as they did so.

Rebecca was molested much as the others had been but there was an acceptance and understanding of the futility of responding. All the women had been subjugated and their spirits broken. They had learned to act like whores and now the physical, if not the mental battle to retain respectability had been lost. Compliance came without a whimper.

The dozen or so women boarded a waiting train and were crowded into a single compartment. During the several hours of their journey the group took it in turns to sit. There was little talk. The women felt shame and were not best disposed to discuss their recent pasts. So far they had survived by complying.

The strategy was working.

The women entered the barracks of the occupying army at Zandvoort, Holland and were de-loused, hosed down and given a pack of clothing. Each woman was allocated a small room, which was furnished with a bed, chair, cabinet, wardrobe and sink. As Rebecca entered her room the escorting soldier spoke to her.

'Unpack your bag and make yourself presentable. You begin work tonight whore.'

Rebecca sat on the edge of the bed in despair. Was her horror to continue so soon? She put her hands in her head and wept yet again. There was movement outside her room and realising that she had yet to do as she had been instructed, rapidly began to empty the bag. There was underwear, nylons and dresses that hid little, two pairs of stiletto shoes and cosmetics. She looked for anything that might be adapted to make a weapon but the Third Reich had been as efficient as ever. The opportunity for a blissful end to her torment didn't present itself.

It was late in the evening when the door opened. The officer was old and bald. He walked into the room, sat on the chair beckoned Rebecca to kneel before him, opened his flies and bid her to begin her work. Rebecca did as ordered and her time as a field whore began.

Chapter 13

AMSTERDAM ON LIBERATION DAY

Rebecca worked at the barracks until the fifth of May 1945 – Liberation Day. It was on that day the Germans deserted the barracks. The servants and field whores were sent to their rooms and waited for the sound of approaching soldiers. There was panic amongst the women. Surely the Gestapo would destroy the 'evidence' of their madness? But why had they not come? Rebecca sat on the floor of her small cell holding her knees in her hands listening to the heavy bombardment. She heard the evacuation of the barracks and the movement of heavy trucks but still they did not come. Then the barracks fell silent. The distant sound of mortars and the rattle of machine guns grew louder as the street battles commenced. Rebecca stayed where she was, ready to accept her fate.

Fate came in the shape of Captain Edward Kinnear of the First Canadian Army. Rebecca froze as she heard the sound of approaching footsteps. 'Better to die than to live like this', she thought. The door swung open and Rebecca closed her eyes and waited for the inevitable.

'Hello', came the surprisingly warm voice. 'Do you speak English? What is your name? Are you OK?'

It was almost three years since anyone had enquired about Rebecca's welfare. She was disorientated and stared into space unable to cope with the concept of liberation and a future life to be lived beyond the shadow of her recent sordid past.

The captain moved towards her cautiously, aware that there were dangers in approaching 'the natives' no matter how friendly, vulnerable or weak their circumstances appeared to be. He checked the immediate area around Rebecca then moved towards her laying aside his sub-machine gun a little distance from her whilst reaching for his pistol and checking for booby traps.

'Shoot me.'

The captain hesitated unsure of what he had heard. 'What is your name?' he repeated.

'Please shoot me. I want to die. Please I beg of you.' She collapsed on the floor hoping for death and redemption.

'Shit', whispered the captain. 'What the hell have the bastards done now?'

Edward Kinnear was not easily distracted from his duty. He looked down at the beautiful young woman and insisted. 'What is your name? I must know your name.' Rebecca looked up into a pair of gentle brown eyes and warm generous mouth. She hesitated then said. 'My name is Rebecca Salomonovich. I am from Hamburg.'

The captain slung his weapon over his shoulder and put his large arms around Rebecca's slender waist and legs and lifted her easily. 'It's time for you to leave this goddam hell hole', he said in disgust. With that carried her out of the cell and into the courtyard. He commandeered a jeep and lifted her into it. Taking the wheel he drove her out of the barracks and into his life. Rebecca Salomonovich was the only woman to escape from the hell that was Zandvoort.

Captain Edward Kinnear took Rebecca to the Red Cross centre at Haarlem. Rebecca thought him to be very kind and considerate and, after her recent past it was not difficult for her to comprehend why. She had put her trust in the captain and he had been as good as his word and found her the refuge she so clearly needed.

Kinnear stood outside the cabin that had been allocated to Rebecca and waited. After a bath and a change of clothing she emerged, as arranged. He looked into her pained eyes. There was a beauty and grace about this young woman. She had been subjected to so much and they had broken her heart but, perhaps, not her spirit. Her identity hung by a thread. That was true. The brutal and dehumanising years had taken away the superstructure which had formally sustained her. But he sensed something extraordinary about her.

He imagined her plight. She would begin by opposing the Nazi's' will, and then, inevitably she would be forced to submit to their demands. She would cocoon her mind from reality in order to retain her dignity. This would not be a clinical detachment for that would have been impossible. It was a Nihilistic survival strategy – no more. Life was without meaning or purpose; values non-existent, morality diminished.

She had not uttered words of recrimination; there were no signs of bitterness, no hate and no vows of vengeance. Her words were serene and beautiful. She was calm, gentle, thankful and courteous. He didn't want to leave her and he knew, by her grace, that she was someone very special and would be loved by someone somewhere. He wanted so much to help

75

her restore her health, re-establish her equilibrium and witness her mental regeneration. But where had she come from?

He shook himself from his thoughts and turned away realising that he had been staring into her beautiful face for longer than etiquette permitted. 'I er, must go now. If you want anything... anything at all', he said faltering over his syntax and falling over his words. 'I will be coming here often over the coming days. I do hope that I can see you?' He blushed and added, 'After all the least I can do is to check that you are in good health. Isn't it?'

Rebecca took his hands in hers. 'Captain', she began. 'Ed', he corrected her.

He saw a deep and grateful smile move across her lips and knew that he was falling in love with her. 'Ed', she corrected herself, 'you do not need to ask. I owe you so much.' He began to interrupt her. 'No, no, no. I do', she interrupted his intended objection. 'Please come to see me whenever you are here.'

Edward Kinnear smiled back at the lady and said. 'You must have family?' He saw something in her face which immediately made him regret his remark. There had been, momentarily, a deep suppressed hurt flash across her face but it was gone in an instant. He would remember the hurt in her eyes for the rest of his life. He had seen a sharper focus to those soft warm brown eyes as that flash of passionate anguish had creased her soul and had given vent through them. They had betrayed her. There was no hate in them. Just a deep hurt.

He began to examine his own conscience and feelings. How credible were the assumptions he was making? He saw Rebecca's unbroken pride and guessed at the abuse that she must have endured and yet he knew that it had not tarnish her soul and that her integrity remained uncompromised. Having fallen into the evil clutches of the Gestapo he knew that she must be deeply scarred. He had seen the blood rush to her cheeks, the torment in her eyes, her instant recoil and how rapidly she had collected herself. What was it? For a moment he had thought her emotionally disconnected. Beneath the sweeping dark eyebrows he had seen no hint of recrimination. No reason to pay penance for past transgressions. Her reputation remained unsullied and he found her stoicism heroic and her indomitable spirit uplifting; yet her candour had not allowed him into her inner sanctum. There was more. Now he understood the wisdom which maintained that it was easier to condemn than to understand.

He thought it magnificent that she was brave enough to face that which she would have preferred to ignore. Her psychological state was not a precondition of his love. She enthralled him. The heady perfume emanating from her body consumed him and he resolved to be with her forever. The inescapable conclusion was that he had fallen in love. She was shrouded in mystery yet open and warm and he felt an insatiable need to care for her. He had wanted to mete out retribution for her but her serenity had reined him in and the significance of that had not eluded him.

Though a patient herself, Rebecca was put to work as a nurse for the allies and she gratefully accepted the goodwill and charity received in exchange for her labours.

Two weeks later Captain Edward Kinnear was wounded in the line of duty and shortly afterwards was returned to Amsterdam. He wrote frequently to Rebecca and she replied dutifully. They arranged to meet in Zandvoort.

Edward Kinnear and Rebecca spent many hours in each other's company. He was most attentive and patient with Rebecca and she was most grateful to him for his care and attention.

He still wore a sling but the wound to his shoulder was healing well and after several weeks he was due to be sent back to England and thence to Canada. He offered to take Rebecca with him on several occasions but she had resolutely declined. Time was short and one day, towards the end of July, he resolved to propose to her.

It was a charming proposal. He and Rebecca strolled along the Zandvoort beach on a warm July evening. She had noted that he was somewhat animated and ill at ease and turned to him. 'Have I said or done something that offends you Edward? I feel that you are a little distant.'

Edward dropped to one knee and brought out a small box from his pocket. He professed his undying love and devotion and swore that he would look after her forever. Rebecca was taken aback and, though flattered; neither accepted nor rejected his offer. She had become fond of the captain and slowly she had begun to confide in him. She was happy and comfortable in his company but she knew that there was no question of love on her part.

She looked down at Edward, took both of his hands and raised him from the sand. 'Edward Kinnear you are my rock, my saviour and the reason that I have found the will to live. Please allow that to be sufficient for the present. Soon I must return to Hamburg', she implored. 'The war will be over soon and I must find my family.' The captain noted that his proposal had not been rejected and took comfort from that. He considered patience to be a virtue, at least for the time being. However he was somewhat perplexed. What was it that she had said? The little history that Rebecca had revealed to him about her past had led him to believe that the Nazis had wiped out her family. He put his good arm around her tenderly and kissed her cheek. He was about to speak when she placed a finger on his lips and smiled. 'Please I need a little longer.' They left the beach and sat watching the gentle sea creep ever nearer to the wall below them. He waited for her to start. It was some time before she did.

She began, hesitatingly, 'I told you that my father and brothers were murdered by the Gestapo, Yes?' The captain nodded. 'But my mother and youngest brother were not. The three of us were not put up against the wall like the others. I do not know why we were not shot.' Rebecca began to relate the story of her capture and subjugation. It was, in her mind, only right to do so at this juncture. She told the story from first to last so that he might better understand her mentality. She needed someone to listen to her. She needed

Edward to know. When she ended she looked into his face searching for his understanding and found it. He moved his lips to hers and they kissed. He came to his senses quickly and asked her forgiveness. She smiled at him and returned his kiss.

'Captain Edward Kinnear you are a good man and I know that it is safe to put my trust in you. You are my rock and I will always be grateful to you. You need never apologise to me. There is one thing, however, that I would ask. Will you help me to get to Hamburg? I must discover the fate of my mother and brother. Please I beg of you. Do what you can.'

It took two weeks for the captain to arrange passage for the two of them. They left Zandvoort on the 4th July 1945.

Chapter 14

REBECCA AND EDWIN KINNEAR IN HAMBURG 1945

The summer sun shone through the glass roof of Hamburg Central Station as Rebecca and Edward walked along the platform. The two had spoken of their lives at length while passing long hours on the train. They had been fortunate to find a compartment to themselves having rationalised that it was better not to speak English in front of the German public. Cities had been bombed, many had died and retribution was more than a possibility. They resolved too that Rebecca alone would speak in public when necessary.

To Edward the hours on the train had seemed but minutes and he treasured every single one of them. They spoke of Edward's home in Hamilton, Ontario. He reminisced about the great lake, the city of Toronto to the north, and his family.

When they disembarked Edward carried their two large suitcases and waited for Rebecca to show him the way. They walked out of the station and hailed a cab. A black Mercedes moved towards them. The driver got out and placed their cases in the boot. He did not speak until they were sitting in the rear seat.

The driver turned towards them. 'Where to?' he asked, as if disinterested in their reply. Rebecca gave him the directions and within ten minutes they had paid the fare and were standing at the frontage of what had once been a butcher's shop. The ruin was the only recognisable building left in the street. The RAF had obliterated the rest.

Edward saw Rebecca swoon and he held her to him. It took a little while for her to recover. 'Here was my home', she said forlornly. 'This was where my beautiful family lived. Here was so much love.' She began to cry and Edward was moved to tears too. They held onto each other tightly amongst the debris.

It was several minutes before they were able to move on. Nothing was said.

Later Edward felt the onset of a cool evening and suggested that they find a place for the night. Rebecca acquiesced reluctantly and the two walked arm in arm down the cobbled streets of the suburbs towards the city centre. They found a room for the night on the third time of asking and paid for three nights.

Edward recognised the awkwardness of the sleeping arrangements and sought to put Rebecca's mind at rest. 'You are tired and need rest. Tomorrow will be a long day for both of us. We must sleep. You take the bed and I will sleep on the floor. I will leave you for a while and will knock when I return.'

Rebecca said, 'You are so kind. I do not know that I deserve so much. God bless you Captain Edward Kinnear.'

Edwards kissed her cheek and whispered in her ear. 'If anyone in this world deserves kindness it is you Rebecca Salomonovich.' He kissed her forehead and left.

When he returned she was asleep in bed. He sat on a chair by her side, and looked into her face. The faithful sentinel remained there until dawn broke.

Rebecca had washed and dressed before she began to poke Edward's good arm. Slowly he gained consciousness and, after a few seconds orientation, he smiled at her and bade her good morning. He washed in a basin of cold water and the two left the place within twenty minutes.

They spent the first hour tracing the steps that Marta and Joel had trodden three years earlier. They had the same result too. No one knew of the Salomonovich's whereabouts. Many were reluctant to talk, some from hate and others from guilt and shame.

It was on the second day that they received information regarding the fate of Marta and Joel. The editor of the local newspaper informed them that the allies had bombed the street in which the Salomonovich's had lived and that the survivors were listed in the paper. They were given a copy of that paper. There was no one by the name of Salomonovich.

It was clear to the couple that there was little point in continuing with their enquiries and, with heavy hearts, returned to Zandvoort after two days in Hamburg.

Within a week the injured captain and Rebecca sailed to England. A fortnight later they were in Hamilton Ontario. They married on Boxing Day 1945.

Chapter 15

GEORGE, JOEL AND RACHAEL

Sir George was a regular visitor to the Bothey and thought Marta and Joel to be both stimulating and fascinating company. George often accompanied his father on an evening. He noted that his father, sensitively, encouraged Marta to talk of her husband and his work. This did not pass by the ever-protective Joel.

One evening the professor pressed Marta a little further than he had previously done. Joel was sitting at the fireplace beside George. He looked up from 'The Times' and lowered the paper slowly.

'Herr Professor', he said in his rapidly developing English, 'You ask many questions about my father but they are not direct questions. Perhaps if you were to come to the point my mother and I could decide whether or not we...'

'Joel', scolded Marta. 'I do apologise Herr Professor.' Marta blushed for her son. 'Joel, we have much to be grateful to the professor for.'

'I know that is so mother but I cannot help but feel that you are often cross examined and that you feel obliged to answer,' Joel replied, in a that voice of strident certainty that he had used so very often since arriving in England.

Marta was about to rebuke Joel again but was interrupted by Sir George.

'The boy is both astute and correct', he said. 'I expected no less of the son on Simon Salomonovich. My dear Marta I had not intended to be so intrusive. Perhaps I have been disingenuous. Oh dear. I do hope not. I do so enjoy our discussions. Joel, you are correct. There is information that you may have that could be of great value but I hope that you do not feel that you have been subjected to subterfuge? That would never do. Oh no!'

Joel hesitated and slowly looked up into the Sir George's eyes. 'Your questions are directed at the wrong person Herr Professor and you will, I hope, permit me to retain a measure of scepticism.'

'That is highly regrettable', began Sir George, but Joel ignored his protestations and continued undeterred without a scintilla of uncertainty. Sir George gave way and listened intently, stung by the criticism but ever alert to the opportunity for revelation.

'Your assumption is correct however', continued Joel. 'I have possession of much information that is of great value. My father took the most remarkable measures to conceal his research. It is not my intention to reveal what he intended not to be known. I will only say that his research in nuclear physics, which he reluctantly discontinued, was not of value to the military in any direct sense.'

'Joel', said George, 'You can't possibly know that.'

Marta and the professor looked at the two fourteen year olds sat on the floor by the hearth. There was tension between them at the best of times. Now Joel displayed open hostility.

Slowly and deliberately, fulminating and enunciating each syllable with a chilling certainty he spoke, fixing George's eyes with certain menace.

'No one will ever tell me what I know, what I can do or say or where I can go ever again. Do you understand that? Do you? My turn is coming. Believe me when the opportunity arrives...'

Marta stopped Joel. She stared, disbelieving that her son could deliver such vitriol to their benefactors.

'I must apologise again Herr Professor', she pleaded, distressed at the destructive mind-set behind her son's bitter invective.

Marta knew enough of the human condition to understand the malignant influence of hate on the psyche. She recognised that unbridled hatred consumes the soul of its victim and leads first to delusion and then down the steep spiral path to self-destruction; a ferocious barrage lurching the neurotic towards the abyss. It seemed that it took little to inflame Joel's hostility and resentment these days. Her own desire for justice was rational, measured and would be lawful. She was desperately worried for the welfare of her son.

Joel stood, deferred to his mother, and placed a hand on her shoulder, then left.

Over the following months the rivalry and bitterness between Joel and George grew. Joel showed little overt affection for Rachael yet found himself deeply attached to her. There was an unspoken indissoluble attachment, a powerful fervour that joined the two spirits; an unspoken, constrained yet powerful intimacy.

George began to hate Joel and buried himself in his studies whenever he was present. He looked for opportunities to meet Rachael when Joel was busy elsewhere.

Sir George was keen that George and Joel should get along. His reasoning was not cynical, though any information gleaned from their rapport would be gratefully received. He recognised Joel's exceptional intellect. For once George had an equal; someone with whom he could converse; someone to exchange views with; someone worthy of his son's company. Joel swiftly discouraged any such expectation.

George resented Joel's easy manner with Rachael and knew that while ever he was around she would be drawn to him. A quiet resentment spawned a malignant hatred of his foe.

It was eighteen months since the shipwreck and Christmas was approaching.

The malignancy festered.

Chapter 16

PSYCHOLOGY

Young George Merrick walked towards Rachael with some trepidation. For the last three years he considered that he had played second fiddle to Joel in her affections. Sir George had remarked to his wife, several times over in recent months, that George was not himself. Quite! He was not. He had changed. George mused that there had been a metamorphosis. Yes, he recognised change and that this particular transition was somewhat less physically spectacular than that which is normally witnessed by the avid lepidopterist, but change he had.

It was inconceivable that George would neglect his research but now there was something else in his life too. It was uncontrollable and this annoyed him intensely. 'How can one think logically and have a sentiment which interferes with one's thought processes?' George recognised that his logic had been susceptible to an 'exterior influence.' He also recognised that 'exterior influence' was unlikely to be the correct term for such a phenomenon. He resolved, therefore, to research such matters. He did so for four hours each day for a period of six months without neglecting his set studies.

Sigmund Freud had clearly taken the leap of faith that only a genius can. George began to understand his own feelings. He recognised his passions and revelled in the new perspective that revealed so much of his inner self. He read criticisms of Freud and researched Adler and Jung recognising that the discipline of psychoanalysis had moved on and that, as in all disciplines, there was always considerable sniping after the master had shown the way. George moved on to current theory and became fascinated by it. Indeed, he deemed it imperative that had done so and considered the discipline surprisingly worthy of his regard.

He remained nervous in Rachael's presence. He recognised that this stemmed from his sense of insecurity and his lack of experience with the female gender.

His upbringing had not included the social graces beyond learning how to greet and address people and the rules of etiquette as applied in the dining room. The incalculability and variability of the human condition were hardly a consideration of Professor and Dr. Merrick. They did not recognise diversity other than to consider it illogical or ill advised.

George was an insular child. He was educated at a boy's school and had rarely spoken to, or interacted with, members of the opposite sex. The only female he spoke to with any regularity, with the exception of his mother, was Nurse Elliot, the district nurse and Mrs. Wattling at the local post office.

When George spoke to Rachael he would generally engage her in an academic discourse asking her to speculate on a given theorem or idea. He had, on one occasion, asked her opinion of a Benjamin Britten violin concerto, which, he pointed out, was written in America by a composer from Lowestoft, just a few miles up the coast. He always left Rachael feeling hollow. It was fair to say that Rachael welcomed her interaction with an intelligent young person of her own age but George's language was, at best, turgid and his perspective on life was unromantic, lacking Joel's passion, zest and smouldering intensity. George saw the sparkle in Rachael's eyes when she greeted Joel and ached to receive the same affection.

Joel and George were both exceptionally intelligent. They lived in the same village and shared a love of science. From Rachael's perspective that was where the similarities ended. George was academically correct, old fashioned, prim and proper. Joel burned on a dangerously short fuse and his eyes barely hid the sea of repressed resentment burning within him. He was exciting, explosive and unpredictable.

George would wish that he could inspect a gull's nest in a cliff face. Joel would climb down the precipice unaided by ropes and take a look just for the hell of it. George would wade in the surf. Joel would swim out well into the bay just to alarm Rachael; a practice frowned upon as irresponsible by George. He would be very correct and precise with Rachael and defer to her. Joel was often dismissive of her presence and rarely accommodated her gender. From Joel's perspective she had a right to be there but she was there of her own volition and those were his terms of his engagement. At the best of times he was amiable.

Rachael Haan was a good-looking girl and between the ages of fourteen and seventeen grew to be as beautiful as her mother had been. Vincent Haan was often heard to say that she was 'the very image of her mother.' She was deeply attached to Joel. Hadn't he saved her father? Hadn't they escaped the Nazis together? She recognised too the burning sense of injustice that they shared and the hope of finding a relative again; he his sister and she, the grandmother that, unknown to her, had already escaped her torment.

They were inextricably linked by their recent pasts and she believed that they would be forever.

Joel had loved his father, his brothers and his sister. Now they were gone. He distanced himself from all but his mother rationalising that if he avoided loving someone new, he would never feel that awful, gnawing pain of loss again. He recognised the danger of intimacy with Rachael and when happy in her company would sometimes disappear abruptly leaving her exasperated as to what it had been that had caused such offence. She had learned not to ask for explanations. These Joel met with obstinacy, sullenness and long periods of isolation.

For three years George had confounded his father, who had little notion of his son's dilemma. The professor's son had always been so consistent and now, regardless of his measured upbringing, he was occasionally inattentive. The boy was a young man for heaven sake, not a child.

George dare not intimate his affection for Rachael and was torn by the prospect of leaving her to go to Cambridge.

He recognised that leaving her for a period could be cathartic on his part but hated the idea of abandoning Rachael to Joel. They had spent many nights together at The Pheasantry reading passages of poetry, debating logic and discussing works of art. George and Joel both had a passion for Turner but, whereas Joel dealt with the soul of the artist and spoke with fervour George assessed each canvass with academic rigour turning to the Dutch masters in an attempt to demonstrate interest and empathy with Rachael's national culture.

Rachael, for her part, loved these evenings and smiled a smile that twisted George's heart painfully. He left for Cambridge in the summer of 1945.

Chapter 17

THE END OF THE WAR - MAY 1945

The victory peal rang out loud from the church steeple and the village hall, decked with red, white and blue buntings, teemed with folk celebrating the end of the war. Streetlights shone brightly. The dark nights of the blackout were over.

Celebrations were muted at The Bothey. Joel held his mother's hand. Marta was dying. Dr. Owen had examined her for what would be the last time. He leaned forward to Marta Salomonovich and put his hand on her forehead. Joel looked at him balefully his eyes welling once again.

Dr. Owen moved to the bedside cabinet and took Marta's wrist. His manner was grave. There was no hiding the truth. He took his stethoscope from around his neck and placed it in his bag then collected his coat from the back of the chair by the door and made to leave. Marta spoke; her diseased lungs demanding concise and succinct communication. Each whispered syllable painfully extracted from her frail body.

'Joel', she began, 'Is that you?' Joel lifted Marta's hand to his face. 'Joel I didn't want to leave you … I will always love you…you must be strong, as we have all been strong… these many days.'

The good doctor turned from the door and walked back to the bedside taking Marta's hand. 'You must rest my dear friend Marta Salomonovich. You must rest.'

Marta attempted to shake her head. 'You have been… a good friend Henry Owen. Such a good friend… but I will speak now.'

Joel wiped his mother's salivating mouth with a handkerchief as she braced herself for her valediction.

'Joel, this I must say to you. I want you to find Rebecca. I know in my heart that she is alive. You must promise me that you will take care of each other.' She stared into Joel's tearful face. 'You must have a good life and carry on the proud name of Salomonovich in memory of your father and your brothers. We do not look for vengeance... we put our trust in God. 'I know that you remember a certain face ... let it not destroy you ... but be sure to let the authorities know of the owner's culpability.' Marta collapsed into a coughing fit.

Dr Owen cautioned, 'Enough for now. Take a sip of water', he said insistently, proffering a glass.

'Later', she replied equally adamant that she would continue. She softened, 'Later my good friend.'

Turning her head to Joel she whispered. 'We have good friends here in England...friends that you can rely on. You must wait before you return to Germany. You must be strong, but you must wait. You are still young'... She lifted her head in an attempt to rise. 'Joel, I know that you do not like the Merricks ... but trust the doctor and Vincent Haan. They care for you ... I'.

Marta Salomonovich stopped mid-sentence, her eyes and mouth wide open. Joel rested her head on the pillow as the doctor came to his side. He put his arm on the boy's shoulder and gave it a compassionate squeeze to align his solidarity.

Joel left the room. Solemnly, Henry Owen followed the procedures that he had carried out so many times over the years then sat with his grieving boy reflecting on their three years of friendship.

Joel re-entered Marta's bedroom and the good doctor followed him some five minutes later. Henry Owen saw that Joel had been crying but now it was a resolute young man that stood before him.

'It would be wise for you to come and stay with me for a few days', offered the doctor. Joel answered rapidly, his course already set.

'I thank you for your offer sir but first I wish to be left alone with my mother.'

The doctor did not consider that this was a good idea at all but knew only too well that he was dealing with a formidable young man and that he had just listened to a statement, not a request. He resolved to go but could not resist saying. 'I will leave you for an hour but if you are not with us soon I shall bring a meal to you and stay with you for company.'

The doctor waited for a response. It was not forthcoming. Joel had not listened to what had been said. He had hoped against hope that his mother would recover but, deep down, he had known that she would not. His options had been weighed. He was ready to act.

Joel disappeared during the five days between the death of his mother and her funeral. The doctor had returned on the night of Marta's death but Joel had departed.

Henry Owen had organised a Jewish funeral for his friend with considerable effort and not a little expense. On the day of the funeral Joel appeared at the graveside as his mother was being lowered into her grave. The doctor looked awestruck at the unkempt young man. Many of the villagers were there to give a last farewell to a woman that they had taken into their midst. The Merricks, Hanson and Hanson, a number of Marta's colleagues and customers and several of the villagers had taken the journey to the Ipswich Jewish cemetery. There too were the grieving Vincent and Rachael Haan.

Rachael looked across the grave towards Joel wanting to share the burden of his grief. She prayed for his recognition but went unrewarded. She recalled her first meeting with Joel. The haunted expression had returned to his face. She thought of her own mother whose body had never been found and knew of the gut wrenching emptiness of great loss. She recalled their intense and strained relationship that she had hoped would blossom with time but Joel's repressed angst shrouded his emotions and all displays of affection and friendship were spurned or avoided.

Fomenting in Joel Salomonovich's mind was a resolution. And only when that resolution had been played out would he be able to consider life again. Aided by his considerable intellect and a maelstrom of seething anger his unwavering course had been set. He would not be staying.

As always Joel appeared aloof, insular and remote. There was silence amongst the onlookers as he walked to the edge of the grave and lowered his eyes. He didn't cry. He stood there; stoically staring into the abyss.

As the Rabbi's words ended he turned to go. Doctor Owen was about to speak to Joel as he walked away but Sir George held his shoulder and shook his head gravely. The good doctor nodded wistfully in agreement. Joel Salomonovich walked out of the lives of those who mourned his mother. He was seventeen.

Chapter 18

RACHAEL ALONE

Rachael was due to go to university in the summer of 1946. Marta had died and Joel had left the year before. Rachael felt that she could not abandon her father who had grieved for his wife and now for his friend and confidant, Marta Salomonovich. Vincent, for his part, felt that Rachael should apply to nearby Cambridge and should do so immediately. He would see her regularly and the break would not be so great.

Rachael resisted her father's advice hoping against hope that Joel would return. She could not imagine him returning and her not being there for him. She deferred her application. A further lonely twelve months passed by. George had pestered her more than she could bear and the sweet natured girl became less than that towards him.

George had visited during the Easter break of his fresher year. He had made the trip from his parent's cottage to The Bothey ostensibly to discuss Benjamin Britten's 'Young person's Guide to the Orchestra' that had been written earlier in the year. He also brought news that Britten, and the renowned tenor Peter Pears were in the process of organising a music festival at nearby Aldeburgh.

George saw the possibility of discussing the subject with Rachael and fervently hoped that Rachael would agree to go to the festival with him when a date was announced. Joel had gone. No one had heard of him for over a year and George was emboldened by this. If there was to be a time to approach Rachael it was now.

Vincent had indicated to his daughter that he had business with his employer and would be late. George delayed his walk until he felt sure that Vincent had left. Rachael had little company now and was not displeased to see George's faltering gait as he entered the cottage. George felt insecure once again and his awkwardness led to yet another unsatisfactory, tense and embarrassing encounter.

Chapter 19

JOEL IN HAMBURG AND AMSTERDAM 1945

Joel Salomonovich seethed with a malignant hatred that gnawed at his heart and seethed in his soul. He recognised the destructive nature of his neurosis yet he had neither the capacity nor the will to convalesce. His destructive path was driven by Mephistopheles and Armageddon itself would not alter his direction.

In August 1945 he travelled to Germany courtesy of a British Army troop ship. He had left Suffolk and hitched a lift to London. There he bought a rail ticket to Dover. It was in that port that he saw an advertisement for interpreters and had been recruited as a 'civvy' by the British Army.

The army took him to Bielefeld in Westphalia. He worked in the barracks at Brackwede and was billeted nearby. When he had earned sufficient money he disappeared without notice and did not leave a forwarding address.

He took a train to Hanover and was fortunate to get a lift from there north to Hamburg. He found lodgings near the Alster Lake, which was within half a mile of the home he had left just a little over three years earlier. He earned money clearing the bombed streets during the day and frequented the bars of the district during the evenings searching for information that might lead him to Rebecca.

He did not make progress for several weeks until one evening while walking on the banks of the Elbe an elderly artist asked him to sit for a drawing. Joel ignored the old man and turned to go.

'You are Salomonovich – no?'

Joel turned abruptly. 'And if I were?' he enquired.

'I never forget a face', the wizened old man went on, taking his pipe from his mouth and tapping it on the pavement. He looked at the product of his last few hours perched on the easel before him and began slowly, clearing his throat as an overture. 'I have observed thousands of faces. That is why I have a talent for caricaturing them.'

Joel was not content with this explanation. 'And the faces that you have not observed?'

'Oh, the war did not diminish your intellect young man and I see that you are not so easy to convince. That is good. However I have recognised you have I not?' He waited but still the answer was not forthcoming. 'The question is, young man, do you recognise me?'

Joel stared at the old man and for the first time recognised him to be Jewish. He scanned the old man's face and suddenly the jigsaw puzzle of cognition revealed the identity of the man before him. He was stunned and asked disbelievingly, 'Herr Goldstein?'

'I see that I am not forgotten after all', croaked the decrepit old man, eyes watering as he spoke. 'Yes it is I Joel Salomonovich.'

'But, but, well I, I saw you shot on the same day that my family were shot. You were in the square. I saw them shoot you.'

'Yes they left me to die like a dog but I am not so easily dispatched.'

Joel looked at the man. He had aged thirty years in the last three. 'You were a good teacher of art. I learned much from you at the school even though, you may well remember, that was not my strength.'

'Oh I remember alright, but you had many other talents and I remember that your art appreciation surpassed all others that I taught.'

Joel noticed the unshaven face, the shaking hands and the bloodshot eyes and suspected that his old pedant had more frequent meetings with bottles of schnapps than with razors.

'I thank you for your intervention on that terrible day sir. You are a very brave man. How many will be able to say that as this city is rebuilt?

'And you escaped?'

'By good fortune we did.'

'And your mother?'

Joel looked down at the wet cobbled street. The old man put his scrawny hand onto his. 'I am sorry. Marta Salomonovich was a good woman.'

Joel shook himself. He was about to explain that Marta and he had been safe in England for three years and that they had lived comfortably at the Bothey but he changed tack and asked.

'I have not seen my sister since that day. I have returned to find her.'

Herr Goldstein hesitated a fraction too long.

Joel sensed it and asked, 'Do you know of anything.' It was the turn of the old man to look down at the cobbles. Joel asked again. 'Do you know of the whereabouts of my sister?'

Herr Goldstein lifted his head and said. 'I can only surmise based on what I have heard and cannot be responsible for the accuracy of my information but ...'

'You look afraid to say it but you must not be. Please tell me. I must know. I need to know.'

The tears flowed down the broken man's face. 'You must listen', he insisted. 'I am reduced to drawing faces in the street. I barely raise enough money to eat. I have had my home taken by others and my attempts at reparation turned down. My wife died before all of this', his arm scribed a circle loosely indicating the ruined city. 'I have lost what family I had and my friends and colleagues have either left the city before the terror or are no more.' He was shaking now and his right hand began to fumble in his coat pocket. 'I live in a small apartment nearby and I go home to my best friend', he pulled out a bottle as he concluded, 'Here he is. This is my companion', he said, taking a swig from the half empty bottle.

Joel was impatient for information. 'But what of my sister? What of Rebecca?'

'I'm coming to that', the poor wretch sighed, wiping his mouth with his ragged coat sleeve. 'As you know I was shot. I was taken to the hospital. There they would not treat me saying that medication was better used for true Germans. True Germans', he repeated. 'What do they know?' Joel shifted feet impatiently. The old man recognised his irritability and moved on. 'It was here that I saw your sister. There were several young women herded into a room. They were medically examined for sexual diseases and the like and those that passed the examination were sent to the coast. I stayed at the hospital long enough to hear that two women were shot and that the rest were transported to Amsterdam.'

'Amsterdam', repeated Joel. So she was not shot?'

'Not at that time. I don't know any more.'

'And you?' said Joel, even more animated and impatient to move on now that he had his news.

'I was taken by colleagues down the Elbe to Kaarssen and convalesced over a number of months in a small cabin in the forest until I was well again.'

'And that is all you know?' said Joel, looking the man squarely in the eyes. He sensed that there was more. 'Yes', he insisted. Joel pressed him further.

'Why were the women taken to the hospital and examined and why were they sent to Amsterdam?'

Abraham Goldstein took another long swig from the schnapps bottle and wheezed. His watery red eyes lowered as he uttered the words. 'Field whores.'

The old man looked agitated as he examined Joel's face. It was transfixed, purple with rage. The old man turned away and began spewing on the cobbles then wiped his unshaven face with his sleeve as was his custom.

Joel came to his senses and moved to help Goldstein. The stench of urine and vomit overpowered him and he recoiled with disgust. He attempted to retrieve his composure but knew that he was too late

'I know. I saw. You are disgusted yes? What do I care? Leave me. It is better that I die. Leave me to live and die with my best friend. He raised the personified bottle to his lips. Joel's hand moved, lightning fast. He caught the bottle and rifled it through the air. It smashed on the wall of a small shop at the far side of the road.

Joel's mind raced ahead to Amsterdam. He would begin in the morning. 'Come', he said offering an arm to raise Abraham Goldstein from the gutter. 'I will carry your easel. 'You need to rest. Let me accompany you to your home.' The two walked for a short while through the wet cobbled streets of the Alt Stadt. Goldstein pulled a key from his pocket as he turned into an alleyway. Joel had not seen the doorway tight behind the corner of a dilapidated building. The door opened and a staircase faced them. It took some time for Goldstein to climb it.

The shabby dimly lit room disgusted Joel as much as the stench of Abraham Goldstein's body and clothing. The smell emanating from the bed made him feel sick to the pit of his stomach. Abraham Goldstein was living out his days in hell. Joel heaved a heavy sigh and opened a window.

'I must go', he muttered, numbed by his surroundings. 'Get a good night's sleep. You will need it my friend. I shall go to Amsterdam and search for Rebecca. When I return I promise that I will call to see you. I owe you a great deal sir. There is hope. Leave the bottle well alone. I will return.' With that Joel left the room and returned to his lodgings.

He lay on the bed fully clothed, thinking. 'Old. Abraham Goldstein. How old would he be? He was, Joel recalled, a little older than his father. That's right. He would be approximately fifty-five. 'One could be forgiven for thinking him seventy-five or even eighty', said Joel out loud. He turned his mind to Amsterdam. Having saved sufficient money for a rail ticket but recognising the importance of preserving the little he had, he resolved to stand by the roadside at first light and hope for a lift. He fell asleep dreaming of Abraham Goldstein, Reinhart Bühler and being reunited with his beloved sister.

It took Joel three days to get to Amsterdam and three months to return to Hamburg. When he returned to Amsterdam he brought a sober Abraham Goldstein with him. It would take a further three years for him to discover Rebecca's fate.

Chapter 20

JOEL IN AMSTERDAM 1948

Abraham Goldstein was not happy. He reposed on a Chesterfield couch looking out across the city of Amsterdam from the penthouse suite of the apartment block he now called home. The hardship and alcohol remained etched into his face but he was clean-shaven, smelt good and wore an expensive suit. Three years. Just three years. Yet it seemed an eternity. An eternity since the wretched squalor of Hamburg.

He turned to Joel and said, 'So, how exactly do you do it?' Where does the money come from? The money rolls in. You bring me to Amsterdam and I move into your flat. Within six months we have an apartment. Within a further year we move here. Where next? The Ritz? Will you take a room or buy the place?'

Joel approached Abraham and placed a huge hand on his shoulder affectionately, then picked up the phone.

Abraham smiled warmly and took the receiver from him. 'A common tactic my friend but I am not so easily diverted. Joel I do not wish to interfere but take care. The world has a nasty habit of kicking those who take it for granted.'

Abraham knew Joel well and sensed his discomfort. 'I am respectable once more and make a living teaching painting to those who will never be able to paint. For that I am grateful to you.' Joel waived the accolade aside. Abraham, as he had already made clear, was not so easily put off.

'And what of you? You who impressed me so much. Such a fine boy. Such a fine man. What is it that has brought you such money?' There was no response. He shrugged his shoulders and pressed his point further. Joel gazed out of the window onto the canal below. 'Tell me that it is legal and I will believe you', Abraham cajoled.

Joel turned slowly towards him speaking kindly but clearly and deliberately.

'No you tell me what is legal and what is not. Tell me what is fair and what is not. Tell me what I have done to the world to be so afflicted.'

'My son', began Abraham, 'for now that is how I think of you, 'you were right when you took me from the sewers and said that there is always hope. There is purpose. Don't throw it all away, I beg of you. Be careful'

'Abraham', said Joel softly, acknowledging the man's concern. 'Soon I must go. I fervently hope that you will accompany me.'

'Go', whispered Abraham. 'But go where?'

'Joel took the old man's hands in his own and spoke softly to him. To America. That is where I must go. I must make money and quickly and that is the best place to do it. As soon as I have discovered Rebecca's fate we will go.'

Abraham looked into Joel's aching heart and pleaded. 'Don't make a mistake. You are running with dangerous people. Of course I will go with you. After all who else do I have? Perhaps the weather will be good for my arthritis.' He looked searchingly at Joel. 'For God's sake, take care Joel.' With that he retired for the night.

Joel was out of the apartment within five minutes. Within ten minutes he was trafficking contraband and raking in a substantial sum from the stake he had taken in the operation.

He returned to the apartment in the early hours of Christmas Eve 1948.

Chapter 21

JOEL MEETS JAN KUYPER

Joel recalled the horror of the days that he and his mother had searched the streets of Hamburg for Rebecca. A macabre encore now took place on the streets of Amsterdam seven days a week. Three years had passed. Initially he struggled with the language but it wasn't long before he was more or less fluent. The populace were friendly and helpful for the most part but no one appeared to have knowledge of the fate of the field whores of Zandvoort. He contacted the British army weekly but nothing was forthcoming.

As promised, after a few weeks, he had returned to Hamburg to see Abraham Goldstein. Old Abraham had responded to Joel's kindness and was making slow progress. After three months Joel brought a presentable Goldstein to Amsterdam and the master began to work for the student.

Amsterdam was not and had never been a centre for the prudish but the German army had had few field whores in the city. Joel hoped that those who had served the Third Reich's men would be spared when the allies arrived but he guessed that many would not have survived to relate their stories. At first he told himself that no news was good news but as the weeks became months he was less sure of that sentiment. He never lost hope. He would not lose hope until he saw the conclusive material evidence establishing the death of Rebecca. It was little more than three years after Joel had arrived in Amsterdam that he met Jan Kuyper.

Jan Kuyper drank heavily and when he did so he became both noisy and indiscreet. This he did on a daily basis between the hours of ten in the evening and two in the morning in 'The Haarlem Bar' in the city centre. Joel walked into the place and walked through a curtain of smoke that took his breath away. He made his way to the counter and sat on a stool asking for a beer as he did so. Joel neither smoked nor drank. His training regimen was awesome. His body a monument to the painful hours he spent lifting weights and running. Joel had worked hard to make his money and he had worked equally hard to hone the rippling muscles of his athletic body.

He stood six foot two and weighed fourteen stones. He had paid grateful demobbed soldiers to teach him armed and unarmed combat. He had learned quickly and would fit the bill adequately if someone was to put an advert in the local paper for an efficient assassin. His brooding demeanour and humourless eyes were a warning to others not to approach without caution. Few did.

His huge forearms nursed an ice cold beer. It would be warm when he left it on the bar.

Staggering from within the smoke filled room emerged the distinctly intoxicated Jan Kuyper. Kuyper cut a diminutive figure and the ravages of time and drink had not added to his stature. The black beret perched to one side of his head resided there permanently and served to hide the burns that he had endured at the hands of the Gestapo. He spoke in a loud whisper as if to tell a secret to everyone present.

'The Germans are gone. Gone. Yes gone. Gone,' he said groping for a cigarette from his coat pocket. He struck a match but forgot to light the cigarette until it was too late and, as the match burned his fingers, he dropped it. He feigned great injury. 'Enough that the Gestapo should burn me without self-inflicted pain. Shhhh', he whispered as he brought a finger to his lips. 'You never know who's listening. You never know.' He turned putting his face close to Joel's. The stench from his mouth almost overpowered him.

'Go home Jan', demanded the barman. 'There are no more drinks for you tonight.'

'Home', mused Jan. 'Home. Where is my home? That shit house that I sleep in? That, that, that …' Jan had forgotten his train of thought and returned to Joel.

'Whores and brothels. Brothels and whores. That's my home now. Oh, where shall we put the homeless Mr Mayor? Where shall we put the likes of old Jan Kuyper? What shall we do with a hero? I know we'll put him in a disused brothel. That will do for him and his kind.' He began to shout, and began to turn purple with the effort of his forced invective. 'Heroes! We were heroes. Do you hear me? Heroes! But then, who cares? Who cares? Heroes, that's what we were.' He placed his arms on the bar and putting his head on them, cried out loud. Slowly he lifted his head and very quietly whispered. 'We did what we could for them, didn't we? We tried didn't we? And what did I get for my trouble?' Jan pulled of his beret revealing a heavily scarred head. 'Yes, they set fire to my head, the bastards.'

Joel had decided to get away from this foul breathed man but something compelled him to stay. Firstly he had used the words 'self-inflicted.' This was not at all in keeping with the vocabulary of most of the tramps he had encountered on his many expeditions into the city. He had spoken of whores and brothels too and the significance of this had not escaped him; and, Mr. Mayor?

To the surprise of the barman and the customers sitting at the bar Joel said. 'I will buy you a drink old man. Sit here', he indicated a table nearby. 'A beer', he ordered, giving the barman, who had already told the drunk that he had sufficient for the night, a steely eye. The barman was about to refuse the young man but there was something about him that made him resist the urge. Few crossed the twenty one year old Joel now.

The barman took the drinks to the table and shook Jan Kuyper awake. 'No need for that. I'm not a rag doll and don't spoil the coat', he warbled. Joel looked at the coat in disgust.

'Now Mr.?' Jan was slow on the uptake and looked puzzled before it dawned on him. 'Don't talk in riddles. You know it's a funny thing about riddles ...' Joel cut him short. 'What do you know of the Gestapo brothels in Amsterdam? I have spoken to officials and they say that the authorities are dealing with all enquiries. They refuse to give me answers. I ask in the streets and again no one knows anything. What do you know old man? I will make it worth your while.' He examined the poor wretch intently seeking affirmation of sanity.

Kuyper was assessing how much he might make from his revelations. 'How badly do you want to know?' he whispered conspiratorially.

Joel knew that feeding drinks to a drunk was akin to pouring money down a sewer. Jan Kuyper was not going to get any more lucid with more drink inside him.

'Let me walk you home and we will discuss it. I see the barman here is fast losing patience with you and we have business to discuss.'

Kuyper downed his beer and noted that Joel was about to leave his. He reached forward but Joel had him by the arm and marched him back through the curtain of smoke and out into the clear night air. 'This way', said Joel, dragging the drunk from his place of worship.

'That's not my way home I ...' Joel cut him short. 'Do you want to deal?' Jan Kuyper indicated that he did. 'Very well. Follow me.'

Joel led the wretch into a dark alleyway. He turned to the old man and whispered menacingly. 'The reward that you get for giving me the information that I seek is that I will not kill you. Do you understand?'

The terrified tramp shouted, 'Help.' Joel punched him in the stomach and he collapsed against the wall. He would have slumped to the ground but Joel held him moving rapidly to one side as he vomited down the front of his coat. 'I don't want to hurt you but you had better tell me what I want to know. What do you know of the Gestapo whores in the Nazi barracks? What do you know?' He picked the man up by his puke sodden coat and knocked his head backwards causing it to hit the wall behind. He heard the crack of bone and stone and saw the shock on the old man's face as he collapsed in a heap on the cobbled pavement.

Joel bent down and put his hands under Kuyper's head and looked into his face. Blood coughed from his mouth. He was delirious and gazed into the distance well beyond Joel's face. 'Why? Why? Why?' Oh why did they do it', he breathed.

'Do what old man? Do what?' demanded Joel.

'All dead. All killed. They slit their throats like the butchers they were. Then they set fire to me ... Me, their reliable informer; the mayor. They made me watch and then set my hair on fire. Why? Why?'

Joel had raised his eyes to the heavens on hearing of the fate of his beloved sister. He considered the information and desperate to glean whatever he could from the old man, raised his head from the pavement. Jan Kuyper's unseeing eyes left him in no doubt that his pain had been relieved.

Joel knelt, almost in prayer; tears falling onto the cobbles that were Jan Kuyper's death bed. Slowly gaining his feet he took a last look at the traitor and began to walk down the alleyway to the corner of the street. He paused, scanned the place then walked away from the city lights. Soon he would be sought. The barman and sundry others had seen he and Kuyper leave the bar together. He would be questioned. It was time to leave Amsterdam. It was time to leave Holland. There was no longer a purpose for him to be there. Now he had no ties. He needed to get far away. America was the place. He knew of the excellent opportunities there. He would wait until he had the resources required to exact his revenge on the perpetrators of the crimes against his family. They would pay. This would be a dish served hot, not cold.

Joel and Abraham Goldstein arrived at Ellis Island, New York on St. Valentine's Day 1949.

Chapter 22

JOEL AND ABRAHAM GO TO THE USA 1948 - 1953

Joel and Abraham stepped out onto Ellis Island clutching one large suitcase each. Stitched into the lining of Joel's coat were a bank account number and a combination code of a safety deposit box.

Joel and Abraham took the ferry and arrived in Manhattan, the fine drizzle welcoming them to the city. He took the concealed paper from his lapel and entered the bank. The cashier was shocked to hear that Joel wished to close the account and take the considerable sum in banknotes and pressed a button beneath the counter for assistance. It was more than an hour later that he emerged from the bank to be greeted by a concerned Abraham Goldstein.

After Kuyper's death Joel had taken great care to cover his tracks. The apartment that he and Abraham Goldstein shared in Amsterdam was vacated and the company informed of a forwarding address in Israel. Joel had taken the cash from the false bottom of his bedroom wardrobe and filled the lining of two huge suitcases with large denomination US dollar bills.

They took a train for Paris and remained there for three days. On the first day Joel opened a bank account. On the second he arranged to send the money he had deposited electronically to a branch in New York. On the third day he and Abraham took the ferry from Calais to Dover. They left Southampton for New York City at the end of January 1949.

In New York Joel bought a car for cash and the two were making their way towards Chicago within three hours of landing. It was four days before they set eyes on Lake Michigan. It took a further four days for Joel to contact someone who could give him two new IDs. Abraham had long since stopped objecting to Joel's actions. Thus Joel Salomonovich became Joel Joseph and Abraham Goldstein became Abraham Turner. Joel had always appreciated paintings by Turner and the old art teacher was flattered by his new name. Joel knew where to get the papers.

He took his money across town depositing most of it in five separate banks. Tracing the man and the money would not be easy. They returned to New York via Niagara Falls, staying there for two weeks. Any trail would be cold by then.

Back in New York Joel and Abraham moved into the Windermere apartment block on the southwest corner of 9th Avenue and 57th Street. They stayed there for two years.

Abraham was pleased that Joel had 'gone legit.' Joel played the stock market and his genius shone through. It was just two years before Joel bought his penthouse apartment on Fifth Avenue. After a further year he had made his first million. Twelve months later he had ten.

The New York Times dubbed Joel 'Young King Midas.' Joel celebrated his success by throwing a party at his eighteenth floor penthouse apartment. The party made 'The New York Times' and 'The Wall Street Journal.' It also made the Canadian press.

Now that Joel had the financial clout and power that he would need he turned his mind to Bühler. He also thought of returning to England. He had missed Rachael since the day he had left. Not once did the wealth that inevitably attracts women persuade him to bed one. Rachael was his woman whether he was with her or not and whether she liked it or not. He had not thought of her as his woman when he had been with her and now it was probably too late but she would always be his woman. He thought of what might have been. He remembered Rachael's face on the canal barge, her terror in the bay and the beautiful smile that flashed across her face whenever she saw him at The Bothey or The Pheasantry. He shivered at the thought of her being married and in someone else's arms.

Abraham was not well. The insidious arthritis and the acute bronchial problems that had afflicted him since his down and out days in Hamburg had, in turn, crippled him and damaged his lungs. Joel got the city's best physicians and had a chauffeur at Abraham's beck and call but the old man eventually retreated to his bed.

One evening Joel sat at the edge of Abraham's bed relating the day's business to him. Abraham waited patiently and said. 'My very good friend; you have made the last years of an old man's life happy ones and I thank you for them' Joel raised his arm to object. Abraham went on, ignoring Joel's protestations.

'No my friend it is always you who takes the centre stage. Be quiet and listen to your old teacher for a change.' Joel smiled, amused at Abraham's rare bout of assertiveness.

'It is time for you to think of your future. What are you to do? I will not be here for much longer.' Joel began to protest again. Abraham raised his voice as loud as he was able. 'Be quiet I said and hear me out goddam it.' Joel sat back on the bed and relented to the avuncular Abraham. 'You are a good man Joel Salomonovich – oh, I know that this name is now forgotten. To me you will always be Joel Salomonovich and tonight I use your proper name.'

Abraham began to cough and Joel put an extra pillow under his head. 'Thank you for your kindness. Now I will continue. How old are you now? Twenty-five? Yes twenty-five. It is true that twenty-five is not old but it isn't young either. It is time that you found a wife. Go Joel. Go.'

Joel stiffened. 'Go where?'

Abraham looked him in the eyes. 'You know where. You have so much love to give, yet so much hate. You are a stubborn man Joel Salomonovich. Stubborn! Follow your heart, which is full of love not your head, which is full of the hate that will destroy you.' He sighed as if conceding defeat. 'Please take the pillow away I must take my medication and sleep. I am weary and oh so very tired. Goodnight.' Joel walked to the door and put his finger on the light switch. He glanced at the bed and smiled at Abraham. 'Goodnight my conscience.'

Abraham smiled and whispered, 'God bless.' Within an hour he had fallen asleep for the last time.

For two days Joel mourned his friend and confident. On the third day he rose from the chair and screamed. It proved cathartic and he began to move on. He planned to take Abraham back to Hamburg and to bury him there and then, yes then he would go to England as Abraham had said he should. But there were other things to settle too.

It took two days to put the wheels in motion. He planned meticulously, used his contacts extensively and left his penthouse at ten o'clock on the Saturday evening. It was five days since the death of his good friend and it was time to take him home.

Joel was twenty-five. For more than ten years SS Obersturmführer Reinhardt Bühler's face had haunted him. There was much to settle. He believed that he had the necessary wealth to execute his plans and he had greased enough palms to wield the influence he would require. The time was right. Joel remembered a passage from the Christian bible. He knew it very well. It was from Romans 12:19. 'Vengeance is mine saith the lord, I will repay.' Joel walked to the window, looked down over Manhattan and spoke out loud. 'Well Lord, you're just about to get a little help.'

Chapter 23

GEORGE AND RACHAEL

Sir George Merrick had informed his 'contacts' at the foreign office within twenty minutes of Joel leaving Marta's funeral. He realised that Joel had been unlikely to part with much information regarding his father's work but steadfastly and patiently had gleaned what he could and had passed it on to the authorities. He had not bargained for the permanence of Joel's absence.

The professor had grown attached to Marta and it was with a genuine sense of loss that he had attended her funeral. He attended his wife's funeral in the following spring and the one funeral that we us must all attend during that same autumn.

George felt the loss of his parents acutely. He had depended on their good council and, now at university, missed them greatly. He drew deeper into himself and worked with a passion, for long hours every day in an attempt to insulate himself from his loss. His only distraction was during university holidays when he afforded himself a few days back at the old cottage, ostensibly to 'tie up affairs', but specifically in the hope of meeting Rachael. She had started at Oxford, much to George's chagrin, the year after he had gone to Cambridge. She read architecture as her father had done at Maastricht University.

After the loss of his parents George yearned to be closer to Rachael. He invited her to his graduation but she was unable to attend. The nineteen year old had a disappointing summer.

George knew that Rachael would be home to spend the summer with her father. He knew that Vincent missed her greatly. Vincent had missed Martha too. He had had the utmost respect for Marta and, having a daughter to bring up, had often sought her wisdom and guidance. They were never intimate but had always been profoundly attached and loyal to one another. Rachael understood the importance of the time Marta spent with her father.

No one could ever replace Ruth and Marta had never intended to. She had been cautious not to intrude between father and daughter but was always on hand to lend assistance when council and support were required. Marta's sure touch was reflected in the warmth and understanding of their relationship. Vincent had never had a closer friend.

The brooding Joel had softened when he saw his mother and Rachael together. Rachael had not replaced Marta's love for Rebecca but Joel saw the joy and contentment that his mother derived from the relationship and the affection that she had for Rachael.

George saw this too and felt increasingly envious of the closeness of the two families. He had been pleased to see the back of Joel, and of Marta.

The two boys had struggled to form a relationship. George was correct, erudite formal and ill at ease in the company of others. Joel was cultured, uninhibited, razor sharp, volatile and unpredictable. George wished Joel to be less sullen and more respectful. Joel wished George would switch off once in a while and drop the far reaching questions and probing enquiries into the meaning of life and beyond. In short Joel found George boring and stuffy. Joel was anything but that.

Now Vincent anticipated the return of his daughter for the summer and, at least for a time, something approaching normality would resume.

And so it was that the student George found himself riding his old and trusty bike along the pathway from the white stone cottage to The Pheasantry to pay a call on Vincent and Rachael Haan. He was pleased to learn that Rachael had returned to Suffolk from Oxford two days previously.

Vincent Haan was chopping firewood in the small yard between The Pheasantry and the old stable block 'I'm very pleased to see you;' he called in his much improved English. George placed his bicycle against the stable wall and bent to take off his bike clips.

'I hope that I find you well sir?' He enquired, nervously scanning the yard in the hope of a glimpse of Rachael.

'I am quite well thank you', replied the courteous Dutchman.

George took note that Vincent Haan was indeed, in rude health. The sandy hair was a little greyer as were his trim smart beard and moustache. Perhaps he stooped a little more than when George had first met him but clearly he had prospered.

The two discussed the weather and Vincent reflected that this was a topic he discussed more frequently since coming to England that at any other time of his life. Vincent updated George on the village gossip, and though that was of was of little interest to him, he smiled and tolerated the banal exchanges. Vincent was about to ask about Cambridge when the stable door opened and Rachael blinked her way into the bright sunlight.

George's heart missed a beat; he blushed and, after saying a quick hello to Rachael, continued to speak with Vincent as if further banalities had been the central purpose of his visit. After a few minutes he turned to Rachael and casually mentioned that he intended to walk to the coast during the afternoon. Rachael thought that that would be very rewarding for George and was pleased that he was keeping well.

She changed the subject leaving George feeling rather awkward and damning his lack of self-confidence. He knew that he had been rebuffed. Rachael had let him down gently but let him down she had. He remained as long as he could, to maintain his dignity, and then left on the pretence that he had an appointment.

George spent the next day pining for Rachael. His unrequited love tormented his soul, gnawed at his consciousness and nourished his neurosis.

Chapter 24

VINCENT AND STANLEY MAINWARING

Vincent was working as an architect for Stanley Mainwaring and Sons, a reputable local architect's firm. Old Stanley Mainwaring had lost both of his sons; one to tuberculosis in November 1940 and the other was missing presumed drowned when HMS Repulse was sunk in December 1941. Since that time he had rarely been seen at the office and Vincent, who had worked there for a little over two years, was left to run the firm by himself.

He engaged a proficient secretary and 'rolled his sleeves up.' There was work to be done and he relished it.

It was a bitter blow to lose Rachael to Oxford. Cambridge would have been much closer and he had begged her to apply there but, uncharacteristically, she had been quite firm about her intention to apply to Oxford. He missed her terribly and compensated for his loss by immersing himself in his work. That work was paying dividends.

He had learned of the death of Ruth's mother and the 'confiscation' of her home soon after their arrival in England. It was another bitter blow for Rachael. He set legal proceedings in place to recover the property but acknowledged that the process would take many years. As always he placed hope behind industry and applied himself to matters that could be influenced.

There was still no news of his brother Rudi. He had been taken by the SS but there was no further information. He feared the worst and as the days went by he began to mourn his last relative.

Vincent had decided that the time was right to 'go it alone.' The opportunity arrived to broach the subject with Mainwaring. He required the old man's signature on several legal papers and arranged to meet with him at his home. Mainwaring had built a fine firm and accumulated a great deal of money from his firm and his wife's inheritance. He had purchased Lord

Allenby's home. 'The Manor House', was an exceptionally pleasant building ideally placed by the river and lake and quite close to the village.

Vincent walked up the long gravel drive and climbed the old stone steps beneath the portico, the tall columns shading the façade from the early summer sun.

He had often cast his architect's eye over the property and thought that the building and grounds were both typically English and perfectly proportioned. From the house the land fell towards the river, which had been dammed during the late eighteenth century to create a sizable lake. The gamekeeper had introduced Vincent to the skills of fishing there and he had become much attached to 'The Manor House', its land, trees, river and lake.

Mainwaring approached Vincent, arms outstretched. 'I trust that I find you very well', was his usual form of address. Vincent smiled apprehensively considering the best way to broach the topic of his leaving the firm. Mainwaring had always been straight with him and Vincent felt greatly indebted to him. He didn't relish his mission.

He began: 'My dear Mr. Mainwaring, I am most grateful to you for giving me the opportunity to ...' He was cut off abruptly with a curt: 'Yes, yes, yes my dear boy. I hope that you do not find me discourteous but I have an appointment with Doctor Owen shortly and am running a little late; and, though that does not excuse my impolite interruption, I do hope that you will tolerate it on this occasion. Vincent I want to talk to you about an urgent matter, which I trust will meet with your approval.'

Mainwaring was not given to abrupt and unmannerly interruptions and Vincent was taken aback by the old man's curious impatience. Vincent had intimated that he had something of some matter to discuss but the old man had been quite adamant, resolute and dismissive. Mainwaring fumbled for the pocket watch in his waistcoat, something he did at regular intervals throughout each day, more from habit than necessity. He drew a deep breath and proceeded. 'As you know I have lost both of my sons. My wife is infirm and I am not in the best of health. No my dear fellow', he protested, as Vincent moved towards him demonstrating his concern, 'No, I am not about to fall dead at the drop of a hat but I do need to plan ahead. I do not have anyone left to run the firm and it is therefore my intention to make you a conditional partner.'

Vincent was about to protest that he had not the means to buy into the firm but Mainwaring waived him away dismissively once again. Perplexed he complied with the kindly gentleman's request. 'My three conditions are as follows,' he continued resolutely. 'I ask you to accept fifty percent on the firm without payment.' Vincent was stunned. 'Half the profits will be paid to me, or my wife in the case of my demise; I shall retire as of this instant, but; the name of the firm shall remain the same for not less than five and twenty years.' He smiled at the thought of that small compensation. 'Yes I would like to be remembered amongst my peers and by the village folk dear boy.' He sat in his green Chesterfield armchair, paused for a moment then lowered his reading glasses to his lap. 'On my demise or my wife's demise, whichever is the latter, you will inherit my share of the firm.' He stopped to gauge Vincent's reaction, and then smiled again. 'You and I have had great sadness in our lives. You, however, still have much to give Vincent Haan and I trust no man more than you. My firm took many years to build. I wish it to flourish in the years to come. Please, I beg you to accept my offer as a great kindness to me.'

Vincent was struck dumb with shock. He had never thought; never dreamed; never anticipated this development. He gulped for air trying to take the magnitude of the offer in. Two year's work and he was to inherit a prosperous business. Stanley Mainwaring had no heirs and he and his wife had no remaining family. There was little else he could do. He was the sole beneficiary. He accepted the proprietor's most generous terms and became a partner in Mainwaring and Sons (Architects) with great pride.

Losing two sons had had a dramatic effect on Stanley Mainwaring. He was a broken man but was of the 'stiff upper lip', generation that 'got on with it.' His emotions were kept in check in public and the only person to have witnessed his personal anguish was Dr. Owen who, having been called out in the early hours one morning, had seen him on his knees, at the rear of his stables sobbing uncontrollably after the death of his elder son. The doctor had retreated unnoticed and the sighting remained unrecorded in the village annals.

Stanley Mainwaring was right about his decision to make Vincent a partner. He was wrong to say that he was unlikely to fall dead at the drop of a hat. Forty-eight hours after signing the partnership agreement he did just that. Within the month his wife had joined him and the Mainwaring's anguish was over.

Mainwaring's will left everything to Vincent, including 'The Manor House' and money, trusting that he would carry out a small number of requests. The trust, faith and esteem with which Vincent had obviously been held weighed heavy on his heart for the remainder of his life. There was small gift for the church renovation fund, sums for several charities and personal gifts to some of the villagers who had appreciated Stanley Mainwaring's fine collection of antiques. Vincent more than complied with Stanley Mainwaring's generous requests.

Chapter 25

GEORGE THE IRASCIBLE PROFESSOR

George Merrick was an exceptional student. At twenty he had a double first at Cambridge and three years later, a doctorate. At twenty-four he had a research fellowship. His working days were long and rewarding. Engrossed in his academic life he had rapidly made a reputation in medicine and genetics.

The university recognised the eccentric genius. He was universally accepted to be, cantankerous, unfeeling and boring. His peers had created a new noun. 'A Merrick.' Its denotation being, a pain in the arse.

Colleagues and students avoided the 'mad scientist,' which was another sobriquet he had acquired. He was irascible and irritable, particularly with the less gifted, and that, in his eyes, was more or less everyone. He could be scathing about the shallowness of other's research and openly critical of methods employed by lesser academics. He lacked any endearing social graces and trampled on the reputations of many of the fine men who had preceded him.

George always put George first, second and third. His massive ego and certainty rendered him immune to criticism. Critics would be proved wrong. It was merely a question of time. This certainty was not confined to his own specialism. George tore through the research of experts in many fields, confounding and astounding while humiliating and humbling. George's father had been knighted. There were precious few who wished the same honour to be bestowed upon the son.

His life would have been one-dimensional were it not for his obsession for Rachael. His unwitnessed passion caused great anguish and many a student became the recipient of his bile when his pain surfaced.

His irascible attitude and shocking manner came to the attention of the authorities and, much to his astonishment; he was reprimanded and warned as to his future conduct. All of this was far beneath George and he subsequently held the authorities in contempt too. The flawed genius withdrew from unnecessary discourse with others and sought solace in his work.

George could not reconcile the inner conflict that burned so deep within his tortured soul. He resolved to visit Rachael and, believing her to be spending time with her father at The Manor House, decided that the sooner he confronted his demons the better. The deluded genius embarked on his emotional apocalypse.

George had never taken driving lessons. His father's old Ford stood rusting beside the old cottage unused for several years. He took the train.

Chapter 26

RACHAEL GOES TO OXFORD

Rachael had chosen Oxford, rather than Cambridge for all the wrong reasons and she regretted the rationale behind her decision. She excelled among 'the dreaming spires' and enjoyed student life. She had needed space and Cambridge was too close to home. George would be a distraction and though her father and she were close his commitment to his newly acquired firm had been absolute. It would have broken Vincent's heart to know it, but he had had much less time with Rachael prior to her leaving home and she had felt it. The time was right to leave and the place to study, she decided, was Oxford.

She had many admirers at Oxford and made friends rapidly but the spectre of Joel clung to her consciousness and inhibited her when the boys made eyes, clinging to the belief that one day he would walk back into her life.

Joel had been gone for more than three years and had given no indication of returning. Yet, when home, Rachael visited The Bothey daily hoping against hope that he would be there. There had been no information as to his whereabouts yet she remained unshakably convinced that he would return.

She had delayed applying for university at eighteen as she waited first at The Pheasantry and later at The Manor. Her father was perplexed. Rachael had always been such a straightforward girl. Now she seemed less sure of herself. He pushed her to apply for university and was disappointed that she had not considered nearby Cambridge. She worked hard and gained a first in architecture during in the summer of 1950.

Rachael returned to Suffolk joining the growing team of architects now working for Mainwaring and Sons. She was happy in her work and loved to be near her father once again but she longed for Joel and resolved to wait for as long as it took.

Chapter 27

ABRAHAM'S WAKE
IN HAMBURG

Joel had Abraham's body flown back to Hamburg. He had brought his friend to America and now he felt obliged to take him home. The porthole seats he had booked for the journeys from New York to London and from London to Hamburg were wasted. Joel was in a trance, deep in thought but unwilling to move on until matters were settled. It seemed that his life had been like that ever since the executions of his father and brothers. Until he had put his friend to rest he lacked the inertia necessary to move forward. His thinking lacked the insight and dynamism that characterised his normal frame of mind.

He, and an ancient rabbi, attended the burial at Hamburg's Ohrlsdorf Cemetery. True Joel Salomonovich and Abraham Goldstein were no more but, as Abraham had remarked just seven days earlier, today his 'proper name' would be used. The service was short and Joel was courteous to the rabbi rewarding him generously for his services. He left to find a place to stay for two nights. It would take that long to say goodbye to his last true friend.

He took a room in a fifth rate hotel on the street where he had met Abraham some four years earlier. It was not a time for opulence. It was a time for nostalgia. He didn't go all the way. The stench and the degradation were unnecessary. The locale sufficed.

On the evening following Abraham's burial Joel drank heavily and returned to the graveyard accompanied by a large bottle of scotch. He sat on the grass and talked to Abraham until the early hours then lay, semi-conscious, by the side of his good friend until mid-morning. He woke struggling to focus on his surroundings and to make sense of them. Eventually he crawled from the damp grass, gave the grave one last look, uttered a fond farewell, and stumbled towards his hotel. He slept for two days.

A collage of memories invaded his sleep. Fond memories of his family: the executions; the lockkeeper and his wife: the jovial captain and his sullen mate and their heroic deaths: the fate of Rebecca: the death of his mother: the ridiculous George Merrick and his infernal, intrusive father; the gentleness and kindness of Vincent Haan and Rachael. The beautiful Rachael.

Bühler's face intruded into each of these scenes, his visage, strangely distorted, moving rapidly towards him in sharp focus then blurring into an amorphous spirit wreaking havoc and chaos as it disappeared into the ether. Bühler appeared from the left and then from the right, screaming as he tore into the scene then leaving it with a demented moan. Joel wanted to be left alone with Rachael but still Bühler came, saliva dripping from his contorted mouth. Joel twisted and turned but the relentless spectre gave no quarter. The unremitting torture continued throughout the two days of his hibernation. Bühler's hideous image continued to haunt the young man. It always would.

When Joel emerged from his room he looked sharp, was impeccably dressed and focussed on the jobs in hand. It was time. Time to move on! The wake was over. The businessman was back in control. He rang the airport and made a reservation for an evening flight to London. He had thought of going overland and sailing but considered travelling anywhere near Amsterdam to be folly. It was just four years since the unfortunate Jan Kuyper incident. Not enough of the Amstel River had flowed under the Magere Bridge.

During the flight Joel thought of Rachael. He saw her as a kindred spirit. She was the one remaining person that he really cared for. Why had he not returned to her before? Would she be married, have children and be happy? Would she be with George? He tried to dismiss these negative thoughts from his mind but, like Bühler's face in his dreams, they continued to bombard his consciousness.

He took a train from Heathrow to Cambridge and a taxi from there to the coast. The familiar shoreline comforted him. He felt strangely at home. New York had never been home and neither had Amsterdam. Hamburg had once been his home but now he felt the pull of this flat land with its winding roads and windmills.

He directed the taxi driver to take him to the coast and now looked down over the bay where he and Rachael had arrived in England and where she had lost her mother. This was the amphitheatre, the crucible in which so much of his life had been forged.

He looked out across the bay. The setting sun painted the sky shades of red and orange and the calm sea looked harmless in its warm glow. 'Not at all like a Turner', he thought.

Chapter 28

1953 REBECCA MOVES TO NEW YORK

Rebecca Kinnear had been a good wife to Edward. He was ever attentive and kind to her but there had been no passion on her part. Perhaps, she mused, any passion that she might have had, had been removed from her soul by the Third Reich. Never the less she felt a tenderness that she had not experienced since living with her mother, father and brothers and for that she was grateful.

Rebecca had seven happy years with Edward before he succumbed to the tuberculosis that destroyed his lungs. She was left alone again. She had a little money and a small town house in the Hamilton suburbs. She had insisted on working, much against Edward's wishes, and had attained a teaching qualification.

Both colleagues and acquaintances respected Rebecca but she had never felt that she belonged in Hamilton or, indeed, in Canada. It wasn't the people it was her, she reflected. But would she feel at home in a country and city that had rejected her? She believed that her parents and brothers to be dead and Germany did not call to her. Poland? She had never known the land of her forefathers. Holland? Never! Again the memories were too painful. A new start was needed; a new start in a new world. She resolved to move to New York. There she could try to build a new life. She would come out of the shadows and begin to live again. New York would offer her opportunities and a chance to live. She looked in the mirror. She felt fifty. She was just twenty-nine.

Rebecca resolved to leave for New York in the summer and began to put her affairs in order. The house was put on the market and she gave notice to her school. It was a cold early spring morning when she went to the railway station to pick up her ticket for New York. She bought 'The National Post' newspaper at the news stand and boarded the train.

It was an hour into the journey before Rebecca decided to read the paper. She unfolded the sheets and stared at a large picture of her little brother. 'Joel.'

Much to the amazement of her fellow passengers the diminutive young woman stood and shouted. 'Joel! Gott seit dank.' She sank back slowly into her seat.

Chapter 29

JOEL RETURNS TO SUFFOLK

Joel had travelled six thousand miles from New York to London, London to Hamburg, Hamburg to London, London to Cambridge and Cambridge to the coast. The remaining half-mile was proving to be the most difficult part of the journey to undertake.

The taxi driver was clearly concerned that his fare was running to a considerably larger sum than he had ever charged before and wasn't at all sure that he was going to receive it. His sharply dressed passenger had got out of his saloon and had walked to the shoreline. This had never happened before. The passenger was clearly not a person to cross and it was with considerable trepidation that he began, 'Sir.'

Joel had been lost in his own thoughts as he stared out to sea, the gentle ripple of the calm water soothing his troubled mind. He turned to the driver. 'Yes of course. How much do I owe you?'

The driver hardly dare say. 'I'm afraid that it's two pounds three shillings and sixpence sir. You see...'

Joel cut him short and gave him four one pound notes. 'Keep the change. I wonder if you could do me a small favour?' The driver's eyes widened as he stared at the four pound notes and then at Joel in astonishment. 'Anything sir. Just as you say sir', his demeanour having been transformed in an instance.

'Good. There is a public house called The Rose and Crown in the village. Take my case there and ask the landlord for a room for the night. I will make it worth your while. Let's say a further pound for the additional trouble?'

The driver couldn't believe his luck and shouted, 'immediately sir. Of course sir. Will that be all sir?' Joel thought for a moment. 'Yes that will be all. There is no rush. Just do as I have asked but be discreet.'

Joel stood on the sand dunes facing the sea breeze and pulled up his coat collar against the chilling wind. He was deep in thought. He had been deep in thought a great deal over recent days.

He didn't want to be recognised which would, inevitably, provide instant gossip for the villagers. Above all he did not want Rachael to know that he was in the vicinity. He rationalised that he needed to know of Rachael's situation before making any move. If she was spoken for he would leave and pay for the silence of those who had had knowledge of his presence. It would be a long night.

The driver returned with the keys to Joel's room at The Rose and Crown. 'There you are sir. Your case is safe behind the bar sir. Will that be all sir? Do you need a lift to the Rose and Crown sir? Free gratis and all that sir.'

'That will be all', Joel replied, patting the driver on the shoulder and handing over the fifth pound note. 'Thank you and goodnight.'

'Thank you and a very good night to you sir', the driver offered. 'And take care of yourself sir; yes, mind how you go sir.'

Joel walked away as the man spoke, already lost in thought. The cold night air bit into his cheeks. He turned away from the coast and walked down the dunes finding refuge from the cold wind behind them. He waited until half past eleven before walking into the village.

Little had changed. The village unexpectedly reassured him as he walked unnoticed towards the public house. Turning up his collar, against recognition rather than the weather, he entered.

Two regulars and the landlord sat drinking in semi-darkness at the back of the room. The landlord, Sam Waldron, rose and came to the bar.

'I don't know as how you got in but I'm afraid that ...' he stopped mid-sentence as he recognised Joel. 'They said you woz ...'

Joel put his finger to his mouth and indicated that the landlord should follow him upstairs. Sam Waldron loved both gossip and money. Joel paid handsomely and Sam decided that he preferred money to gossip.

Chapter 30

REBECCA IN NEW YORK

The New York rain fell heavily as Rebecca left Grand Central Railway Station. The sky was an unremitting grey and the weather forecasters would have an easy time of it for the next few days. She called a cab and was grateful to be relieved of the two heavy suitcases she carried. All her possessions were in those two cases. She had sold her home lock, stock and barrel. She had nothing from her life in Hamburg and had accumulated few Hamilton acquisitions. The contents of her cases consisted of her clothes and a photograph of Edward Kinnear.

'The Murray Hill Hotel please', she asked politely. 'It's on …'

'I know where it is lady', interrupted the less than polite cab driver.

She wiped the window to get her first view of New York but the condensation was heavy and the driving rain didn't help.

The Murray Hill was on 28th Street between Park Avenue and Lexington, a few blocks from the station. The short trip took almost ten minutes during which the cab driver sounded his horn in an irate manner at ten second intervals. Paying off the cab was a merciful relief.

The Murray Hill was less than grand but Rebecca rationalised that it would suffice for a couple of nights until she found lodgings – or Joel. Impatient to be on the move she left her room within minutes, leaving her cases unpacked.

Joel. She was excited. She would see Joel. Did he know that she was alive? She rather doubted it. How had he escaped the bombing of their home? Had her mother? Her brain ached with the pace of her thoughts, the ramifications, the dimensions, the reunion and …

She had sat on the bed to steadied herself. 'Enough', she had said out loud. 'It is time to emulate my mother. It's time to be pragmatic. Time to take control and to carefully consider the best way forward. To be pragmatic. To be Marta Salomonovich.'

Rebecca bathed and put on a clean long cream skirt and sweater. Ever since Edward Kinnear had released her from the Zandvoort barracks she had worn clean conservative clothes. After those wretched years in her cell wearing provocative low necklines and high hemlines and stockings and lingerie that frequently went without a wash for days on end, she considered the conservative clothes she now wore to be a luxury that she could afford at any price.

She checked herself in the mirror, took the elevator and arrived in the lobby within minutes. She walked to the reception desk and asked for assistance.

'This may take a few moments', she said apologetically, 'but I need a moment of someone's time.'

A good percentage of New Yorkers have little time to give and the receptionist was no exception. 'Harry', he beckoned to a young man smoking a cigarette and taking a break from the pressures of mopping the floor. 'This lady's from out a town and needs a hand. Got five?'

'I've always got five for a lady', he smiled as he lifted both eyebrows and sashayed across the lobby. The young man put a comb through his hair with one swoop of his hand and put his face towards Rebecca's. She was repulsed by his nauseous behaviour and almost turned on her heels but she desperately needed information.

The undeterred Rudolph Valentino gazed deeper into her eyes. 'And?' he whispered.

'It's nothing really. I just want to know the best way to get to Ninth Avenue.'

'Ninth lady? Where on Ninth? It a long road.' She showed him the address and he gave out a low whistle. 'You know people there lady?'

Rebecca tried not to show her impatience. She would have taken a cab but her resources were limited and she needed to conserve what she had. 'Please, I just need to know where I can catch a train or bus to this address.'

'Why don't you ring? Save you time and money.'

Rebecca bit her lip again and wondered whether to cut her loses and try elsewhere. Perhaps at a store or perhaps she could find a policeman?

'Ok, listen. The subway is just around the corner here.' He took her by the arm and walked her to the door. It took him thirty seconds to tell her all that she had wanted to know. Before he could strike up any further conversation she thanked him and left. She prayed that Valentino was a one off. Somehow she doubted it.

The subway took a little working out but she recognised the station that the floor mopper had said she should alight at and, within minutes, took the escalator to Ninth Avenue and a heavy drizzle. Soon she stood outside the Windermere shaking with excitement.

According to the newspaper article Joel's party had been held at the Windermere. It seemed an obvious starting point. Rebecca had retained the paper she had read on the train and had brought it with her. She looked at the façade of the building then walked into the magnificent marble lobby and reflected. 'All this time my little brother. All this time you have been here. All this time!'

The grey uniformed concierge was not at all impressed by the young woman or her questions. He looked at Rebecca's clothes and, believed he 'had her number'. 'I'm sorry lady but unless you've an appointment, a letter or an invitation...' He left the sentence in the air as he raised both arms feigning empathy. 'It is not our policy to give out names and the numbers of apartments. If you want to leave a note I'll make sure that it's delivered.'

'But could you not check to see if he is here. Please, tell him that Rebecca Salom...'

The concierge raised his arms again and smiled, 'I am afraid that Mr. Joseph ain't here.' He observed the consternation on Rebecca's face. 'Look lady, (the 'lady' came with a heavy coat of laboured irony), 'I shouldn't tell you nothing you know but, like, is it important?' Rebecca missed the point of the question.

'Yes it is very important.'

'Just how important?' Again she missed the point.

'As I say, very important.' The concierge was beginning to lose patience. 'Lady, what's it worth?'

Slowly the penny dropped. 'Oh! Well I don't have ...' She began to scramble for her handbag and pulled out a five dollar bill. The concierge snapped it from her hand like a striking cobra simultaneously scanning the room and hoping that no one had spotted his latest transaction. He turned back to Rebecca, clearly nervous and frustrated by her naïvity.

'Mr. Joseph has gone to Europe. He left last night. I'm sorry if you've come far but I can't help you no more.'

Rebecca thought that this was little enough information for, what was, for her, a considerable sum. She began to walk away, then, on impulse, turned and asked, 'Where in Europe and for how long?' She noted the concierge's look of alarm and despair once again. For the second time within the hour Rebecca's arm was held as she was taken to an exit.

At the doorway he whispered, 'It said Hamburg on the cases lady. That must be where they are going to bury Mr. Turner. I'm not sure that Mr. Joseph will be coming back at all. Now off you go and don't say I said a word. Understand?'

They went through the revolving door and exited on the sidewalk together. He turned to her once again. 'This is free gratis'; he appeared pleased with his philanthropy. 'Mr. Turner was an old friend of Mr. Joseph's from before the war. He died on Monday. Mr. Joseph is taking him home to be buried and he ain't returning. Poor old Abraham Turner', he said without much feeling. The concierge considered it time for her to leave. 'There, I've given you more than five dollars' worth. Goodbye and don't come back. Do you hear?' With that he disappeared through the revolving doors with his ill-gotten gains.

Rebecca returned to her room, her mind in turmoil. How could she contact Joel? Clearly he could be traced now that she had a lead. His high profile as a businessman would leave a paper trail. But she was desperate to meet him and meet him now. What if he had disappeared again? The possibilities and permutations peppered her rapidly and hard. Perhaps she should wait for him to return but the concierge had said that he wouldn't. She needed Joel. Waiting was not an option.

Her mind turned to Joel's 'old friend' who had died. Who was this old friend from Hamburg? She had never heard of an Abraham Turner. For that matter she had never heard of Joel Joseph. So was Abraham Turner a sobriquet too?

Turner? Turner? Something triggered her thought. What was it? Her eyes widened as it struck her. Joel had always loved the paintings of Turner. Joseph Turner. Joel Joseph and Abraham Turner. Who was Abraham Turner? There were many Abraham's amongst Hamburg's Jewish community but none that she could remember as being a close friend of Joel. The only one that she could call to mind was a former art teacher of hers. She would never forget Abraham Goldstein. It was Abraham who had remonstrated with the Nazis in that wretched square in Hamburg where her father and brothers were murdered as she was being dragged away from her mother and Joel. It could not be this Abraham; he had been shot by the officer at close range and his chest had burst open. She had been dragged over his dead body as he lay in that filthy street. She looked to the ceiling and repeated. 'So, exactly who was Abraham Turner?'

Rebecca considered the works of 'The Painter of Light', Joseph Turner. 'Shades of Darkness, the Evening Deluge', 'Rain, Steam and Speed,' 'Chichester Canal' and 'The Dancing Temeraire.' The paintings had great atmosphere created by the contrasting effects of the light and their sombre colours. The outlines of the subjects lost definition and were shrouded in steam, haze, mist or cloud. Perhaps, reflected Rebecca, the irony is that the amorphous nature was a metaphor for a man who had a need to change his name. Perhaps it wasn't ironic at all. It was Joel and Joel was Joel no matter what he gave as his second name.

She bought a ticket to Hamburg.

Chapter 31

REBECCA IN HAMBURG

Rebecca purchased a deposit key and left her luggage in a locker at Hamburg airport. She was exhausted from the long journey but knew that time was of the essence and that she must move quickly.

If Joel Joseph, or Salomonovich, was going to bury his friend Abraham Turner, or whatever his real surname was, she was going to attend the funeral. This was her one chance to meet Joel. If Abraham was an old friend she felt sure that she knew where in Hamburg that funeral would take place.

The Portuguese Jewish Cemetery in König Strasse was the oldest Jewish cemetery in Hamburg, famous for its epitaphs in Hebrew and Portuguese and the beautiful craftsmanship of the stonemasons. She made enquiries at the main gate and was disappointed with the result. Still resolute she interrogated the gatekeeper. He was an accommodating old soul and noted the urgency of Rebecca's enquiries.

'Wait here for a moment', he said, smiling warmly. 'I'll see what I can do.'

Rebecca waited six long minutes before the kindly old gentleman returned.

'There was a funeral this morning for an Abraham Goldstein but that was at Ohrlsdorf Cemetery. I'm afraid that you have missed it. It is now almost one o'clock.'

Rebecca thanked the guardian of Hamburg's Jewish souls and ran to the gate. By one twenty five she was at Ohrlsdorf. It took a further twenty minutes to find assistance and locate the grave of Abraham Goldstein.

She stood beside the new grave. Where was Joel? She had missed him. Not two hours earlier he had stood on the very spot where she was standing. Just two hours. 'Of course', she said out loud, 'Abraham Goldstein, the teacher. The art teacher. Abraham Turner. Turner! Of course. He survived.'

Rebecca retired to a nearby bench and sat with her head in her hands. She didn't understand it at all. She had seen Abraham Goldstein shot. At least, that Abraham Goldstein. The art teacher. And now this. Joel had gone. She had missed her brother. She wept for more than an hour, and then, with the pragmatism inherited from her mother, resolved to find lodgings and decide on her next strategy.

Had Rebecca stayed at the graveside for a further hour she would have met the drunken friend of Abraham Goldstein and could have watched him sleep by the side of the grave until the morning came.

As it was she returned to the grave on the following day and sat nearby throughout the morning, and well into the afternoon, hoping against hope that Joel would return. Had she returned twenty minutes earlier she would have witnessed a drunk making his way back to his room in the old quarters.

Rebecca returned to New York and began her search back at The Windermere. The concierge was not pleased to see her.

Joel Joseph had become Joel Salomonovich once again and was living in rural England. His New York connection was severed by his 'associates' and he disappeared from corporate view. Joel was lost to Rebecca once again.

Chapter 32

GEORGE ASKS RACHAEL
A QUESTION

It being the summer recess George had decided to spend time at the family cottage. He would take work back with him to Suffolk and, on evenings, sit on his father's chair, at his father's desk, in his father's study. He felt content there.

The dimly lit room had been a restful place to retreat to since the deaths of his parents.

It was on his third day back at the cottage that he had run into Rachael. He was cycling to the village bakery when he saw her leave the post office. He contrived the meeting by cycling around the back of the Rose and Crown and arriving in front of her as she began the walk back to the Manor House.

Rachael smiled and George melted.

'Hello George, I hope that you are well', she enquired. George blustered.

'Quite well thank you Rachael. May I carry your groceries?'

The load was not heavy but she handed it over and he placed it in the basket, sitting above the front wheel of his bicycle. They walked side by side during which time George was careful to ask much about how her father was and to express the extent of his esteem for that gentleman. Rachael felt that it was a little overdone but was responded gratefully for his enquiries.

'Rachael', he began awkwardly, 'I have tickets for the Aldeburgh Festival. The English Opera Group is singing and Benjamin Britten is conducting. It is very exciting and I'm sure that you would enjoy it. Do come.'

Rachael had not had much artistic stimulation since leaving Oxford and she rather liked Britten. George, she felt, would be a little tiresome but she considered that having said no to him so often that, on this occasion, she would relent; and, perhaps, it would be good to get out. She acquiesced rather than accepted.

George was elated and eagerly outlined the itinerary for the day. The tickets, he had said, were for Friday and that would be in three days' time. He would call for her at 8:15 a.m. Within an hour of leaving Rachael he was frantically attempting to purchase two tickets for the concert. It took him two days.

Chapter 33

JOEL'S RETURN

Sam Waldron would have benefited from a good grooming and a decent shave. He was unkempt at the best of times. His shirt was clean but it hadn't seen an iron for weeks. The front of his waistcoat was as shiny as the back, it being smoothed away by constant rubbing as he leaned for long hours on his own bar. The Rose and Crown landlord's fiery red face was more a result of the huge quantities of ale he imbibed than of any exertion and his complexion contrasted sharply with the white stubble that was a permanent feature on his face. A tuft of white hair sprung from his chest and out of his open necked collarless shirt. His huge red arms were covered in thick white hair. In his youth he had boxed as 'Sam Waldron - The Suffolk Punch', and he had had a kick like one too. Villagers considered it unwise to cross Sam. His temper was apt to get the best of him. He had a leather belt around his waist and it was common knowledge that his wife, Beatty, knew what it felt like.

Sam nodded for Joel to follow him as he walked to the foot of the stairs. He turned abruptly, sensing that Joel was not following. He looked at the young man. Joel looked down at his cases and the truculent host grudgingly lifted them and climbed the stairs.

Sam put the case down to open the door. 'This is the best we 'ave', he said as he threw the door open and lifted the case in. Joel hadn't spoken and this put Sam on edge. Sam didn't like feeling uncomfortable. He turned to Joel and walked towards him. This was a strategy he used to cower those he considered fit subjects for his menace. Joel surprised Sam by taking a step towards him offering him his hand. Sam's natural reaction was to reciprocate. Joel took Sam's hand and grasped it, squeezed tight and brought his nose to within an inch of Sam's. Sam writhed in agony. Calmly Joel began. 'I want you to remember this, so listen very carefully.' The grip became tighter still and Sam was staring wide-eyed at the powerful young man with the unflinching face.

'I have paid you well and I expect to get what I have paid for, do you understand? You will not cross me.' The last sentence was delivered with great certainty. Sam was sweating profusely. The young man's eyes pierced his own and for the first time in his life he felt a victim's terror. Joel went on, his vice-like grip remaining firm. He placed his arm around the terrified Sam and took him to the door. 'I want supper now and breakfast at six-fifteen. Both are to be served in this room. I shall leave at seven o'clock. You have never seen me. Is that clear?' Sam would have agreed to anything at that moment. He just wanted his hand back. 'God the pain!' He nodded compliance and Joel let the hand go. Most people place an injured hand under an armpit for relief from pain – Sam was no exception.

'Now sit.' Sam sat immediately. Joel asked several questions about the village, none of which he had the slightest interest in knowing the answers to.

He moved on to the village folk mentioning The Merricks, Dr. Owen, The Haans and several other good citizens. He elicited much, sifted out the chaff and discovered what he needed to know. 'Go now and remember what I said.' Sam needed no further encouragement. He scurried out of the room.

At seven sharp Joel left for the railway station. He deposited his suitcases and walked through the back lanes to The Manor House. He approached the building at seven-fifteen.

Joel knew that Vincent was a creature of habit and, he surmised, it was most likely that he and Rachael would be breakfasting at that hour. This was the best opportunity for him to be sure that Rachael would be at home.

He walked around the back of the building and peered in through the kitchen window unobserved. Vincent sat eating his breakfast of toast and English marmalade, a new delight to him since arriving in Suffolk. Rachael was preparing to leave and was fussing over her father.

He heard Vincent say, 'Don't worry. I have managed by myself for many years. I'm sure that I can survive for a day or so. Go and enjoy yourself. You deserve it.' Rachael put her arms around her father and hugged him.'

Joel knew that when he met Rachael they must be alone. Why, he didn't know; but alone they must be. He retreated to a copse of sycamore adjacent to the driveway and waited for her to appear. This she did within the minute.

A pheasant screeched as it took off from the undergrowth and Rachael turned towards the copse. Her eyes rested on Joel and a quiver of fear and tremor of excitement rushed through her body. The star crossed couple gazed into one another's eyes. Both were petrified and unable to speak.

Rachael saw the hurt that remained in Joel's deep languid eyes. Heathcliff was still troubled but at least he had returned to his Catherine. The dam burst, Rachael dropped her basket and she ran towards Joel. She began to speak but Joel took her in his arms and kissed her on the lips. They remained in each other's arms, Rachael's head resting on Joel's thumping breast. He held her tight afraid of losing her again. She lifted her head to speak but he placed his lips on hers again unable to resist the woman he considered his own. It was some time before she spoke. 'Tell me that you are not going away again. Promise me that if you do go that you will take me with you.'

Joel saw her pain and her devotion and held her close again. 'I promise that I will never leave you again my darling. Never, ever, ever.'

George had risen early that morning excited at the prospect of taking Rachael to Aldeburgh. He had dressed smartly and eagerly paced his father's study looking at several of his research papers before placing them back in the correct files. Time moved slowly. Eventually he had had enough and decided to surprise Rachael by waiting for her at the end of the Manor House drive.

He saw her leave the Manor and was about to call to her when he saw a figure moving in the trees and decided to hold his tongue. He slipped quietly behind an old oak. There his world collapsed as he slid into despair. All possibilities ended there. He watched the couple embrace, listened to their avowals of love as he sold his soul to Mephistopheles for the promise of retribution.

Rachael had agreed to meet him. She had told him that she had not seen Joel for years, yet when his back was turned, there they were, cavorting in the woods, happy as you like, laughing at him behind his back. All this time! All this time they had been laughing at him. They would pay. Somehow, some place, some time they would pay.

Joel had said that he would never leave Rachael. 'Never, ever, ever', George had heard him. He took the Aldeburgh tickets from his pocket, tore them asunder and threw them into the long grass. By lunchtime he was back in Cambridge abusing research students for their stupid antics, the shallowness of their understanding and their lack of dedication.

The broken young man turned away from his torment, away from society and into the singular world of scientific research for the next thirty years always believing that if he had never loved Rachael he never would have died that day. He would not waste his affection again.

Chapter 34

VINCENT, RACHAEL AND JOEL

Joel and Rachael were deeply in love and, as is the case for those suffering from that condition and wrapped in each other's arms, they were unaware of time slipping by and of their surroundings. It was some time before Rachael saw her basket on the ground. She shrieked, 'George!' Joel turned around expecting to see George Merrick then, puzzled, he turned back to Rachael. 'I'm sorry?' he enquired, 'What about George?'

Rachael hurriedly explained that she was due to meet George and was going to Aldeburgh with him when Joel had appeared from the copse. She was twenty minutes late already. Whatever would George think?

Yet George had not called on her to find out why she was late. That was odd.

The breeze was freshening and she shivered. Joel, ever attentive now, took Rachael's coat from her basket and put it over her shoulders. She thanked him with a kiss.

'I must apologise to George. I must go to him and say how sorry I am', she said.

Joel bent down and picked up two pieces of torn paper which had blown to his feet and replied solemnly. 'He knows that you're not coming Rachael.'

'How can he?' She said, looking quizzically at Joel. Joel didn't reply. He hesitated before putting parts of two tickets for Aldeburgh into her hands.

'Oh Joel, he was here.'

The couple walked to the railway station. According to Mr. Thomas Wilkes, the ticket master, only two villagers had caught the train that morning. 'No miss', he said to Rachael in his all-knowing voice, 'only Walker Iredale, you know, the lapsed Yorkshire man', (he grinned at his ingenuity), 'the one that made furniture before the war? Yes, and young Grace Hopkinson, always a nice girl, she was off to Colchester to see her aunt. Her aunt is ill you see ...'

Neither Rachael nor Joel wanted to see. Joel abruptly interrupted what could have been an hour's spiel, if Thomas Wilkes had had his way. They left for George's cottage.

'That's strange' observed Rachael, as they walked through the Merrick's small orchard.

'What is', said George.

'The car! The old car has gone.'

'So, he's driven it somewhere.'

'Joel, he can't drive! I've let him down and now he's taken the car. I hope that he is all right. I've found you and I'm so happy but I wish that I could say something to George. I'm afraid that he is going to be very annoyed.'

Joel nodded, unpersuaded. They walked back to the Manor House and Joel spotted the trampled grass behind the oak where George had hidden. He thought it best not to enlighten Rachael.

Vincent Haan was delighted to see Joel, the boy who had saved his life in the bay eleven years earlier. This was the boy that he knew had his daughter's heart. He only needed to see her flashing eyes and happiness when Joel was around her to know the truth of that. Rachael had had a heavy heart for many months and Vincent knew that neither he nor Doctor Owen could lighten it. Now he saw Rachael vibrant, alive and excited once more, just as she had been before Joel had gone away.

Joel noted that Vincent's sandy hair was thinner now and that his hairline had receded. Other than that, and his ever-expanding girth, Vincent looked good for his fifty years.

Vincent appraised Joel's appearance too. Driven, successful yet still unfulfilled. Expensive haircut, sharp suit and Italian shoes. Gold wristwatch and expensive ring. He reflected that the last time that he had seen such quality clothing and adornments they had been worn by his wife and mother-in-law before the war.

'You have prospered Herr Haan', offered Joel as he sat at the dining room table. 'I have been lucky', Vincent replied modestly. Rachael was about to rebuke her father for this self-deprecating remark but Vincent held his hand up in protestation. 'Yes, yes, yes, I have worked hard but I have been lucky too.'

Vincent related the story of his time working for Mainwaring and Sons and the good fortune that he had had. He paused for a little while, smiled and asked, 'And you Joel?'

Joel noted the openness of the question. Vincent was a charming man and not one to pry.

'I am well sir', was all he offered in response.

Vincent recognised Joel's reluctance to discuss his recent past and moved on.

'You look well and that is fine to see', Vincent observed. 'The Bothey is in good order. I have made sure of that but I do hope that you will accept our hospitality, it would give me great pleasure.'

Rachael looked longingly into Joel's eyes and he acceded to her silent plea.

'Thank you very much sir. It is kind of you.' He looked Vincent in the eye and said, 'But I will not be staying here for long.'

Vincent turned to look at his cherished daughter's face. She was smiling.

'When I say 'not staying here for long' I refer to the Manor House sir. You see I have asked Rachael to marry me and it is my intention, with your permission sir, to live at The Pheasantry.'

Vincent rose and put his arms around the fiancéd couple and shouted out loud.

'This has made me happier than I ever imagined I could be since, since well ...' he nodded acknowledging the response that his sombre observation had elicited. 'This calls for a celebratory drink.' He went into the dining room cabinet took out three glasses and opened a bottle of champagne that he had been pleased to accept from a grateful customer.

He raised his glass and proposed a toast. 'To you both. My beautiful daughter Rachael, who looks more like her mother every day, and to my future son in law. I am the happiest a father can be. God bless you both.' Vincent calmed a little and exclaimed. 'I have another toast. Rachael, to the memory of your mother, how proud of you she would have been. Joel, to your mother too, my special friend, Marta Salomonovich; a gracious lady. We will always remember their kindness and their goodness.'

Joel and Rachael were married in December 1955. Rachael died in childbirth nine months later. The child was a boy. Simon Reuben Benjamin Salomonovich. Joel, like Orpheus, entered hell to beg for the return of his Eurydice, his Rachael. He too failed.

Vincent Haan died within six weeks. The coroner's report stated that the cause was a heart attack. The truth was that Vincent Haan died of a broken heart. Mainwaring and Sons was in need of a new owner and The Manor a new tenant. Joel added both to his ever-expanding portfolio.

Chapter 35

1957 REBECCA FINDS JOEL

It was in October 1957 that Joel got his first break. He had been on the trail of SS Obersturmführer Bühler for more than twelve months. Since Rachael's death, finding Bühler had become his sole obsession. Fifteen years earlier Bühler had asked Joel to remember his face; now a photograph of it was before him. He guessed that Bühler would have been in his early twenties when he had had his father and brothers shot. The picture was of a man in his late thirties. Never the less it was Bühler. Joel had seen his face every night since he and his mother had left Hamburg on that cursed train. He knew Bühler's face when he saw it.

Reinhardt Bühler was a successful importer going by the name of Hans Kohler. He had purloined several works of art during the war and it was the sale of these, and the assistance of post war Nazi organisations which dedicated themselves to aiding their heroes after the war, that had set him up in business. He had done well; too well. His photograph was printed in 'Der Spiegel' and he was recognised. Were it not for the labyrinthine network of the post war Nazis he would have been exposed and apprehended. As it was he slipped out of the country and returned to the Argentine, disappearing into the backcloth of the suburbs of Buenos Aires.

Life in Argentina had not suited Bühler and he longed to return to his home town of Munich. It was in the winter of 1953 that he had got his wish. He slipped back into Germany via Italy and Austria and bought a remote abandoned isolation hospital to the north of the city. He converted the hospital into a hotel and lived a modest existence away from the glare of publicity.

Joel had been in contact with the Simon Wiesenthal organisation and they had raised Bühler's profile. He offered a reward of five thousand pounds for information leading to his arrest. The offer of a reward was placed in 'The Times', 'The New York Times', 'Der Spiegel', and the 'Clarín' in Buenos Aries.

Rebecca was sitting in her apartment in Brooklyn when she read about the reward for Bühler. Like Joel his face was not one that she was likely to forget. She picked up the phone and rang the contact number provided. It was a young woman's voice at the end of the line.

'What is the nature of your information?' the young reporter asked. Rebecca did not have any recent information and blustered.

'I am sorry. This information is for the person offering the reward and for him or her alone.'

Loretta Russell was not at all impressed by Rebecca's evasion, having already listened to all too many weird and wonderful calls offering patently false information. Loretta got used to the format of these cranks, as she called them. First they offered the aforesaid weird and wonderful information which could not be substantiated. Then, realising that cash was not forthcoming offered her a rich variety of abuse. This, to her, sounded like another crank; and yet, there was some genuine resonance compelling her to persist.

She hesitated then asked, 'What's your name?'

It was Rebecca's turn to hesitate. 'Rebecca Kinnear. Please listen to me', she almost whispered, 'I know that you will have received many false calls but were any of those callers able to tell you anything about SS Obersturmführer Reinhardt Bühler?'

Rebecca had already revealed more than all the previous claimants put together. Loretta Russell looked at the news sheet in front of her. It read: Reinhardt Bühler of the SS. Where the hell did this lady get the Obersturmführer bit? It was worth giving her a little more time.

'So, the advert asks for information. You say that you have some but that you are not willing to give it to me. Where does that leave me lady?'

Rebecca understood only too well. She had nothing to report on Bühler since she had last seen him in 1942. Thirteen-year-old information wouldn't be of much use to anyone.

Loretta Russell's initial enthusiasm was waning. 'Lady?'

Rebecca began to tell the story of the executions of her family in Hamburg and gave a graphic description of Bühler. 'Oh yes the photograph is not a particularly good one but it is Bühler, that is for sure,' she added.

Loretta Russell was busy. Rebecca's story was interesting but there was nothing new in it. 'Look, give me your address and your telephone number and I'll keep you on file. If anything comes up I'll get back to you.' She scribbled a few notes and hung up.

Rebecca knew that she was clutching at straws but this was one more straw, one more possibility amongst the hundreds that she had explored in order to find Joel.

Rebecca's information had remained dormant for several months before Loretta Russell was asked to review the information that she had on Bühler for an article on fugitive Nazis. The piece made 'The New York Times.'

Joel had many contacts and it was from New York that he took a call.

'Hello Spencer', he shouted down a crackling line, 'Where are you calling from? The moon?'

Spencer Hume had been Joel's trusted head of security in New York. He spoke Joel's language, removed obstacles clinically, calmed turbulent waters efficiently and moved rapidly when solutions were needed. He recruited only the best and gained a reputation for his dispassionate distaste of those who failed. He was Joel's eyes and ears and was one of very few to have earned the respect of his equally dispassionate boss. Even so, Spencer knew that Joel Joseph's edicts were not to be questioned. Joel did not require advice. He demanded action. Spencer had the attributes to provide an invaluable, if sometimes barely legal, service.

Few people knew of Joel's movements. Spencer did.

'What do you have Spencer?'

'It may be something, it may be nothing but here it is. You were looking for one Reinhardt Bühler, yes?'

The smile left Joel's face, 'go on', he croaked. He took a deep breath and sat back in the Chesterfield wondering why information regarding Bühler would come from the other side of the Atlantic.

Spencer was pleased to have his master's attention. 'A dame called, where is it? Oh yeh. Loretta Russell. She wrote an article in The Times; the New York Times that is. She claims to have spoken to a woman who witnessed some of Bühler's executions. Sounds like he was quite a guy. Apparently he executed dozens of Jews in Hamburg. I know that there is nothing new here but I rang the reporter and she reckons that her witness was gen.' He read out Rebecca's account of the executions.

Joel considered Spencer's rendition and recognised that the informant must have been present when his father and brothers were killed. She must have been present when Abraham Goldstein was shot too. Yes, there was almost a hundred there at the time but she must have been one of them. That alone was sufficient reason for action.

Excitedly he said 'Thanks Spencer. What is the name of the reporter again?'

Spencer looked at his notebook. 'Loretta Russell and I have her number.' Spencer Hume recited the number.

'Thanks again Spencer look me up when you cross the pond. And Spencer; the name of the informant?'

Again Spencer had cause to refer to his notebook. Rebecca. Rebecca Kinnear Anyways Joel I, Joel, Joel ...'

The phone had gone dead.

Could it be? Could it just be?

Joel had slammed down the receiver. He lifted it again immediately and dialled rapidly. Loretta Russell was on leave and her number could not be given to anyone. Joel asked that she ring him, and then rang Spencer back.

'Hi, what happened? I was …' Joel interrupted him. 'Spencer I have a job for you. Get your people onto Loretta Russell and find out the address of this Rebecca Kinnear. I want to know who she is. This is important Spencer don't let me down; do you hear? Don't screw it up.'

Spencer heard loud and clear. For many years when Joel Joseph had told people to jump they had jumped. Now he heard his old boss's strident tone again and he responded as he always had.

'You got it Joel. I'm on it. Give me an hour and I'll get back to you.'

Spencer moved incisively. Joel's Manhattan communication centre remained as efficient as ever. Spencer needed the best he had. Marcus Eliot was such. Within twenty minutes of being given his remit Eliot had relieved his expense account of a few dollars and 'bought' Loretta Russell's phone number. In turn he had paid that lady to phone her desk in order to obtain Rebecca Kinnear's phone number; had taken her return call and had got back to Spencer.

Spencer knew he had the right man in Marcus Eliot. It was no surprise that he had his information within half an hour but sensing the importance of Rebecca Kinnear, had decided to interview her personally.

The apartment building was not in the most salubrious part of Brooklyn and the lift stank of urine but Spencer ignored it. He had been born and brought up in much worse. He got out at the fifth floor and walked along the long dark corridor to room 523.

He knocked twice. A chain bolt slid into its channel on the inside of the door and it opened slowly.

It was a woman at the door. She was clearly nervous. Spencer estimated that she would be in her early thirties despite the greying hair, sallow complexion and hollow cheeks.

'Mrs. Kinnear?'

'Yes?' Rebecca answered tentatively.

'Do you remember ringing a reporter called Loretta Russell about a man called Reinhardt Bühler a few months ago?'

Rebecca's eyes opened wide and Spencer could see that she had once been quite beautiful. What the hell had happened to her? He noted how animated she had become. 'May I come in?'

Rebecca stared through Spencer, then, collecting herself, apologised and opened the door. He was surprised. The sparsely decorated room was spotlessly clean and tastefully furnished.

He took a seat but declined the coffee he was offered. Time was short. He began.

'Mrs. Kinnear I have a friend who lives in England', Rebecca's heart dropped a beat, she knew of no one from England. Spencer noted her anguish. 'My friend is German. He originated from Hamburg.' Rebecca was attentive again. He continued. 'My friend is called Joel Joseph. Have you ever heard of him?'

Spencer caught her as she began to slip from the couch. It was several seconds before she had recovered sufficiently for him to continue. He brought her a drink of water from the kitchen then, sitting beside her, looked at his watch anxiously. He had to get back to Joel and pretty soon. It was an hour and half since he had promised to return Joel's call and Joel did not like to be kept waiting. He hoped that the lady's story was worth the effort of finding her.

'Lady, I'm sorry, Mrs. Kinnear, I really don't want to push you but I have a deadline? Do you know Joel Joseph?'

Rebecca pulled a cushion to her stomach and held it tight. 'I don't know for sure', she whispered, 'I have tried to meet him because of who he may be.'

This confused Spencer and he began to consider ringing Joel to tell him that the lady was gaga. He gave it a last shot. 'Lady', he didn't apologise for the nomenclature this time, 'Lady, who do you think he is and what the hell has this to do with Reinhardt Bühler?' He was standing now, impatient to leave.

Rebecca stared at the floor once again, and then said, 'I believe that Joel Joseph is my brother.' Spencer's impatience abated. 'I was separated from him during the war and Reinhardt Bühler was the man responsible for the executions of our father and of our brothers.'

Rebecca moved quickly, more quickly than Spencer imagined she could. She knelt before him and taking his hands in hers, pleading with him.

'Oh sir, if you know the whereabouts of Joel please tell me. I beg of you please tell me.'

Spencer was not easily shocked but this he had not anticipated. 'Ma'am', the 'lady' had gone now, 'how do you know this man to be your brother. Were you called Joseph? Was that your name?'

Rebecca was desperate to hear of Joel but her intelligence did not fail her. Joel would have changed his name for a reason. She would not be responsible for any harm that might befall him as a result any indiscretion. Spencer was thinking fast too. What harm could it do to put her on the phone? He considered the angles and what to say to Joel. He looked at his wrist again. Where had the last fifteen minutes gone? Damn it, the only thing to do was to put the woman on the phone and hope to God that this really was Joel's sister. What if she wasn't? What was the worst Joel could think of him? This woman might sound cranky to start with but then she could tell him what she knew of Bühler. That was the original deal. Wasn't it?

Rebecca's eyes still pleaded with Spencer. 'Ok, we'll ring England and you can talk to Joel Joseph. Where's the phone?' He dialled collect and an excitable Joel answered immediately.

'Do you know where she is? Have you found her?' he shouted. 'Goddam it Spencer where have you been?'

Spencer drew a deep breath before beginning. 'Joel I have the lady with me now. It took a little time. There were complications and…'

Joel's spoke slowly and softly but he cut Spencer off midstream as effectively as if he had cut his throat.

'Put her on Spencer. Put her on now.'

Spencer offered the handset to Rebecca.

Joel and Rebecca sat a continent apart with phones to their ears. For a few seconds neither could speak. It was Rebecca who broke the silence. 'Joel. Joel is that really you?'

Joel Salomonovich had not heard his sister's voice since she had been dragged from the square by Bühler's henchmen years earlier. Rebecca had been eighteen then. There was no mistaking the thirty-four year olds voice even though the line crackled like an old film.

There had been no answer. Slowly and warily Rebecca repeated. 'Is that you Joel? Joel, is it really you?'

The floodgates opened and Joel drew on every nerve and sinew to speak.

'Rebecca it is Joel. My God! My God! Where have you been? What are you doing in New York? I thought you were dead. Then I heard ...'

The conversation continued for half an hour before Joel asked Rebecca to put Spencer back on the line. Spencer's demeanour had lightened considerably having recognised the success of his mission. He took the phone from Rebecca.

'Spencer?'

Spencer braced himself. He sensed that Joel was back to his magnificent decisive best. There would be action this day.

'Spencer, the lady is my sister. I want her over here as quickly as you can arrange it, savvy? She won't be coming back to that hellhole. Help her to take what she wants and get her on a plane. Pull strings but get her on a plane and I mean now. And Spencer, make sure that she is very well looked after. Capice?'

Spencer had been used to jumping when Joel rumbled. Down the chain others would jump with equal alacrity as Spencer snapped his fingers. He gave the phone back to Rebecca, with considerably more precision and care than when he had taken it from her. He left her speaking excitedly with her brother figuring that the longer she was on the line the more time he had to get things moving and avoid Joel's inevitable wrath at being kept waiting. He had a hard taskmaster.

It was five to noon on the following day when Rebecca flew out of New York with two of Spencer's best men sitting one row back. Marcus Eliot and George Kowalski weren't in the habit of 'slipping up'. Not ever. Spencer intended to deliver his charge safely to England and to deliver himself from the possibility of reprisals.

Eliot shadowed Rebecca as she went through the Heathrow customs. Kowalski moved on ahead spotting Joel across the concourse. He shook hands with Joel and pointed to the descending escalator. 'There she is, just as Spencer said sir. Will there be anything else?' Joel whispered a 'Thank you, no', as he stared at the escalator unable to contain his emotions. He wiped his eyes as he began to walk. He broke into a run then stopped abruptly.

Spencer's men had delivered their charge and took the ascending escalator. Mission accomplished.

Joel stopped a yard short of Rebecca as she dropped her one small case and opened her arms. Joel swept her off her feet, hugging his sister tightly as tears sprung from the dam that had been built over so many years. No words were spoken. None were needed. The two surviving members of the Salomonovich family clung to each other afraid to let the other go.

Eventually Joel whispered. 'You must be very tired after your journey. Come, I have a car waiting.' He picked up Rebecca's case, put his arm through hers and walked into the Heathrow night. The bright lights of the terminal lit the slanting rain but neither noticed the weather. Joel's chauffeur saw to the case as he held the rear door open. Joel climbed in beside her.

The journey from Heathrow to Cambridge was long and the traffic heavy but time, like the weather, went unnoticed.

Joel broke the news of the death of their mother and related the story of the train, the barge and their shipwreck. He told the story of the Haans and of Ruth's, cruel fate. He spoke of Rachael, her death and of the birth of his son Simon. Rebecca's eyes were wide open despite not having slept for many hours. A curious mixture of joy and melancholy pervaded the atmosphere. The litany continued unabated.

Rebecca was anxious to know about her newly discovered nephew. She ached to hold him. They turned to the executions and Reinhardt Bühler and Rebecca saw the appalling hatred that burned within her brother. She stroked his arm to soothe his wrath. She had not seen this Joel before. He softened again when he spoke of Abraham Goldstein.

Rebecca spoke of Edward Kinnear and of their visit to Abraham Goldstein's grave. Joel raged at the bad luck that they had had when they had missed each other in New York and Hamburg. Rebecca didn't let his hands go. She couldn't bear to, not after so long. It was past midnight when the car drew up the drive of the floodlit Manor House.

Rebecca turned to Joel. 'Is this really all yours my little brother? Mother, father, Benjamin and Reuben would have been so proud of you.' Joel neglected to tell Rebecca that he had a place in Long Island worth ten times as much or that just one signature in Zurich would release over twenty million pounds. He also neglected to mention the death of the unfortunate Jan Kuyper. Rebecca, in turn had neglected to inform Joel of the nature of her imprisonment. Joel knew that she had. Rebecca also knew that making a fortune was not always the cleanest of professions.

Neither had considered the language that they had spoken in. It had been German.

Chapter 36

JOEL, REBECCA AND SIMON 1953 – 1983

Joel, Rebecca and Simon lived together at the Manor House. Simon was not a strong child and suffered from pneumonia at the age of seven and this resulted in respiratory problems throughout his life. Rebecca was a most attentive aunt and loved the boy as her own.

Joel had finance meetings in London every Thursday and researched the Wiesenthal information on possible links to Bühler during the remaining weekdays. The three spent their time together, mostly at The Manor House at weekends. Joel missed Rachael. He had had her to himself for less than a year. It had been all too short.

He felt, on more than one occasion, that he had got close to Bühler but it was clear that his contacts were one step ahead of the game and he had the capacity and the network to go to ground when required. Joel had set up an extensive network of detectives and informers but the trail had never the less gone cold.

The months turned into years and still nothing. Joel's fortune grew but money had become meaningless to him now. He began to miss his meetings in London and talked to his chief of staff on the phone rather than make the tedious journey into the city.

Simon went to East Anglia University near Norwich in 1970 and studied architecture, the discipline that his Grandfather Vincent and mother Rachael had studied many years before. It was during Simon's last year, in 1973 that he brought home a beautiful fellow student called Laura Van Buren. Laura was born of Jewish Dutch parents who had fled to England before the Nazi invasion of Holland. They had fled Amsterdam on the first of May 1940 just ten days before the Nazis had marched in.

Michael Van Buren had been a jeweller and a successful one too. He and his wife Emma were well educated, industrious, of good manners and gentle decorum. The elderly couple had settled in Canterbury and into the English way of life. They were happy and contented and had no thoughts of returning to live in their native country after the war was over. Laura was their only child and she was quite as intelligent as she was beautiful. Joel and Rebecca were delighted that Simon had brought such a girl to their home. Joel saw that Laura's eyes sparkled with life, as Rachael's had, and she disarmed him with her charm.

Simon and Laura married in 1974 much to the delight of Laura's parents and Joel and Rebecca. The Van Buren's and Joel became grandparents in the summer of 1975 when Simon and Laura's daughter, Julia, was born.

The pneumonia that Simon had contracted as a boy had caused irreversible damage to his lungs and in the winter of 1979 he succumbed to it. Laura's parents were elderly and though wealthy did not have the energy required to raise a young child. The obvious solution was for Laura to bring Julia to The Manor House. The place was large and the heartbroken Joel and Rebecca doted on the child. Laura thought of Rebecca as a close confidant and the two grew ever closer.

Julia grew more beautiful each day and was a happy child, excelling at school. Joel would have spoiled her were it not for Rebecca's good sense. Never the less Julia had everything that a young girl could want. Laura and Rebecca kept Julia's feet on the ground often chastising the grandfather's largesse.

Julia went to Oxford in October 1993.

Chapter 37

GEORGE'S DECENT INTO HELL 1954 – 1984

George's callous disregard for his fellow academics and his seditious tendencies grew ever more scandalous. The truth was that he found others tiresome and their conversations unrewarding. He remained supremely aloof and confident in his intellect, barely maintaining civil relationships with his colleagues.

George's mentality rarely permitted idleness but the instant he ceased work the inevitable melancholy returned. He sat at his father's desk in the cottage meditating on the cause of his anger and raging at his perceived loss of Rachael.

His incongruent machination continued unabated, the origin was inflated as his anger intensified, sharpening the consciousness of his perceived alienation, and strengthening the power of his resistance to acceptance.

The intractable problem caused him to become increasingly morose and bitter. His perspective of others grew increasingly negative as he considered his own superiority. His mindset became evermore destructive and harmful. A spirit of fault-finding; an unsatisfied temper; a constant irritability and the poisonous gall of resentment sent him spiralling into paranoia.

Though conscious of and well versed in, the phenomena of his destructive path, the addict ploughed the cancerous furrow with imperious indifference. Irritable, scathing, petulant and indifferent to the needs of others he demanded retribution. Humourless, aloof and unsympathetic he cut a sad uncollegiate figure. Distant and uncommunicative, his brusque manner demanded fealty. He assessed undergraduates work with sour contempt, dismissing their passionate intensity as trivial and undeserving. His tortured mind, abject despair and unsmiling insular world offered a bleak insight into his terrifying vanity, arrogance and the abyss of his despair. His uncommunicative eyes hid his utter anguish and fulminating uncompromising hostility to his cause. His fiery intensity brooked no discussion or argument. The tortuous struggle for his soul was lost. The malevolent wind had turned.

He was summoned to appear before the vice chancellor once more and was reprimanded but again he escaped the censorship that a lesser being might have suffered. Darkness descended on the young man. It did not invade or incapacitate his intellect; rather it twisted and corroded his morality. His genius was not compromised. Mephistopheles beckoned and imbued him with his malign spirit. George Merrick's soul died and he rode roughshod with the Devil and four horses over the detritus that he considered humanity to be. He had the passion for destruction, the capacity to inject his venom and the means to vent his hatred.

George Merrick was not given to wistful thinking; he was only concerned with the possible. However, in his terms the impossible often became the possible, which invariably became the probable; and the probable a reality when his genius was engaged.

There was a solution somewhere. He could win. There had to be a way.

Two men, both with fierce intellects and driven by hatred set about their quests simultaneously. Joel Salomonovich sought revenge for his father, brothers and Rebecca. Bühler would pay. George Merrick sought revenge for the loss of Rachael. Joel Salomonovich would be punished. But that was insufficient for George; he still pined for Rachael, and that presented an impossible position. Underestimating Joel Salomonovich would be not at all wise.

George angled his research towards his goals. It would take years to complete his work. He began in earnest and worked tirelessly for the next thirty years.

Chapter 38

JULIA MEETS GEORGE MERRICK

Julia Salomonovich was as beautiful as her great grandmother Ruth Haan and her grandmother Rachael had been. The resemblance was quite striking. Rachael had looked uncannily like her mother Ruth but Julia and Rachael could well have been mistaken for identical twins at the same age. To Joel his wife and granddaughter were clones sculptured from the mythical Maastricht marble quarry of Haan. And more, Julia's natural grace and elegance, her smile and expressions, her passions and idiosyncratic movements were a constant reminder to Joel of his tragic loss of Rachael and Simon. His heart experienced great love for his granddaughter and great sadness at the memory of his darling wife and son. How proud would Marta Salomonovich have been to know that she had such a wonderful great granddaughter?

Julia was five foot six, had long black luxuriant hair and an olive complexion. Her large brown eyes were as tender as they were beautiful. They sparkled with the vitality of youth. Her nose was small and her mouth full. Her neck was long, graceful and slender. Her large breasts were accentuated by the narrowness of her waistline and petite frame. Her legs were long, taut and sensuous. More than this, Julia was desirable. Whatever it was that attracted men to women, she had it in spades. She was a feminine female. Beautiful, attractive and sexy as hell.

She dressed conservatively but well. Her clothes were feminine but never risqué. Laura and Rebecca had instilled a sense of propriety in the young woman and she had valued and heeded their advice.

It was easy to understand the transfer of poise and deportment from Ruth to Rachael. It was somewhat puzzling to witness the same between Rachael and Julia as Rachael had died so young and Julia had not known her. Nature and nurture. In the past Joel had had more time for nurture. He now had just cause to rethink the equation.

At twenty-two the world was at Julia Salomonovich's feet. She got a first in classics at Oxford, had attained a tennis blue, was an excellent pianist, had the temperament of a saint, a winning personality and was popular with her peer group. The love, affection and the money bestowed upon her by her mother Laura, Rebecca, Joel and Grandpa and Nana van Buren might well have spoilt her. It hadn't.

It was in the summer of 1996 that a fellow student visited her. He was one Gerhard Severin of Koblenz. The pair had completed their studies at Oxford and Gerhard had remained behind in England to spend a little time with Julia and her family at The Manor House before returning to Germany. Gerhard was fond of Julia. Their relationship had been purely platonic until now but Gerhard was beginning to have second thoughts about that as he began to feel the reality of being parted from Julia at the end of their last term together.

In the morning he would return to Koblenz. Yes, Julia would be visiting him soon but he knew that he must declare himself as soon as the opportunity presented itself.

Julia and Gerhard sat in the Rose and Crown public house enjoying evening drinks and discussing the reciprocal arrangements for Julia's visit to Germany.

The Rose and Crown was a much-changed place since the demise of Sam Waldron. When he had been landlord only the unwise drank at the place after dusk. Now the villagers frequented it in numbers. The friendly landlord and landlady, and the ambiance that they had fostered, had changed the fortunes of the place and the village was the better for it.

Julia laughed, 'You know Gerhard it would be easy to travel with you and I understand that but I can't come with you tomorrow. My grandfather insists that I go with him and Aunt Rebecca to Hamburg. I have promised him many times, and mother agrees, that it is important that one understands one's roots. The Nazis executed my great grandfather and my grandfather's two elder brothers in Hamburg during the war and I know that he is drawn to the place. He has visited many times with Aunt Rebecca and my mother over recent years.' She rose, 'It's late, and we must be going. You have to rise early in the morning'

Gerhard stood and said, 'It's a beautiful night. Shall we walk along the river and down by the lake? It's not much out of our way and I would like to see it one more time before I leave.' Julia acceded and the pair left the premises offering a general 'goodnight' to the pleasant company.

The full moon cast a romantic light on the couple and Julia, not unaware of her friend's feelings, sought diplomacy from the night air. 'How different it is with girl friends' she mused. There wouldn't be complications and there would be little danger of their friendship being lost forever. Gerhard was so dear to her and she prayed that he would remain her friend and understand that her feelings towards him would always remain platonic.

They had left the road and were walking along the path which led to the lake when they heard a scuffling noise nearby in the undergrowth. The moon was hidden behind a cloud and it was quite dark. Nervously they stopped to listen. Again there was a rustle, then quiet once again. Soon they were able to make out the shape of an elderly gentleman some forty or so yards ahead of them. Bent almost double, stick in hand, he slowly made his way towards them. The chap looked all in. He took a few paces at a time then leaned on his stick while he caught his breath. He did not notice the young couple until they was almost upon him. Julia had walked the old path many times during her twenty-two years. She had never encountered anyone coming from the direction of The Manor House so late in the evening. The old man was quite out of breath and both Julia and Gerhard were concerned for his well-being.

The venerable gentleman was short with the young pair. 'I thank you for your concern but my welfare in not your business', he chided as they enquired after his health. Julia glanced at Gerhard and, though both were slighted by the curt response they had received for their polite enquiry, chose to fulfil their moral responsibility rather than take offence recognising that age had its privileges even if they were, as is so often the case, abused.

The man faltered and Julia and Gerhard took him by the arm and assisted him back to the road. They sat him on a bench outside the Rose and Crown. At that moment the moon appeared from behind the clouds and the pale light lit the forecourt of the inn.

Professor George Merrick stared into the eyes of Rachael Haan. He stared in disbelief, uncomprehendingly. Was he dreaming? What kind of cruel joke had the devil in store for him now? It was twilight, die Demmarung, my god Gotterdammerung, the twilight of the gods. Was this Valhalla? For only the second time in his long painful life George Merrick was speechless. It was the same two visions, though an eon separated their manifestations and both had rendered him mute. The white moon accentuated his pallid complexion and Julia and Gerhard feared for the mystery man's health.

'Are you alright? Shall I get help? Where are you going? May we take you?'

All the questions remained unanswered. The old man continued to stare at Julia as if he had seen a ghost, his arthritic fingers wrapped tightly around his antler head walking stick as if he needed to hold on to his sanity by holding on to something of the material world.

Julia saw uncomprehending amazement and disbelief in the man's pained face. It was a frightening expression that she would never forget. Was he hallucinating? Had he had a mild heart attack? A stroke perhaps?

It took a few moments for George Merrick to recover himself and regain his equilibrium. The shock of seeing Rachael had punctured his cardio vascular system and taken his breath away. It had short circuited his neurons and blown a fuse in his nervous system. It had awoken a long lost hope and had dashed it as he recovered his composure. He took a deep breath, thanked the young man for his concern, ignored the young woman and lifted his fragile frame from the bench waiving away the young folk's attempts to render further assistance.

'Thank you', he whispered, 'I am quite well.' He paused recognising that he had not enquired who his would be saviours were. 'My car is across the road and I do not have far to go. May I ask the names of my aides?' He enquired again avoiding the young woman's eyes.

Gerhard began with his introduction but the old man wasn't listening, he only had ears for the young woman. 'My name is Julia Salomonovich', she began. 'I live just past the lake over there at The Manor House. Have you been down to the lake?'

The old man could hold back no longer, feeling compelled to look at Julia. He avoided her question. The man made Julia feel strangely ill at ease, but she continued undaunted. 'Let us see you to your car but I really think that you ought to …'

The old man interrupted her abruptly. 'I am quite well, really, he shouted irritably.' Recognising the sharpness of his voice he softened and added; 'I shall be off in a moment. Thank you once again for your concern. Concern for the elderly, I fear, is a rare quality amongst the young these days.' He smiled an awkward smile, hobbled across the road and, opening the door of his car, bid them good night. The vintage Austin spluttered and left sedately.

Julia raised her eyebrows as she looked at Gerhard. 'What an oddball. What was he doing walking from the lake so late in the evening? It is too late for one so old and infirm to be out in the country.' She turned towards home.

'Come on it's too late for us too. You have to be off early in the morning and I need my beauty sleep.'

Gerhard understood English colloquialisms very well indeed but said to himself, 'No you don't Julia Salomonovich. That is one thing that you certainly do not need.' He damned his luck when he considered the fact that what he intended to be a romantic walk by the lake had become a bizarre encounter with a foolish ancient relic who ought to know better than to be wandering through the woods late at night.

Julia could not sleep. The old gentleman. Who was he? What was he doing down by the lake so late in the evening. She would mention it to her grandfather in the morning. She would never forget his face and the shock and disbelief that pervaded his countenance when he alighted upon her. What had he seen that had elicited such a response? What had she said or done? She tried to recall. He cut such a lonely figure. There was a great sadness etched into his face. His image haunted her night.

In a bedroom not ten yards away the image of Bühler was interrupting her grandfather's sleep once more.

Chapter 39

JOEL DISCOVERS JULIA'S MEETING WITH GEORGE

Julia woke early and was assisting her mother and her Aunt Rebecca to make an early breakfast for the departing Gerhard when her grandfather entered. As was his custom, had taken his 'English constitutional' around the lake and arrived in the kitchen in time to catch Gerhard, Julia, Laura and Rebecca discussing the previous evening's events.

'What man?' he had interjected. 'Oh really grandpa, you are the limit', said Julia, approaching Joel and giving her grandfather a hug. 'We were just gossiping about yesterday evening.'

'Well if it's a secret between the four of you and I am not part of the conspiracy I shall sit on my own in the corner and not concern myself with any you.' Julia trilled. 'Very well grandpa.' There was short silence before she laughed out loud and kissed Joel on the cheek. 'Big baby', she whispered in his ear.

The game was over and the four members of the family laughed together as Gerhard, who was quite mystified by their sense of humour, looked on. He had felt that a family feud was about to erupt, gave a sigh of relief and made a mental note concerning the strangeness of the English and their strange sense of humour; the irony of Joel, Rebecca and Laura's original nationality not being lost on him.

'So?' said Joel, waiting. 'What of yesterday evening?'

Julia related the story of the old man walking from the lakeside to the village and, though surprised, Joel showed no more than a mild interest in her story. It was when Gerhard interjected with his sobriquet for the man that Joel stiffened.

'I believe it was the 'Nutty Professor', he said, recalling a film that he and Julia had recently seen.

Joel's demeanour changed. Gerhard believed that he was witnessing another charade but Julia caught his hand as he was about to expound his views on English humour. Joel's face was like thunder. He questioned the young pair as to the man's appearance and build. He suspected that the 'old man' was George Merrick but it was not until Julia mentioned that he had left in an old Austin saloon that Joel had his confirmation.

George Merrick! He made his apologies to Laura and Rebecca and left the kitchen without eating, leaving Julia, Laura and Rebecca aghast and Gerhard less sure of his understanding of the English psyche.

Chapter 40

FRASER HUME IS BRIEFED

Fraser Hume dealt in quality. If anyone in his team had fouled up they were not given a second opportunity. But fouling up was very rare indeed. Spencer Hume only recruited the very best. Fraser Hume was such a one. If Spencer's son hadn't the qualities required he wouldn't have got the job. Clear and simple!

Fraser replaced his father, as top man, on merit and there was unanimous consent on that point throughout Joel's organisation. It was Fraser that Joel Salomonovich sent for now.

Joel was fuming as he entered his study. 'What the fuck was Merrick up to?' If he went near Julia again he'd 'knock his fucking brains out.' Joel seethed at the thought of Merrick seeing his granddaughter and he knew the reaction that that encounter would have elicited. Julia was Rachael's double. Had he seen her before? Was he stalking her? How probable was it that they had met by accident? He picked up the phone and rang the communications centre of his London headquarters. The return call came within minutes.

The centre was reporting that a Professor George Merrick, who had privileged access to the business magnate Sir Nicholas Hansen's mainframe, was searching for information regarding Joel Salomonovich, Joel Joseph and Reinhardt Bühler.

Fraser Hume, like his father before him, had witnessed Joel Joseph's wrath before. His 'associates' had not. That evening the four stood in Joel's Manor House office listening to him fulminate. The air was blue and the message crystal clear. A huge desk and five metres separated the one from the four. That was uncomfortably close for the four and the huge desk represented a flimsy barrier.

Joel lowered himself stiffly into the chesterfield chair, and then beckoned the others to approach. They moved cautiously.

'Listen, and listen carefully. I want to know what that bastard Merrick is up to. Find him. Frighten him and put a tail on him. I want to know when he eats, when he breathes and when he shits. I want to know every goddam thing he does. Got it?' Fraser Hume and his men were quick to respond. 'Got it.' They nodded compliance vigorously to negate any possibility of the slightest misunderstanding.

'We missed him this morning, we got the information a fraction too late but we have his place watched. He hasn't returned', offered Fraser. Joel tapped his right fist into his left palm slowly but deliberately. 'Find him gentlemen. Find him.' With that he turned to the fire and the four took it that they had been dismissed.

Joel and Rebecca had intended to fly to Hamburg with Julia but Joel considered that he had more pressing matters to deal with now. Recognising Chopin's Polonaise in F-Sharp Minor he walked to the music room and put his head around the door.

'Grandpa?' Julia sat at the Steinway grand.

'I am very sorry. You will forgive an old man sweetheart?' The smile that had so often melted the hard man's heart worked its spell once more.

Julia had felt the aftershock of Joel's wrath. The whole household had. The eruption had been as violent as it was sudden, the pumice destroying all in its path. And, though not directed at anyone present and the epicentre somewhat distant, the air of malevolence, menace and foreboding now hung in each and every room like a curse.

Julia lowered her eyes and whispered. 'Once again the grandpa that I know and love becomes the enigma that others say he is. I defend you and say that they do not know you but, sometimes, I believe that it is I who does not know you. I do not ask for answers. We have shared so much. But I don't understand. I don't suppose that I will ever understand. Promise me that, one day, I will. Promise me.

A sacred promise was given. Joel smiled with great affection and with a heavy heart left the room in silence.

Julia sighed and looked down at the keyboard but the mood had changed and she shut the piano lid. What had Chopin said about Liszt's F-Sharpe Minor Polonaise? Oh yes! 'It portrays the lurid hours that precede a hurricane.'

Quite!

Chapter 41

GEORGE ASSESSES JOEL'S LIFE

George Merrick sat in his father's study. He had returned to the old place less and less frequently as the years went by. He loved the bay that had brought Rachael to him. For many years he had toiled along the paths that he had cycled as a boy. He smelt the sweet air emanating from the oaks, the elms and the silver birch of the woodlands. This, he knew, was the most humanising experience of his existence. He tried to resist but the pull was too strong and he was inexorably drawn to the place of his nascent passion and endless torment.

Rachael had sent George an invitation to her wedding. He hadn't replied. George had heard of the birth of a child and the death of Rachael and he had suffered the anguish of both. He hated Joel Salomonovich and swore vengeance for taking Rachael away from him. Joel Salomonovich was rich and powerful. He had moved in high places and had great influence. He was a difficult target and yet there was one avenue that George had identified as a possible weakness. One small chink in the man's armour. Why did he never return to New York or Amsterdam? Was he hiding something? And if so, what?

This theme had arisen regularly over many years but he had been unable to discover any wrongdoing. He had looked over the lake towards The Manor House. Many a night he had trembled with rage and shaken his fist at the edifice and his nemesis within. Oh to have been with Rachael at The Pheasantry and later at his parent's cottage. If not for Joel Salomonovich she would have been his and she would have been alive today.

Since the dark cloud of Rachael's death had descended on him George had been immersed and consumed by research but he was often drawn by an unaccountable need to be near The Pheasantry and The Manor House. The professor was driven by facts and hard logic. There was little or no place for sentimentality. Except here. Here was another dimension. The rules of his daily life did not apply here. They hadn't since he first met Rachael in the village hall those many years before. The pragmatic George; the unromantic George; the soulless George. None had a place here. The irascible, straight-laced, driven, logical, consistent and coherent George had always taken on a quite different persona in Rachael's presence. In her presence his sure-footed certainty deserted him, his confidence and irrepressible energy evaporated as his father had observed on that wonderful day when the sea had brought her to him. Even then, after so many years and when so close to her infamous rendezvous with Joel, George was unstable and dangerously melancholic. Rachael had been everything to him and that damned Salomonovich had taken her away from him and killed her as sure as if he had stuck a knife between her ribs.

Having reached the lake he had sat in the folly glaring at the Manor House until the lights burned bright. Swearing a demonic invective he left his vantage point as the mist swept in quickly from either side. There was a dawning realisation that he had left things a little too late that inauspicious evening. Given that his health had deteriorated over recent months, this had been unwise. The return trek through the woods had proved difficult and he had struggled to get his breath, which had caused him to stop on several occasions. 'And the damned arthritis hadn't helped either.' He had stood in the moonlight catching his breath and looking down at the gnarled hands holding the antler handle walking stick and had delivered a pledge.

'Soon, and it must be very soon, I will put my experiment to use.' He had whispered as if to another close by.

He had stumbled onto the path and almost staggered into the young couple taking the evening air.

George Merrick's mind was cold, calculating and clinical yet meeting Julia Salomonovich had temporarily disorientated him. For a moment he had suspended rational thought and had held a tenuous hold on reality as he saw Rachael Haan before his very eyes. True he was quick to disabuse himself of the notion but his mutilated passion awoke and shattered his equilibrium. This phenomenon had occurred just once before in his life. It was the same image that had returned to haunt him now. He had recoiled. He knew that he had and he knew that it had been noted. He had seen the girl's reaction. He had displayed irritability when she asked after his well-being. He had begun to respond in his usual acerbic and abrupt manner but the irruption had been stemmed by her ethereal touch and his rancour had subsided. He had recognised the strangeness of that and its origin. Consumed by her beauty and elegance he then withdrew his invective and found refuge in false disinterest. He had curtly thanked the couple, pointing out the inadequacies of similar aged people as a distraction while doing so, and had left them to their evening.

Professor George Merrick sat in his father's study and began to plan. He considered the futility of approaching Julia; the possibility of her informing Joel of the old man by the lake; the nature of his recent research and the limited timescale within which he could operate.

His mind went back to The Bothey and the evenings spent there with his father, Marta and Joel. He remembered the gentle probing questions of his father and the answers he had elicited from Marta despite the intermittent editing by Joel. He must remember it all. What could he learn from this information? He began to search the desk. Surely his father would have... no his duty was to report ... but then again Sir George had always been meticulous in his recording of minutia. No, not the desk; he had emptied that. Ah yes, the old chest in the loft. Sir George had replaced the trap door with a winding staircase to make the loft space more accessible; his arthritis and age militating against flexion.

George was pleased that he had for precisely the same reason. He climbed the stairs and walked to the chest. It took less than a minute to locate a small book. He took his treasure from the chest and returned to the study.

The book was a chronological record of events pertinent to Sir George's reports to the war office between 1941 and his death in 1950. George sat and read the book from cover to cover making notes as he devoured its contents. He was fascinated by the detailed and methodical questioning of Martha and Joel and bemused by the lack of bounty and meagre gleanings it had procured. George saw, as his father had before him, Joel's hand in the responses that Marta had given. Never rude, never defensive but always vague and rarely rewarding. But this was not what George was looking for. Now he wanted to garner information about Joel's past.

How he wished he had read this log long before. Some of the reports he had witnessed first-hand but much more had been recorded at times when he and Joel had not been present. SS Obersturmführer Reinhardt Bühler was as much a nemesis to Salomonovich as Salomonovich was to himself, he observed. How old would the man be if he were alive today? Sixty? Seventy? 'It is the good that die young', he thought out loud. Audibly exasperating, when in his own company, was something that annoyed him intensely; but it happened now with ever increasing regularity.

On the morning after the incident with Julia and Gerhard he caught the seven thirty train to Cambridge. He arrived in his rooms at eight twenty-five and packed immediately. It was fortunate that he had left early; Joel Salomonovich had hammered at the old cottage door at seven forty-five that morning intent on discovering why George Merrick had been on his property during the previous evening and why he had approached his granddaughter. He also arrived wishing to mutilate 'the bastard', into the bargain.

Chapter 42

SIR NICHOLAS HANSON

George Merrick did not have friends as such but he had made a great deal of money from his inventions and research and had had the good sense to invest it well. His work had enhanced the fortunes of many wealthy and powerful figures in society and it was from these movers and shakers that he now sought favours. He knew the power that information and knowledge wielded and the complex infrastructure required to keep magnates at the top of the food chain.

George also knew that those who wielded power were the wealthy, politicians or aristocrats all of whom had labyrinthine connections. He knew too that power was maintained by knowledge. Knowledge of the political, financial and commercial world. Knowledge of relationships; who did what and who knew who? It took a great deal to get on the inside but once there, the wheels, which needed regular maintenance in the form of corporate hospitality and favours, were oiled and a place at the table was laid.

All magnates have information gathering departments at the core of their operations. They act as the barometers, thermometers and altimeters that inform decisions and confirm directions. Banks of complex computers run sophisticated software twenty four seven. Agents across the world feed minutia into their data banks, processes information and spit out significant detail on request. Without this arm an empire works in the dark and mistakes can be very expensive.

The pilot of Sir Nicholas Hansen's AW 139 helicopter approached the helipad perched high above his yacht. The two hundred and ninety foot 'Miranda' was not an easy target to miss. She cruised at 16 knots and was heading for the Amalfi coast and would anchor in the bay there during the time that it took for Sir Richard to shower and change. The 'Miranda' was a floating telecommunication, business and entertainment centre. Swimming pools were located on two decks; one indoor and one out. It had a thirty-seater cinema, a fitness suite, Turkish baths, staterooms, a library and a conference room. The Miranda had four decks the lower one accommodating the thirty-two crew who looked after thirty-two possible guests.

Sir Nicholas looked through one of the six porthole windows of the 139, still talking to London. He completed his conversation before descending the two steps onto the helipad. A trap door was opened for him and he took the lift down to the yacht's telecommunication centre, waiving away his valet's greeting as he did so.

He had left Westminster at three o'clock that afternoon after a profitable meeting with a permanent secretary, to entertain a Greek shipping magnate on, and off, the Amalfi coast. Dinner would be at seven in the evening. The journey had included a chauffeur driven Rolls to a skyscraper, a lift to its helipad, a short trip to Heathrow, his Lear Jet to Rome and his chopper to the 'Miranda.' He would make a couple of calls and go to his rooms to change for the evening, take his launch to his jetty and walk the fifty yards through his gardens, between the acacia and bougainvillea into his villa. Cognac in hand he would stroll down the hallways past the portraits of his late Italian wife Francesca and his late and lamented daughter Miranda to meet his honoured guest in the library.

Communications. Always communications. In helicopters, jets, yachts and villas. The powerful have a lust for information and a pathological need to keep reins tight in hand. Sir Nicholas was as a driven man. His empire was his life. He could no more live without it than he could live without the blood in his veins. He ran the show. He and he alone possessed of the keys. He liked it that way.

After the preliminaries he and the impressed visiting magnate strolled to the jetty and took his launch to 'The Miranda.'

He had changed and now walked to the afterdeck, taking a little of the Mediterranean air before dining with his guest. His mobile vibrated at his thigh. The number was limited and the call would be accepted.

'H', he answered.

'Ah my dear boy, I see that you still go by the same sobriquet. I trust that you are well and that you have not forgotten an old man?'

Sir Nicholas hadn't forgotten but the voice of his former professor was not what he needed just now. He feigned interest. 'Hello George. What a pleasant surprise.'

The old man dismissed the nicety, as was his nature, and pressed on. 'You will, of course, remember that you asked me to ring you if there was anything that you could for me in return for the pharmaceutical problems you wished me to look at?'

Sir Nicholas waited.

'I recall that I solved some small problem that your people were having difficulty with.'

Sir Nicholas recalled all too well and the problem had been far from small. He hadn't expected a response to his invitation so soon and, just now, it was proving irritating. He cut to the chase. 'What can I do for you George?'

The professor sensed his 'window' would be short. 'I would very much like to access your mainframe dear boy. Perhaps, say, for a day or two. I recognise that you will limit my access. That is not a problem. I need to work as soon as possible. Shall we say tomorrow at your London headquarters?'

Sir Nicholas thought for an instant and made his decision. He could not foresee a problem; especially as he intended to provide the professor with an 'assistant' who would supervise his every move and detail his every entry.

He boarded the launch and headed to his villa and began to think of his meeting with the Greek but smiled as he reflected on his old mentor. 'What is the old bastard up to now', he thought. 'Sorting out his bloody pittance of a pension I shouldn't wonder.' He laughed but, as always, he would take precautions. Information was power and power shared was power diluted. Sir Nicholas never let his guard slip. Not even for his former professor.

George packed his bags and left his Cambridge rooms post haste. He reckoned that it was a good time to move. He reckoned correctly. Fraser's men were at his doorway just five minutes after he had left.

At nine in the morning, on the following day, George was sitting in a lavish sixteenth story reception room in London tapping his fingers and waiting to be given access to Sir Nicholas Hansen's telecommunication centre. The efficiency of the authentication's complex procedures left him fuming at the unnecessary bureaucracy that had cast its shadow over his academic work for so many years. He was shown into a small room and given access to a PC.

'Call me if I can be of any assistance sir', smiled the immaculately presented young woman who had been given the surveillance assignment. George returned her smile, understood her role and sat down to work.

The amiable 'assistant' left the room and took up her position behind the one-way mirror, logged on and watched George's every move, as instructed.

George resisted the urge to smile at the mirror.

Chapter 43

A DISH BEST SERVED COLD

George tapped into the Hansen Corporation's mainframe and watched the information rattle from the printer. He began with the feedback on Simon Salomonovich. He sifted through pages of information about his background and his work. Much of it was general information and known to George. He quickly became irritated by the reams of detail. It was two hours before he picked up on a piece regarding Simon Salomonovich's execution. The order had been from one SS Obersturmführer Reinhardt Bühler. Who was Bühler? He fascinated George no less because he obviously interested Joel. Here was the man who had all but destroyed Joel Salomonovich. This was the man that Joel Salomonovich had left home to find after the death of his mother. Now some of this began to make sense.

He fed Bühler's name into the mainframe. Within seconds the printer broke the silence again and issued the following:

SS Obersturmführer Reinhardt Bühler
Born on 11th November 1918 the son of SS Obersturmführer Wilhelm Richard Bühler of Augsburg, Bavaria, killed by the Soviets during the atrocities in the aftermath of Operation Barbarossa in December 1941. Mother, Ursula von Kleist – committed suicide 28th August 1920.

Army career: Enlisted 1936. SS from 1939. Wanted by the War Crimes Commission for personally killing over seventy men, women and children. Also for ordering the murder of several thousand others.

Disappeared 1945, believed to have taken the ratline to Argentina organised by Kameradenwerk. He surfaced as Hans Kohler in 1953 as an importer. Recognised and disappeared again without trace. Whereabouts unknown. Presumed dead – unproven. Case remains open on the Wiesenthal files.

George considered the ratline; the route out of Germany after the war and the Kameradenwerk, the organisation which many Nazis had used to escape from Germany. The Kameradenwerk. Yes, there must be some way to contact them. Somehow, somewhere; there must be someone. Someone who knew of Bühler. Wiesenthal hadn't found him. George would. There had been sightings in Munich and again in Augsburg but the trails, which were never more than lukewarm, went cold very quickly on each occasion. George made a note to ring a colleague in Munich.

What of Joel Salomonovich? He had disappeared from view when he had left Suffolk after his mother's funeral. Where had he been? George hit more keys. Joel Salomonovich had worked for the army as an interpreter at the Brackwede barracks in Bielefeld and had then disappeared from the radar. A Joel Salomonovich had paid for the funeral of one Abraham Goldstein who had died in New York and was buried in Hamburg. George noted it.

It took Professor George Merrick two hours to link Joel Salomonovich to Joel Joseph, and Abraham Goldstein to Abraham Turner. It took another two to deduce that Joel had been in Amsterdam at the time of Jan Kuyper's murder. The photo fit of the man who had bought Kuyper a drink was a pretty fair representation. The Harlem barman was to be congratulated.

If only the authorities had access to such information, pondered George. My god, what the hell else was filed away in those endless annals of the so called super highway? He read his notebook again making chronological plans of action in the margins. He had much to do.

George pushed a few more keys, got what he wanted and made appointments with a former student who worked at the foreign office and with a former colleague in Munich. Satisfied with his research he booked tickets for Munich and a car from Hertz for the following day. He met the man from the foreign office in the evening and by morning had landed at Franz Josef Strauss airport.

Sir Nicholas Hansen had already been briefed. George was well aware that he had been. Sir Nicholas had a shrewd idea that the professor too would know that he had been.

Chapter 44

JOEL SENDS JULIA AWAY

'Where the hell has he got to?' Joel always tempered his language in Rebecca's presence. The two sat on the bench seat in the bay window of the drawing room of The Manor House. The rain beat down on the windowpanes on a day that had hardly got light. The lake was barely discernible in the grey and amber glow of the autumn noon. God, how he hated England in November even if there was an evocation of a Turner to be had in the endless mists.

Rebecca reached out to touch her brother and held his hand. She was now in her seventies and fragile but she and she alone could pacify and comfort Joel. They talked of their parents, Simon and Marta and their brothers Reuben and Benjamin. They moved on to Simon Benjamin Reuben Salomonovich a much-loved son and nephew. They never tired of talking about their family. Joel spoke of his beloved Rachael who Rebecca had never met and wished so dearly that she had. 'Life's like that isn't it? he mused. 'You know two people for most of your life and sometimes they were not even on the planet at the time. And yet they seem to belong together. Mother and my son Simon are such examples. I knew them both what seems now so long ago. How can they not have known each other?' He pulled himself up. 'Drivel. I speak like the old man that I am. Rebecca for the first time in my life I am beginning to feel my age.'

Julia and her mother found the two together. 'Are we interrupting?' Laura enquired. She was assured that they were not. 'Gerhard rang and would like to know when we are going to Germany. Have you decided yet?' asked Julia. Joel looked at Rebecca. 'Your aunt and I have decided that we can't go to Hamburg at present liebchen. Perhaps...' Joel was thinking on his feet ... 'Perhaps it would be a good idea for you to visit Gerhard. He lives with his family I believe?' Joel looked for agreement from his daughter in law. Laura smiled understanding the inference.

Julia smiled too and gave her grandfather a hug. 'Yes he does grandpa. You seem keen to be rid of me? What are you planning in that wise old head of yours?' She kissed her grandfather's forehead as she spoke.

Joel walked to the desk telephone. 'Oh nothing really but Aunt Rebecca and I thought we might go to London and conclude some business. I really have neglected my duties of late. It doesn't do the staff any harm to see the old man about the place for a day or two.'

'Frightening the life out them I shouldn't wonder', Julia trilled.

Joel picked up the phone. 'I don't want you driving all the way to Koblenz again. Your aunt and I leave tomorrow morning' – this came as a surprise to Rebecca who kept a disciplined silence – 'when do you wish to go?'

Julia wasn't fooled. 'It's the old man isn't it?' Joel had the demeanour and skills of a poker player. Rebecca had not. She had glanced at Rebecca and that had been sufficient to confirm her suspicions.

'You want me out of the way. Why? Who is that man?'

Joel's face remained in poker mode. 'He is someone that your grandmother and I knew many years ago. Over the years I have crossed him from time to time. Never in person. My contacts have been concerned about his interest in my affairs. It seems the man has some sort of neurosis. An unresolved vendetta of some sort. I don't think that it's anything to worry about liebchen and we are really going to London. Really. I just don't want you to be alone in the house next week. Especially if he is walking about in the woods. Verstehen?'

Julia nodded her understanding. She was keen to go to Germany; she always was. She had a strange affinity for the country. She was less keen to see the amorous Gerhard. Friend Gerhard? – good. Amorous Gerhard? – bad. She pondered for a moment as Joel lifted the handset. 'OK, I'll go.'

Joel dialled Stansted. There was a flight to Frankfurt the following morning. He booked Julia in and hired a car from Hertz. 'Just fifty miles driving on this side and fifty miles on the other side. That doesn't sound so difficult does it? Remember...' Julia cut him off. 'I know grandpa. They drive on the right side of the road there.' She gave both the elderly siblings and her mother a hug and left to pack.

A taxi picked up Julia at eight thirty the following morning. Joel and Rebecca waved as it disappeared behind the sycamore copse that hid The Manor House from the road. The driver stopped as he reached the junction, and then pulled out onto the northbound route towards Woodbridge. A white Astra pulled out from the kerbside a hundred metres further down the road and fell in behind the cab. The driver had established that the 'target' had indeed a ticket on the eleven fifteen Stansted flight to Frankfurt.

Julia picked up a black BMW roadster from Hertz at the Flughafen Frankfurt am Main south of the city and hit the E35 north to Koblenz. Now a black Porsche fell in behind her. The German private detective agencies were obviously paid better than their British counterparts.

Details of Julia's whereabouts were relayed to George Merrick and he filed the information away into the personal computer between his ears. It was time to move. He picked up the phone.

Chapter 45

GEORGE MERRICK IN MUNICH

George Merrick was in considerable pain. The arthritic old man always felt fractious after being cooped up on a commercial jet airliner. He grimaced as he left his seat. The young stewardess moved in order to help him. His irritability surfaced despite the insidious unremitting pain. 'Don't. I can manage. If airlines gave as much care to their passengers as farmers do their battery hens then I wouldn't have had a problem in the first place', he thundered, venting his spleen. 'Herzlich Willcommen? I really don't think so.'

The stewardess was young but fortunately well-seasoned. She knew an awkward customer when she saw one and backed off, smiling politely as she turned her attention to other more amenable passengers, her thoughts remaining undisclosed.

Within half an hour George was sat in a hired, Munich made, BMW heading southwest from the Franz Josef Strauß airport. He drove along the E53, skirted the northern suburbs of Munich, and then took the E52, now heading northwest, past Dachau towards Augsburg. He passed Augsburg airport to the north of the city then turned off the autobahn and parked at the Rastplatz just short of the Augsburg Naturpark. He pulled up behind a black Mercedes parked on the slip road which led back onto the autobahn. The driver got out and walked to the BMW driver's door. George lowered the window.

'Herzlich Willcommen Herr Professor', offered the smiling driver. George did not return the smile hoping that all the 'Herzlich Willcommens had now run their course.

'You will forgive me Walter if I do not get out of the car. I fear that if I did I would have great difficulty getting back into it.' Walter Krantz acknowledged the professor's difficulty. 'None of us are getting any younger', said the fifty two year old. The older man's reply was sour and curt. 'Quite.'

Walter Krantz had once been a dashing young man but in recent years he had put on four extra stones and, although time had been kind to him in the sense that and he had been left with a full head of raven hair, he looked far from youthful. A husband who had caught him *in flagrante* had broken his nose. It had not set straight and for a man of such vanity it hurt him more now than it did when it had been hit thirteen years earlier. There were many more occasions when he might have suffered the same fate but for luck, a decent sense of timing and a nifty bit of footwork. Walter Krantz had worked hard and had played hard all his life and every last bit of it was etched into his careworn face. He stood nervously, shifting from foot to foot.

'Kompt sofort. Let's be on our way.'

Krantz, relieved at getting the awkwardness of the renewed acquaintance out of the way, no matter how temporarily, started the Mercedes and the professor followed. The road climbed steeply through the trees of the Naturpark. The Mercedes and BMW turned off the road and pulled higher up a long winding gravel path. Half way along they came upon a huge sign nailed to a tree. It bore the legend Der Tannenbaum Clinic. A large chalet stood in a clearing some two hundred metres or so ahead. The cars approached the building and circled the fountain in the centre of the island of the gravelled forecourt.

Walter Krantz parked the Mercedes and walked to the side of the building, opening large double gates. The BMW slipped through and he locked them behind him. The BMW pulled away once again. 'This way', he indicated walking ahead of the car. George parked in a wooded barn a good hundred metres to the rear of the chalet.

'I trust that this is adequate George.' George murmured that it was. Krantz carried George's luggage as they walked through the trees to a small door at the rear of the clinic. Walter unlocked it then closed it behind him. He and George were now in the south annex of the chalet. This was connected to the main building by one corridor. There was one key and that belonged to the owner of the place. Walter Krantz.

Krantz opened a door and turned on the light. 'I trust the room is to your liking?' There was no answer. After a moment George asked, 'And my laboratory? Krantz was pleased with the request and opened an adjoining door. 'Das, mein freund, ist heir.' George gave the room a summary appraisal. The laboratory would be adequate.

'Everything that you asked for is here', said Krantz, eager to impress his guest after putting a great deal into the enterprise. 'The best has been bought and your materials have travelled a somewhat circuitous route to get here. All is well my friend. I have delivered my part of the bargain. All that I ask is that you are successful in your endeavours and that you are able to repay me before I get much older. I too am anxious to start again.' If Professor George Merrick was impressed or grateful it was not discernible. Krantz pressed no further.

'And our associate?' asked George.

'He is next door. I thought that you might rest before ...' Krantz looked at George and knew that he had thought wrongly. Irritability surfaced in George's eyes once more. 'Of course', deferred Krantz, 'Er kompt sofort.' He left.

After a few moments there was a soft knock on the door and Walter Krantz entered followed by an old man. His piercing blue eyes were watery now and his hair that had once been Aryan blonde was now grey but George recognised him from the photographs taken many years earlier. The man's gait belied his years but it was former Obersturmführer Reinhardt Bühler; of that there was no doubt.

Professor George Merrick had dropped out of sight, as Bühler had done before him. Neither would be seen for some time. The professor began work that evening and worked from dawn until dusk for the next eight months.

It was July before George returned to England. He believed that he was ready.

Chapter 46

FELIX ELDER

Felix Elder stretched upwards his fingers easily finding the crevice above. He pulled himself onto the ledge and sat looking down one hundred and thirty feet to the valley beneath.

This was the Mendips not the Himalayas. This was very easy not at all the severe or virtually impossible climbs that he took for granted on expeditions. This was recreation. It was hardly a strenuous examination of his climbing skills. It was a country stroll for an Olympic marathon runner. Never the less Felix was at ease with himself, as he always was when out in the countryside, and that was always a good omen.

Very little impressed Felix. Thrills and excitement had to be extreme to have an impact. Paragliding was the prosaic domain of the holidaymaker and the bungee jumper a fairground customer feebly masquerading as an adventurer or daredevil. No, Felix craved the ultimate. He stuck his fist up at life and challenged it to do its worst. His adversaries, whether organic or inanimate, would always come off second best. Nothing fazed him. Everything was surmountable. Everything that is except finding the time to earn the money to finance his exploits.

Now that capacity – the capacity to earn and save over a period of time – that had proved nigh on impossible. That was not a challenge. It was an inconvenience. Financing his exploits was a perennial problem. Forming a relationship was a problem. Cities, socialising, even shaving and washing were problems most of the time. Indeed conformity in general caused him great irritation.

Felix was a loner. His notion of fun was to rise at six. Run ten miles, pump iron and climb. Climb until he reached heaven itself.

There was more than one dimension to his existence if you searched deeper into his psyche. But one would have to delve very deep indeed if one were to find the definitive Felix. The narrowness of his activities did not define the man. His complexity was apparent only to those few souls who were mad enough to share his experiences on his madcap expeditions.

A commando without an army, a galloping renegade, a free spirit. Black belt karate, judo, aikido, jujitsu and kendo. A kick boxer and a wrestler. A fighting machine. He had been wrongly dismissed from the army for risking the life of others. He took the fall. He knew that he shouldn't have but was time to leave the organisation anyway. He had learned what he had wanted to know and needed to leave before the stifling rigour of obeying daft orders and cowing to authority affected his sanity.

Felix came from a well to do family from Buckinghamshire. His father had died when he was young and his mother as he had entered his teens. A reluctant aunt adopted the youth. She was married without children and had deceived her husband into believing that she could not conceive. The truth was that she was a hedonistic child of the seventies and needed the freedom of youth. The same was true even as she approached her fiftieth birthday. The aunt had moved to the Cotswolds with her wealthy husband then abandoned him and Felix to return to 'the scene' in London. He was sent to a prestigious boarding school in the Lake District and was received at 'home' when the occasion necessitated.

Felix thrived in adversity. He became head boy, a natural leader of men, captained the first fifteen rugby team waltzed through his Duke of Edinburgh Gold Award and graduated to Cambridge University.

He studied microbiology and was fascinated by the lectures of one Professor George Merrick who he viewed as an eccentric and, though not a fellow traveller, a man of stature, of depth and intellect and above all, of individuality. Felix hated the prosaic, the bucolic and the mundane. He craved the god given right to be different; to be an individual and not to be contained by other people's conservative conventions. He was born twenty years too late. The students of his years demonstrated, if that is what you could call it, against fees and conditions that affected themselves; not the problems of third world hunger, poverty, war, man's inhumanity to man or the iniquities and inequalities of society. Today it was about them. Felix needed radical insurgency, dissent and rebellion.

An office job would have been an anathema to Felix. How did folk live like that? He needed the drug of fear, danger and the unexpected. He demanded an edge; the possibility of a dark abyss should he fail; the absence of a safety net; to lock horns with the very devil himself.

Once he had been 'holed up' in a cavern seeking protection from a monsoon on a small reef off Sumatra. Three of the seven on the expedition had perished after being shipwrecked. The other three were dealing with Felix's contempt. They were shaking with fear.

'Why did you come on this trip when it is very clear that you are not suited to it?' he enquired of the one 'bravo' throwing up over the rocks that protected them from the raging sea.

'You bastard. Three dead and you ask that. You are inhuman?' raged the young man. 'Do you not understand what has happened here?'

Calmly Felix replied, 'I do.' He paused, and then added, 'I also know myself.'

'Know yourself? What is that supposed to mean?'

'Everything', he had replied, in that same laconic dispassionate fashion that toyed with other's emotions.

'I asked you a question', the young man demanded.

Felix did not look up for several seconds. Then slowly raising his head he stared into the very soul of his inquisitor. The young man squirmed at the intensity of Felix's gaze and, for the first time, recognised the power and brooding danger of his fellow traveller.

'The first person that one should know is oneself. The most important person to know is oneself. Intimately. Few people do. Even fewer use this knowledge to plan their actions and their lives. Most people kid themselves. You', he looked across at the others, 'you have all kidded yourselves into believing that you were prepared for this expedition. You are romantics. What has happened was always on the cards. Life is a risk when you put yourself on the front line.' He turned to the squirming youth who had confronted him. 'You are not a front line person. Savvy? Now you panic. Now you are scared. Examine yourself. Who are you? What did you come here for? What did you wish to discover? You are ill prepared and that is foolish. That gets others killed and we have witnessed the evidence.'

The young man broke down as he recognised the truth.

Felix looked at the three frightened 'explorers.'

'Stay here. I will return.'

'But where, I mean how will you ...?'

'OK you go. Tell me now what you are going to do and I will know not to return for you', he threatened.

He turned to see three bowed heads in the shadows. When they looked up again he had gone. Twenty-seven hours later the storm had abated and he had returned with a boat and crew. He never revealed how he had achieved this miracle but the legend of Felix Elder grew stronger.

Felix pumped iron for a purpose – not for fun. When not on an expedition he would withdraw into himself for a short time; then pump iron again. His muscular physique was a tribute to his dedication to training not to steroids. His muscles were made from the sweat of exertion; they were not taken from a bottle. He did not think of his body as a temple, though he neither drank alcohol nor smoked. It was more of a fortress; a stronghold. And it had a purpose. He didn't pump iron to look good like those tanned Californian beach bums. The painfully acquired chiselled body was not fashioned to attract the attention of a few passing women. It was to provide him with the tools and weapons required to survive extreme conditions and the demands he would subject himself to.

It was New Year's Eve and his few acquaintances were with their friends or at family get-togethers. Felix appreciated the fact that some folk liked such entertainment. He knew that, had he been in company, he would have been frustrated by the inevitable small talk. Better to stay clear. On a whim he caught a train to the Mendips. From the small station at Yatton he walked the eight miles to Cheddar Gorge and within an hour was beginning to climb the familiar cliffs of his youth. No ropes necessary!

Felix sat at on the edge of a cliff observing a peregrine hovering high above its prey when the overhang gave way. He fell thirty feet hitting his temple on the limestone. That would have ended his life there and then but for a small bush growing out of the cliff face, which tangled with his backpack and stopped further descent. He lay there unmoving for a moment until, slowly, the weight of his body became too much for the bush. The branches bent further and further until they gave way. He spiralled through the air and landed softly on a sandy slope between two huge boulders. Down the valley he rolled until he came to the next ledge. His clothing caught on the overhang and he turned slowly in mid-air suspended above the deep gorge. Unconscious he swung there for more than eleven hours.

It was elderly morning hikers who raised the alarm. The venerable group followed the well-trodden path which ran by the narrow fast flowing river which since the ice age had been carving its way through the chalky grassland valley. They stopped for a well-earned rest to take in the heady perfume of the marjoram and wild thyme.

It was a moustachioed retired colonel, still eagle eyed at almost eighty, who caught a glint of something almost half way up the cliff face. A second flash confirmed the direction in which to point his field glasses.

There, clearly unconscious, was a man hanging from the precipice. The colonel signalled the alarm and, summoning his military discipline, ordered the group to implement his commands. He assumed control, 'like in the good old days', and others obeyed the emergent leader to the letter.

The dismayed leader of the troop, like so many appointed leaders who are only effective when the going is good, acceded to the colonel's assumed seniority. Now there was the need for a real leader – someone who could think rather than an apparatchik who could, at best, implement policy.

Folk were dispatched with point and purpose and within the hour the rescue helicopter had winched Felix aboard. The crew were in contact with the Royal Infirmary at Bristol and preparations to receive Felix were being made.

Professor George Merrick was duly informed as leader of an experimental research programme investigating persistent vegetative state and coma phenomena. He left Cambridge immediately and arrived in Bristol later that evening.

Felix Elder was put on a life support system. The prognosis was far from promising.

Chapter 47

JULIA GOES TO KOBLENZ

Three weeks after arriving home from her strained time with Gerhard in Germany Julia Salomonovich sat in the Manor House kitchen with the phone to her ear. She couldn't believe what she was hearing. Gerhard was speaking from Germany. He was upbraiding her for having been to an Oxford reunion and sharing the same room as several other students, male and female, overnight before driving home the following morning. This she felt not to be Gerhard's concern.

Joel had listened to her chiding him. 'Problems?' he asked.

'I think so', she replied pensively. She outlined the situation to him and asked, 'Why is everything so complicated when it's a man and a woman who are friends? What would you do, oh wise one?'

Joel laughed. 'People need to know where they stand. I know that you have a certain affection for Gerhard and I know too that you do not love him.'

'How do you know? How can you be so certain?' She asked, alarmed at her transparency.

'Julia. I loved your grandmother. She was the most beautiful woman that I ever saw. When other women were in the room I saw only her. I cared for her. I wouldn't let anyone hurt her. She made me laugh, she made me smile but above all she completed me. I loved every moment that I was with her. I hated being separated from her – no matter how brief a time that was. She gave me a reason to live and memories that have sustained me over these many years and I will recall them to my dying day. And you? You tire of Gerhard when he visits for a day or two too long. I do not see the sparkle of love in your eyes nor the warmth and passion of the embrace of one afflicted by love. No liebchen, you are not in love.'

Julia was stunned. 'You really did love her didn't you grandpa', she said softly, taking his hand between hers and stroking it compassionately. Joel nodded stoically holding back a tear.

'I shall go to Koblenz again and explain my feelings to Gerhard more clearly. You are right. It is time but I do hope that he understands and that we can remain friends. I don't want to lose him but it can't go on like this any longer.

Julia set off for Germany two days later. A red Peugeot had replaced the white Astra that had previously followed her but the driver had retained his job.

Chapter 48

PETER FOSSARD

He lay silent. The translucent remains of Peter Fossard's malignant body lay wasted. Crucified. Worse than crucified. Crucifixion takes hours; maybe days. This had taken months. The end was near. Mercifully, the macabre bitter end was near.

It was mid-December. There would be no Christmas.

He felt soon, in his very sinews he knew it would be soon, that he would embrace death. Engulfed, relieved, forsaken, frightened but delivered from his hell on earth. Delivered from the abject misery and the pain of his finale. Free from the morphine that dulled his mind. Free from the incontinence that robbed him of his dignity.

He was ready to go. He had fought a titanic struggle but it was over. He comprehended that inevitable fact and was now prepared to concede defeat.

But he knew too that he would never see his beloved wife and daughters again. They were the reason for his dogged fight; his survival thus far; his scrap with the almighty for his body if not his soul. He had struggle against all the odds. A lingering martyrdom.

But now the epic fight was over. He was resigned to rest in peace. His time had come and he had made his peace with God and with the world. He saw the injustice of it all but had accepted the inevitability of his circumstances.

Peter turned his head. He scanned the windows yet could barely make out the hospital garden. The late autumn wind had cleaned all but the most stubborn leaves from the trees. The drizzle ran down the misty windowpanes and washed the remnants of colour from the drab canvas. Dusk approached and he wondered if he would see another dawn.

'Come on. Get yourself together', he breathed to himself. 'Nothing can be done.' The effort to speak was too much for him, so he thought through the rest of his monologue. 'Remember, all that you have left now is your dignity.' He closed his eyes remembering the incontinence and the smell of his emaciated body. 'Perhaps not even that, but then… then, importantly, the memory you will leave behind, with Sarah and the kids.'

He drifted back to happier days. Days he thought would last forever. Days of tenderness and love. Days of endless summers, parties and wine. Days that had been lived; his loving wife and lovely daughters all of whom he was so proud.

Staring into the abyss he thought of Sarah. He felt her beautiful hazel brown eyes engage his?

It was May 1975. Peter was 26 and single. Six feet two inches tall, an olive Mediterranean complexion and a Roman nose that, if he had been less extrovert and less confident within himself, would have wounded him more than it did.

He was well built, fairly good-looking with a penchant for looking at himself in mirrors. Mostly he chose to ignore the nose.

'I'm Peter, six foot two with eyes of blue, and look at you.' This piercing, evocative overture, this prelude to love, this wooing exposé which Peter was want to submit under the influence of an alcoholic beverage or two was aimed at one Sarah Bennett; affectionately referred to as Sarah Bernhardt.

'Well thank you kind sir.' She replied, equally inebriated.

'I guess I'll be taking you home young lady?' he ventured.

'Guess again', she replied curtly.

These lines were recalled at dinner parties, weddings and family gatherings throughout the thirty years of Peter and Sarah's marriage. Sometimes a fall back at times of discomfort and stress, sometimes under the influence of alcohol and generally a requirement after a contretemps or poignant moment. De rigueur.

At the rugby club the couple thrived and were clearly popular and well loved. Peter had been a decent inside centre well known for his dedication to the club, passionate love of the game and dispassionate tackling of opponents.

He was an opening bowler and dependable middle order batsman who performed with panache; a man to be reckoned with when the going got tough. It often did. A man one could rely on when your back was against the wall; a four-handicap golfer, a man of culture; an architect; a man for all seasons.

Peter was a curious mixture of dominating adventurer yet receptive and attentive friend; a man who knew what he wanted in life but one who was ever mindful of the underdog.

Sarah had been happy too. A twenty-two year old graduate in ancient history at Bristol University, she had met Peter at an alumni reunion.

Peter, at twenty-six, had left the university the year before Sarah had begun and neither were citizens of Bristol. Perhaps the only opportunity for the two to meet was at that reunion. The romantic Sarah had always believed that their meeting was meant to be. A fatalist and romantic at heart.

Chloe was born just a year after they had been married and Lucy fifteen months later. Peter became a proud family man. The girls idolised Sarah who was able to share so much of their lives and Peter loved to watch the three of them together. He thanked God every day for the luck he had had in meeting Sarah. The girls were clever and looked very much like their mother. Both too were graduates of Bristol University and, over the five-years when the girls were students, Peter and Sarah had loved to go back to the old Alma Mater whenever the opportunity arose just to walk around the place arm in arm.

Both girls were now married and had successful careers. They lived away but were very close, ringing almost every evening to discuss their days and to keep in touch with family affairs. Peter missed them very much but had accepted the inevitability of their departure and had looked forward to seeing grandchildren in the near future.

Peter's friend, Mike Tyler, had pleaded with Peter to go to the reunion that summer. He had insisted that Peter, being the recipient of a recent Dear John letter from an attractive blonde was not, in itself, a reason to 'go morbid.' Peter reluctantly agreed to go and Mike reminded the happy couple of his cupidity whenever he was in need. Mike was very often in need.

Sarah mothered Mike. He had been a bachelor for the first twelve years of their marriage. He had then married an Australian girl who had developed amnesia and had forgotten to tell him that she had already married some two years earlier. There were months of legal hassle before she upped and left taking all but the rented flat and his clothes back to the antipodes.

'Never again', lasted for five weeks. Peter was to be his best man for a second time. Before both occasions he had offered his grave misgivings about the unions. Mike had been 'walking into things' for as long as Peter could remember. He hadn't a clue when it came to relationships with women. He had always been a lost cause.

Mike met his second femme fatale soon after his first 'wife' left and was married to her for two torrid years. This time it was he who did the leaving. This, he felt, to be most reasonable as he was beginning to believe that the only man in the town not to have slept with his wife over the last eighteen months of their marriage was himself. When he checked their bank accounts it appeared to him that her budget for gifts, clothes and perfumes had been similar to that of The Queen of Sheba in the weeks prior to her visiting King Solomon.

He had been divorced for eight penniless years and for the second time in his life he had been given the opportunity to repent at leisure. Mike mistook the Fossard's fridge for his own, knew the couch intimately and the girls still called him 'Uncle Mikey'.

Sarah was a very attractive fifty-two years old. At five six she was the smallest member of the family. Petite and feminine her blonde hair was longer than suits most women of her age but it looked well on her. Her fair, fresh complexion and blue eyes radiated health and warmth. She smiled a smile that captivated all. One flash of those beautiful white teeth, between those oh so kissable lips, disarmed the most awkward of bureaucrats.

Her long slender neck, small shoulders and slender waist went rarely unnoticed by red blooded men. She was a feminine female. The way she walked, the way she sat, the way she smelled and the way she talked all the way down from the slender wrists and perfectly manicured nails to the shapely legs and the beautiful size four feet.

She had a penchant for fine porcelain and Peter spent many hours scouring the streets of foreign climes seeking elegant pieces when away from her on business. How he missed her at those wretched seminars and conferences or during those visits abroad. He enjoyed the travel but he yearned to have the love of his life by his side to share his experiences.

Peter lay in pain thinking of her. He thought of the first night that they had made love.

It was May, two months after they had met. Peter had taken Sarah home to her flat and had climbed the narrow stairwell on several occasions. He had wooed her gently. They has kissed and caressed in the car and on the stairwell each evening before he returned to his flat. They had smooched and cuddled in the cinema and even behind the pavilion between innings. But that night....that night they had laughed in unison. They had caught each other looking and smiling; they had clung to each other and instinctively moved a little closer. They had felt the warmth and receptiveness of each other. They had fallen in love.

Both knew it. There was no mistaking it. Every movement suggested it. Positive followed positive. A deep spiritual stirring engulfed the pair and their moment had come.

They sat in the car. 'So, I'll see you up?'

'Coffee?'

'Please'.

This was the first time that Peter had been invited to the flat on an evening. They climbed the narrow stairs and excitedly Sarah fumbled for her keys feeling a large hand caressing her neck. She turned and kissed him lightly on the lips. A gentle quiver ricocheted down his spine and he bent to return her affection. They smiled.

She opened the door and took off her coat and made her way to the small kitchenette. She didn't make it. He held her close.

'I thought you wanted coffee?'

'I lied. Did you?'

'Well I...'

'Did you?'

'I like coffee', she offered.

'That's not what I asked,' he breathed, drawing her closer.

'I know', she said.

'Then, Sarah Bennett', he said in his best policeman's voice, 'did you or did you not tell a lie on the night of the twenty-fifth of May 1975 in the vicinity of your flat? Yes or No?

'Yes.' She laughed, and then reflecting, looked into his eyes and said tenderly. 'Yes I did.'

One small word. 'Yes.' The door was open and she had let him in.

Confident in her acquiescence he kissed her lips, her neck and her shoulders in turn. His hand caressed her back through the sleeveless silk top and moved slowly forwards. He cupped her breast; his heart hammering. She put her hand on his as if to remove it. She hesitated then withdrew her hand. Putting her arms around his excited body she accepted his affection, submitted to his caress and ached for his love.

He moved his hand down to her waist under her top and onto her bra. Moving the strap to the side he held her breast.

He whispered in her ear. 'I love you'. He had known that this was what he had wanted to say but didn't believe that he would ever have what it takes to say it. In the end it didn't take anything at all. It was so easy, so right; so very right.

She looked down at his hand caressing her breast beneath the top. She raised her head, then, slowly, her eyes lifted to look to him for a lead.

'God she is beautiful', he thought.

He kissed her eyes, her cheek and ears, and then returned to her neck.

They would have remained there had the phone not rung.

'Leave it', he said sharply as he took her hand and led her to the bedroom.

They made love. He was gentle and considerate. She was inexperienced and took her cues from him. She was a virgin giving herself to a man that she truly loved and admired. She had always imagined that this situation could be seedy, tacky, and unlovely. She had been wrong.

They would never know how long that phone rang for. They were wrapped up in each other and they neither heard nor saw anything but the other.

He drew her to him once again. She quivered as their naked bodies entwined. There was just the two of them. The world had been left behind, as if a curtain had closed behind them.

Soon another curtain would close, this time parting Peter from Sarah and they would meet no more. Never again would he hold his darling Sarah in his arms. Never again would he watch her, admiring her beauty and grace and knowing that she was his. Soon it would be over.

Peter lost consciousness moments before Sarah and Mike Tyler entered the room. She might have been a little earlier but, as always, she took a few extra moments in the waiting room steeling herself, wiping away the tears that burnt her cheeks and fixing the smile that she had taught herself to perform each and every time she entered that small horrid room.

She took a deep breath and slowly releasing it opened the door. An overhead lamp lit the room softly and she sighed at the sight of what remained of her beloved Peter.

Mike stayed back as Sarah walked slowly towards the bed. She made sure that he was still breathing and placed her lips on what was once his handsome face.

'Sleep darling. I love you. I will forever'. She sat, looked up at Mike, her eyes welling up once more and dropped her eyes praying for what she knew could not possibly be delivered.

After a miserable hour, which seemed like five, Sarah stirred. She sat at the bedside, touching Peter's wasted arm for all of that time. She remembered the rugby matches and the golf club dinners when she had been so proud to see him walk up to claim his trophy. The dinner dances where he had chatted to people so easily and, somehow, made them feel good about themselves; his dancing, which made everyone laugh and the evenings at home, sharing an easy chair by the fireside. Then there was Christmas Eve and putting Lucy and Chloe's presents under the tree. So many memories.

She stirred from her daze and recognised that she had been staring at some point in the corner of the room, unseeing for an eternity.

Slowly and sadly she rose from the chair with that same, familiar, dreaded dilemma. She had neither the will nor the capacity to endure longer vigils; but how she hated the leaving. And this leaving was becoming more and more difficult as the long unendurable, unceasing, unremitting days came and went.

She kissed Peter's forehead, then, lovingly, touched his arm, as if to reassure him, and, from the darkest recess of her mind said: 'Goodnight sweet prince, and flights of angels sing thee to thy rest.'

Head bowed she shuffled slowly out of the room turning for one last look.

Chapter 49

A QUESTION

Sarah closed the door of Peter's room and stood there for a moment. Still with head bowed, she turned away slowly. She was looking at two large black shoes. Her eyes travelled gradually upwards until she was looking into the face of an elderly gentleman. The man had white hair, a white moustache, a pallid complexion and gleaming white false teeth. He had an intelligent but severe face, was bent with rheumatism or arthritis and was dressed in a dark suit with a spotted dickey bow around his scrawny neck. His close proximity alarmed her. Clearly the man did not communicate easily and he must have stood silently as she paused at the door. Most folk would have indicated their presence. He had not. The man disturbed her.

'Mrs. Fossard', croaked the old man.

'I'm afraid that I am not able to talk just now', she replied, pleased to see that Mike Tyler was walking along the corridor towards them. 'I don't wish to be rude', she continued, wiping her eyes with a white handkerchief, 'but I really must go now.'

'Please', insisted the old man as he put his hand on Sarah's arm.

Mike Tyler arrived at the scene and noted Sarah's concern.

'Can I help you?' he asked sharply.

'No, I don't think that you can.' He hadn't turned to address Mike Tyler. His eyes were fixed on Sarah. He went on. 'But I believe that I can help you madam.'

'I must go. Really', Sarah insisted.

'But it is most important that I talk with you', he said urgently. 'Please give me a moment.'

Mike wondered whether to be rude or not. He wasn't going to give the old guy much more latitude.

'At least take my card. One moment please. I will write a little note.' The old man fumbled for a pencil and after eventually finding professorial pair of glasses, wrote a few words.

Mike indicated his impatience on seeing Sarah's discomfort.

'We must go', he insisted, taking Sarah by the arm.

The old man gave him a steely eye then turned to Sarah. 'Please ring me. It is most important.'

Nothing, other than Peter, at this moment in time was of any importance to Sarah. She took the card as Mike shepherded her away down the corridor with a terse, 'Goodbye.'

After a few steps Mike turned to see the old man deep in conversation with another man in a sharp grey pinstripe business suit.

'Ah, Walter, there you are. A problem', issued the old man. The two men entered the lift adjacent to Peter's room.

Mike turned his attention to Sarah wondering what the old man had wanted, who Walter, the man in the pinstripes was, and where the lift was taking them.

Sarah sobbed and Mike put his arm around her shoulder to comfort her. Within a very few hours they were both going to lose the best friend that they had ever had.

Later that evening Sarah Fossard was sitting at her bedroom dressing table, in her primrose silk dressing gown, having had a long hot bath. She almost always showered but felt that a bath would relax her aching limbs and help her to prepare for her return to the hospital that evening.

She brushed her long blonde hair and wondered whether or not it was time to have it cut. Perhaps she was a little old for having that length of hair. God, she felt it. Peter had always loved it.

She had said, 'You only love me for my hair.'

He had replied, 'True. Cut it and I leave you.'

She smiled at the memory and then reflected on how much she would miss those intimate exchanges.

She reached down to the handbag at her feet. Rummaging around, in what Peter was wont to call the 'repository of all things animal and mineral;' she noticed the business card handed to her by the old, insensitive man at the hospital earlier that afternoon.

The print read: Professor George Merrick. That was all. This was a strange business card indeed. No address, no place of business and no telephone numbers were listed.

George Merrick was a cautious old man. When he distributed a card it contained precisely that information he wished to be conveyed to the recipient; neither more nor less. The card provided him with a space to enter any such information. A four-inch long, sharpened pencil, always located in the top pocket of his jacket, scribed the knowledge to be imparted. A ballpoint pen had on one occasion leaked and ruined his jacket. George had never to learn a lesson twice. Indeed, the missive on the card was testament to that very fact.

Sarah gave a cursory glance at the card and began to dress. She put on a smart black suit and resumed her place at the dressing table. As she reached forward to pick up her pearl earrings she noted the business card again. She reached into her handbag and took out her reading spectacles. Faintly, written under the printed heading was a short message.

'I can save your husband. You must allow me to help. This is very serious. You know that you must explore all possibilities. This is the only one. Ring me immediately. There is no time to lose.'

Save Peter! What on earth was he talking about? She knew that Peter was very close to death. Not even God could bring him back now. What nonsense! What absurd macabre nonsense! Did the man not understand the pain she was going through? Did he not comprehend her agony? Why would he torture her so with rubbish like this? And yet, and yet. Professor Merrick. Was he a real professor or just some sort of crank?

Cryogenics. Was it cryogenics? Was it salvation of the spiritual entity? Perhaps the man was a religious maniac. What on earth was the man talking about?

Sarah had an excellent brain. Perhaps she had not reached her full potential in life. There were many academic avenues that she would like to have explored but her family had been more than compensation for that. Her family was everything and she regretted not one moment of her life with Peter and the girls. She began to think of a way forward. How could she establish the credentials of the old man without having to meet with him?

Professor! If he was a professor he must have, or have had, a university. Who would know about a Professor George Merrick? Who at Bristol University, her old alma mater, would know of his field of research? Chris Adams. Yes, Chris Adams. Chris had played rugby with Peter at the university. He was younger than Peter but older than Sarah. He had been a contemporary of both. Chris worked for seven years in industry before returning to Bristol and academia. He was the one to ring. Peter had his number. He rang him occasionally.

She walked across the hallway into the study sitting at Peter's desk. She looked for the small telephone book but couldn't find it. Suddenly it came to her. The PC! Everything had been transferred to the PC. She switched on and waited impatiently. A thought flashed across her mind and she clicked the Internet icon.

Professor George Merrick she typed. The result amazed her. She sat her eyes transfixed to the screen. There was a picture of the man. It was the same man. Much younger but the same man for sure. There he stood at a pedestal, on a stage, the proud recipient of the Nobel Prize for chemistry.

A Nobel Prize winner at the hospital? Why would a Nobel Prize winner stop her in a corridor? And why was he so insistent that he needed to speak to her?

She looked at his resume. It was amazing. The man was a genius. The things he had invented and discovered was astonishing. Why had she not heard of him?

She picked up the telephone and rang Chris Adams. Chris was an ebullient chap who teased Sarah about having married the wrong man. It was just as well that his wife, Charlotte, understood the game they played.

'Chris Adams here. Who is speaking please?' the man with the Constable Country accent asked.

'Hi Chris, this is Sarah.'

Chris sighed, waiting to be told of the death of his dear friend Peter.

'Hi Sarah. How are you?' he said instantly regretting his stupidity.

'Chris, I want to ask you something. Something that may, or may not, be of importance. Perhaps I'm being stupid. I don't know. I don't think that I know anything anymore.'

'Tell me. Anything that I can do, you know?' he replied, breathing hard and beginning to feel hot under the collar.

'Professor George Merrick. What do you know of him?' she asked.

Now Chris Adams had thought of many things that dear Sarah Fossard might say to him on this particular occasion but that was not one of them.

'George Merrick? *The* George Merrick? Oh, well oh. I mean, well let's see, er. How do I begin? Why?'

'I don't want to be rude Chris but if you could just give me a short synopsis', she implored.

Was he really having this conversation or was this a surreal narcoleptic episode? It was only yesterday that he had read how widespread narcolepsy was. Charlotte asked him if he would like a glass of sherry. He shrugged his shoulders at her and said, 'A large brandy please. It's Sarah on the phone', he offered.

'Give her all my love', said Charlotte with some feeling and handed him an extra-large brandy. He threw it down in one.

'Sarah, George Merrick is one of the geniuses of the twentieth century. He was a student and don at Cambridge. A double first I believe. He was a child genius. He devoted his entire life to science. No family. He never married.

There was a rumour that he had a tragic love affair or had been rejected and took it badly. Something akin to that no doubt. So anyway he devoted his life or re-devoted his life to science. Cutting edge man and on so many fronts. Only Conan Doyle and he have fitted so much into one lifetime. How sad that when he goes all that goes with him.'

He instantly recognised his faux pas.

'I'm sorry Sarah. Me and my big mouth. You know me. As tactless as they come. Look I don't know what this is about but would you like me to ...?'

'No. I'm going to the hospital to see Peter now. Thank you for your help Chris. You don't need to apologise and we all hold you very dearly in our hearts. All my very best to Charlotte. I must go', she said, barely making it to the end of the sentence.

'Anything you want Sarah. All you have to do is ask', he choked.

'I know; I'll speak to you soon. Good bye', and with that she put down the receiver.

She panicked. One of the foremost brains in the world had said that he could save Peter. She knew that his fate was already sealed but she had not listened to the old man in the hospital earlier and every avenue ought to have been explored. There was a desperate need to cling to any passing straw and she had not done so. Perhaps the professor would be at the hospital. She rang the number on the card.

'Hello. This is George Merrick.', the old man's voice croaked again.

Sarah froze for a moment.

The sage answered for her. 'I hope that this is Mrs Fossard. Yes?'

Sarah came to her senses. 'Yes. You wished to speak with me Professor.'

'I see you have researched a little. Good in one sense but it has taken too long. I must see you immediately.' The excitement in his voice caused him to lose his breath. He stopped to take in a little air before asking, 'Where are you now?'

'I am about to leave for the hospital. I will be there in a little over fifteen minutes.' Sarah was caught up in the pace of the phone call and was rapidly firing her words into the phone. 'What is this all about professor?'

'There isn't time. Get here as soon as you are able please. Come to your husband's room. Come quickly. Yes?

'Yes.'

'And Mrs. Fossard. Come alone and bring both your husband's and your own passports.'

'What'? She was now beginning to believe that this could be a hoax.

Merrick's voice was curt. 'Bring them', he shouted as he slammed down the phone. He reached for his chest to ease the pain of his breathing.

Sarah threw the handset onto the bed, collected her coat from the wardrobe, two passports from the living room cabinet and ran down the stairs. The red Mercedes SLK 120 was in the driveway. She reversed down the drive sharply causing a green S Type Jaguar to swerve violently the driver shaking a cathartic unseen fist at her. The horn of the evading car blared loudly through the winter air. Perhaps the driver had found resolution. Unchecked, she pulled away, the automatic switching through the gears smoothly.

What had happened? Here she was, driving in a suit picked for the mourning of her husband and driving, not to see her dying husband, but to meet an eccentric professor who had asked her to bring passports and wished to speak to her about the offer of a miracle.

She shook her head, realising that she was now clutching at those damn straws again and broke the speed limit.

Chapter 50

METAMORPHOSIS

Sarah Fossard had always been very particular about her appearance. Not this time. Windswept she arrived at the hospital and walked quickly through the automatic doors and into the reception area. She turned right purposefully and made her way to the lift. After an interminable wait it arrived. She walked forward then stepped back apologising to those disembarking for having blocked their way.

Her pulse was racing as she stepped into the lift. She wanted the fourth floor. Surely the elderly couple who shared the lift would not want to stop before her?

'Second floor dear' asked the lady, smiling almost apologetically.

'Of course' she replied, returning her smile.

Sarah Fossard was a lady. She had been brought up to respect others, especially the elderly. Pressure or no pressure her instincts and etiquette remained intact.

The lift stopped on the second floor and the elderly couple stopped to bid Sarah a good evening. With good grace she returned in kind. At last she reached the fourth floor and the doors opened.

George Merrick stood in the corridor. He beckoned Sarah to follow him. Clearly impatient and tense he waved his hand in dismissal of her questioning face.

'Please follow me. I cannot speak until I am absolutely sure that it is safe to do so. Please.'

The old man struggled to speak. It would have been clear to Sarah that the arthritic Merrick was not used to walking at his current quick tempo, had she not been stunned by the evening's events.

George Merrick's face had a reddish purple hue and he wheezed audibly as he toiled along the corridors.

At last he reached the door to a single room and ushered her in.

Merrick held the door open and she entered turning immediately back towards the incoming professor. Her eyes met his in supplication. 'Please', she begged, dabbing at the rivulet weaving its weary path down her cheeks.

'Mrs. Fossard', a foreign voice came from behind her. She jumped.

'I am sorry to startle you so.'

The professor cut off further peripheral discussion with the unexpected and alarming third party.

'This is Walter Krantz. He is the director of a small infirmary in Germany. 'All that I have to say can wait. There is one imperative if you are to save your husband.'

'Save Peter', she screamed incredulously. 'I have spoken to the most eminent...'

'There is no time. Look at me. I can save your husband's life. There is but one way and I have it. Do you understand?'

Sarah, bent double by the emotional stream coursing through her veins, nodded meekly.

'Go on', she whispered, as though responding after a considerable punch in the solar plexus.

'Good', said Merrick. It was the voice of a spoilt intolerant child being granted a parental caprice.

'I need you to sign these release documents. We are all leaving with immediate effect. The authorities know that we are leaving. They do not, however, know why we are leaving. They believe that it is to take your husband home to die. We are not. We are taking him to Munich so that he may live. Please sign these documents here and here.' He pointed to the relevant spaces for her signature. He then pushed a buzzer on the wall and a posse of folk in white smocks entered the room, clearly having waited in the wings for the go ahead.

Professor Merrick spoke rapidly barking orders at all present. He had donned an unassailable aura and his commands and gestures were breathtakingly arrogant and pointed. He was well prepared. He glowed. This was the culmination of a lifetimes' work. This was his hour. All he had to do was get the damn man to the infirmary in Munich in time.

Sarah, still shocked, found her voice. 'His things ...'

Krantz cut her off as he left the room ... 'Are now of no use.' He looked at her for a moment and left.

Sarah decided to let events take their course. She was out of her depth and out of her mind. What the hell was happening?

Merrick barked a few further orders and the foot soldiers left the room each of them clearly well briefed.

Walter Krantz took Sarah by the arm and they walked rapidly towards the lift.

'All will be answered before we get to the plane. You have to trust the great man. Be assured your husband is in the hands of the best there is.'

'But where are we going to. He said Munich?'

Krantz smiled a lukewarm smile that made Sarah's flesh crawl. 'OK. First Bristol airport then, you are correct, Munich.' She looked to speak again but Krantz had his index finger at his lips. 'We must act first; not talk.' She relented.

Sarah was somewhat desensitised by the appalling situation but recognised a philanderer when one took her by the arm. She made a mental note not to be left alone with Krantz. He had that lounge lizard way with him that made women feel vulnerable and part of a game where their role was to be the prey. She didn't like it. She took her mobile from her bag and rang Mike Tyler as she walked along the corridors and out of the building.

'Damn', she said under her breath. Sarah was not given to oaths but she sure felt like one now. 'Damn. Where was Mike? He'd promised to be there for her and now she needed him desperately. His mobile was ringing but he wasn't answering.

Walter Krantz opened the door of the black BMW and helped Sarah into the car. Again she felt the unwelcome contact with Krantz. He watched as she swung her nyloned legs into the back seat. God, how she hated that slick urbanity that trailed lechers. She hoped that he was not to be a fellow traveller.

Krantz smiled at her and sat in front with the driver rapidly tapping directions into the satnav. 'Go', he shouted and the BMW accelerated away.

She would be breaking the speed limit twice on the same evening.

On the short trip across town to the airport she rang Mike Tyler half a dozen times. No reply. The car sped on.

The party were expected and passed through customs without delay. On the tarmac stood a Lear Jet. They got out of the car and walked towards it. Was she really going to Munich? Where was Peter? How was he to travel? What was to happen at the other side? There were so many imponderables. Was this a calamitous misjudgement? She couldn't handle it.

An elderly female medic descended the steps of the jet and approached her. 'Hello. Come with me', she offered politely in a light German accent. 'I'm Sylvia. I will be travelling with you. She took Sarah by the arm and assisted her to climb the steps into the jet.

The Lear 45 Jet was the largest light jet in service. It had a cruising speed of 534 miles per hour and a range of 2,100 miles, plenty of miles in hand for the journey. As Sarah walked into the five-foot wide cabin she noted that the four rear seats had been converted into two beds. There was a further four seats ahead and she was shown to the front starboard one by a handsome young man in a blue uniform with a surfeit of gold braiding. 'Please', he said as he conveyed her to her seat. He smiled and left for the cabin. She sunk into the deep upholstered cream leather seat still shaking.

Sylvia Ergbruder offered Sarah what she believed to be a glass of water and a mild sedative. Mild it was not! She accepted it gratefully and was asleep within the minute.

Chapter 51

FELIX TRAVELS FROM BRISTOL TO MUNICH

The helicopter taking Felix Elder's body to hospital had three men on board; the pilot, a medic and the crazy guy who had abseiled down to the ledge on which Felix had come to rest. This was not the regular crew. These were the employees of one Sir Nicholas Hansen.

Felix Elder's brain had ceased to function. He was clinically dead; in a vegetative state. The hospital came on the line to the pilot enquiring about the nature of the injuries to ensure that the appropriate staff and theatre was made available if necessary.

The pilot responded. 'No problems Bristol, just a few scrapes and bruises. Over.'

Bristol came back. 'Lucky man. What's your ETA, over?'

'We don't have one Bristol. He reckons he's OK and is not coming in. Sounds like a real hard case. We have tried to insist but he's having none of it. It's just like fishing. We've caught a big one but we had to let it go. Over.'

The airwaves buzzed with activity for several minutes before Bristol accepted the man's right to go where he wanted to go. Where he actually went was Munich. Sir Nicholas had repaid his debt to the professor in full.

Chapter 52

WALTER KRANTZ ABDUCTS JULIA SALOMONOVICH

Julia Salomonovich had decided to drive to Koblenz. The journey to Harwich took less than twenty minutes and the ferry time six hours to the Hook of Holland. She had left the Manor House at six a.m. and took the 6:45 ferry. She had left the Dutch port by 2 p.m. local time. The journey to Koblenz would take a further three and a half hours. She crossed the Netherlands and was, as always pleased to pass by Venlo and into Germany. Many of the Dutch spoke English but Julia spoke German fluently and felt very much more at home there. She skirted Monchengladbach taking the E35 just south of Cologne, and then followed the autobahn southeast past Bonn following the Rhine towards Koblenz. Gerhard lived in Montabaur now, approximately ten miles northeast of Koblenz. She would arrive in time for the evening meal.

Half an hour short of her destination she stopped at a familiar Rasthof, just north of Dierdorf. She had always called Gerhard half an hour before her arrival as a courtesy. She noted the black Porsche pulling into the car park behind her and one of the two men leaving it and making his way to the toilets at the rear of the building. Was it her imagination? Did she always have a black Porsche in her rear view mirror? It certainly felt like it on her past three visits to Germany. Still Germany was teeming with black Porsches. She turned away from the bright lights and took her phone from her bag.

As always Julia had pulled in well away from the facilities. She hated the places. Yes, German Rasthofs were a thousand times better than the appalling British motorway service cafes but still she had never felt sufficiently desperate to eat while travelling.

Folk have a sixth sense when things are about to implode and Gerhard was no exception. 'Julia, I'm so pleased that you have come but is everything alright?' he enquired hopefully. 'Oh Gerhard I'm so close', she answered, partially betraying her motive for her journey. 'Not now. I'll see you in a short time. OK?' There was no reply and Julia snapped her phone shut as she saw the black Porsche retake the autobahn.

Julia sighed and walked to the rear of her silver BMW. She lifted the boot to take out a bottle of Evian water. It was her last conscious thought. An arm came from behind her and she spun around into the embrace of Walter Krantz. To a distant observer it may well have looked like a father kissing his daughter goodbye before seeing her into his car. The reality was that a chloroformed handkerchief had covered Julia's nose and mouth until she had succumbed.

Krantz took Julia to the passenger door, opened it and sat her in the seat, swinging her legs in then closing the door. Within seconds he was driving along the autobahn. They followed the black Porsche for a few miles before pulling off at Ausfahrt 37. The Porsche continued along the autobahn for a further two hundred metres before inexplicably exploding. There would be no witnesses to relate the fate of Julia Salomonovich.

Later that evening Walter Krantz drove Julia's car to a remote spot near the infirmary and met George Merrick. The professor stared at the young woman for some time before Krantz said, 'Professor, er George, we must move quickly.'

They took hold of Julia and swung her from her own car into the rear seat of the hired car. Krantz wedged a large stone under the accelerator of her BMW and, standing with one foot on the ground outside the car and the other on the clutch pointed the car at a distant bend jumped clear. The car accelerated into a granite wall of rock at a little over sixty miles per hour. The architects of the accident followed the BMW and approached the hissing wreck with caution.

Krantz found difficulty in opening the driver's door but eventually did so exiting the car holding the large stone. He threw it deep into the forest and returned to George. George and Walter Krantz nodded to each other pleased with their endeavour. They returned to the hired car and George pulled away sedately confident that they had been unobserved.

At the village, less than a mile ahead, Krantz got out and collected his own car, from a public car park. George waited fifteen minutes before following Walter to the infirmary.

Anyone enquiring about Walter Krantz's day would be informed that he had taken a day off work and only returned to the infirmary in the evening.

Professor George Merrick had arrived at the place desperately seeking help for a young woman who had had a car accident down the road. To all intents and purposes he had never been to the place before.

Julia Salomonovich and Felix Elder were now guests of Professor George Merrick and Walter Krantz. The last guest had yet to arrive.

Chapter 53

THE FOSSARDS LAND IN MUNICH

Two hours after Walter Krantz had returned from the Rhineland with Julia the Lear jet landed in Munich. Peter and Sarah Fossard were placed on stretchers and within minutes were racing to the infirmary each in newly registered black Mercedes vans.

Sarah stirred and was given an injection. It was easier that way. To an observer two casualties had left the Lear on stretchers. After three kilometres the cars stopped. Peter was trolleyed into the back of a waiting ambulance and Sarah was bundled into a dark green Range Rover. A blindfold was placed over her eyes and smelling salts under her nose.

She reacted dramatically coughing and shaking her head. She reached up to remove the blindfold from her face. Two hands gently restrained her.

'I'm afraid that we are obliged to take precautions Mrs. Fossard', came Krantz's all too near and familiar voice. 'I hope that you do not mind. It is for your own good, believe me', he whispered in her ear.

She knew the type and guessed that his eyes would be straying. She folded her arms and hunched forward wondering what the hell had happened to her since she boarded the jet.

'Have I slept? Are we in Germany? When will I know what is happening? For God's sake this is unbearable.' She broke down and sobbed uncontrollably.

She regretted it immediately as Krantz put his arm around her as if to comfort her. She shrugged him off with, 'Please, I will be alright soon. Just let me be.'

Krantz' arm had acted as a wakeup call. Sarah found a new resolve. She would be pragmatic. She steeled herself. No more whimpering. Enough self- pity!

'Thank you', she said regaining her composure and moving away from the aging lothario.

The Range Rover had slowed and was encountering rougher and steeper terrain. The ambulance followed it up the steep incline. Forty minutes after leaving the jet, and three and a half hours after leaving the hospital in Bristol, they had arrived at the infirmary located between Munich and Augsburg.

As they entered the building Krantz removed Sarah's blindfold. Florescent tubes lit the reception area brightly and she blinked as her eyes adjusted to the unforgiving light.

'Where is Peter? How is he?' she enquired of Krantz as the ambulance entered the entrance to the rear of the infirmary. Krantz had an earpiece fitted and was clearly in contact with others. He ceased issuing orders.

'He is as well as he was when we left. There is no imminent danger.'

'No imminent danger', thought Sarah. 'He's at death's door.' She tempered her response. 'I must see him immediately. Please.'

Krantz turned towards her as they walked down a short dark corridor. They stopped. 'Within twenty minutes you will have seen your husband and his future will be in your hands, I assure you. 'But you must be patient for just a few minutes more. Soon the professor will answer all your questions. Just a few more moments.'

He pushed open the adjacent door open and waived her through. She looked deep into Krantz's eyes looking for answers. Nothing! She walked through the door.

Chapter 54

DEAD OR ALIVE?

Sarah Fossard sat nursing a hot polystyrene cup of latte. She looked for Sylvia. No sign. All the personnel were different. There was much activity but the British side of the operation had clearly remained in Britain or, at least, disappeared from view. She recognised only Walter Krantz. 'And where was the nutty professor?' she thought.

She didn't have to think for long. Professor George Merrick emptied himself into the room with his familiar awkward gait. 'Please follow me', he instructed; not waiting for a response. Sarah and Walter Krantz complied.

Sarah was fading fast. She needed some semblance of normality. Above all she needed Peter. 'What next? How many more doors? How many more ...?'

They entered a small softly lit room where Peter lay. He had been out for several hours but had 'opportunely' awoken.

'Sarah', he moaned almost deliriously. She came within the compass of his rapidly deteriorating eyesight.

She held his tiny hand. 'I'm here sweetheart, I'm here my darling.' She brought his hand slowly to her face.

Merrick began. 'What I have to say to you is not for the ears of any other. I cannot begin without your complete agreement upon this point.'

Sarah nodded and recognised that Peter was not considered to be in on any decision making process going by the professor's body language. She was determined that he would be.

'This, as you know, is Walter Krantz; he is the director of this privately run infirmary. The infirmary has research laboratories and, for many months, they have been made available to me by a certain organisation. Enough of that. To the point. I have a proposition to make to you. It will astound you and I therefore, recommend that you do not react hastily or without considering the content and the full extent of my discourse. Do not leap to conclusions or dismiss my offer until you have heard me through and comprehended its ramifications.'

Sarah hadn't turned towards the professor as he spoke and he recognising the significance of that he deferred to her obdurate insistence that the central character in the decision making was to be Peter.

He turned to Peter frustrated at the banalities of lesser mortals and began again.

'What I am about to offer you ought to take long and careful thought but, not to put too fine a point on it, you do not have that time for that.

Sarah thought that statement unnecessarily cruel and looked hard at the professor. Did he not recognise his insensitivity?

He turned to her. 'No more', he said, 'We must speak frankly and act boldly. You must understand the timescale.'

'Sir', he said, ensuring that he turned occasionally to Peter but still directing his words at Sarah. 'We believe you to have no more than thirty-six hours. If you have not decided within four hours to agree to my proposition I cannot help you. I believe that all will be lost. This is the procedure. I will speak. Please do not interrupt me until I have finished, no matter how fabulous the proposition may be.' He turned again to Peter. You may tire sir. If you do I trust that you will put your faith in your wife and allow her to make any decisions on your behalf. I am sure that she has your trust and your welfare at heart. Do I have that affirmation?' Peter nodded almost imperceptibly.

'Good', the professor continued as he began to pace the room. Sarah shot a withering glace at him as she recognised that Peter would be unable to track his path. He rarely relented but expediency was an imperative and he returned to the bedside. 'I'm sorry', he smiled, looking first at Peter and then Sarah. Noting Sarah's nod of acceptance of his weak apology, he went on.

'I told you that I was going to be frank', he said. Sarah braced herself. 'Your body cannot be repaired. It will never work again. Within two days it will cease to function. Termination is inevitable.'

Sarah looked aghast. The callous, clinical pronouncement of Peter's death could not have been clearer. She had been told not to interrupt but then again she had also been told that Peter was going to be made well again. Was this just a cruel, elaborate, sadistic joke? The professor's indifference to Peter's feelings was the final straw. She began to protest.

Merrick's hand was in her face waiving away her protestations. 'I said enough. You must listen if you are to save your husband.'

Sarah was stunned. Now he was going to be saved! What the hell! 'God help me.' The punch bag slumped. Her innards twisting, her body aching as she fought to keep a grip on her sanity.

'Have you heard of transmutation?'

'Yes, of course', she gathered herself, remembering her university days.

Now she was frightened 'Don't tell me we have an alchemist amongst us. God, no, not a crank', she thought

'I see I have someone before me with a little knowledge, which is often, as I am sure you know more than a little dangerous. Let me tell you that that, indeed, in my experience, it is often far more dangerous than having no knowledge at all. I anticipated your scepticism however.' The professor was driven by a powerful urge to act out the dramatic revelation of his accumulated knowledge.

It was Mark Antony that rose in the Roman Forum, appearing by kind permission of Brutus. He prepared to deliver his skilful rhetoric to the baying crowd. Firstly he would illustrate his good intent to his would be, fellow travellers. Secondly, having captured his listener's ears, it was essential that he incrementally dismember the practices of his foes. Lastly he would point out that he had contributed to the enlightenment of society and that he was virtuous by having done so.

Then, and only then could he credibly present his solution to Sarah.

'Fear not. I am not about to deliver a treatise on Christian Rosencrantz, and the alchemical. Sulphur, salt and mercury have I none. Such are the incongruous materials of cult and mysticism. You cannot believe that I would deal with the patently absurd. I am a man of science; a man of mathematics, physics and biochemistry.' He paused and looked at Sarah, pointedly ignoring both Peter and Walter Krantz. He knew where the decision lay.

Sarah Bennett had been an astute young girl. Sarah Fossard was an astute wife and mother. She saw that Merrick was pitching the ball straight at her and herself alone. She was the target audience and no amount of prompting was going to change that. She stared on in fascination feeling that the professor was one step, or perhaps a whole flight of steps ahead of her. He probably knew what she had just thought and that … It was no good second-guessing this guy. She knew only too well that she was out of his intellectual league and that he would have all the bases covered. He was impressive. Even in the drum tight pernicious atmosphere of the room she saw him as many had seen him before: a formidable opponent and a driven genius. God he was as impressive as he was awful.

He allowed her the time to think the thoughts that he knew her to be rationalising; then went on. 'Yes. I want you to put away all such foolish thought and concentrate on what I say, and only on that. Do not draw hasty conclusions. Think of the ramifications. Many will not occur to you immediately. Some will come in time; others will not manifest themselves until they are being experienced. Many may not be recognised until sometime after they have been experienced.'

He saw her bewilderment. 'Stay with me.'

The maestro took centre stage. He had no libretto and he certainly wasn't acting.

He began: 'There are many people who present dissertations and doctoring to the world either academically or informally. There is often wisdom and a core of validity in their conclusions. They pique our interest and arouse our senses. Often the research is well disciplined, perspicacious

193

and has a certain sagacity. Rarely is it enlightening and important. When it is; oh what joy. But a rara avis. George Merrick's trance like demeanour added gravitas to the delivery.

'Pure research must start with a clean slate. Unknown in politics and a rare too during recent years where the big buck, celebrity and fame appear to be the craved grail. Many begin their research with entrenched views and are burdened by dogma. They barrage us with an avalanche of illusion and metaphor. We hear a ragbag of clichés most of them nigh on incomprehensible. Their apocalyptic predictions, replete with emotive montages, have scant regard for fact. If we are prepared to take the dubious leaps of faith that they offer us we are transported into transcendental consciousness that is a dangerous cocktail for the uneducated. The obduracy and intractability of these superficial characters tender us the unrealistic and the unobtainable. How credible is the assumption that this or that product is good for us? How credible is sponsored research? How credible I ask you? We are asked to suspend belief in what we know to be true, honest, just and right and to follow the conman, the charlatan and the quack. I categorically and vehemently denounce them. The bitter irony is that not only do they make fools of so many but that they also put the genuine article under suspicion.'

End of part one. The demolition of his fellow scientists.

'I have a very different offering', he continued. What I am shortly to present to you is the distillation of a lifetimes' work. My classic, nay, my quintessential opus. I have adduced the evidence over many years. It is irrefutable. Only the constraints of technology have hindered my progress.'

'I will add here that I have an unblemished reputation and that my work has, and will, continue to change the world. I am not a boffin who satisfies himself with personal enlightenment' an old duffer who learns so much and shares so little. My work benefits mankind.' He paused to allow the impact of his wisdom to permeate Sarah's consciousness.

'Only Walter and myself know of the information that I am about to impart. In years to come the world will know of it.'

Walter Krantz's had been named and though, normally, Sarah would look in the direction of someone mentioned in her company, out of politeness, she did not. She was transfixed, as anyone would be, by the naked power, the persuasive, fervent, tenacious and unrelenting fire of Merrick's delivery. Krantz hadn't noticed the discourtesy either. He knew the broad content of the professor's essay but he too was caught up by in the passionate intensity of the missive to notice.

End of part two. His own unique qualities and magnificent references had been submitted.

Initially Sarah was sharing her attention between Peter and the amazing rhetoric of the professor but now, even in Peter's hour of need, the professor held her undivided attention for the whole of his soliloquy. She felt guilty at her neglect. Peter's eyes were closed. A slight movement of his thumb told her that he was still with her.

Professor Merrick had mesmerised Sarah, so powerful was his dramatic denunciation of cant, humbug and the unworthy. So incredibly compelling had been his advocacy of his own work that the riveting vividness of his discourse had distracted her from her dying husband. She felt ashamed.

Merrick noted her sentiments. 'But alas', he said, 'The unpalatable fact is that nothing is shaped in the crucible of debate and rhetoric.' In a fit of righteous fury he seethed. 'Indeed much of my criticism bares that very motif. You may ask; is the money and time spent on my research worth it when so much needs to be achieved in the world? I will answer that the human cost is incalculable and that none of that was my doing. I feel no moral anguish. Is it reprehensible to spend so much money on such an enterprise? What of this fiscal insanity? I will answer that my faculty's patron has spent more on Beluga and champagne than I have spent on my research. This is the pinnacle of my achievements. No other person has stretched the boundaries of science more than I.'

Peter groaned and the nurse was called. He resisted the shot of morphine recognising that he may well not hear the rest of the story if he took it. The nurse left, Krantz giving an imperceptible nod to dismiss her.

Peter spoke in a wheezing staccato voice. 'What is this about? What is going on?'

Sarah touched his brow and smiled helplessly. She turned to the professor intending to ask for the diatribe to end. To indicate that she had the gist of his coruscating discourse, but he cut her short.

'I will explain in simple terms. Do I have your attention?' Sarah remained his audience.

'I prefaced my remarks by asking you to think of the ramifications. I also noted your face when I used the word transmutation and the shame you felt at neglecting your husband, even for a few seconds. If you love your husband, and that is patently apparent, you will do precisely as I suggest.'

Merrick braced himself. Sarah noted the increased gravitas once again and took a deep breath. This must be big if it was going to top that which had preceded it.

'What I am about to impart is for your ears only. Transmutation, as you appear to be aware, concerns the anatomical change of substances. Sarah stared at the professor. 'I see I do have your attention Mrs. Fossard. The common perception is that the old alchemists sought to change lead into gold. I regret to inform you that my research has nothing to do with that particular art.'

'All research must be tried and tested. It was true that I said that all my work has been tried and tested but there are levels of testing are there not?' The question was rhetorical and the professor moved on.

'I have recorded one hundred percent success with mice, rats, cats, dogs and a chimpanzee.' Sara noted the singular in the latter animal listed. George Merrick noted that she had.

'So what you are suggesting is that Peter will act as a guinea pig?

'Precisely. But what is the choice?' At last he turned to Peter. 'I can offer him the opportunity to see his grandchildren grow up. To look after his wife in her old age. He can guarantee her security long after he would have died naturally. I cannot offer him life in the body he has, that is beyond repair, but I can offer him a new life in another.

As the professor leaned over the bed talking to Peter, Walter Krantz was looking at Sarah. This was not his usual leer; he was looking intently to examine her reaction to the proposition.

Sarah was shocked beyond belief. She swooned and the anticipating Krantz placed a chair behind her.

'Thank you Walter', said the professor, in a matter of fact way, belying the atmosphere in the room.

'I trust you are giving serious consideration to my proposition', he resumed. 'I want the questions to come from you. We have a little time it seems.' The statement clearly indicated the opposite and that time was of the essence. The effect on Sarah was exactly as Merrick had anticipated. He was squeezing the last vestiges of resistance from Sarah. The coup de gras was not far away.

A thought flashed across Sarah's mind. 'Who?' she asked.

'Who indeed', he countered. 'Think. Perhaps it could have been Einstein, Mozart or Leonardo in another age. Imagine the possibilities. To save genius and place it in the body of a young and fit body.' Krantz recognised that he had failed to mention the possibilities of transmuting another Hitler or Stalin and the abuses that advanced science always brought along with it.

Sarah could not have foreseen this. She had searched her memory for medical homeopathic and faith healing revelations. She had imagined several possibilities but not this. Her mind was working overtime and she knew that the professor was scrutinising her face to assess when she would be up to pace with developments. She repeated. Who?'

Merrick and Krantz looked at each other and then at Sarah.

Merrick spoke, 'That is the catch. We had hoped to find someone not dissimilar to your husband. We have not been able to do so.'

'You must have someone or there would not be any purpose to our being here', Sarah whispered, desperately attempting to rationalise the situation and finding it impenetrable. She saw that Peter was in pain and recognised that time was short indeed. His lungs had begun to make the dreadful wheezing noise that heralds the end. The death rattle had begun. He would, she thought, be dead within twenty-four hours.

'More like twelve', said Professor George Merrick.

Sarah stared in disbelief once again. The professor knew her every thought. He wasn't that flight of steps in front of her that she had believed earlier; he was in another dimension. George Merrick had calculated her every thought. He had been through the logical processes that her mind would follow. She was educated. She was rational. She was sensible. He knew what she would think. All options had been considered and plotted. She was following his particular path as precisely as he had believed she would.

Sarah was thinking of the new man that Peter was to be. Would he be old or young, handsome or not so handsome, tall or small, black or white? Oh, educated or ... for the second time within a few minutes she felt ashamed.

What was she thinking? Was it what Peter wanted? Could it really be successful? Did that matter anyway? How would Peter cope?

'There are too many questions that do not have answers are there not, my dear?' It was the first time that George Merrick had used familiar language in her presence. If the truth were known, it was only one of the rare times that he had ever used it. He took both of Sarah's hands in his. You are exhausted and confused but we must make a decision very soon. We will leave you to discuss our proposition. I know only too well. It is life or death.' He turned to Peter. 'The choice is yours sir. I must now go to check if there is a need to make adjustments to our affairs. I will answer your remaining questions when I return.'

Sarah turned to Merrick. She looked him in the eye, a considerable feat in itself.' Who?' She said pointedly.

'That's the problem, said Krantz. People don't line up to be donors for our programme you understand. First our donor must have a functioning body. Secondly the donor must be free of disease and heart trouble; there is no point in transmuting to a donor who is likely to die. We won't get volunteers from the general public. There are, I imagine, very few folk walking about with full body donor cards in their pockets. I have been able to finance the good professor for some time now and we have been most diligent and proactive but, in the absence of a Burke and Hare kind of organisation, I suspect that we are going to have to take what comes when a subject such as Peter comes along. We do not have a catalogue for you to peruse.'

Sarah's imagination ran rife. Again she knew that the professor had registered that it had.

George Merrick stopped at the door. 'I will leave you with one last thought. People are what they because of what they think, what they believe and what they value. They are the sum of their relationships, their experiences and their memories. A man of eighty would not have married his wife of eighty had he been twenty at the time. No, they love each other because they were young together and shared their lives. When someone dies, all that is left to their loved ones are memories.'

Krantz continued in his less than poetic style. 'The only donor we can use is one who is in a vegetative state. As I said, we won't get volunteers. The body must be fully functioning. Ideally it will be a healthy body. The brain and its patterns, the long term memory blocks, the mind and the soul if you like, may not function but as long as there is no neurological damage we have an acceptable donor.'

'There is a further problem of course', said the professor.

'And that is?' enquired Sarah, barely believing that she had.

'Permission from the donor or a relative,' explained Krantz.

She should have seen that one coming. 'Oh yes of course. And you have someone?' She said.

'We have one and one only. As you can imagine we have scoured the world for information of others but no luck so far.'

'Why are you still searching? Is it for others or is there something that you are not telling me about the man you have? Is he a psychopath or something?

'That would not matter', said the professor, who was stood at the door with Krantz, holding the handle and ready to leave. 'The man would have a whole new set of thought and memories. No the fact is that we don't have a man.' He paused before dropping his bombshell. 'We only have a woman.'

Sarah gaped at the two men as they closed the door behind them. It was a good thirty seconds or more before she closed her mouth and looked down at Peter for help. Peter could not assist her now. He was falling away rapidly. His breathing had become increasingly strained and the nurse, who had entered the room immediately after the two men had left, patted Sarah on the arm with the assurance of many years' experience. She injected morphine.

'How long?' asked Sarah.

'Frau Fossard, we do not talk in term of time.'

'How long?' she repeated.

'I could get into trouble and I really can't say with any certainty', she whispered.

'What is your name', she enquired.

'I am Nurse Gudrun Hackemann', she replied

'Guess Gudrun, please guess,' she implored.

'Hours I think. I am going home soon. It is six o'clock. I would be surprised to see him with us tomorrow. I am so very sorry. You did press me.' Sarah nodded her agreement. 'I will leave you with your husband now.' The nurse squeezed Sarah's arm to offer further comfort. Please push the button if you need anything. Would you like coffee or tea?'

'Thank you, but no', replied Sarah. 'I am very grateful to you.' She turned to the comatose Peter and whispered. 'You've left me and now I have to make the decision alone. It's so cruel. Why? Why? Why? It is so unfair. What can I do? If I say no – you die. If I say yes…' She broke down for the umpteenth time that evening despite her resolution to stand firm and do the best that she could for Peter.

Gudrun Hackemann was relieved to get out of the room. She reported directly to Walter Krantz as she had been instructed to do.

Krantz smiled. He looked across at the professor.

'It is so small', remarked Krantz, nodding towards a device connected to a laptop on the trolley he was pushing. 'The computer to which it is attached is small too', replied the professor as he continued to adjust the apparatus. 'How big should it be Walter? What size vessel accommodates a megabyte or a gigabyte; or a million gigabytes come to that?'

Krantz floundered. 'Quite', was all that the professor offered. 'We have given them the allotted time to stew on their dilemma. 'The coup-de-gras is nigh I believe.

Peter was fading fast when Gudrun Hackemann returned to the room some fifteen minutes later. She feigned to check the apparatus, recorded something on the chart at the end of the bed, smiled at Sarah reassuringly, and then left.

She reported back to Walter Krantz that Peter Fossard was deteriorating rapidly and that Sarah was in urgent need of assistance. She turned smartly on her heels ready to return to lend support to Sarah.

'Thank you', said Krantz, halting her progress. 'You have worked diligently. I see that you are tired and are in need of a break. I have arranged cover for you. You can take your break now. You will not be required for another hour.'

'But Herr Director', she objected, 'I.'

Krantz cut her off.

'Please, we will see you presently.'

Gudrun Hackemann was a professional and was more than put out at being informed that she would not be required at such a critical time. She considered the situation and decided that it would be unwise to argue with the director in front of the strange professor. She left for the refectory determined to confront Walter Krantz at the first opportunity.

Krantz unlocked the door next to Peter Fossard's room and entered.

There on a trolley bed laid a beautiful young woman. She wore a white smock. They were ready. Only the disintegrating Fossards were left to be dealt with.

Sarah Fossard sat holding her husband's hand. She didn't move as the professor approached her.

It was the George Merrick who broke the silence after a few 'respectful' seconds. 'It is time. The decision was not so difficult was it? What were the alternatives? Death and an eternity without your beloved husband. Seriously - Death? Could you really choose that for him? I think not. Yes, there is only one answer and, before you ask, we do not have a late arrival. It is time. There is no turning back.'

Sarah hadn't finally made her decision until that moment but the professor's measured words and certainty somehow reassured her.

'You always seem to know best professor', she uttered hoarsely, now totally disarmed. The psychological attack had been clinical.

'It will be necessary for you to leave the room I am afraid.'

Sarah was about to object but again that same authoritative hand waived her away and so she turned to look at what remained of Peter Fossard, her one true love; her husband. This was it. If she did not agree, he died. If the experiment failed he died. If the experiment worked he would look so different and the consequences of her decision may lead to God knows what.

She was defeated and could take no more.

Sarah opened the door to leave. Walter Krantz stood outside the door with a trolley bed. A white linen sheet covered the clear profile of the body that lay upon it. 'Please', she almost begged. Krantz hesitated but relented and granted her request. He pulled the sheet aside and Sarah swooned as she looked down on the beautiful face of Julia Salomonovich. Immune to further horrors she lowered her head and walked away utterly defeated. It would be some time before she reflected on that dreadful scene; before she questioned why the director of such an august establishment pushed beds around his own infirmary.

She made her way along the short corridor to the rest room sat down and took the last tissue from her bag. Her mind was in turmoil. The condition of the woman on the trolley bed was worse. She was about to lose her mind.

Sarah needed more tissues and walked back along the corridor towards the operating room. Again that was strange. It wasn't an operating room! There was no one around. That, in itself, was odd. The corridor had appeared busy a little earlier. Perhaps the nurse was in another room with a patient. She retraced her steps to the small kitchenette by the rest room and fed the coffee machine. The place was silent. How many hospitals were silent?

She called out, 'Is anyone there?' There was no response. She resolved to open the adjacent door. The room was empty save for a bed and cabinet. She tried the next door. That was locked.

'Entchuldigen darf ich Sie helfen', came a voice from immediately behind her. The coffee cup and saucer dropped to the floor as she jumped in fright; her right hand holding her chest as she caught her breath.

The janitor was very old and smiled at her with broken teeth.

'Bitte', he said indicating that he wished to pass her.

Sarah had a passing acquaintance with the German language but this was not going to be a time for her to use it. She returned to the rest room and sat.

She remembered her mobile and attempted to contact Mike Tyler but couldn't get a signal. The old janitor cleared up the mess Sarah had made when dropping the coffee and smiled as he passed her on his way out. Sarah smiled the smile that the relatives of the terminally ill or injured give to others. Polite but dreadful, empty and forlorn.

Her mind took her back over many years and, as she reminisced, a thunderbolt struck her. Merrick had said that they would. What had he said? Think of the ramifications. Many will not occur to you immediately. Some will come with time; others will not manifest themselves until they are being experienced. Some may not be recognised until long after they have been experienced.

This one had been recognised. Sarah had thought of her two daughters, Chloe and Lucy. 'My God', she whispered, 'What have I done? Faust! My God. Faust! I've sold Peter's soul to the very devil himself.

She struggled with the concept of her daughter's relationship with a young woman who was their father. Was the young woman younger than her daughters? Would they accept him? How would they introduce her to their family and friends? Her family and friends? Mike Tyler? Chris Adams? Merrick had foreseen all of this. He knew.

She burst into tears and sobbed her heart out. There was no one to there to comfort her.

After twenty minutes Peter's door opened. She walked to it quickly. Walter Krantz wheeled the trolley past her as she arrived. The professor was closing the door.

'Tell me', she implored him. She grabbed his arms and begged, 'Please.'

Professor George Merrick was not used to failure. He was not arrogant; he was merely certain that if he had said something would occur then it surely would.

He said, slightly baffled but unhurt, 'You did not doubt me did you? Of course the procedure went as I expected it to. Oh yes, quite as I had anticipated.'

This was hardly the compassionate and informative response that Sarah had hoped to elicit. She had no idea how to respond. She lifted her head slowly and stared into George Merrick's watery old, demonic eyes.

'And Peter?'

'Now that is something that we must come to terms with Mrs. Fossard. When you say Peter to whom do you refer? If you mean the body of the man who was your husband I regret to inform you that it has ceased to function and, as such, is no more,' She flinched at the cold, callous, dispassionate delivery of his words. She felt feint as he took her by the arm.

He continued, 'However if you mean the spirit and soul of your husband she is convalescing and is as well as can be expected in the circumstances. She is asleep and needs rest. You will be able to visit her very soon and then, very shortly, we must be prepared to travel again.

'But', she began.

'No buts. All is well. Has not everything that I predicted come to be?' He didn't wait for an answer. Sarah knew that every word he had spoken was true but she had yet to encounter Peter in his new guise and she craved first hand evidence. But the professor was always right and he exuded competence and precision and she needed him to support her so much that she complied without further interruption. She walked to the rest room and crumpled into the armchair.

Walter Krantz arrived at the coffee machine and brought a latte to her. She thanked him.

She thought of Faust. What was the price? Had she sold Peter to the devil? Where were they going to next? Why were they moving? Where were the personnel? She couldn't handle it at all. Suddenly she felt very tired, Walter Krantz's voice became incoherent her vision blurred and she slipped into a deep sleep.

Walter Krantz served a strong 'mild sedative.' He had lingered by the coffee machine talking to her until Sarah slumped and had succumbed to the drug. He picked her up in his arms, pleased that her face fell against his own. He could see her breasts gently rising as she breathed deeply and that old feeling began to course through his veins once more. 'Behave yourself Walter' he thought. 'Not long now and then I shall have all the time in the world.' He put her down on the bed in the room that Sarah had found empty. 'What a pity. Just a little too old but a beauty just the same. She would have made an excellent patient twenty-five years ago. She must have been very sexy when she was young.' He reached down to the hem of her skirt and pulled it down over her knees. 'What a pity', he repeated to himself as he left the room.

Sarah Fossard had been sedated for the journey to come. Walter Krantz was grateful that she had been. It had been a mistake to wheel Julia Salomonovich in as she had left the room; he should have checked that she had left beforehand. It had also been a mistake to allow Sarah Fossard a look under the sheet too. He considered it unwise to inform the professor of his unfortunate indiscretions.

It was out of character for the professor to be anxious, but he was. Walter Krantz noticed the beads of perspiration on his brow as he entered the room. The professor noted that he had.

'I will run through it one more time Walter. Let us bring the second donor into the room as we talk. There must be no mishaps. Krantz unlocked the door of the adjacent room.

Have the travel arrangement been activated?' Krantz nodded as they wheeled out a young man on a trolley bed into the corridor then into the 'operating' room. 'The two women will be picked up and taken to the 'other place' within the next few minutes. Sarah Fossard has been sedated for the journey. Julia Salomonovich will be sedated too after you have examined her. I hope that that this will not take long George. It will take, perhaps, some hours for them to get to Innsbruck. It is beginning to snow quite heavily.'

The professor had not known about the snow. 'This must not change anything', he said, clearly concerned that an incalculable was now manifest. He looked into Krantz's face and waited for confirmation. Krantz shook his head.

'Good', the professor said recognising the hesitancy in Krantz's voice. 'One last point: I trust that Peter Fossard's autopsy has been organised and that a speedy cremation will follow. Loose ends my dear boy. Loose ends! We ignore them at our peril.'

Krantz gave assurances that all was well once again, partially to convince himself. The professor sensed that there was something disturbing Krantz.

'The snow Walter. It worries you? Is that it?'

Krantz nodded. It can be bad at this time of year George and the forecast is not good.'

George Merrick screwed his eyes tight as he examined Krantz's face. There is little we can do about the weather Walter.' He looked hard at his partner once again. 'You will be sure to inform me if there are any further problems.' He held Walter Krantz's face for a moment before moving on.

Is everything well Walter? I mean everything? I need to know now if it is not so.' Krantz nodded. 'It is just that we are so close now but do not worry; I will keep my nerve. You can be sure of that.'

George Merrick had never left anything to chance. He calculated and he executed; he didn't gamble. Walter Krantz could become a liability.

'I want you to check Sarah Fossard, the body of Peter Fossard, the staff and the other patients Walter; one last check before the demise of Professor George Merrick. A troubled Walter Krantz left to do the professor's bidding. Still the professor felt uneasy about any 'loose ends' that his accomplice might leave. There was something Krantz wasn't admitting. He knew it in his bones.

It was seven minutes before Krantz returned. A long seven minutes for the usually calm George Merrick.

'Where have you been?' he demanded, then immediately rescinded his rasping challenge with a softening coda. 'Yes, I understand there are difficulties.'

'I am sorry George. All is not well. The nurse has returned before she was due.'

George Merrick's considerable brain engaged the problem. 'No matter' he said, after no more than a few seconds reflection, 'Just be sure that this door is locked at all times. I have to examine Julia Salomonovich before she is sedated.'

Chapter 55

AWAKENING

There was movement. The suggestion of eyes rolling beneath eyelids; a subtle change in the rhythm of breathing indicating consciousness; the deathly pallor giving way to a living complexion and the visage expressing emotion. The changes were gradual but each aspect was observed and recorded by Professor George Merrick. The complex array of electrodes gleaned their information and fed it into the computer for analysis. The pulse was increasing and the blood pressure began to rise.

Metamorphosis. The professor's smiled a rare smile. He knew that, no matter how temporary, he had achieved what had been hitherto impossible. Success, no matter how brief, had been attained. All that remained to be ascertained was the stability of the subject. That would be established shortly.

Her mouth began to move and the tongue slowly licked her lips. Her body's slight movements signalled awareness but the mind lingered on the edge of sleep. This was a living sleep; a different sleep. This sleep had replaced the painful unrest that had prevailed for the past weeks. Here was a refreshed body soon to rise brightly and start a new day.

Something moved. The slightest movement of a hand beneath the white linen sheet. She was dreaming. Dreaming of floating in a warm sea. Now in a safe room. A womb perhaps? Being reborn, reincarnated. The chrysalis was cracking and the metamorphosis was nearing completion.

Her face felt the flow of air from the air conditioning over its surface and her nose sniffed a perfumed fragrance. She became faintly aware of a movement close by and her eyes flickered and closed again. There was recognition of an awakening but a willingness to be reconciled to sleep.

Then realisation. Cold realisation! Stemming from the back of her mind, down the long convoluted corridors of her memory banks and gushing into the mainstream of consciousness, the terrifying truth hurtled towards stark reality. Her eyes flashed open and she stared into the small hospital room.

A young woman sat at the side of the bed. She dropped the clipboard that she was holding as she recorded her notes and stared in disbelief at the young woman lying in the bed.

'What the ...? How? She froze. For the first time in her professional career, the nurse panicked. It was a momentary lapse. Rapidly collecting herself she reached for the remote control above the bed.

'Everything is fine. Everything is fine. Just relax and take it easy. Take your time. Take your time', she reassured the patient, wishing that someone would reassure her that she wasn't dreaming.

The patient moved an unfamiliar tongue over unfamiliar teeth in an unfamiliar mouth. Her memory was returning, slowly but surely.

The appalling, unrelenting, fearful pain had gone. The agony that was the last rites of cancer had ceased. Now there was relief. There was stiffness as a result of lying inert for a few days, but no more than that. The arthritic index finger on the right hand had ceased to throb and it bent quite easily where it had stubbornly refused to do so for the past twenty two years.

The nurse smiled as she wiped the patient's brow uttering further words of reassurance. There was a confused look on the patient's face. Everything felt odd. Different. Strange.

The patient looked at the nurse. She had long auburn hair. It was brushed back and held in a ponytail by a yellow elastic band. She was small and petite. She observed the nurse taking particular note of her feminine finely manicured varnished nails. Her hands were tiny and slender. Her pendant earrings swung to and fro and lower a pair of small pert breasts stood out proudly.

Suddenly there was a wave of anguish and terror. Then uneasiness, an adrenaline tidal wave surged through her body. Then a terrible sense of foreboding overtook her.

Very slowly she raised her hand to her face. She began at her temple, brushed over her cheek and down to her chin. The skin was smooth and soft. It was the face of a young woman. She closed his eyes and gave an inward scream. She sighed and feigned sleep.

Professor Merrick was travelling as fast as his gammy leg would allow. He had hoped to get to Julia Salomonovich before the nurse. He opened the door and saw that he had not. The nurse was mopping the brow of the 'client.'

'Please leave us for the moment', he whispered. The nurse looked him questioningly.

'Herr Professor?' she said delighted to be the one to report the miracle of Julia Salomonovich's recovery.

The professor feigned a nonchalant countenance. 'Yes, it was as we had expected all along. Trauma.'

'Trauma?' repeated Nurse Hackemann. 'Are you quite sure Herr Professor, I really...'

'Quite sure thank you nurse', he replied curtly. 'I think that you can rely on my judgement. Yes?'

'Herr Professor I really didn't mean to …'

Again the nurse was cut off mid-sentence.

'Good, then that will be all for the moment.'

'You wish me to leave the room Herr Professor?'

'Quite.'

'I am sorry I don't understand.'

'I mean yes, of course I wish to examine the patient. Kindly leave the room.'

'I do not wish to be rude Herr Professor but I am confused and am sure that this is not the usual protocol.

At that moment Walter Krantz entered the room. The professor caught two pairs of eyes and took messages from both.

'Nurse, I'm so sorry, I don't know your name', the professor said, lying in as charming a voice as he could muster.

'Hackemann', she replied.

'Yes, Nurse Hackemann. Perhaps you do not know it', he said, glancing in the direction of Walter Krantz, who was shaking his head and smiling at her, 'I am here to extend my research. We have developed new treatments and new techniques. I really need the time with my patient. Please', he insisted, shuffling her out of the room.

'As you wish but are you sure that you don't need assistance. It is most irregular…'

'Quite sure. Quite, quite sure. Thank you but I do need a little time to speak with my patient.'

His patient! Really! The nurse felt hurt. 'This professor!'

Since the patient had been brought to the hospital after a car accident seven days ago there had been no sign that a recovery would be possible. There had been no sign of life and experience had told Nurse Hackemann that there would not be in the future.

No one had visited the beautiful young woman during that time. She lay there without so much as mark on her body. The impact of the car accident had been dramatic on the mind but negligible on the body. She lay unconscious and hope was all but extinguished. The good nurse reflected that she had seen many remarkable recoveries in her sixteen-year career. But this was quite different.

She walked along the corridor, into the small staff rest room and poured herself a black coffee reflecting further on the curious circumstances that related to the beautiful young woman. According to the admission sheet the accident had taken place on the road leading to the infirmary. Most vehicles that used that road were travelling to or from the infirmary. It was true that the roads led to the Hauptstrasse and from thence to the autobahn but there were much a better routes for tourists. Why would the young woman travel along that road?

And again, the only apparent casualty was the young woman. Was it a hit and run? And if so why were the police not swarming all over the place?

She had been taken from the wreckage by an old professor who was fortunately travelling to the small infirmary. The professor had rushed into the infirmary and had asked for help to bring the young woman from his car. How he had managed to get her from the wreckage and into his car in the first place was something of a mystery too. He certainly did not seem to be in any physical condition to carry her. Two porters had had to rush out into the snow with a stretcher and she had been trolleyed into a small room that was opportunely available. Spare beds were not at all common in the small sanatorium.

It was strange too that the patient was not transferred to a hospital that dealt with such emergencies. This was a nursing hospital and had limited facilities or staff to cope with accidents. It was also fortunate too that the director of the hospital had been present on the night of the accident. It was he that appeared to take charge of the admission. She made a mental note to ask him about later that evening after their lovemaking.

Another quandary, niggling at the back of her mind, was the nationality of the woman. According to the admission staff there were no belongings that indicated who she was. Surely someone would have brought the contents of her car, and more specifically the contents of her handbag, to the infirmary?

Gudrun Hackemann loved to shop for clothes. It was her hobby; her therapy. She bought fashion magazines regularly. She observed other women's attire with careless scrutiny and educated interest. She knew clothes and the clothes that the woman had been wearing had definitely been British. Was she British?

The ground floor of the infirmary had sixteen single rooms. This was the area that she covered. It was not onerous; most of the patients were well able to look after themselves. The other occupants were, for the most part, elderly and most treated the place as somewhere to rest at the inclement time of the year. They complained of ailments and paid a great deal to be heard. All the patients, or clients as the director referred to them, were extremely well heeled. This was not an altruistic, benevolent institution. It served the wealthy well and they paid through the nose for that service.

That was another thing, who was paying for the young woman? Normal policy would have been to transfer her to the city hospital as soon as possible. The reason that she had been admitted at the infirmary in the first place was because the accident had happened nearby and the professor was on his way there.

No. Instead the woman was given special attention. It was clear that she was in a vegetative state but it was equally clear that the director and this mysterious professor had hopes that she would recover.

The director had given her specific instructions that the professor was to be assisted and his requests complied with. This in itself was strange. The director had been most formal with her when delivering these instructions.

This was not his normal manner with her, she mused. And again, how fortunate that the very professor who had brought her to the infirmary was an expert in the field that she needed.

There had been no mention of new medicines, techniques or developments up to this point, yet she had to agree that this professor had produced a miracle. There had not been any signs of a recovery. Not one. No hope. Yet there she had been eyes open and clearly conscious. Only one hour ago, just before her break, the young woman had appeared to be a hopeless case. She had checked all the vital signs carefully before leaving and they were as they had been for over a week. When she returned the story was so very different.

The professor and director had been leaving the room as she had walked unnoticed down the corridor towards them. They had been alone. She had entered another client's room well before she got to them. She thought that the young woman must have just been attended by the professor. It had been a little more than two minutes later that she had entered the young woman's room. She was alone. The nurse could not believe her eyes. The computer instruments were indicating that the 'client' was sleeping peacefully and that all was well. The pulse a little racy 'but, hey, this was the healthiest 'client' in the building.'

Her eyes had left the instruments and she had turned to the 'client.' She noticed the eye movement and, shocked, immediately pushed the remote control for assistance. She had sat for a moment stunned staring in disbelief at the patient.

It had been strange that the person entering the door was not a doctor but the old professor. It was equally odd that she had been asked to leave the room and no other nurse appointed to take over. Clearly a nurse could have been of assistance and she would dearly have loved to assist the conscious young woman that lay in the bed. She felt pushed out. It was she who had spent the long hours with the patient. It was she who had monitored her over the past week.

How strange that the professor, who had after all, had rescued the young woman from her car, maintained that he had no idea who she was. Surely he would have found identity papers in her handbag? Her family could then be informed. And what of that? No one had visited her. Didn't she have family? Friends? Colleagues? Surely this beautiful young woman would have someone who cared for her. There must be someone searching the hospitals of the area for her. Surely they would have heard of the accident. It was strange, yet again, that she had not heard or seen reports of the accident or the mention of the young woman's accident in the newspapers.

'Oh, there you are nurse.' It was the professor.

'I want the 'patient' to rest. Please do not disturb her until I call you', he said. He waited as if to be sure that his words had been fully comprehended.

'Yes Herr Professor', she answered coldly, a point not missed by George Merrick.

The director appeared and nodded in the direction of the professor. He flashed his clipboard in response to the director and he in turn gave, what looked to the nurse, to be a nod of affirmation.

'Stranger and stranger', she thought. 'How is the young woman going to rest if the two of them are in the room? And what is going on between the two of them?'

Her pager buzzed and she walked along the narrow corridor to tend the needs of one of her more 'conventional clients.' Perplexed, she spoke to herself. 'It's very odd. So very, very odd.' She stopped and stared back along the corridor and shook her head, puzzled.

'There are many questions that you are going to answer this evening Walter Krantz. That is if you are at all interested in our sleeping arrangements for the night.'

Chapter 56

THE NEW JULIA

Professor Sir George Merrick was a genius of that there was no doubt. He remained aloof from less distinguished academics, barely recognising them as colleagues. He was considered to be a brilliant beyond genius, to possess an extraordinary fertile and productive mind and to have the knowledge of the Bodleian Library, fully referenced at his disposal. He was also considered to be rude, often uncommunicative, usually dismissive of others and always humourless. He had devoted his life to science. His excitement was the relentless pursuit of knowledge and his fun the satisfaction of discovery.

But this success would be different. Now all was possible, and for only the second time in his life he felt alive and in touch with his emotions. He felt light, heady and young though his old frame militated against leaping into the air and bounding around the room. But soon ... very soon ...

The professor collected himself. 'Just a little longer. Be patient. It is logical to allow Miss Salomonovich to awaken naturally to reduce the impact of the inevitable trauma. I will stay at the bedside and analyse the data from here', deduced the professor. For the first time, and only briefly, he took the opportunity to celebrate his success. 'At last! At long last! Now my research may continue. Now I can have that which I should have always had and my research will go on indefinitely.'

He looked down at the patient on the bed. She was beautiful. Her long black hair was neatly brushed and tied back in the ponytail that Nurse Hackemann had groomed every day for the past week. She wore a white smock that tied at the neck and lay under a single white linen sheet.

The young woman was aware of another in the room. Her eyes opened ever so slightly, closed and opened again. They were so heavy. It took several attempts to roll back her eyelids and still they hung heavily. She stared at a cream ceiling. She sensed movement and turned her head to the side and saw an old man. He had very thin white hair and a frail almost emaciated body that was bent forward, his lizard neck almost horizontal with rheumatoid arthritis and old age. His almost translucent yellow pallor indicated anaemia and it contrasted starkly with his bright white false teeth. His right arm shook uncontrollably at times and this clearly irritated him. His irascible nature was etched in his face.

As the young woman looked at the old man she was aware of yet another in the room. As she turned her head again the sheet fell a little. Her hand moved to her long slender neck. The neck was not at all recognisable to the patient and the look that she received from the second man was not one that she had received before either. She felt nauseous and shocked.

The man was in his late forties. He was short, stocky and wore a dark pin striped grey suit. He looked down at her and she turned away. He spoke in English with a heavy German accent, his voice deep, patronising and sugary sweet. It was Walter Krantz.

'You are back in the land of the living. It is a miracle but you are back', said the hospital director.

'The professor is indeed a genius but I never...' his voice tailed off.

However, I am anxious to have confirmation. Can you tell it to me? Can you give me the password? I must have the proof.'

'Herr Director', objected the professor. 'I know that you are anxious for validation but I think that we can allow a few more moments for the patient to gather her wits.'

The woman stared, first at the director and then at the professor; unable to absorb the unbelievable truth.

She tried to speak but something prevented her. A strange larynx perhaps? A mental blockage? A strange jaw, teeth and tongue? Was it any wonder that the merest utterance was taking so long to be delivered? The mouth tried to shape a word. Her tongue licked her full lips as if her mouth was dry.

'Take your time my dear. All in good time', said the professor as he moved to the head of the bed to observe and record information from the numerous monitors. He too spoke in English. There was a slight accent, which the 'client' could not identify. 'Not West Country but...' Then she recoiled as the professor's hand brushed past her to the glass of water on the cabinet by her side.

'The electrodes have served their purpose. I have all the data I require. I will detach them now. All is well.' He offered a glass of water to the woman but her eyes stared through him.

She attempted to speak. 'What was that?' asked the professor. 'She is trying to say something. Go ahead please. Go ahead. In your own time.'

The woman was rapidly regaining her faculties. A thousand memories had coursed through the millions of strands of her memory. She focussed on the professor's eyes and mouthed one word.

In a high-pitched voice, which surprised her considerably, she uttered 'Metamorphosis.'

The director looked at the woman and, smiling with huge relief and satisfaction, turned to the professor.

'Genius. Pure genius', he acclaimed. 'Metamorphosis. That is correct.'

'You doubted? Herr Director you doubted me?' demanded the professor, seemingly offended.

The director knew that the professor was one of the most intellectually gifted scientists of the century but even now, at the scene of the revelation of his success, when the evidence lay before him, he paused and uttered, 'I admit that I did. I will never make the same mistake again Herr Professor.'

The director paged the nurse. When she entered the room he took her to one side and whispered several instructions to her. She looked questioningly at the professor. The professor noted swift non-verbal communication between the two and turned away satisfied with what he had seen.

The nurse ached to understand how the young woman had recovered so rapidly. To enquire what the catalyst had been. And, furthermore, to know why a woman, so recently after having regained consciousness was been taken off her drip feed and electronic monitoring apparatus. At first she thought to protest but clearly the professor and director were in full command of the situation and, after all, it was the professor's genius that had brought the young woman 'back from the dead.' She considered that thought for a moment.

The professor broke the uneasy silence pervading the room. 'I believe that we should let our patient rest. It has been a very tiring day for her and I am sure that we would all benefit from a break. Herr Director it is almost nineteen hundred hours. It is past your time of duty. Go home – it has been a long day for us all. And you too nurse – it is past your time too', he said in perfect German.

'But … the nurse interjected… but the client? Surely you need help at this time.'

'It is kind of you to volunteer but the next shift will be here presently and I have one or two details I must attend to too', the professor chided.

There was an almost imperceptible nod of the head from the professor to the director.

'It is no trouble', the nurse offered, but quite suddenly she was taken by the arm and led to the doorway by the director. Did she imagine that the director was been given orders by the professor? How could a professor, who, after all, had only arrived at the place a week ago, be dictating the welfare of a 'client' when the director himself was present?'

'It is a bitter night, wrap up well. We don't want you to catch a cold do we now', the professor cajoled in his usual patronising fashion. He smiled in an attempt to soften the statement. The nurse looked into the cold, driven eyes of a man on a mission.

'The journey to the valley is difficult enough in this snow. It is dark and you need to have your wits about you. We don't want to be blamed for an accident by sending you home tired, do we now Herr Director?'

'Nein', offered the director, looking a little flustered. 'I will take Nurse Hackemann back to the village after her work. I pass her home on the way to my house on an evening. This is no problem for me and it will set your mind at rest.'

Again she noted a nod between the two men. 'Later', she thought.

The professor knew that the director took Gudrun Hackemann home each evening. He also knew that her house was far from 'on his way home.' He knew too that the director often entered Gudrun's woodland chalet and that he left from there for the hospital on many a morning. The director and nurse could not have imagined how the professor might have come by this information, but then, there was much that they would not believe about Professor George Merrick.

Walter Krantz's wife had long given up hope on her philandering husband and had only remained with him for the sake of her children. Her youngest was to go to Berlin University in the September, which was just seven months hence. When her daughter left, she too would leave.

Her husband and the nurse thought their clandestine liaisons had been discreet and they had remained just so for the four months of their relationship. It was the village florist who first recognised their affair. She it was who asked the director's wife if she had liked the flowers that her husband had bought for her. The director's wife quickly changed the subject but was clearly disturbed. It had begun again. He had promised so many times.

It didn't take long before the gossiping florist had discovered where the flowers were going to and she dispersed her knowledge in the time-honoured village manner of swearing everyone she told to secrecy. As is common in many villages news spread widely and rapidly. It was surprising that the lovers themselves had not realised the extent to which their illicit rendezvous were known.

The director moved to go.

'So, gutte nacht, schlaft gut. Sleep well. It has been a long day', offered the professor.

'Gutte nacht George', said the director, who then rapidly recognising his error added, 'Bis Morgan Herr Professor.'

The nurse noted a look of admonishment that fleetingly crossed the professor's face as the director called him by name. 'Goodnight', she offered curtly.

With this the director ushered Gudrun Hackemann from the room.

The professor went quickly to the door and saw the nurses animated actions as she began to cross-examine her lover. They fairly bustled down the corridor as he led her by the arm.

'Thank God. At last they have gone.'

It was the last time either of them would see the professor or the beautiful terrified young woman.

The professor closed the door and turned to the young woman in the bed.

'You heard it all?' he enquired.

A barely discernible nod indicated that she had.

'My part of the bargain is done. Now it is your turn. We must work together.'

The professor sat down on the bedside chair.

'All has been arranged. The transfer will take place within the hour. You and Sarah will be in Austria by dawn and in the nursing home before first light. If all is well, and it will be, we can begin our work within hours. I know that you are desperately wondering about a plethora of information and anxious for knowledge of your situation and the whereabouts of your wife but I do not have the time now. You must be patient for a little while longer. It is vital that you do not speak about the recent phenomenon. That was a condition if you recall?'

The young woman nodded as the professor moved away writing rapid notes. After a few moments he pressed the pager then turned to the patient.

'As I promised, your torment and pain has gone has it not? Yes it has gone', he said, the question being rhetorical. 'You were on the very edge of death and now you are well. Soon you will be as good as new and you will be thirty-five years younger too. All is well I think.'

A nurse entered the room.

'Nurse Lessing I presume.' The professor introduced himself as the patient turned her head to see who the new entrant was. 'You are new here, yes?'

Trudy Lessing smiled warmly. 'My first day Herr Doctor. Can I be of any assistance? The director said that I should report to you.'

'Yes. The director told me that this would be your first shift. Welcome to the infirmary.' She smiled a thank you. 'This patient is transferring to a nursing home to be nearer her family. An ambulance will be here at twenty hundred hours. Please prepare her belongings and inform the porter. Thank you.'

The nurse smiled. 'I will inform the office and get the paperwork immediately Herr Doctor.' She turned to go.

'That won't be necessary. I have already done so', replied the professor. 'So, if you will do as I ask we will both make our appointed times.'

The nurse caught the professor's curtness and responded quickly. 'As you wish Herr Doctor. Of course.' The nurse was happy to please the venerable old doctor and went about his bidding.

The professor held a syringe in his hand and turning to the bed whispered. 'Sleep for now. The days ahead will be long and difficult. Sleep.' He left.

Chapter 57

TWO WITNESSES DIE

Gudrun Hackemann walked out of the hospital bombarding the director with questions. She was in rapid-fire mode and the director was deflecting the flak with considerable experience, skill and obduracy.

'Well it is all very odd to me', she was saying. 'Walter, who is the professor?'

'Why do you ask?' answered Walter Krantz, keeping a respectable distance from Gudrun. Both of them had observed a strict protocol and had kept a professional relationship whilst at the hospital. There was no point in advertising their attachment.

Besides', thought the director, 'soon I will have the money to leave this damned place and start life anew and soon our relationship will be severed.'

She turned to him. 'He seems to have a hold on you. What is it? I can't put my finger on it but I have never seen you like this.'

'I thought you had relented and let it go. Really, it's nothing', he replied unconvincingly.

They reached the black Mercedes saloon and got in. Her hand immediately moved onto the inside of his upper leg.

'I think I will ask you that again a little later', she cooed.

'I won't say', he replied in his silly, lovemaking voice.

'Oh, I think that you will. Believe me you really, really will.'

Walter drove down the narrow winding mountain road. The snow was falling heavily now and the windscreen wipers were working overtime. The headlights shone brightly into the driving snow and they were relieved when the car turned the last steep bend and reached the main road which led to the village.

Approximately a kilometre before the village Krantz turned off the road. The narrow tree lined lane allowed for single file traffic only and had small lay-bys acting as passing bays. They past three small chalets and soon the lane ended at an ancient five bar gate. The old wooden gates were never closed. Gudrun feared that they would disintegrate is she tried to close them. The car travelled along the rutted driveway and under a lean-to canopy that protected it from the worst of the weather.

The couple embraced in the car. Gudrun returned to his inner thigh and he put his hand on her breast. She wore a thick woollen overcoat. He calculated that more fun was to be had indoors. He took her hand from his thigh and whispered in her ear.

'Come on. It's cold outside and I know how to make you warm.'

'I'm still going to make you tell me', she said, licking her lips.

'Tell you what?' he teased.

'You know what I'm talking about. Your mysterious professor', she insisted as they walked through the snow to the door of the chalet.

'Which professor would that be then?'

They laughed as she opened the door. As she did so the telephone rang. Perhaps it was her mother. She had been meaning to ring. She ran to the telephone and picked up the receiver. It was her last act on earth.

The explosion ripped through the chalet killing both of them. The blast tore half of the roof away and ripped away three quarters of the front elevation of the building. Furniture was flung over a hundred metres into the air landing in neighbouring gardens and along the lane. There would be little left to bury.

Chapter 58

THE EXPLOSION

The young nurse entered the small hospital ward room.

'All is prepared Herr Doctor. The ambulance has arrived and the porters will be here in a few moments.'

The professor had a telephone in his hand. He took it from his ear and replaced it slowly and precisely taking a deep breath and exhaling slowly and deliberately.

He stared into the distance for a short while and then, as if the nurse's words registered he mumbled, 'Thank you very much. That will be all.'

The nurse smiled and turned smartly leaving the room to attend to her other 'clients.'

The professor left the room too. He first called at reception to confirm that the staff knew to collect a certain Felix Elder at six in the morning prompt. They were also informed that he was in room fourteen. As always he demanded efficiency and precision. On no account was Mr. Elder to be disturbed during the remainder of the evening.

The professor was not a happy man. He loathed leaving his destiny in the hands of others. Things were not precisely as he had planned them and he knew that gremlins were attracted to adapted plans.

If that interfering Nurse Hackemann had only returned a few minutes later, as she had been instructed to do, all would be well. Krantz would have switched the machine and he would then have assumed the persona of Felix Elder and would have been on the road to Innsbruck with the Fossards. Krantz and Hackemann would have then gone to her place, as they always did, and that would have been that. Now the place would have the police asking their stupid questions about that idiot Krantz.

Krantz! It was three days earlier that he had discovered the affair between Walter Krantz and Nurse Gudrun Hackemann. He had followed her home until she had left the road for her chalet and walked on foot following her at a distance. He had lost her for a moment but caught up just in time to see her enter her front door. He left immediately.

Early the following day he had seen the nurse arrive at the infirmary. He observed her as she took a clean smock from the laundry stack. He saw her put her bag in her locker and put her coat on a hanger in the staff room. It was quite simple really. He waited a while, took her front door key from her pocket and drove into the village.

He entered a small café and bought himself a cup of black coffee and sat for a little while. When the old lady who had served him went into the cellar he made a quick exit via the back door. Once outside he recovered an overcoat and trilby that he had placed amongst a small copse during the previous evening. In the unlikely event of prying eyes it was unlikely that someone would be able to identify him.

He made his way behind the stone wall which ran parallel to the old lane, and, always extremely vigilant, made his way up Nurse Hackeman's driveway. The path was well gritted and he was pleased to note that he would not be leaving footprints in the snow. He opened the front door taking his shoes off as he did so.

He opened the sitting room door and walked straight to the telephone. He hesitated and looked out of the window nervously. No one! He took the simple explosive device he had prepared from his overcoat pocket and a timer from under his trilby. It took him less than two minutes from entering the premises to leaving them. He returned by the same route. He then removed the overcoat and trilby in the copse beyond the wall and placed them in a carrier bag before opening the gate, checking the footpath and emerging back into the village. The whole exercise had taken a little over eight minutes. He then re-entered the café.

The landlady was just returning from the cellar. She asked him if he was waiting for more coffee. His German was excellent and he was well able to speak in the area's colloquial accent but he replied with a laboured 'Nein Danke.' This the landlady would relate to a police officer the following day. He returned to his car. Before getting in he changed his socks and his shoes. There would be carpet fibres on his socks and the soles of his shoes. He checked to make sure that he was not being observed, and then drove back to the infirmary.

At the infirmary he took the carrier bag from the boot of his car and entered the boiler house next to the rear entrance. He threw the bag and its contents into the inferno and left.

There was no one in the staff rest room when he arrived and it was easy for him to slip the key back into the right hand pocket of Gudrun Hackemann's coat. It was all so simple and straightforward.

Everything had gone 'like clockwork' as Walter Krantz had observed earlier in the evening until that interfering bloody nurse had stepped in.

She wouldn't interfere again.

Now the project had acquired a new dimension, one that George Merrick did not like and was not familiar with. Chance! He analysed the facts and identified only one way forward. He put the wheels in motion and acted swiftly reflecting on the fact that all the spy stuff three days earlier may well have been wasted.

The police may well identify Professor George Merrick as a suspect in the case of the exploding chalet but even if they were to trace him to the infirmary they would soon discover that he had had a heart attack and that his body had been found on the floor of his room in the infirmary.

Chapter 59

A SECOND METAMORPHOSIS

The professor entered the room where Felix Elder lay. The handsome young man was attached to a life support machine. The professor pushed his bed alongside so that his head was adjacent to Felix's. He turned the handle at the end of the second trolley until its height corresponded with that of the scanner and connected a myriad of probes between the scanner and Felix, Felix and himself and he and the scanner. All that remained was to connect the whole circuit to his laptop. This he did with some difficulty as his arthritic fingers almost lacked the dexterity required.

He checked the apparatus thoroughly and picked a remote control from the cabinet at the side of the bed. The time was right. All had been checked. He stopped for a moment then said out loud, 'Goodbye you old cripple. Goodbye you ugly old wizened bastard. Goodbye Professor George Merrick. Hello Felix Elder.'

With that he squeezed his hand and immediately lost consciousness leaving the dry old sack of his worn out body. It was nine o'clock in the evening. The snow continued to fall.

At three o'clock in the morning Felix Elder opened his eyes. George Merrick stared out from behind them. He felt amazingly well but then Felix was an astonishing guy. After all Felix had survived a minor operation and it was highly unlikely that it would affect his constitution.

He moved his hands to his head and removed the probes adroitly. He observed the suppleness of his fingers. It took a moment for him to sit up and, as he did so, he noted his fine muscular arms and large hands. Gone were the arthritic fingers and the puny white limbs. His tongue moved around his palate. It was a long time since he had had his own teeth. God he felt well. If he felt like this after what he'd been through, God knows how good it was going to feel later. He could breathe. Not in the little burning gasps that he had taken for so many years. No, these were huge intakes of air billowing out his lungs.

He stopped himself. The professor's cold logical mind was at work within Felix Elder's brain. This is gratuitous. 'It is time to move', he said to himself. He stood for a moment, checking that he had his balance. No problem there. What a guy Felix had been. What a constitution. Enough! He looked down at the old man on the floor. He was barely breathing. He placed a pillow over the old man's head and held it there for a short time. The wheezing old fellow had gasped his last breath and the room fell silent.

Felix lifted the body of the old professor with ease and walked to the door with his light burden. He pulled the door slightly ajar and peered out. There was movement in the corridor. He pulled the door too. He waited a short time then pulled at the door once again. The corridor was clear. It took just three paces to cross the corridor with the lifeless body in his arms. Still holding the emaciated corpse he opened the door to George Merrick's room. He placed the old man on the floor and prepared to leave.

He looked down at his old shell and was shocked at what he saw. 'Goodbye old man', he considered for a moment then smiled. 'To paraphrase Mark Twain; reports of my death will be greatly exaggerated.' He hit the panic button on the wall and quickly returned to Felix Elder's room.

He closed the door gently and listened intently. Nothing yet. He replaced the apparatus that had been connected to Felix, laid back, and waited.

Suddenly there was a commotion outside the next room and eventually a pass key was inserted in the lock.

It appeared that Professor George Merrick had had a heart attack. The newspaper would report the fact over the next few days in most of the major cities of the world. An eccentric genius. A loss to the world of science. Felix would take great pleasure in reading his obituaries.

He lay back on the bed and coupled up the life support apparatus and drip feed. At last he had time. Not time to be spent frivolously testing his new powers. It was difficult to curb his enthusiasm, even for such a rational thinker, and he knew that now was not the time for action. Now was a time for reflection and analysis.

Felix considered his accomplishment. The metamorphosis of both he and Julia had been complete successes. Now the woman he always coveted was within his grasp and he was a dashingly handsome and very intelligent candidate for the post of partner. 'It's just a matter of time', he told himself.

But there were loose ends. Walter Krantz and Gudrun Hackemann were accounted for. That left Julia Salomonovich and Sarah Fossard. There should have been only one other person who knew of his transmutation, his metamorphosis. By necessity there had been six. Five too many. Walter Krantz and the interfering nurse were no more. Now all that remained were Sarah Fossard, Julia Salomonovich and Reinhardt Bühler. Could he count on them not to talk? He believed that he could not.

He closed his eyes. Perhaps feigning deep sleep would be the toughest act of the evening.

On Saturday 10th December at six a.m. precisely, the ambulance left Munich with Felix Elder on board; destination Innsbruck.

Chapter 60

JULIA AND SARAH ARRIVE AT INNSBRUCK

Julia Salomonovich and Sarah Fossard arrived at the small convalescence home in Innsbruck at the same moment that Felix Elder left Munich. The snowfall had turned into a blizzard and progress had been very slow. The ambulance driver had remarked that the fall was the heaviest that he had seen for many years and that it looked like there was much more to come. Soon the road to the autobahns would become impassable.

Julia and Sarah had been sedated and were both out cold. It is doubtful if either could have mustered a word to say had they not been so. The horror and fear that both had suffered over the past two days was appalling enough. When coupled with the steady stream of tranquillisers and sedative cocktails they were being fed and the long weeks of dealing with Peter's cancer it was unlikely that either would be able to muster the blink of an eye.

It was, perhaps, a godsend that they had slept. They would need it.

Helmut Maier had paced back and forth across the front porch of the home. He was last in contact with the ambulance less than fifteen minutes earlier. The driver had reported then that he was no more than two kilometres away but still they had not shown. Maier's staff had had the driveway of the home cleared several times during the evening but no amount of salt and spadework appeared to be sufficient to combat the heavy drifting.

Maier demanded punctuality and obedience in all things and at all times. If someone did not comply with his strict code of conduct then he ceased to have any dealings with them. It had always been the same with him. The Wehrmacht had been an excellent teacher. The SS a fine master.

Of course there were heavy snowdrifts. That was to be expected but nature should have been accounted for. The ambulance was due and it should have arrived by now. Someone was at fault.

He was about to pick up his mobile as he saw the flashing lights of a snowplough. The ambulance followed in its wake.

'Gott seit dank!' He swore.

Maier ranted at the driver for several moments during which time the two women were transferred to adjacent rooms.

Sarah had regained consciousness in the ambulance but had neither the energy nor the will to engage in conversation with the drivers. She opened her eyes at one point and gained a reference for the conversation between driver and co-driver but they were so heavy she closed them once again. On arrival at the home she was taken out of the ambulance first and had assumed that she and Julia would be put in the same room. The door closed and she waited for some time before realising that those were not to be the domestic arrangements. They lay her on the bed fully clothed in the black tailored suit that she had worn since leaving for the hospital in Bristol.

Sarah came too with a hangover. She got up and went to the washbasin and looked in the mirror. 'What a sight.' Her handbag was at the foot of the bed and she reached down to pick it up. A wave of nausea hit her and she had to sit for a moment to collect herself. She went to the toilet and vomited.

Peter. Where had they taken Peter?

She washed her face and brushed her hair and felt a little better for having done so. Picking up her bag, she left to enquire as to Peter's whereabouts. Meeting him was going to be difficult but she had to see him. She looked at her wrist and was amazed to find that it was already half past three in the afternoon.

'What kind of sedatives do these people use', she thought.

She opened the door and looked along the oak panelled hallway and made her way past the bottom of the huge staircase. The place appeared deserted. She walked down towards the front door. As she did so the ambulance driver walked in, covered in snow.

'Entchuldigen aber ... Oh I am sorry, I don't have the English ... er ... you are not ... er...' he pointed at the door.

'No, no', she replied smiling, 'I was looking for my... that is for the young lady who came with me. Do you know which room she is in?'

'Ja, bitte', he indicated for her to follow.

The young man and Sarah retraced her steps back across the hall. Passing the door to her own room she noted that Peter had been put in the next room. She thanked the driver and watched him walk away until he was out of sight before opening the door.

Chapter 61

FELIX BEGINS HIS JOURNEY TO INNSBRUCK

The weather had not improved and the ambulance taking Felix Elder to Innsbruck was stuck in heavy traffic caused by an accident on the autobahn. The driver picked up his mobile from the dashboard and rang Innsbruck. The number was engaged.

The driver was nervous, 'Herr Maier will go crazy. You know how he is. We must let him know that we will have to find a place to stop. We can't go on for the moment. Get me the map', he indicated the glove compartment to his co-driver. 'Where are we exactly?'

The driver's mate peered at the small road atlas in the dim light of the cab. After a few moments he had got his reference, 'We have hardly begun our journey we must turn back. We must think of the patient. We are less than ten kilometres south of Hohenbrunn. We have travelled only thirty kilometres and have been going for over an hour now.' He examined the road atlas again. In another ten kilometres there is a Rasthof. If they have rooms I suggest that we stay there until we receive further orders. We cannot go on. It's impossible.'

They pulled into the first Parkplatz that they came to and the driver attempted to contact Innsbruck once more. Again the line was engaged.

The driver looked upwards as if seeking inspiration. 'What the hell do we do now?' His mate shrugged his shoulders. 'Well I'm going for a piss to start with', he moaned, 'You never know when we'll get another chance in this weather and the Rasthof is still some way ahead.' The two clambered out of the ambulance cab and made for the nearest bushes.

It took Felix Elder less than three seconds to take control of the vehicle. The engine kicked in and he sped out of the Parkplatz, back end slipping and sliding as he powered away.

The driver and his mate were startled as they heard and then saw the ambulance disappear.

'Quick ring the police', screamed the driver.

'On what?' replied his mate.

'No, no, no. Not the cell phones too?'

A flashing blue light and blaring siren eased the traffic for Felix but still he made alarmingly sluggish progress. Soon the ambulance would be reported stolen. He had little time before it would have to be ditched.

'The bitch.' George Merrick had rarely resorted to coarse language. Felix Elder thought of Nurse Gudrun Hackemann and did so now.

Chapter 62

SARAH MEETS JULIA

Sarah was about to enter Julia's room when she heard a ring tone coming from the room opposite. The door was ajar and she instinctively felt the urge to listen.

An old man sat on the end of the bed, his back to the door. He spoke in English with a thick German accent.

'Yes I understand, but the price is now much higher my friend.' Clearly someone wasn't happy to be paying the higher price.

Sarah turned towards Julia's room once again. She squeezed open the door and entered. As she was about to close the door she heard the old man say 'Julia Salomonovich.' She froze and held the door ajar to listen. She was able to pick up snippets of the conversation but what she had already heard had sent shivers running down her spine.

For so many years she had lived in suburban peace and normality. Now all was chaos. She appeared to inhabit a fantastic and horrific twilight world, which blurred the boundaries between reality and the macabre. She continued to listen.

'My friend it is only you and I now', the old man continued. 'Krantz is disposed of? Already - good? 'Yes they are here. No they won't be going anywhere soon. I can finish it now if you wish... yes I will wait until you arrive ... as you wish ... I understand that you can learn from the girl Salomonovich but to keep her alive? Is that wise? Yes I am aware who is in charge. May I remind you of who it was that supplied the means my friend ... Krantz was a fool...I hope that you understand that I am not.' There was a silence between the two men. Then, 'So you will arrive tomorrow afternoon now... Yes, I understand that... and remember my friend if anything was to happen to me ... the authorities will receive information from my contacts ... No I have not compromised our position. They will only know where to find my information if I ... enough... I have already said. I am not a fool... Ja, verstahen... Aufeidersehen.' Reinhardt Bühler put the phone down.

Sarah couldn't move. The fear and uncertainty that had been her constant companion for so long returned with vengeance. It took time for her to close the door silently. She stood with her back to it listening and hoping to gain some equilibrium. She attempted to make sense of the snippets she had overheard. Regardless of details she and Julia were in danger.

Who was the old man? His inferences were clear. Crystal clear. But who the hell was he? One thing, and one thing only was for certain; it was time to leave. She would try to rationalise things later. But for now! Now it was time to get as far away from the rest home as possible.

Peter? How could she take Peter, or, at least, God! Julia with her? Could she walk? Would she want to? Where would she go? God, what had she done?

She whispered. 'Hello. Are you there?' A distinctly feminine voice replied,

'Sarah.'

The voice was not one that either woman recognised. 'Is that really you?'

'It's me Sarah. My God it's me.'

Sarah walked to the bedside stumbling in the dark as she did so. She reached down and found the bedside table lamp. After a short fumble she found the switch and turned it on.

The amber lampshade softened the light. Julia looked up into her best friend's eyes. Sarah steeled herself and looked down into the face of a stranger. The two froze as if in a trance. Julia reached up to embrace Sarah.

Sarah opened her arms to the stranger and held her close. Julia felt a wave of euphoria, relief and comfort on seeing Sarah at last.

Sarah wanted to hold Peter and tell him how frightened she was but recognised that her own fears were hardly paramount. She moved Julia to arms- length and looked at her. My God you are so beautiful ... and so young.'

Julia blushed. It was the first time that anyone had called her beautiful.

Is it really you? What do I say to you? I'm sorry. It was so selfish of me. I didn't want to lose you. I ...' Julia put a finger across Sarah's lips.

'Shush, shush. I'm alive. Before, I didn't have an option...' her line faltered as Sarah began to comprehend the significance of it.

'No, no, I ...' she began, and then recognised that she was making the same mistake over again raised her arms to the heavens and screamed a silent scream. She felt helpless. She couldn't think. 'Where was her Peter? Where was her rock?' What was her reference point? She held Julia close recognising that her needs were far greater than her own.

Sarah released Julia and began, 'We are in danger we must go. Are you able to walk? This is so awkward, so strange. I don't know what to do or what to say. I know that you must have so much to say but that must be for later.'

'For someone who should be dead by now I feel amazingly well. We must have been given something. I don't know how long I have been conscious but it hasn't been for long. I lay here in the dark alone and frightened, trying to remember. I have heard snippets of conversations but that is all. Sarah, I was in agony. Then I went to sleep. I woke in a strange room and that terrible pain had gone. The professor and Herr Krantz were triumphant but I felt that I was playing a bit part in their sideshow as they celebrated their success. I was a kind of Eliza Doolittle. I felt used and abused, unimportant and dispensable. They gave me something and all I can remember is being in an ambulance.

I woke later here in the dark perhaps twenty minutes ago. I was terrified and have laid here unable to make myself ... to... to even touch my body let alone discover if I can walk. But, my God, the terrible pain has gone. Sarah', she said taking her arm, 'What has happened? Why are we in danger?'

'We have a little time. You must stand and try to walk. I will help you and tell you what I know.'

Sarah began by relating her initial meeting with the professor in the corridor of the hospital in Bristol. Julia moved back the bedcovers as she did so and looked down at her long elegant legs. 'My God', she uttered in disbelief. She began to sit up but immediately lowered her head back onto the pillow.

'Does it hurt darling?' Sarah asked, feeling stupid for having called the stranger 'darling.'

'No, it's not that.'

'What then?'

'It's this body. God. My God ...' she closed with a whimper. 'I have two large heavy breasts stuck out in front of me. Usually when I sit up my whole body comes with me. When I tried to get up they, they ...' she began to cry.

'Now I'm crying. I never cry. Everything is so damn different. My voice, my eyesight, my body, my teeth and even my feelings. I feel so ...'

Sarah reached forward and held Julia to her. 'You missed out 'my hormones.' That's oestrogen pumping through your body darling, not testosterone. Already I am learning. I wanted you to carry on as Peter. I was determined that we would try to ... oh I don't really know what I am saying. One thing is clear you cannot live as Peter. You cannot live as a man. I don't know what I was thinking?'

Sarah continued pouring out the story of the last few days. The flight from England to Munich; the journey from Munich to Innsbruck; the telephone call that she had just overheard and the fear that something had happened to Walter Krantz.

Sarah helped Julia to the edge of the bed. She sat there for a moment as Sarah walked to the light switch near the doorway. The room lit up brightly.

Sarah walked past the bed to the dressing table mirror. 'Look.'

Slowly Julia turned towards the mirror, her eyes closed by fear. She took a deep breath and opened them. There facing her was a beautiful young, sad woman. She gasped. Even in the white smock it was clear that she was quite stunning.

Sarah, resigned, said, 'You see what I mean? If you had any masculine features at all you could... but, well how can you live as anything other than as a woman.'

Julia had not taken her eyes from her reflection but now, inevitably looked down her body. Even covered by the heavy smock there was no mistaking her feminine features.

Sarah smiled reassuringly recognising Julia's shock and trauma. There wasn't time for this. She began to look through the wardrobes and cupboards but they were empty. It was then that she saw a tan suitcase under the bed. She looked at it and, as a matter of course, was about to ask for it to be lifted onto the bed for her. She stopped. 'Stupid of me', she said. Julia missed the significance of the comment unable to tear her eyes from the mirror.

Sarah put the suitcase on the bed and opened it. She quickly rifled through it looking for something suitable for Julia. 'A cocktail dress, an evening dress, a few tops and skirts, bras and pants', now she had Julia's attention.

'I'm not...'

'Look in the mirror again. What do you see?' Sarah pointed first at the mirror and then at Julia. 'Who are you now? I know that you have Peter's mind but you cannot dress his mind. It is this body that you inhabit and it is this body that we must dress.'

Julia had now turned her attention from the mirror to the suitcase. 'My god are those really my clothes?' She looked at the tiny cocktail dress and high sling back shoes and sighed. 'Some things ok – others, never.'

Sarah handed her a thick woollen jumper and a pair of blue Levi jeans. Julia looked somewhat relieved. She then handed her a white bra. Julia shook her head in blank refusal.

'Not ever', she rebelled.

'I'm afraid my darling that you must, believe me. You must.'

Julia was not impressed and folded her arms. Realising that she was now cradling her breasts she unfolded them immediately. 'This is impossible!'

'Please trust me', Sarah's voice was urgent.

Julia stared into Sarah's pleading eyes. 'God she is wonderful', she thought and nodded reluctantly.

Sarah helped her to her feet. She was surprisingly steady on her feet but needed a little help to walk. She began slowly and after a few lengths of the room was able to go travel unaided. Sarah did not know how far they would have to walk but clearly there was no alternative. Peter's problem solving mind had already begun to function in Julia's brain.

'Sarah. What have you got?'

'A plan you mean?'

She nodded.

'Nothing really. I have my mobile and if I can get to a directory I will get a taxi to pick us up. The roads are not good, the snow is quite deep but there must be transport somewhere. Perhaps there are keys for a car? Quickly you must dress.' She looked into Julia's handbag. 'Good, money and a passport', she whispered to herself.

'How are we to get past their guards? Have you thought of that? Julia asked, knowing that this sort of thing was not at all Sarah's field or strength.

'We are not prisoners', she replied.

Julia looked at Sarah in disbelief. 'Then why all the spy stuff? Why are we whispering? Why are we trying to make a getaway when we could take our time and recuperate here?'

Sarah outlined the telephone call that she had overheard. 'According to that conversation the old man, the professor and the two of us are the only ones who know of the experiment and they intend to keep it like that. The old man is not aware that we will be leaving. As far as he is concerned there is no reason for us to worry and he believes us to be sedated. As long as we avoid running into him we should be ok.'

Julia thought this through then turned quickly to Sarah. She was interrupted by her own hair as her ponytail swished around her neck. Shocked she reached to push it behind her. She felt her long slender neck and her heart dropped again. It was several seconds before she was able to speak. Her tongue brushed across her perfectly formed teeth as she looked down at her tiny hands. She collected herself and began.

'Even though no one else knows of the experiment it is possible that the old man has left a message that he is to be informed if we are seen. There is no percentage in ringing reception. The old man probably owns the place. Why were we transferred from Munich? Think of that. Why are we here in Innsbruck? Where are all the personnel that we met in Munich? What did they know? What of the nurse? We know what happened to Walter Krantz. I think the professor needs to check on his experiment and that he will then dispose of us too.'

Sarah visibly receded into the easy chair at the side of the bed. 'Those were my thoughts too. I had hoped that they wouldn't be yours.'

'Look Sarah, 'I should be dead. Whatever it takes. Right? Think of Chloe and Lucy. They need you.'

'They need us', Sarah repeated, reaching for Julia's hands.

Julia disappeared behind a screen to dress. She pulled the string at the top of the smock and pulled it over her head. Slowly she looked down. There stood two large beautiful breasts. The dark nipples stood out proudly from them. The amazingly tiny pants fit perfectly. The bra proved awkward and felt uncomfortable. She was pleased with its considerable functional effect.

'Sarah', she said coming out from behind the screen. 'Is this right' Sarah looked her over. A deeply disturbed Sarah replied in a hurried whisper. 'Yes. Hurry, I just want to get away from this place.'

Julia pulled on the jeans, the jumper and a pair of socks and approached Sarah who was checking the suitcase. 'We must take your clothes. We may need them.' She threw a pair of shoes onto the bed.

'Those are the most sensible I could find. Hardly a heel on them. Your bag.'

Julia turned to look at the handbag that Sarah was pointing to. 'Your passport is in the bag. Bring it.'

'I don't need the bag', she insisted, reaching in for the passport.

Sarah stared at him and said slowly, 'Oh but you do. Bring it.'

Julia suddenly felt nauseous and out of her depth. She slung the bag over her shoulder as Sarah went to the door. She pulled at the strap of her bra, which had fallen, from her shoulder. 'Trussed up like a bloody ...' Her litany trailed off as she failed to think of a suitable end to the sentence.

Sarah took the suitcase to the door. 'I will carry the case. It is light. I have left the heavier things behind. You may be younger but I believe that I am stronger than you. I can manage the case dear?'

Julia looked down at her breasts and noted that the nipples were clearly influencing the contours of the heavy sweater. The two women stared at each other and in unison thought, 'Mike Tyler.'

Mike Tyler's usual comment on seeing such a sight was always the same... 'It must be cold tonight.'

'As soon as we're clear, we'll ring him. We're going to need him now', Julia whispered. Sarah nodded in agreement. Julia opened the door and held it ajar.

'All clear', she said, clearly having taken charge of the situation. 'Let's go.' Sarah picked up the suitcase, took a deep breath and opened the door.

Julia was not amused by the fact that it was Sarah carrying the case. It was all wrong. Everything was so bloody wrong!

Chapter 63

FELIX MEETS ASTRID SCHWARZ

Felix knew that he had no more than fifteen minutes to dump the ambulance. True he had the two driver's mobile phones but it wouldn't take long for them to borrow one. Neither would it take long for them to track him down. He was in an ambulance, on an autobahn with lights flashing and a siren screaming. He would have to dress soon and that too would take time.

Damn it, he had to take the ambulance. The driver and his mate were going to stop or return to Munich. He couldn't do that. His bridges had been burned there! He was supposed to be unconscious. They would discover that he was not if he returned to the infirmary. They would discover much more too. It was far too risky. He had to press on. There was no alternative. He needed to get over the border and away from the questions that would inevitably be asked.

Once afforded the opportunity the professor had calculated that he had to take the vehicle. Thankfully he had been given the break he required and violence had been avoided. As far as the driver and his mate were concerned a person unknown had stolen their ambulance and kidnapped their unconscious passenger.

He drove for a few kilometres before he saw the lights of a Rasthof service station. He pulled in behind the filling station kiosk. There was a holdall on the floor beside the bed. He reached in and pulled out Felix's clothes. The fellow certainly travelled light. He put on a white tea shirt, and put a red sweatshirt over that. He then donned a pair of worn blue jeans while checking the dark window. Good, no one there. He waited until he felt that it was safe to leave and, picking up his holdall and leather jacket opened the door quietly and walked away abandoning the ambulance to the elements. He made his way to the restaurant.

God he felt good. He strode out across the car park taking a huge deep breath as he entered the large timber building. He joined the self-service queue and ordered a coffee. Taking his mug to a seat in the corner he began to rationalise his position keeping an eye out for the inevitable police car.

Firstly, no one knew who he was. Only the driver and his paramedic mate would recognise him and they were unlikely to arrive. Even if they could he would keep himself well out of their way.

The police would come and they would find the ambulance. What then? What could they do? Nothing! They would be looking for an unconscious man. He was unlikely to be chasing about a service station. No, he was quite safe.

Next. How to get to Innsbruck? Hitch a lift? That was possible. Take a vehicle? No, that would be a clear signal to the police. Hitching was going to be it. He turned towards the folk in the restaurant and looked for a suitable candidate.

There were several truck drivers. He made a note of the three most affable looking. He noticed a young woman looking in his direction. As he caught her eye she glanced away. He thought no more about it. He looked around again. There was a group of three young men but what would they want with an old ... wait, he wasn't old. Perhaps they would... he caught the young woman looking in his direction again. Old habits die hard and he looked behind him checking that her attention had not been given to someone else.

He couldn't believe it. Was she flirting with him? It certainly seemed so. No one had ever done that before. He felt the empowerment of that and experienced feelings that he had never had to interpret before. He pondered. We are the sum of our experiences and some are enabled to gain those experiences only because of their physical appearance and the strengths or weaknesses which that baggage brings with it. How much more powerful would that truth be for women?

Perhaps the new Julia Salomonovich would discover the truth of that over the coming months. Certainly doors were opened for the beautiful; and the handsome come to that. This had never happened to the professor in all of his wretched life. It happened to the new Felix within five minutes of being let loose on society.

'Lucky bastard', Felix observed. He estimated that the young woman would be in her early twenties. She had long blonde hair which she swept back regularly to keep it from her face. She was very pretty but not especially beautiful, he judged. She wore a thick red and white cable sweater and black jeans that scarcely concealed the curvaceous figure beneath them.

Again the woman looked in his direction and smiled. She raised an inviting eyebrow. Felix felt very warm. He squirmed a little before regaining his senses. He was handsome, well-built and fit. The woman clearly had good taste. All he needed was confidence. 'How difficult could it be?' He had seen countless undergraduates make fools of themselves. How much wiser was he? He smiled and walked to her table with his coffee in hand.

'Do I know you?' he enquired.

'Oh, you are English', she said in a lilting Tyrolean accent. 'I'm sorry,' she lied. 'I thought that you were someone else.'

'Ironically I am', he replied.

'I'm sorry?' she said, puzzled.

'No matter. Are you travelling alone? May I buy you another cup of coffee?

'Ja und Ja Danke' she laughed. 'Meine name ist Astrid und Sie?' She proffered her hand. Felix felt her tiny hand slip into his huge grip. He held it lightly as they shook. He remained calm and didn't betray the emotional turmoil that he was experiencing. There was no reason to tell her his name. 'Mike. Mike Mitchell. He was pleased with the alliteration.

Felix returned with the coffee and sat opposite her.

'And you. Do you also travel alone Mike?'

He looked at the young smiling face and lied again reflecting that once you got started it became infectious. 'Yes, my wallet has been stolen and the only way that I can get to Innsbruck is by hitching I'm afraid. I will meet friends there and be able to get money. I have just a little.'

'What will you do in Innsbruck?' she said, engaging his eyes as they had never been engaged before. He was suddenly aware of a long forgotten feeling springing from deep within him. He was becoming aroused. He felt the flush of youth and passion. He reached under the table and felt his erection, flinching in amazement. The size! My God!

She was surprised to see his face so animated and said, 'What is it? Are you well?' she smiled and gave him a coquettish look that almost made him lose control. 'God the emotions of youth run high.' It's no wonder his undergraduates couldn't damn well study properly. He remembered that someone had said that youth was wasted on the young. 'Well', he reflected, 'that may be true of youth but it's not about to be wasted on me this time around.'

Astrid was staring at him. 'Oh I'm sorry', he said, 'I was just... er... I was just thinking, I don't suppose that you are going in the direction of Innsbruck are you.'

Felix felt that she was quite relaxed about the enquiry. If only his erection would subside he would ask her how soon she intended to renew her journey.

'Actually I live near the Innsbruck airport close to Kranebitten. I can take you to Innsbruck if you wish.' Again he caught her flashing young eyes looking deeply into his. He adjusted his sitting position once again. As with his former students who were distracted by sex he too was now being distracted and he fought hard to rationalise his thoughts.

Putting his bag in front of his crotch, he stood and offered to go. 'Are you ready?' he asked. He thought that he caught a little smile of satisfaction at the corner of her mouth as she stood. 'Good', she said. 'It's stopped snowing.

Chapter 64

FLIGHT

Julia and Sarah walked towards reception. There was no one at the desk and they slipped past with some relief. They donned their coats as they walked out into the freezing cold. The snow had been cleared from the pavements and, under normal circumstances, they would have made reasonable progress but Julia was having difficulty walking on her tiny feet. She was clearly weak from her recent inactivity and 'the damn shoes' weren't helping her either.

They walked for a few hundred metres before they came to the main road. The two women were already tired and were now very cold. They held each other's hand to maintain their balance. They said little, unable to voice their thoughts.

Julia was experiencing unbelievable feelings. Her body movement was different. Her steps were smaller than normal and she recognised that she didn't have the strength that she had formally had. Now Sarah was a good two inches taller than she was. In her former guise she was six two. Sarah was five eight. She estimated that she must now be five six at best. Sarah had heels on and it was strange looking up at her.

They came to a filling station and walked in cautiously. The young man at the counter glanced Julia over and she squirmed. God she had seen him look directly at her breasts. Is that what men did? 'Yes I suppose I did', she reflected. 'But', she thought, I'm wearing a thick sweater and a coat?' There wasn't time.

Sarah had approached the man unaware of Julia's feeling on her first contact with a man.

'Bitte', she began trying to remember a little of her school German, 'Wo ist der telefon buch?'

As so very often in the areas surrounding tourist resorts in Austria, Switzerland and Germany, when the accent was recognisably English the reply was too.

'Please, over there, but can I be of assistance to you?'

Sarah smiled for the first time in several weeks. At last, a little luck.

The young man smiled waiting for an answer.

'Thank you', she replied, returning his smile, 'May I use your telephone. My...' She pointed at her mobile... 'is not working. Krank. Ja?' The cashier dialled for a taxi for Sarah, it was clear that he was familiar with whoever was at the other end of the line. He went off on a lengthy and largely indecipherable spiel and then offered the phone to her, pleased with his altruism.

Julia had turned away from the counter and stood by the door staring down the road anxiously. Sarah, sensitive to Julia's predicament, had moved close to support her. When the phone was proffered she took it with a generous smile and a sincere 'Danke.' The call lasted no more than a few seconds.

'He said that the car will be here soon.' She glanced back at the kiosk cashier, offered him a further smile and shouted a grateful 'Danke. Aufeidersehen', as they left.

The two women sheltered behind the filling station nervously scanning the road. Both wanted to speak but neither could bring themselves to do so. Each had taken furtive glances at the other since their surreal reunion. Julia wanted to take Sarah in her arms and tell her that everything would be well, as Peter had always done, but she could not bring herself to do it. An invisible barrier had been erected. The parameters of their relationship had changed and they needed to form another, and soon.

Sarah saw a woman, young enough to be her daughter. She recognised that her mind had, as Peter had said to her when her mother had died, 'gone into neutral', a temporary state of mind that the bereaved and other similarly anguished folk seek refuge in when life becomes unbearable, unmanageable and beyond endurance.

The stranger was no stranger. She had shared her life with her and knew her intimate secrets and nuances and shared her memories and her hopes. Yet she found difficulty to communicate, let alone to relate to her now. Sarah was nearing the edge and Julia knew it.

The wind had changed direction and the air felt lighter and less chilly as the taxi drew onto the filling station's forecourt. Julia tapped Sarah on the shoulder and lifted the case.

'My turn. Come on. It's time to leave this damn place.'

The two got in and turned nervously scanning the road through the rear window to see if they were being followed. They were not.

At the same time that the women were driven away from the service station Reinhardt Bühler knocked on Julia's door in the rest home. He knocked several times before pushing the door ajar and whispering, 'Miss Salomonovich? Hello.' He stepped into the room and in the dim light saw a figure still sleeping in the bed. He closed the door gently behind himself. 'The sedation was far too strong', he declared to himself. 'Perhaps a little later.'

Julia Salomonovich had remembered Peter Fossard's old trick of putting a pillow under the sheets to act as a dummy when left for an illicit smoke from his summer school dormitory. It had worked then and it had worked now. It was simple but effective.

Chapter 65

FELIX AND ASTRID IN ROSENHEIM

Felix Elder was both apprehensive and excited. George Merrick had rarely experienced either of those emotions. They left the restaurant and made their way to her car. The puce Volkswagen Beetle pulled away sedately and they were soon on the autobahn heading towards Rosenheim.

Astrid turned on the radio and listened for the travel news. 'The roads are good as far as Rosenheim but the Austrian border is not yet clear. Let us hope for the best.'

Felix felt more comfortable with his holdall covering his crotch. He took the opportunity to look at Astrid as she drove. She smiled a lot and was very much at ease in his company. He would have relaxed too if it was not for the sex thing. He reflected that here were two young intelligent people who could have a perfectly reasonable discourse but that this was now impossible due to an instinctive urge to fornicate. Taken at face value the situation was ridiculous. As a professor he could not understand it. As a young man it was quite simple and seemed only too natural. Progress was slow and would have been tortuous were it not for their chemistry, excitement and fascination.

Traffic stood on the autobahn and it was clear that the journey would take many hours. Astrid was listening intently to the traffic news. 'I don't know if you understood that but it seems that the road at the border is unlikely to be cleared until tomorrow morning.'

Felix rapidly recalculated, reconfigured and recalibrated his proposed programme. Irritated because others had caused the need for changes he asked,

'Why are the authorities not prepared for the snow?'

'It is not just the snow', Astrid replied surprised by his manner of speaking. 'It is true to say that the snow is the heaviest that we have had for

239

many years but there have been accidents and some folk are sleeping in cars at the side of the road. There is no way to pass. What shall we do?'

It was clear to Felix that any attempt to progress further would prove futile. They would gain little by pressing ahead.

Astrid saw the sense of that rationale too. 'Well it looks like you will have the pleasure of my company for the evening. What, I wonder, does Rosenheim have to offer?'

The two laughed. Felix smiled at her as she took the Ausfahrt off the autobahn. There was the nagging doubt about Innsbruck but all had seemed well according to Bühler. It was clear that he had to get there as soon as possible but wishing was not going to improve matters. No, he was pursuing the correct course of action. And yet ... He knew that he should concentrate on his mission. It made sense. It was logical. He recognised that Astrid was a distraction. There would be others perhaps more suitable. He understood that testosterone was surging through his muscular body and that his decision-making was being warped. He had anticipated that. What he hadn't anticipated was the strength of the urges and their ability to disrupt the logical thought processes. Knowledge and experience were counting for little and he had to get his head around that. An old head was on young shoulders but how could he compete with the chemistry of his body and the natural rhythm of life? He considered the conundrum.

Sex education teaches kids to have sex and the number of illegitimacies have increased as a result of it. Cigarette packets state that the contents kill and the young take up smoking. Alcohol and drug abuse information is widely available but education does not translate into action. Children are taught to be aware of the environment yet it is the parents who turn off the lights and turn off the taps. To know is insufficient. Education and applied knowledge are rarely fellow travellers and come a poor second to the hormones of youth. Logic cuts no ice. Rational thought is overwhelmed, swamped by hormonal activity. What is transparent to those whose passions have subsided is kaleidoscopic to the young.

'Nevertheless', he thought, 'I really can't travel further, can I?' There wasn't a heliport or a secret passageway into Austria available. So why not spend a pleasant evening in the town and who knows? Again he became conscious of the swelling between his legs. Didn't it ever go down?

She broke the silence as they entered Rosenheim. 'Shall we eat? Do you have money?'

He nodded. 'Yes I have a little. Enough to eat.'

'But not to sleep?'

'I will manage. Don't worry about me.' He imagined that Felix Elder would have had much tighter squeezes than sleeping in a bus or railway station.

They drove along Munchner Strasse looking for a place to eat. Set in the snow the Bavarian buildings reminded Felix of the Christmas postcards he had collected as a child. He reflected on the lateness of the spring.

'What about here', she said, stopping at the Hotel Hirsch.

'To eat?'

'To sleep too. I'll take the bed and you take whatever is left', she said, giving him some form of modern communication that he had not deciphered but recognised that he ought to have. 'It's not as it used to be', he mused. 'Girls are certainly more forward than they were in the old professor's day.' At least girls had certainly been more reserved with George Merrick in his student days some fifty years ago than had Astrid had been with Felix. Fifty years! If Astrid knew that he was in his seventies. My God!

Again there was a need to adjust his groin. Didn't the thing ever take time off? They parked the car by the roadside, made their way up the flight of steps and entered the hotel.

'Just a moment', said Felix. 'I don't know how to put this exactly but might I suggest that you hand over some money... for appearances you know.'

'Oh, how very old fashioned you are. You are surprisingly proper but I'm paying by credit card. OK?' He smiled and nodded. 'Ok.' He had always disliked the 'American OK.' Now he minded less.

They took a room on the first floor.

'I need a shower and clean clothes', she said adding, 'and I need you out of the room sir.'

Felix laughed, 'Very well my lady. Will that be all my lady?' They laughed. 'Seriously', he went on, I must buy a few things. I'll see what the town has to offer. See you presently.'

He left Astrid sitting on the edge of the bed brushing her hair. Her English was quite good but she had not heard a young man speak English as Felix had.

He sounded very correct and much older than his years. He had winced at some of the music that she had played in the car yet it was very popular music and not at all heavy. His leather coat and worn blue jeans told her that he was cool but his language was strangely archaic. What had he just said? I will see you presently. That did not seem at all usual for such a cool guy. Still, he was gorgeous and built like a tank. He had those magical qualities that most women required of men. He was good looking; a good listener and attentive; put her at ease and was clearly both competent and confident. In short she had felt special in his company.

She laid her clean set of clothes on the bed and slipped into the shower deep in thought. Decisions might need to be made.

Felix made his way across the street to a small supermarket. He bought a pack of razors, a toothbrush and toothpaste. He did not know when Felix had last shaved but it must have been at least a couple of days since. George Merrick had hadn't had much facial hair. His light sandy hair colour and patchy growth had prevented him growing the beard that would have saved him so much time on a morning. Felix's stub was black, dense and even. Perhaps he would grow a full set some time? In the meantime he would shave.

He called in at the apoteke a little further down the street and bought condoms nervously looking through the myriad of types available hoping to find something unexotic. That done he doubled back towards the hotel taking his mobile from his jacket pocket.

'Hello. This is George ... I know it doesn't sound like me. Do you think I should sound like an old man? Listen. Is everything well? Good... You have checked the two women? Good. There is a change of plan. It may well be that I cannot get to you until tomorrow afternoon. Let them rest this evening. God knows they've had enough tranquillisers and sedatives to make them sleep for a fortnight. However, a little more for breakfast I think. Until tomorrow.'

Fantastic! All was going to plan. Thinking of the superlative 'fantastic' gave him considerable food for thought.

He had often grimaced at the endless superlatives used by his undergraduates. Great, fabulous, fantastic and mega had often described the prosaic and unworthy. Perhaps he had been a little harsh. Life certainly could be very agreeable. Fantastic even!

He marvelled at the spring in his step and his zest for life. He combed his thick black hair and took the hotel steps three at a time.

Chapter 66

Julia and Sarah

Julia Salomonovich and Sarah Fossard sat in the beige Mercedes taxi in silence bewildered, shocked and exhausted. Sarah reflected on the past forty-eight hours. She had tried to suppress her hurt and anger for Julia's sake. She knew that she had made a mess of things but was sustained by the thought that if she had not made the decision Peter would have died. It was little enough consolation.

Julia was considering their next move. Where would they go now? Home was out of the question. Chloe and Lucy must be warned to stay clear of the place and Mike Tyler too. The professor had killed or had at least had had someone killed. There was no reason to suppose that he would not do so again. No, they must have something to bargain with, but what?

She pictured the old man coming towards her with a weapon. Surely he was too frail? Perhaps he would have an accomplice? Surely not! His secret was too valuable and it was clear that he wasn't going to share it with world. At least not yet. No, it would have to be a trap, a device, an accident or a bomb. My God this was a nightmare.

She felt that they didn't have much going for them but, then again, she was alive and, by any measure, she most certainly would not have been were it not for the professor's genius. It was a double-edged sword. If he had refused the operation Sarah would not be in danger. Or would she? If they knew of the professor's intentions then surely they would not have walked out of the hospital alive. An 'accident' might well have been contrived. The more she thought about the problem the more intractable it appeared to be.

She looked down at her body again, 'God knows what my reaction is going to be when I inspect my undercarriage.' For the umpteenth time she suppressed her feelings. She displaced them by working on strategies for survival. Sarah's safety was paramount. She must come out of this for the sake of her daughters. The consequences of suppression would have to be dealt with later.

They arrived at the airport at Kranebitten north of Innsbruck. Sarah paid off the taxi and they made their way to the booking office. The next plane to England was a flight to London at five past seven, within an hour, but that was fully booked. The clerk looked down at her computer screen.

'Yes', she offered, 'we have a flight tomorrow at half past six in the morning. It goes to Birmingham.'

'Is there nothing before that? Sarah almost pleaded'

'I'm afraid not madam.'

As they moved away from the counter Julia said, 'It's our only chance. He hadn't even arrived at the rest home when we left. We could have gone anywhere. He has to track us and that will take time.'

Sarah countered. 'The airport would be a good bet. Perhaps we should go to the railway station.'

'True but the airport only seems logical because that is where we decided to go. He has to guess where we are.' Julia was trying to kid herself. 'Look, we'll go into the departure lounge. He'll have to buy a ticket to get in and passenger details are privileged information. He will have to take a huge gamble. Then again we can recognise the old man. What can he do to us in an airport? We can always call the police.'

'And say what precisely. Who is going to believe our story?'

Julia held Sarah by the shoulders to comfort her. She was trembling and it was clear that she couldn't go on for much longer. 'We don't have to tell our story to anyone. All we need to say is that a madman is following us.'

Sarah looked at Julia. 'Then we book the flight?' Julia had already turned to the counter.

Chapter 67

DELAYED IN ROSENHEIM

When Felix Elder returned to the hotel room Astrid was sitting at the dressing table brushing her hair. She had showered and changed and looked fresh and revived. The transformation was amazing. Gone were the chunky cable jumper and jeans. She wore a short slashed necked black silk dress. She turned towards him.

'Did you get what you went for?' she asked.

'Yes' he breathed, his heart missing several beats. 'Now I can shave and brush my teeth', he added, sagely omitted to mention the condoms.

She walked past him on her way to the door. 'You can have the sofa and the top cover from the bed tonight. I will be at the bar when you are ready. Ich habe durst!' He pulled his top over his head and she turned to look. 'Very impressive', she laughed looking at his muscled torso.

He put an index finger over each nipple and said, 'No looking. Anyway you're thirsty. Off you go' She left laughing.

Felix was amazed that he had begun to develop a sense of humour. It certainly hadn't been there before.

It was his first opportunity to inspect his new body. He turned on the main light and opened the wardrobe doors. A full-length mirror was fixed to the inside of one of the doors. He threw his sweatshirt and tee shirt on the bed and checked out his pectoral and abdominal muscles. He knew that it must have taken considerable time and dedication to hone the definition of his pecs and six-pack. He bent his right arm and watched the bicep bulge. He felt the hardness with his left hand. 'Rock', he said, 'I'm made of rock. My God, how the hell am I going to maintain such a physique?' He made a mental note to buy weight-training equipment. The very idea of training had appalled him before but now there was a different perspective and it appeared rational.

He moved to unbuckle his thick black leather belt, undid the brass top button of his jeans, a garment he had never previously worn, and pulled

245

down the zip. He knew that he had an erection but wasn't prepared for what came next. The brief white pants that he had slipped on in the dark in the ambulance strained to restrain his equipment. The bulge was enormous. It was in stark contrast to the puny affair that he had possessed for the past seventy years. He turned sideways to look at his profile. The bulge didn't look any smaller. His strong legs were covered with black hair. He checked out his calves, his quads and his hamstrings before moving up to his buttocks. 'Solid as a rock', he said, giving them a sharp smack. His eyes descended to his pants once again and he pulled them down over his erect penis. There it was in all its splendour. He stood looking at the image for a while then moved his hand down his body to take himself in hand.

'My Lord', he said, conscious that his vocabulary and idioms were in considerable need of review.

He was also conscious of the time and quickly showered and shaved. Shaving a strange face was something of a challenge but he managed to succeed in not cutting himself, acknowledging that it would take time to adapt to his new refined fine motor skills. He changed into a clean cream casual shirt and pair of green chinos. The phone rang. 'Yes', he said. Astrid wondered if he had drowned in the bath. He laughed, 'Sorry, I won't be long.'

Thirty seconds later he left the room and made for the bar. Astrid sat on a bar stool talking to the barman. She was clearly comfortable speaking with strangers. Her greeting surprised him. She leaned towards him and kissed him on the lips. He flushed a little and had his complexion not been quite so dark his embarrassment would have been more obvious. Astrid noted his reaction and felt warmth from his unexpected vulnerability. He certainly was a man of mystery, she thought.

Felix regained control and ordered drinks. They left the bar and moved to the restaurant and were shown a table in the corner of the room. He began to drink his glass of Pils but was not impressed. Neither George Merrick nor Felix Elder had anything more than a very occasional drink. They ordered and began to eat.

'Tell me all about Michael Mitchell', she began. 'Who is he?'

'Guess', he said in a mysterious whisper. He really didn't know where this sense of humour was coming from but it seemed appropriate and it was certainly fun.

'Oh I don't know', she began. I think that you are a soldier of fortune on the one hand, yet on the other … she hesitated … I believe that you are something that requires intelligence… yet… yet…you really speak like an old school master sometimes. I don't know the English accents so well, though I did spend time in Suffolk during my second undergraduate year.'

'Really', Felix interrupted, almost telling her that Suffolk was his home county. He stopped himself in time. 'Go on.'

'You are reserved. No, unsure of something. I saw that in your face when you asked me to continue.' Felix saw the sparkling intelligence in her eyes when he had spotted her looking at him in the Rastplatz. He hadn't bargained for her being quite so bright. 'Am I right', she asked.

'No but I can understand your line of thought. I have an academic background but I am a climber by trade. I work freelance.' He saw that she was going to continue and interrupted her. 'So, now it is my turn. Who is Astrid ... I don't even know your last name.'

'Schwartz.'

'Schwartz. Oh! How do you do Miss Black?'

She laughed and was about to continue her interrogation when he interrupted her again. 'And you? What about you?'

'It's your turn to guess.'

'Guess. Guess', he feigned hurt. 'The great Holmes does not guess young lady.'

Her eyes sparkled excitedly.

'You are an artist. No a student of art. Yes, a postgraduate of Munich University. A Master's degree perhaps?' I believe that you have been painting very recently. He caught her eyes, which confirmed his guess. 'Furthermore Miss Black, your home is in Munich but your parents live near Innsbruck. You are twenty-three years of age and single.' Her mouth dropped open in amazement.

'But how...' He waived her interruption aside. 'Elementary my dear Miss Black, elementary. She moved closer to him as he poured her a glass of Mosel Spätlese. Astrid inched her face towards him. 'Go on Mr. Holmes', she said seductively. 'What else do you know about me?'

'Oh, when one possesses such deductive powers as I there is little that one cannot discover', he continued. 'For instance you only dine with very handsome, intelligent and interesting men when in Rosenheim.' She shrilled with laughter. He lowered his voice. 'And you are very beautiful, I know that too.' She stopped laughing and paused for a moment. Her smile dropped and Felix saw that she was reassessing her situation. The smile was back on her face in an instant. The almost imperceptible flicker of contemplation would have gone undetected by one with lesser forensic observational powers.

'Well Mr. Holmes, may I ask how you came to your conclusions? I don't see any evidence. Perhaps it is guesswork all along. Perhaps you are quite wrong.'

Felix was well into his part. He had never before engaged in such a conversation. Never had he felt so light and so happy. The conversation was inane. That was true. It was unlikely to profit mankind. That was equally true; but it was fun. Fun! A concept well known to his under achieving undergraduates but not previously to himself.

'No Miss Black', he continued with his part, 'It is you who have underestimated the great Holmes.'

Astrid was intrigued and lapsed into German. 'Bitte erzhalen.'

'An explanation? Naturlich. Are all the main characters gathered around the great fireplace?' They looked around the room as if to confirm as much.

'Good. The great Sherlock will reveal all.' They both took a sip of their wine and Astrid put her hand on his knee. Again she saw that look of uncertainty in his face. What was that? It took away his confidence and she warmed to him further.

He knew that she had observed his lapse and saw her reaction to his vulnerability. He knew that, paradoxically, it left her vulnerable too.

He began his revelation. 'Your fingernails have been cleaned but I noticed earlier that you had paint underneath them.'

She thought for a second. 'I may have been painting my house. What is it that you call that?'

'Decorating?'

'Yes, decorating. How do you know that I was not decorating?'

'Elementary Miss Black. I can recognise artist's oil paint when I see it.'

She was fascinated now. 'Go on. How do you know the rest?'

'It is so simple. On the back seat of your car there is a textbook and an alumni magazine. This not only indicates that you were an undergraduate but that you are remaining in contact with students who have left. An alumni magazine is circulated to postgraduates, as a rule, I believe.'

Astrid was enraptured by the wonderful personality that was Felix Elder. Here was a man of charm, wit and intelligence; someone who disarmed her with his old fashioned courtesy, discourse and wit. She felt safe with him, comfortable and important. He was exciting and had clearly lived life to the full. He was handsome and had a serious body. He excited her. She stared unashamedly into his piercing blue eyes.

'Your car's registration plate begins with the letter M which stands for Munich. It is a fair assessment that it is where you reside. You travel to Innsbruck with a flowering plant on the back seat carefully wedged between your coat and holdall. This I believe to be a gift for your mother who lives nearby in Kranebitten.'

She interrupted him. 'I told you I was going there. That's not fair', she pouted.

'How I gain my information is irrelevant', he said waiving away her protestations and looking down his nose at her with mock dismissal. 'And so to the final part of my analysis. How do I know that you are twenty-three and single? That is easy. You left your passport on the desk in our room.'

She didn't see it at first. Then it struck. She convulsed with laughter and scorned, 'that's cheating and I thought that you would not stoop to such... oh yes, that's how you found I was a student and oh, you big cheat.' She squeezed his lips together between her index finger and thumb in mock anger. He protested his innocence.

They laughed uncontrollably. Then she moved towards him and kissed him on the lips again. It was long and passionate and earned them an ovation from the other diners.

Felix stood and bowed and Astrid followed with a curtsy. This brought a peel of laughter and further applause.

Felix and Astrid made to leave. He stopped at the door to address the diners.

'What is the German word for honeymoon?'

'Honeymoon ist gut', was the response from an elderly gentleman. 'Gute Nacht. Schlaft Gut.'

Astrid held Felix's hand to go but he turned her to him and kissed her once again. There was a sigh of approval as they left the room.

They walked through reception and into the waiting lift. Once the doors had closed they held each other again and kissed. Felix protested. 'This is the slowest lift I have ever had the misfortune to ride in.' They fell into fits of laughter again. 'God', Felix thought. 'I am enjoying this.

'Honeymoon? Why did you tell them that?' She said searching his face.

'Because it made them feel good. It did, didn't it?'

Astrid held him tight. It had certainly made her 'feel good.'

He opened the door and made way for her to enter. She walked past the bed to the window and drew the curtains. Felix watched her more excited than he had ever been before. She pushed her hands through her hair sensuously and Felix's wide grin disappeared as he nervously tried to anticipate what she would do next and how he should respond. Was this it? At the age of seventy plus was he finally going to lose his virginity?

Her eyes travelled downwards and she whispered, 'I can tell that you're pleased to see me.'

He blushed as he walked towards her.

Chapter 68

JULIA AND SARAH AT INNSBRUCK AIRPORT

Julia and Sarah looked at the distant snowy escarpment of the Tyrol from the upper floor departure lounge of Innsbruck airport. Julia lifted the case from the floor. 'My turn again. Come on we need a coffee and a place to call a home for the next eleven hours.'

The airport was quite small by international standards and the choice of seating arrangements limited. They found a place and took their coffee to a small table at the back of café which offered them a full view of the entrance. They felt a little more secure now they had found a quiet niche.

Sarah spoke first. 'I didn't pack. All I have is what I am standing in. I haven't changes since, well since, since when? When did all this begin?'

Julia took a few moments to reflect. 'We left Bristol for Munich on Thursday. We travelled to Innsbruck on Friday. We slept most of the day today and today is Saturday. It will be Sunday lunchtime when we arrive in Birmingham. Four days! My god just four days. It seems like months.'

Sarah held her coffee in both hands and looked at Julia. 'And now what? What on earth do we do now?' Julia was about to speak when unmistakable cognisance flashed across Sarah's face. To Peter Fossard the expression would have been so familiar. It was a realisation, a visualisation, a dawning or moment of clarity. Julia knew when Sarah had one of her flashes of inspiration.

'Sarah. What is it? What do you have?' she urged her impatiently, knowing that when Sarah was so moved it was unlikely to be the result of a peremptory caprice.

Sarah assimilated her thoughts and attempted to unscramble the flash of insight that had struck her. 'Of course. I heard it before we left the home.'

She was almost speaking to herself; the frantic trawl through her memory leaving her breathless.

'Sarah', Julia beseeched; attempting to elicit an overdue response.

She stared hard into Julia's face. 'The old man in the home. What was it that I overheard? He said, '...and remember my friend if anything was to happen to me ...the authorities will receive information within twenty-four hours. I am not a fool.'

Julia saw the sense of it. 'We have a card at last. The trouble is getting home, lodging a letter somewhere and being able to contact Merrick before he gets to us.' She stopped for a moment. 'Or there's always the police?'

Sarah looked at him. She didn't have to speak.

'I know, I know. Who is going to believe us? That's it then.' They sat quietly for a moment.

'Julia', said Sarah. Both froze. 'I know, I know. Somehow I haven't been able to call you that; call you anything come to that. Calling you Peter would be as strange as calling you Julia. But, well, there is no point in calling you Peter anymore is there?' she said, looking for confirmation. 'It's no use hoping that you could pass for Peter. I think that I am beginning to see that now.'

Again there was silence. Julia reflected on her circumstances. 'We'll save that for later. Ring Mike, we need him to fetch us from Birmingham.'

'But.'

'I know. Look, for now he doesn't need to know anything and neither does Lucy or Chloe, it will only complicate matters.'

Sarah was about to interrupt her but Julia cut her short. 'I know, things couldn't be much more complicated.'

Sarah reached into her bag for her mobile and rang Mike. She knew it wasn't 'kranken' or whatever. That explanation had just ... no matter.

At last Mike answered. Sarah began, 'Where have you been? I've been ringing you for three days.'

'Oh, hello Sarah, I'm very well thanks. It's so nice to hear your sweet voice again.' She apologised, 'Where have you been. I went to the hospital and they said ...'

Sarah interrupted him. 'Please don't ask questions Mike. No recriminations. We are in Innsbruck and will be arriving at Birmingham airport at one o'clock tomorrow afternoon can you be there to pick us up?'

Mike Tyler wondered if Sarah had lost her sanity. He had been to the hospital and had been informed that Sarah had taken Peter home for his remaining days. Mike had gone to the Fossard's home and found it locked. He had then picked up a message on his answer phone saying that Sarah had taken Peter to Germany in a last ditch attempt to save him. Save him for God's sake! The man had hours to live. He tried to ring her mobile but could only get a weird buzzing and a message saying that some satellite couldn't be found. Now he had discovered that she had gone off to Austria. She couldn't have taken Peter from there so where the hell was he, or his body now? None

of it made sense. Sarah just wouldn't have left Peter. But she had said we …
The imperative struck him.

'Sarah. Peter. Is he …' he hesitated.

'Mike', she chided, 'I know that things seem very strange but I will
explain as soon as I can. Will you be there for us?'

'As always Sarah.'

'And Mike, not a word to anyone, and that includes Lucy and Chloe.
Do you understand?'

'I'll be there Sarah but I do have one question. 'Are you safe? Sarah.
Sarah'. The line had gone dead.

Chapter 69

A NIGHT IN ROSENHEIM

Felix had never felt out of his depth. He did now. Astrid stood beside the bed smiling provocatively; he was hot, under pressure, couldn't think straight and had a little more empathy with his undergraduates than he had ever previously.

Astrid was hesitant. Having signalled her acquiescence in the sacred feminine semaphore, she had anticipated a swift and impatient assault. He had stayed his ground. 'God this mystery man was cool! What was it about him? He was young, handsome, intelligent and exciting yet responsible and without the affectations of her former lovers. And, oh, she thought, sexy as hell.'

She smiled remembering a line from an old American movie. 'Cat got your tongue?'

She smiled as he walked slowly towards her, his heart pounding. He took her in his arms and kissed her. When their lips parted he held her little closer still scenting her fragrant hair and feeling her lithe body in his arms. A new sensation. A wonderful supple sensation. A sensation denied to him by Joel Salomonovich.

Astrid was surprised by Felix's gentlemanly manner. A reserved Englishman. Surely such a notion was a thing of a bygone age judging by their standards in Ibiza, the south coast of Spain and most other places where British youth gathered to party. Had she mistaken his coyness for coolness? She decided to make the first move. Her hand moved to his crotch and he almost hit the ceiling. She closed her eyes and moaned that she wanted him.

Lacking knowledge of procedures and protocol in love making delayed Felix's response by no more than a nanosecond. Any time widening his knowledge by researching sexual engagement would have been lost on him. Felix did what most men do in his predicament; he went into autopilot and discovered that things occurred as and when, dictated by their hormones.

Indeed, he was to reflect later, that prescient knowledge would only have lessened his experience. Astrid was certainly tactile and had a fertile imagination and that, he concluded, was what really counted. They slept much later.

Chapter 70

MIKE TYLER'S STORY

Mike Tyler was at his wits end. The more he considered Sarah's recent incoherent ramblings the more he believed her to have had a nervous breakdown. It was the only explanation. When someone near to one is dying they grieve, he rationalised. When they die they mourn. That was the natural order of things. What they don't do is fly off to Europe, disappear from sight and leave their whereabouts unknown to those nearest and dearest to them.

Mike had visited Peter with Sarah only three days earlier. It was transparently obvious that Peter was close to death. Mike, being Mike, had not been impressed with the approach of the old man and his 'crony' as they had left Peter's room and, ever protective of Sarah, resolved to visit the hospital once again that evening in order to prevent a further unsolicited approach.

Sarah had said that she would go home, change and return to the hospital later in the evening. Mike had been delayed for a short time but on arrival was informed that Peter had been taken home. This was a considerable shock. He had assumed that Sarah had been updated on the impending death and had wanted Peter to die at the home they had shared for over twenty years; somewhere familiar to him. Shocked that Peter could be moved at all he had left immediately recognising the dreadful pressure that Sarah would be under.

There was no one at the house. He phoned Chloe then Lucy, both were in transit on the way to the hospital, neither knew of Peter and Sarah's whereabouts. He agreed to meet Peter's daughters at the hospital's reception desk.

Chloe and Lucy had been through purgatory during recent weeks. Both had suffered greatly. Their father meant everything to them and they were now rendered numb and unresponsive to an unconcerned world. The weeks had drawn into months and each month had seemed like a year. The dreadful toll was visible in their young faces.

Mike had arrived at the hospital first and had made further enquiries of the receptionist.

'I'm sorry Mr. Tyler but I can only give information to members of the family', she offered apologetically. Mike understood but was not at all amused. He understood the hospital's rationale. He understood that the receptionist was merely applying the proscribed protocol. He recognised that his own heightened anxieties intensified his tension and should be controlled. Still the vitriol, blessedly not aimed at an individual but none the less delivered with some venom, came forth.

He apologised. 'Look I know that it's not your fault but ... I'm sorry.' He left the desk and took a chair. 'But for God's sake, how many people ask after the health of a relative or friend with malice in mind? And who checks to find out if relatives are who they say they are anyway? And further, someone with an ulterior motive in mind is highly unlikely to confess that they barely know the person they are enquiring about. Was it not more likely that they would lie? What was the point? The residue of bitterness and gall leached into his destructive mind set leaving him feeling empty and hopelessly forsaken.

Chloe and Lucy arrived. Chloe asked about her father at the desk. The receptionist reached under the counter and placed an envelope in her hands. Frustrated Mike watched Chloe open the envelope. She read the contents to Lucy and Mike.

It read: To the family of Peter Fossard. Mrs. Fossard has decided to take her husband to Germany for medical treatment. The treatment is a radical departure from traditional methods and must be administered without delay. Mrs. Fossard informs me that she will make contact with her family at the earliest opportunity but considering the circumstances, this will not be possible for a little time. Please understand that the best possible care will be taken of Mr. Fossard. I also ask you not to discuss this letter with anyone. The work is experimental but I am sure that you will agree it is quite certainly his only hope. Mrs. Fossard wishes you to know that although the steps she has taken are highly irregular it is her wish that I begin proceedings with immediate effect.

Professor George Merrick had not signed the letter.

Mike immediately thought of the old man who had approached Sarah at the hospital. What had she fallen for? A quack? My God! And Germany! Why Germany for god's sake?

Mike was for going to the police but Chloe held his arm. 'She is doing what anyone would do Uncle Mikey. She is giving dad one more chance. I know that it's weird and ...' she lost her ability to find the words at that point and wondered away to a bench at the far side of the room sobbing. Lucy joined her.

'OK', rationalised Mike, 'if everything is above board, why did your mother not phone either of you?'

Neither woman was in a fit state to reply. The question was left hanging in the air.

Lucy went to stay with Chloe. They needed each other desperately. Mike resolved to stay at home to man the telephone. If Sarah rang he would be there for her. The three kept in contact with one another throughout the following day.

Mike wanted to call the police but Chloe and Lucy still clung to the hope that their mother had acting in the best interests of their father. They knew she always had and they knew that she would now.

It was on the third day that Mike resolved to go to the police station, regardless of Chloe and Lucy's protestations, and it was on his way there that he had taken Sarah's call on his mobile.

Now he was more perplexed than ever. Why was he expressly forbidden to talk to Chloe and Lucy about their mother's phone call? His brain was overheating. He couldn't think straight. The stress of the situation was clouding his judgement and angst rendered his thought processes impotent.

Now he sat staring at the wall waiting for the time to set off for the airport in Birmingham. It couldn't come soon enough.

Chapter 71

MIKE TYLER'S CONCERN

Mike Tyler had never done drugs but he guessed that continued heavy use would have left him feeling pretty much as he felt now. There was a reality somewhere to the fore but however much he attempted to perceive it the damn thing evaporated and formed elsewhere. He sat in Birmingham airport car park and began to analyse the possibilities of the whereabouts of his best friend. Like a drunk desperately trying to focus he took a deep breath and paused to think things through before failing to assemble the elements of his deliberations. It was no good. There was no logical explanation other than that Sarah had gone mad.

What had she said? 'Can you be there to pick us up?' Will you be there for us?' Us. Us. Us. Who the hell were us? Peter was either dead or on his deathbed … somewhere. Who the hell was she with? Why had she decided to take a trip to Innsbruck? Euthanasia? Wasn't it legal there? Is that why she had left? Surely not! Peter had little enough time left and was in agony but a decision like that would surely have been made much earlier on in his illness and Sarah would have consulted him for certain.

That still didn't answer the question, who the hell was she bringing back with her? Perhaps it was a mistake. Perhaps, after so many years of marriage, she was just used to talking in the plural. Even so, none of this made sense. Chloe and Lucy. What of Chloe and Lucy? Would a sane Sarah, a rational woman, a loving mother, leave her two precious daughters in the dark with regard to the fate of their father? Of course not! It was clear. Sarah had gone over the edge. He would do her bidding – get her home – assess her mental state then ring the doctor. It was for her own good.

He had rationalised the situation at length and had reached his conclusion.

Never-the-less it was an irresolute Mike Tyler who left his car and walked rapidly towards arrivals.

Chapter 72

BIRMINGHAM AIRPORT

Sarah sat in the aisle seat and ordered two large glasses of cognac. Julia sat facing the porthole lost in thought. The bizarre circumstances of her own plight weren't her only concern. She knew that she couldn't rest or rationalise her thoughts until Sarah was safe and Chloe and Lucy acquainted with her new stark reality. Those were her real concerns and bugger her own living hell.

She offered the cognac to Julia and they touched glasses, as they always had. Julia took a deep slug. She replaced the breath that had been taken away by the burning alcohol with a deep intake of air. Peter Fossard could drink spirits with the best of them. Clearly Julia could not.

Julia put her glass down and took Sarah's hands in hers. 'I'll still see you safe Sarah. I promise. I always have and I always will.' The plane began to descend into the mist shrouding Birmingham. Sarah was not a good traveller and landing would normally have occupied her thoughts but she was lost in considerations and reflections far beyond her normal parameters. She knew that Julia meant well and that it was Peter that was talking through her. She also began to recognise that Julia could not possibly live up to the expectations she had of Peter.

Sarah and Julia passed through customs and arrived at the carousel within minutes. 'Good, the case is here', whispered Julia, still unacquainted with her new voice. A large arm moved rapidly in front of her and she jumped back defensively. 'I've got it young lady. There you are.' An athletic middle aged man, having being nudged by his wife, had assisted the 'young lady' with her suitcase. He smiled at his prompted chivalry with some satisfaction. Julia stared unable to utter a word and Sarah, on seeing her unease, intervened thanking the man and his wife for their consideration.

Sarah took Julia by the arm and marched her towards the exit. 'It happens! Sometimes it happens', was all she could say.

Recovering herself Julia swallowed hard. 'It never happened to me before and I was just so gob smacked I couldn't think of what to say. This is going to be even more difficult than I imagined. My God! A little thing like that! What next?

Sarah reminded her. 'It's Mike Tyler next.'

Chapter 73

FELIX TO INNSBRUCK

Felix woke the next morning feeling considerably different to any other morning he had experienced. There was no pain. No aches. No difficulty in moving. And there was a beautiful young woman's face not six inches from his own. Astrid was stirring slowly and Felix watched her come alive little by little. The irony registered loud and clear. He had watched Julia do something similar on the previous day. It was time to go.

'Astrid. Come on it's time to move.' Astrid's hand moved to his crotch. Didn't the woman ever give up? He checked his watch. Eight o'clock. The logical thing was to keep his appointment in Austria. Logic had always informed his actions. He was expected in Innsbruck and the traffic should be moving by now. But then again. Damn the woman. Ten minutes wouldn't harm anything.

'Where the hell has my logic gone?' he groaned to himself. He knew the answer. It was between his legs and in someone else's care.

It was almost nine thirty before Felix and Astrid hit the road. They travelled south along the E60 entering Austria at Kufstein. 'The Austrians clear feet of snow where the English have difficulty with inches', observed Felix. Astrid nodded her approval of her countrymen.

The sixty-five mile journey took a little under two hours. 'Will I see you again?' asked a subdued Astrid. Felix had addressed this problem in advance. Machiavellian solutions came there many. Astrid had awoken the unknown Felix and he was reluctant to throw away a useful card. He would back it both ways. There would be no farewell; just a gentle aufwiedersehen: A promise of a return in the not too distant future and a suggestion of attachment. That would suffice.

Felix knew that his destiny lay elsewhere and that his plan was nearing completion but Astrid could prove useful and there was no point in burning this particularly thrilling bridge. Felix felt no guilt. He never had and he wasn't about to start now.

'As you know', sighed a reflective Astrid, 'I go to Kranebitten. It is quite close. It is near the airport where my parents live. If you wish…' Felix cut her off. 'I must meet my friends. Perhaps some other time?' He saw her downcast face and laughed to lighten the mood as he kissed her temple.

Felix opened his mobile and spoke briefly. 'Hello, it's … me. I trust that you are all well?' Again Astrid noted the strangely conservative quaintness of his address. The boy wonder spoke like one of her seventy-year-old professors for heaven's sake.

Reinhardt Bühler had answered Felix's call. 'Maier here.' He listened to Felix briefly before he whispered 'I believe that you are not alone. Is that correct?'

'Perfectly correct my friend. Perfectly correct. I wonder if you would be so good as to pick me up. I am with a friend and I really don't want to put her to the trouble of taking me into the city. She has already been most kind to me and I must not put her to further trouble.'

Astrid began to protest but Felix raised a large hand and smiled.

The couple drove on for a further quarter of an hour before pulling into the appointed rendezvous Rastplatz. The awkward parting took no more than five minutes and was witnessed by an elderly gentleman with piercing blue eyes who sat in an adjacent black Mercedes.

Felix enjoyed the experience. He kissed Astrid passionately, waived aside her fears of them not meeting again and opened the car door. 'I have your number. I will phone you tonight. Aufwiedersehen. The puce beetle rounded the distant bushes and disappeared along the autobahn.

Felix stood in the drizzle smiling at the occupant of the black Mercedes. The occupant was not amused. In his day young men had fought for the Fatherland and the sublime Hitler. Duty and discipline were demanded and the price of failure was high. He looked across at the unworthy young man with contempt. 'In his day … In his day …'

The impertinent parasite smiled as he approached. Bühler snarled and the driver's window ascended as he turned away in disgust to avoid communication and contamination.

Amazingly the fool tapped on his windscreen. 'In his day …' Reinhardt Bühler's rage was never far from the surface. He threw his door open and demanded to know what the hell the oaf wanted.

'Helmut Maier I believe.' Bühler stared hard at the young man. 'What do you want? Who are you?' he demanded. The young man's index finger waived in front of Maier's face. 'The question is, Herr Maier, who are you? Not who am I.' He laughed out loud at the ashen face before him. 'It is just my little joke Herr Helmut Maier or shall I call you Obersturmführer Reinhart Bühler.'

Bühler made to leave. Felix then uttered a single word that halted him in his tracks.

'Metamorphosis.'

The penny dropped and Bühler stared at Felix in disbelief. 'Herr Professor Merrick?'

'The very same. Your faculties are slowing down old man. The same may not be said about the excellent Felix Elder. On the contrary his are much improved of late. And now you will be kind enough to take me to our sleeping friends. I trust that they are comfortable?'

The car pulled away from the Rastplatz and glided onto the autobahn. They travelled south turning onto the E13 at Mattrei am Brenner as Bühler interrogated Felix as exactingly and thoroughly as he had interrogated so many unfortunates during the war.

'My share of the profits are nothing to me', he spat. 'I will trade it all for the opportunity to, shall we say, change my personality.'

Felix smiled. As always the brain of George Merrick was, as Sarah Fossard had once observed, not just a step ahead of the game but a whole flight of stairs in advance of the competition. Felix knew his quarry. He also knew that Bühler was no fool.

'There are several difficulties there my friend. Firstly we do not have a suitable donor. Secondly and advisedly, I do not have the device with me. Who knows what calamity may befall it in such circumstances?' He caught Bühler's concern. 'Do not fear my friend, it is safe. And thirdly I am not at all sure that I wish to dispense my largesse. This was certainly not included in the extensive package I offered you at an earlier date.'

The Mercedes turned towards Gschnitz and began to climb. Bühler was thinking. Felix knew where he was going with it.

'The arrangements stand my dear Reinhart', cajoled Felix.

The Mercedes stopped. 'Eight million Euros, it is all that I have. I will just have sufficient to live on if you give me the opportunity. And I will include the Innsbruck rest home', he added desperately.

'Reinhart, Reinhart, Reinhardt, I know that you have always been an altruist. I know that you have a soft and gentle nature but, you see, I really don't. I have transacted business with you and that is that. No more and no less. Furthermore, you have already crossed me once so how do I know that I can trust you again?'

Bühler stared at Felix. 'What in God's name does that mean crossed you? I procured ...'

Felix warmed to his task. 'It means old chap that you have already lied to me. Exporting, especially exporting illegal contraband, drugs and arms is a highly rewarding business is it not? You lost a great deal in the early days. Gambling is not your forte, I would keep off it were I you, but you remain more than well-heeled and are worth at least double what you claim. Quite an inauspicious start to negotiations wouldn't you say?' Bühler struggled with the term 'well-heeled', but he understood the meaning well enough and knew too that Felix was playing with him. An alternative strategy would be required. A bartering position defined. He thought he might have it. The four strategies already considered by Bühler and their counter strategies had already been accounted for by the brain of Professor George Merrick. Felix Elder had recalled them. 'Just so', he laughed to himself.

Bühler started the car and drove the remaining mile or so to the hotel frantically considering further options and searching for any levers to pull in the light of new developments. Felix Elder would offer him none.

Bühler drove to the front of the home taking his reserved parking place in the forecourt. Turning to Felix he began on another tack. 'You know when a man is on your hook Herr Professor. You fish well. What is it that I can do for you that will convince you that I am suitable for your Metamorphosis? You plan meticulously. You know where you are going with all of this. Don't play with me. Tell me your terms. Money? Conditions? Favours? I am ready to oblige; I have many contacts my friend. I will gamble.'

Felix laughed. It was so obvious. Strategy one. The direct approach. Worldly goods. 'Ah, now my dear Reinhardt, 'I am quite sure that you will recall that I advised you against gambling', mocked Felix.

'Don't', screamed Bühler, attempting to contain his rage then suddenly recognising that he was weakening his bargaining position. His temper temporarily subsided. 'Just ... just don't play with me', he whispered.

Felix was well pleased with his method. 'I will consider your proposition', he offered as he opened the car door. 'But remember this; no mistakes from here on in. Do you understand?' Bühler nodded in meek obedience.

The pair walked across the gravel forecourt and into the building. Felix was shown to his room and within five minutes had rejoined Bühler at the reception desk. 'Well', began Felix, it's time to see how our guests are. They have been sedated for long enough.'

Bühler led the way to what had been Julia's room. The sun filtered through the curtains. The shape in the bed didn't fool anyone. Felix stared at Bühler. 'Try the next room. If you've fouled up already Bühler!'

Felix pointed to the door and Bühler responded. The next room's door was thrown open. The room was empty. Felix looked hard at Bühler. 'Well?'

Bühler was in disarray. He had planned so effectively. He couldn't believe his own eyes.

'I planned it all. It was perfect. They travelled from England to Munich by the Lear Jet I provided. We changed the staff after the journey and before they left for Innsbruck. They were sedated in the ambulance so that they could not talk to the drivers. They were transferred here where no one knows of their existence. The drivers have since been sacked under the pretence of them being late. There is no connection with the English couple and the outside world. They did not even know that they were in danger. There is no reason for them to escape. They were sedated again. One is weak from the 'operation' and surely cannot walk far. Why would they leave? How have they left' They ...'

Felix stopped abruptly. The diatribe was not of current consequence. He paced the room identifying and assessing his options. They were limited. There was no imminent danger. He examined the consequences. He remained safe. Never the less ... Already having recalibrated his intentions, he conceived the need for a sacrificial lamb. Bühler had never been considered in any other role. Perhaps the sacrifice would be brought forward.

'When did you last see them? When last did anyone actually see them? Find out.' Felix screamed. He rose menacingly in front of the old man. 'Idiot!'

He caught Bühler's hand as it flashed towards him and crushed it as he lowered Bühler to his knees. He spoke slowly emphasising each individual word. 'Let me tell you what you will do now. Since you can't even lock a door I had better take charge. First you will pull on all your so called connections', he caught Bühler's eye as he released his hand. Bühler placed his injured hand under his armpit in an attempt to assuage the pain. Felix took hold of Bühler's left arm then and slung him against the door. The old man looked terrified as Felix Elder towered threateningly over him. The hard stare and threatening tone relented as Felix's volatility subsided. He placed a hand on Bühler's shoulder. Bühler had expected a blow and flinched as he did so. Felix had already considered his options. He would need Bühler.

'I am aware that you will not allow me personal access to your contacts but you will never the less avail me of their services. Do you understand? Secondly you will put all local airports, ports and railway stations under surveillance. I want to know where they have been, where they are now and where they are going.' Felix turned on his heels. 'Don't fail me Bühler.'

Felix made to leave but turned back to the miserable Bühler. 'A bleak future awaits you if you fail my friend. On the other hand reincarnation may be your reward should you succeed. And with respect to a donor? I may just have one. It is time to call in all of your favours. Get them going Bühler. All of them. The whole fucking Third Reich if you have to.'

Bühler's animated face searched Felix's eyes looking for sincerity or betrayal and found neither. His tormentor held all the cards and was a master at playing them. He hesitated; then, nodding acquiescence and an acknowledgement of an unwritten contract left the room shuffling in a manner not unknown to the former arthritic George Merrick.

Felix waited for the door to close before lifting the chair at the side of the bed and hurling it at the wall mirror. It smashed into a thousand pieces. Bühler heard the crash through the door. It was followed by several Anglo Saxon expletives. He went about his business as briskly as his frame would allow.

Chapter 74

JULIA AND SARAH MEET MIKE TYLER

Julia, still walking with some difficulty, exited the airport some sixty seconds before Sarah. She walked past Mike Tyler unrecognised and stopped by the taxi stand. Sarah, for all her bravado, fell into Mike's arms. At last here was someone familiar. Someone that belonged to the day before her nightmare began.

After a brief embrace Mike pulled back and stared into Sarah's eyes, hoping to find sanity. 'I know that you have waited a long time Mike but before I begin I want us to sit down somewhere comfortable so that I can give you all the details.' She saw the coming protestations and held up her hand to Mike's face.

'I know, I know. Where is Peter? What of Chloe and Lucy? Trust me. I know that you have waited and fretted but give me a few minutes more. That is all I ask. We must leave here immediately.'

Mike looked around him. Was she been followed? What was the imperative? For God's sake would someone explain what the fuck was going on before he exploded?

They began to walk swiftly across the tiled floor past the newspaper stand towards the car park. Sarah suddenly froze and felt in her handbag. She took out her purse and offering change to the lady at the stand, took the newspaper from her and began to read. Mike watched her. Sarah had insisted that they leave immediately. It had been imperative. There had been considerable urgency in her request. Now she had stopped to buy and read a newspaper. He walked around in front of her and took hold of both of her arms. He was about to remonstrate with her but saw that Sarah's face was contorted in disbelief.

'Sarah, Sarah, what the hell is going on? Look, you're giving me the creeps.' This was a surreal and macabre play being acted out before him. He was a detached onlooker, a member of the audience. He wasn't really there at all was he? Surely he would wake up soon?

'Sarah, for God's sake', how many times had he blasphemed over the past few days? 'What is it? Please talk to me. Tell me what's going on before I lose it.'

He saw the fog lift from Sarah's eyes and a hint of recalculation. Sarah came out of her trance. 'Soon Mike, soon. We must go and quickly.'

Mike Tyler threw up both arms high into the air and screamed a silent scream. This wasn't a nightmare. This really was happening.

They reached Mike's car but before opening it he took a deep breath and lowering his voice as a nurse might to a confused geriatric. He offered an unconvincing, 'Alright, I'll wait but tell me one thing Sarah; are you in danger?'

Sarah replied. 'Perhaps I was but ... perhaps, no. Well I don't believe that I am now.'

Exasperated Mike decided to let things be. Sarah clearly needed help. He had lost the will to ask further questions. For one whose life had been in such turmoil Sarah was remarkably full of purpose and he resigned himself to wait for her to relate her story when her faculties returned. It was a strange thing though; she seemed to be quite sane no matter how off the wall her behaviour was. Then again how many people feel the urgent need to get out of a place, and get out of it fast, then stop to purchase The Daily Telegraph? Exactly! None!

They pulled out of the car park and made their way out of the terminal. Near the exit Sarah asked Mike to stop and she got out to remove her coat. As she did so she noted a taxi pulling in behind them.

Mike took the M42. The taxi followed at a distance. Julia excited the driver by asking him to, 'Follow the car parked on the exit road.' To which he had replied in broad Brummie, 'At last. No one ever has ever asked me to that before lady. I hope that you are secret service. We could do with a bit of excitement in these parts.'

Sarah opened the newspaper and began to read it again. Mike had to catch his breath to prevent yet another profanity leaving his lips. Sarah read the second article on the front page before turning to the obituary column. The front page read:

The death of Professor George Merrick was announced yesterday. The emeritus professor of Cambridge University was working in Munich at the time of his death. He had been in poor health for a number of years but his death was unexpected.

Sarah scanned the extensive coverage in the obituary columns. It appeared, to the correspondent that the professor had evidently died of 'natural causes.' The article ran on listing the achievements of the professor and citing his considerable standing amongst academics. The correspondent argued that it was quite impossible to imagine why Professor George Merrick had not been knighted. His father had been and it was clear that the son had been more productive than the father. Clearly the writer was ignorant of George Merrick's irascible nature and the contempt that he had held for his fellow man. These were the reason that submissions for his knighthood had been figuratively black balled on four occasions.

Sarah asked Mike to pull over at Junction 4 near Solihull. They took the A3400 south towards Hockley Heath for a couple of miles pulling into the car park of a small hotel. Mike began. 'Sarah I ...' She interrupted him immediately.

'Please Mike, you have been so good. Just wait a few moments longer and I will explain all. If there is accommodation we will take two rooms.' Mike was past profanities and past questioning Sarah. He acquiesced throwing both arms into the air once again.

They entered the hotel and were greeted by a smart elderly lady who informed them that, indeed, four of her eight rooms were vacant; it not being the 'busy period you know.' Mike noticed a beautiful young woman paying off a taxi in the forecourt. He still had a roving eye, even amidst the unending chaos.

The young woman entered the small reception hall, put down her case and waited for Sarah and Mike to complete their transactions. The landlady offered to show Sarah and Mike to their rooms, informed the waiting young lady that she wouldn't be 'a tick', and led Sarah and Mike up the winding staircase.

Julia watched them disappear before moving to the reception desk.

The landlady informed Sarah and Mike about the hotel's domestic arrangements and sundry other frustrating details before leaving the two on the landing. Sarah turned to Mike and said. 'Mike, I will be with you in five minutes. Just five minutes. I need to freshen up. OK? Then, I promise I will tell you everything. You won't believe it but... well...' Both doors closed. Sarah listened at her door and satisfied that the corridor was clear reopened it.

She descended the staircase and met Julia at the reception desk.

Julia had just finished furnishing her details and had already booked in. She thanked the landlady and asked her not to go to the trouble of showing her to her room. She could find her own way and her case was not heavy. It would be no trouble at all. Julia and Sarah climbed the stairs together and walked along the landing. Julia opened her door and she and Sarah went into the room. Julia put her case down on the bed and went to the window.

'There's no need to look out of the window. He won't be coming', smiled Sarah. Julia turned from the window and looked at her questioning her certainty.

'Merrick's dead. The two reasons I thought it right to stay here was to set Mike straight before he bursts and to reassess our position. We must get to Chloe and Lucy as soon as possible but you do see my point?' She stared at Julia seeking affirmation.

Shocked by the news she was still assimilating Julia demanded. 'How do you know about Merrick?' Sarah offered her the Daily Telegraph. Julia saw the photograph and read the short front-page article. She slumped to the bed relieved of her fears for Sarah's safety. The women held onto each other for a few moments before Sarah broke the silence. 'Wait here. I'll see Mike and try to tell him what we have been through, though I'm quite sure he'll have me certified as soon as I utter my first words.

'The bastard's dead Sarah.'

'Yes I know. We're safe', she replied, not grasping the full implication of Julia's words for a moment. Then it was Sarah's turn for the much used profanity of the day.

'Oh my God! He's taken it with him. The science, the machine, the ...'

'Yes, this is it. I'm here, Julia Salomonovich is here and now I'm here to stay.' Julia slumped back onto the bed. They both heard Mike knocking at Sarah's door. Sarah held Julia briefly then left.

Bewildered and confused Mike Tyler had paced his room for the whole five minutes of his tenancy. Enough was enough. Distraught at Sarah's understandable trauma and perplexed by her strange behaviour his agitation had triggered an angst ridden perambulation. He had been shocked beyond belief since Sarah had left the hospital just three days ago. He sensed Sarah's intense vulnerability and understood his duty and responsibility in that regard. Peter would have expected no less. And yet, on the surface, she showed no visible anguish, panic, or distress. How could that be? Between which organic layers was grief and sorrow to be found? Where the heartache and the misery? No such manifestations were evident. On the contrary she had seemed resolute and purposeful. But what purpose could possibly be driving her onwards?

Denial! She was in denial. Perhaps she had succumbed, capitulated, collapsed and accept the reality that Peter had died. He resolved to be there for her whenever; dutiful, supportive, dependable and faithful.

She had been decisive and alarmingly strident when convincing him to leave the airport 'post haste' but she had contradicted her petition when stopping at the news stand to purchase The Daily Telegraph. Then, when challenged, she had stopped to read the damn newspaper. Full of purpose once again, she had insisted that they get a move on. When he had driven to the exit she had insisted that he stop while she got out to remove her coat. That being done she had urged him onwards once more. Stop, start, stop start. This behaviour, however bizarre, did not characterise the pained widow he knew she must be. On the contrary her appearance, demeanour and deportment all suggested that her psyche was positive, constructive and structured regardless of her staccato tempo.

He must see her now and demand to know what was going on. The time had come. He acknowledged his responsibility and knew that Peter would have expected no less of him. He opened the door and took a step into the corridor wondering what could possibly happen next when Sarah came out of the room opposite her own? Once again he threw up his hands in despair.

'What the hell is going on Sarah? What were you doing in that room? Who's in there? I want to know Sarah and I want to know now. You seem to be treating this like some huge game and I am beginning to lose my sense of reason.'

Sarah pushed past him and made her way into his room and sat on the bed.

Mike followed her in and shut the door. She pointed to the armchair. 'You had better sit down Mike.' He acquiesced meekly. 'When I have told you what has happened since I last saw you just three days ago you won't have any reason left to lose.'

Chapter 75

FRASER AND BÜHLER

Fraser Hume was not amused. He had spent the past months combing Europe for Bühler and was not happy at the thought of wasting the New York Giants season ticket he had waited three years to acquire. When he got that son of a bitch Bühler, he was going to pay in hide.

Fraser had his best men with him. Connor John, Leroy Gomez and Tony Molinaro. They were feeling pretty much the same way as he did. It was late on a Friday evening when Leroy took a call. 'Twenty-four carat my man'. He put the phone down and jived his way back to the dimly lit card school.

'Call'. Fraser waited to see Molinaro's cards. 'Bluffing Tony? I never thought you had it in you and guess what? You didn't.' He raked in the money before turning to Gomez. 'I'm hoping that twenty-four carat means what I think it does and that you're not as crap at bluffing as Tony. What have you got?'

'Well boss man, it's like this.' began Leroy. Remember we put the squeeze on that guy in Munich?' Spencer remembered that a little pressure had been put on a small time crook called Wolfgang Friedler; if, that is, you call hanging the unfortunate Herr Friedler upside down from a five-story window to be 'a little pressure.'

Fraser had contacts with the local police but was conscious that informing them or 'putting the word out on the street' would have been as subtle as a one of those cheap sounding German sirens. Bühler had always had a sensitive nose and had kept one step ahead of retribution during a lifetime. To do that required sympathisers, smart organisers and luck. Bühler had had all three in spades.

Fraser's men had been patient. They knew that they had to be. This wasn't a 'breaking down the front door job' as Leroy Gomez had so aptly put it.

Tony Molinaro smiled. 'You're full of shit Leroy,' Connor John offered. 'You got the floor, use it.'

Leroy loved the banter. He continued. 'This Friedler guy, you know the one who doesn't like hanging out of windows? He has it that Bühler's 'hangs out' near Augsburg. Says that he comes into town, by which I mean München town, most every Friday night. Has done for years. Got two interests. Gay bars and nowhere.'

'How's that Leroy?' Molinaro asked the question that had been on the Connor John's lips. Fraser interrupted. 'Let him talk and for God's sake Leroy, get to the point.

Leroy Gomez loved centre stage and there was no rush. He pushed his fingers through his huge afro as, what he referred to as, his 'winning smile' appeared beneath his Mexican 'tash.

'That's it man. He's got a neat trick. He vanishes; evaporates; disappears. He just leaves the planet. No one knows where the fuck he goes. Next time he's seen is the next Friday. I'll tell you this for free man... it just don't make no sense.'

Leroy sat, pleased with his performance but uneasy with his rare inability to procure the goods for Fraser.

Tony eased his chair back. 'It does if you have the right connections Leroy. Back of a shop. Shazam! Organisation der ehemaligen SS –Angehörigen.'

Leroy understood well. 'Yeah well Odessa or no Odessa no one ain't seen shit nor hide of him outside the funny place.'

Fraser looked at the others, resolute. 'Gentlemen, we move quickly and, Leroy, we also move cautiously. Capice?'

Chapter 76

MIKE TYLER'S SHOCK

Mike Tyler sat on the bed his long legs stretching out before him. 'Sarah, if the time is good for you it's more than good enough for me. Give.'

Sarah began perambulating as Mike had done some minutes before, wondering where to begin. She decided to start at the beginning and the long-suffering Mike would have to patient. This would take a little more time than she had anticipated. She sat at the edge of the bed, stared at the ceiling, took a huge breath and began.

'The old man at the hospital.' Mike had an annoying habit of interrupting folk when they were relaying a story. At such a juncture he would usually have made a comment about the cheek of the man or what he would like to have said to him. On this occasion he remained silent.

Sarah went on to relate how she had found Professor Merrick's card in her handbag and how she had met the professor and Walter Krantz at the hospital later that evening. Again, amazingly, no admonishment came from the usually garrulous Mike. Even the professor's mention of offering Peter a chance to live, though causing him to stare questioningly into Sarah's face, elicited no verbal response. Sarah knew this could only get tougher.

She spoke of her sedated flight to Munich knowing that the climax of her story would come long before the end of it. She would have to assume that Mike wouldn't ring for a strait jacket before she could relate the whole of her sorry tale.

She took yet another deep breath and explained the concept of the metamorphosis experiment the professor had offered. Mike shot off the bed and began shaking his head.

'What are you talking about? The man's clearly mad.' He had lasted well but couldn't suppress or suspend his pent up emotions further.

Sarah waited. 'Do you want to hear this or not Mike?'

273

Mike Tyler walked to the window, looked out without seeing and turned back to Sarah. She had never spoken to him in such a tone before. He was hurt.

He settled again but almost hit the ceiling when Julia Salomonovich's part in the process was introduced but he saw Sarah begin to rise, apologised and promised to restrain himself once more. Soon, he believed, Sarah would point out that the experiment hadn't worked and that Peter had died and that she had had a bleeding breakdown. Then he would take her home to Chloe and Lucy, who, he almost shouted out loud, she hadn't even bloody mentioned yet.

Sarah went on, resolute and determined to finish. She resumed where she had left off. Peter had faded and it had been left to her to make the decision.

'There was only one option', she cried, taking Mike's hands in hers. 'What else could I do? Peter would have died within hours. I agreed and the experiment took place.'

Mike again felt that he could fill in the rest of the detail. The experiment failed and now Sarah hadn't the nerve to return home. To his surprise she continued detailing the ambulance journey to Innsbruck

'Why Innsbruck? For what purpose Sarah?'

'To cover their tracks. All the way through they were covering their tracks. The personnel changed at each and every stage and destination. No one other than Merrick and Krantz knew more than the tiny part they played. The staff at Innsbruck allowed us to walk away because they knew nothing.

'You walked away. Away from where Sarah?' She was losing her chronology and subsequently losing Mike's fading credulity. She stopped to think for a moment. It wasn't easy. She continued, starting with her overhearing Bühler's telephone conversation. She had gone to Peter's room and there she was.

Mike stood up. 'Sarah, you're asking me to believe, to believe, my God Sarah.' It hit him like a bolt. 'Sarah, if Mike is now Julia Salomonovich as you say he is, where is he - she now?' Mike sounded like a bridge player who had just played his ace of trumps. He smiled and moved to put his arm around the wounded shell of the woman he had admired so much for so many years. He thought her silence to be a long overdue recognition and acceptance of the new harsh reality. He wanted to tell her that he knew that she had done what she had thought to be for the best for Peter and that she was now in safe hands. Surely she would come home to grieve and to convalesce. He took a huge; much needed breath to summon the strength to speak.

She interrupted him before he had time to begin. 'Mike, the experiment was successful. You asked me where Julia Salomonovich is now. You see, that is what I have been trying to tell you for the past twenty minutes. I didn't want to relate all that has happened. God knows. I just wanted to explain, to prepare you, to to …' She walked to the door and opened it.

Mike Tyler opened his eyes wide with dawning realisation. Sarah nodded.

'Are you saying that Peter is next door? The room you came out of just now?' Mike saw his opportunity to make Sarah face reality. 'Show me.'

Sarah left the room. Mike looked out through the window onto the heathland stretching towards the M40. He wished he and Sarah were on it heading for the M5 and Bristol.

'Mike'. Mike turned to see the beautiful young woman that he had seen in the reception hall a little earlier.

'I'm sorry', he stuttered, always unable to turn off the charm, 'Do I know you? Sarah I thought that you … he froze. 'You're not suggesting? You can't be serious. I … I … what am I supposed to say. This is all just too ridiculous. No.'

Julia dressed in a thick woollen jumper and jeans, worn to hide her figure as best she could, walked into the room and sat on the stool by the dressing table. She looked out of the window nervously. 'Mike, it's not a trick, and it's not a joke. Ask me anything about your life. Anything. I know the answer. Michael Tyler I know you better than any other living person. Give me a test. Do you think that I've been spending the last three days reading your autobiography? Maybe I'm a fraud and I have researched your background for years. Ask yourself the question. Why would I do that? Why would Julia Salomonovich do that? For what purpose? And why would Sarah prove such a willing accomplice? Think man. Go on ask me anything.'

Mike stared at the young woman transfixed. It was some moments before he found the equilibrium to reply coherently. 'OK. Rugby, yeh? What position did I play?' Julia cut him off. 'Mike, try something that only you and I would know.' Mike felt that the question had been avoided and demanded an answer.

'OK, if that's what you want. Flanker at …' Mike burst in. 'See that's not right at all. I played in the centre. You see Sarah; you see', he screamed.

Julia continued. 'I was going to say Bozo, yes that's what I call you when you act dim, Bozo, that you played at flanker at school, fly half for the university third team, centre for the second team and played just once at centre alongside me in the first team. Don't get ideas above your station – Bozo. At cricket you batted like every ball needed the skin knocking off it and subsequently averaged three in the one season that you made the university second team and you were never called upon by Henry Winter, captain of the second team, to bowl one ball, though you frequently told him that you ought to have been. I have just spoken a thousand words without a full stop and have done so without taking a breath, making me the world's longest circumlocutionist, and I say this without going round the church to find the steeple, nay, without beating about the bush, prevaricating in any sort of way, procrastinating, or filibustering. Indeed I hope that I have been quite succinct, believing brevity to be of the essence of, so to speak, etcetera.'

Mike stared in disbelief. 'Where did you get that from?'

'Another tough one hey? The last bit you mean? First year rag week. An extract from the third sketch of a dismal set of four. Sounded funny as hell when you'd had ten pints and a couple of whiskey chasers. Look Mike I know that it's going to take time.' He saw the irony. 'Bloody hell Mike it's me that needs the time and I'm bloody counselling you. I'm the one that's lumbered with this.' Julia pointed to her body and immediately wished she hadn't. 'Tell you what.' Julia looked at Sarah. Sarah knew that this was going to be good. 'I've seen you in the buff a million times. Want me to go into detail?'

Mike stared hard into Sarah's eyes for help. 'It's Peter Mike. He really is in there; still fighting, still shining through.' Something remained and she clung on to that she knew would be transient.

Julia began again. You want more 'past glory stories?' Mike shook visibly. Relating reckless stories of their younger days had always carried the title of 'past glory stories.' Mike's eyes became ever wider with disbelief. Julia was concluding. 'And how about this one Mr. Tyler. How many people have you told about what happened on the night of the alumni party? You will recall that I hoped to spend the night with Sarah? Mike, I for one remember that night very well. At least until two in the morning, that is.'

'Blind drunk you sat with your backside out of the second story window defecating, yes that's the word you used when I asked you what the hell you were doing, defecating on the path two stories below. Peter, aka me, returning from the appropriate place for such a function, caught you as you began to fall backwards towards that which you had deposited moments earlier. For some reason you had neglected to use toilet paper for the appropriate purpose and had thrown the blankets off the bed. There you reposed, if that is the word, on white linen sheets. The sheets were not white in the morning.

'Next morning I called you the shithouse you were and took your sheets to the laundrette on Swift Street, you know the one where you took one sock at a time and ogled the tits of that thick blonde. Remember? Remind me again about how you repaid me. Oh yes! You threw up on my floor when coming to find out where your sheets had gone. Sarah didn't know the entire story but she sure as hell does now. She does remember, however, that you put her off staying at my flat that night. We spent the night in the common room back at the university.'

Julia's words were sharp and focussed, clear and well directed but her actions militated against animation. She remained quite motionless as she related their shared history.

'And here's another thing Mike, I thank you for taking me to the party where I met Sarah. I do remember that you had to persuade me to go. But does that entitle you to the entire contents of our fridge forever? Sarah, Chloe and Lucy seem to think so. Me? I think that you are a Bozo. Are there any more questions? I know all the answers Mike and again, I ask you, why would I do this if it wasn't true? What possible reason? Why would Sarah lie to you? What would our motive be? Where is Peter? Why is Sarah with me when she should be with Peter? Think man.'

The 'Think man', did it. Not just the words; the idiom. Peter had delivered it to Mike often. There was a dawning reality awakening in Mike's fevered mind. He sat down quietly on the bed, stunned.

Sarah sat beside him and put her arm around him hoping to comfort him. 'I know. You thought that I was mad. Truth be known, I'm still not at all sure of it myself. You're stunned. I'm stunned. Think of Julia. Yes Julia. I've tried calling her Peter but do you really believe that you can call her Peter when you look at her? Believe me I've tried. Just look.'

Julia remained sat at the stool not wishing to be looked at by anyone, least of all by Mike Tyler. He had absolutely no intention of moving any more than was absolutely necessary. Mike couldn't take his eyes from her. It was as unnerving as it was traumatic.

Changing the subject Julia offered. 'The question now is; where do we go from here? How do we approach Chloe and Lucy? I hope that you can see that although they were our first concern we must tread cautiously. They've been through enough. What's best for them? Who knows! Sarah is working on that one. I've tried and failed.'

The room fell silent all three wishing one of the others would offer a second miracle.

I imagine that you know of the death of the nutty professor Mike?' Julia glanced at Sarah.

Sarah took over the narrative relating the death of the professor and the loss of the device he had invented. Now Julia would remain Julia and that was an end to that.

'So that was the reason for The Daily Telegraph? I thought you'd gone nuts. I'm still not sure that you haven't.' Julia and Sarah began to protest but Mike raised his arms. 'Sorry, you know what I meant.'

Sarah continued, 'So now we are safe, at least we believe ourselves to be so. We don't have a madman chasing us. It's over. Now we have to rebuild our lives; starting tomorrow. Tonight we need a good night's sleep. We're going to need it. There is so much to do.'

Sarah felt that it was time to move on and that there was little more to be gained from mulling over the details. A period of reflection was needed.

'Come on Julia give the man time to think. All of us have had precious little time for that and poor old Mike is floundering. He's still not sure if it's all an elaborate hoax.'

Julia glanced nervously towards Mike during the awkward silence that followed. He was staring at her and rapidly avoided her eyes, which left her feeling uncomfortable. She lowered her own eyes and thought, 'I know Mike; Drop dead gorgeous.' The women left him shell-shocked and trying to grasp a new reality.

Julia and Sarah met in Julia's room. Sarah struck up first. 'It will take longer than I thought. He just can't take it in and we need him desperately. We need a man.'

Julia looked hurt. 'We need a physical man then. Someone we can trust. Someone reliable. We have the first and second, let's hope that we have the third too.' The women looked at each other as Sarah went on. 'I know. I know, it's Mike and Mike is, well Mike. 'He's going to have to come up trumps', said Julia, becoming a little more accustomed to hearing her new voice. She flashed her tongue across her perfect teeth and reflected that none had been drilled back into place after being knocked out by a lock-forward. That particular numb pain which often accompanied Peter's everyday life had disappeared. 'Pain is insidious', she reflected. 'Painlessness goes unnoticed. Count your blessings.'

Peter had often observed that floor got lower every year', by which he meant that it was more difficult to bend. Now as she picked up the increasingly significant handbag from the carpet she noted the ease with which that simple movement was achieved.

It was Sarah who broke the silence. 'So, where do we start tomorrow?'

Julia outlined her thoughts and Sarah agreed. It was time for an early night. It had been a very long day. They had spoken with Mike for more than two hours. Sarah left Julia alone and went to her room still fretting over her next major task. How on earth would she be able to break the news to Lucy and Chloe?

Chapter 77

JOEL AND IAN SMITH

Laura Salomonovich was a concerned mother. Julia had never gone more than forty-eight hours or so without contacting her when in England and rarely more than twenty-four hours when abroad. Her mobile had been switched off too and that she would never allow under normal circumstances. Like most of her generation her mobile phone was in constant use. Laura decided to ring Joel.

Joel and Rebecca had told Julia the truth. They had gone to London. Joel had had several meetings with several key personnel in his organisation and was pleased that he had put the chief executive's job in the experienced hands of an elderly ex-Zimbabwean with the unlikely moniker of Ian Smith. Joel had put great faith in the man and he had been proved right to do so, on more than one occasion.

The last of his meetings was over and handshakes were exchanged as the boardroom vacated. Ian asked for a moment of Joel's time and Joel sat on the edge of the long highly polished mahogany board room table. 'Mr. Salomonovich', he began. 'Please, Joel, my name is Joel.'

'Thank you. Joel, I hesitate to bring up personal matters and perhaps I am prying a little but one or two things have been brought to my notice lately and I think that you should know about them. I don't pretend to understand their significance. Shall I proceed?' Joel nodded uneasily. 'Oh dear', Ian continued. 'I sound like a junior on the first floor. Anyway this is what I have.'

'As you know our communications department monitors much more than our equities and businesses. The super highway is teaming with…' Joel cut him short. 'Cut the bullshit Ian. Just say it.'

Ian Smith grimaced and went ahead. 'Someone is checking you out big style Joel. Someone wants to know about your past, your present and your plans for the future. If I said Joel Joseph and Abraham Turner would you know who I was talking about?'

Cognisance failed to register on Joel's poker face. What about Jan Kuyper, Bielefeld, Hamburg or Amsterdam? Do any of those ring a bell? I hesitate when I introduce Simon Wiesenthal and Obersturmführer Reinhart Bühler of the SS. I see they don't concern you... good I...' Ian Smith stopped as Joel raised his hand and pointed to the drinks fountain. 'Water Ian.'

Joel's blood pressure had shot up and his face glowed scarlet. He required Ian Smith's assistance. The poker face was not necessary. He took the proffered glass and drank it in one. The phone shattered the silence. Ian lifted the receiver and delivered it to Joel. 'It's for you.'

Joel, still visibly shaking, put the phone to his ear. 'Yes. Fraser you are just the man...What? When? Look, locate him and do nothing till I get there. And

Fraser?' There was a short silence. Then, 'I understand you Joel. Don't mess up, right?'

'OK Ian, I know he's checking me out; has been for a little while. Hansen Yeh?'

Ian Smith should have known. Joel Salomonovich appeared to know pretty much everything. He knew that there were communication lines between his boss and certain staff. There had to be. A circle within the circle; A Praetorian Guard protecting the main man. 'That's the strange thing Joel; Why Nicholas Hansen's lot? Oh, I know that we have had a few skirmishes over information in the past. A little tit for tat but nothing like this. I can't see what's in it for them. Can you?'

The poker face retuned until the phone rang again. Ian passed it to Joel. 'It's for you again.'

It was Laura. She was concerned about Julia. She had gone to Germany but Gerhard had rung to say that she had not arrived. They had had a 'little tiff' on the phone and he had assumed that she had taken a room for the night somewhere nearby or that she had returned home. He had been ringing her mobile for the past twenty-four hours.

Joel put the phone down. Ian recognised that however distressing the news he had just delivered to Joel it did had not taken precedence over the appalling magnitude of his latest missive. Joel looked old and drawn. Ian went for the water jug again and turned to offer the broken man a last drink.

There stood Joel Salomonovich tall and straight, resolved and unbent. Vitality had returned to his eyes and Ian Smith began to understand how this man had built his huge empire. Joel had had a great shock but he had recovered quickly and now, imbued with his mother's pragmatism and a fire burning in his belly, he was preparing for battle.

Joel uttered the oaths he had sworn more than sixty years earlier. 'Sic vis pacem para bellum. Culpe poenae par esto.' Ian Smith drew deep from the well of his experience and said nothing.

Chapter 78

FELIX MELTS INTO THE BACKGROUND

Felix Elder put George Merrick's considerable intellect into overdrive. He assessed the probabilities and calibrated his options with the logical, precise and systematic analytical dexterity that had led him through the frontiers of science many times before. No fact was omitted from his scrutiny. He would reach 'the' conclusion and then put his plan into action efficiently.

He considered that the likelihood to be that Bühler would find the whereabouts of Julia and Sarah within a few days. There were only so many places they would go. Why was it necessary to find them immediately now that they had gone? What could they do? Go to the police? Who would they accuse? The distinguished recently demised Professor George Merrick? How would they know the exact location of the infirmary in Munich? Who could they ask for directions? If they went to the home in Innsbruck, what would they find? An efficiently run caring establishment. No, Julia Salomonovich and Sarah Fossard were not the immediate problem. Indeed, a period of calm would be advisable. He would allow his quarry to settle and Julia Salomonovich the time to accept her new reality.

He turned his thoughts to Joel Salomonovich. He would know that George Merrick had had something to do with Julia's disappearance by now. He recognised Joel's intuitive intelligence. The bastard was sharp and had the uncanny knack of jumping to the right conclusions. But so what? The professor, his old rival, had died.

Again he reassessed his machinations dispassionately. He had sold his soul to Mephistopheles for an extension to his life, perhaps even immortality itself. He had dispatched Walter Krantz and Gudrun Hackemann and snatched Felix Elder's body. He had played God with the bodies and souls of Peter

Fossard and Julia Salomonovich, but even Joel Salomonovich himself couldn't chase him to the gates of hell.

There was no timescale imperative. He could go about his business unhindered. He would first destroy the miraculous device; the blueprint of which was embedded in the labyrinthine convolutions of his memory banks, and then deal with Bühler. Both had served their purposes.

There was Nicholas Hansen too but he had no knowledge of Felix Elder either. Oh, they may tarnish the name of George Merrick but that gentleman had died.

Then there was Sarah Fossard and Julia Salomonovich. He had plans for both of them too.

Chapter 79

JULIA ALONE

Julia had not been Julia, alone and compos mentis before. She was still not sure that she was in full possession of her faculties. She sat at the dressing table, looked in the mirror weeping tears of despair. She considered oestrogen to be pretty heady stuff.

It took a little while before she stirred, the appalling magnitude of her predicament inhibiting her thought processes and causing untypical inertia. How could she jettison her past? The fact was that before a new perspective could be woven into the fabric of her life her corrosive sense of inadequacy would have to be conquered. She must embraced the new reality and comprehend the powerful impulses and irrational urges militating against her experience. She understood the unpalatable fact that it would be necessary for her to surrender to the inevitable; to the impetus of her seismic leap; to let go of the past and to embrace a new future. It would be impossible to delude herself any longer. It was clear that she should succumb to her feelings, and embrace the new Julia.

She sighed audibly. She had no infrastructure to sustain her. How could she bypass her consciousness? She clung on to veneer of normality but her psyche stoked rebellion. The frenetic battle and emotional struggle for her stability, her suppressed hurt and anger at her masculine defenestration caused her to weep bitterly.

With the dawn came a fresh uncertainty and the chilly air of reality; a recognition for some semblance of normality to maintain her. The incontrovertible truth was that she must now draw a curtain across the past. So little remained of the fabric of her former mentality. She must erase the initial ignominy and abhorrence she had felt and conquer her reasoning, take on board a whole new corpus of etiquette, comprehend new protocols and reconcile herself to her body.

Where on the previous evening she had been corkscrewing in an emotional maelstrom, a sanguine acceptance descended. The chaotic aftermath had been quelled. She had recoiled in horror. Dismantled, her identity had hung by a thread but she had survived. Still, unaccountably, her sensibilities were disturbed by the belief that someone would denounce her as a fake. How could they?

Her life, there was no doubt, would be heavily constrained but having internalised her feelings she believed that she would not have to compromise her integrity. Some values would remain non-negotiable but changes there must be. She would never again be confident of her sexuality.

Nevertheless her body pulsated with life and vitality. Peter Fossard had been a shell of a man wracked by pain and fear. He should be cold and in the grave, or hot in the furnace. Wasn't her current predicament an improvement on that? She would put her trust in her instincts; however tenuous her belief that those instincts were indeed hers. To what degree had she relied on her experience in the past? How much would be of use to her now? She had begun to have unexperienced memories which she imagined to be lingering in the convolutions of Julia Salomonovich's mind. Would they come to her aide?

She stirred from her miasma looking into the open suitcase lying on the floor. Sarah had not packed in her usual impeccable manner. The clothes were in need of hanging and she began the mundane task. She flicked her tongue across her beautifully even teeth, one experience that she now relished, as she picked up a hanger that had fallen from the bed. How easily she had done that. No pain; no ache; no grunt. The inescapable fact was that she was suppler than she had ever been. She placed her legs together and reached down to her toes. Her hamstrings dealt with the task admirably. She placed her left arm over her right shoulder and took her other hand which she had placed behind her. The task, which Peter Fossard had found impossible, was derisibly easy.

Her new weight distribution created a need for a new sense of equilibrium. She considered the locomotion of her new frame. She noted her slender arms, tiny wrists and fingers once again and remembered the difficulty she had had in lifting the moderate weight of the suitcase. The pitch of her voice was becoming more familiar to her as were her tiny feet and shoes; the ones that she couldn't see when she stood up straight because of her bosom. She had already decided that her thick long black hair, which Sarah had fastened back in a ponytail at Innsbruck airport, was going to have to go as she didn't have a clue how to deal with it. Now she was struck by the size and weight of Julia Salomonovich's clothes. There was nothing to them. They were modest, thank God, though that may well have resulted from Sarah's selection of them but, nevertheless, they were tiny. This was December. These were Julia's winter clothes. And in the summer? Another blasphemy passed her lips.

She stared long and hard at the face in the mirror. She was quite beautiful. She didn't feel at all narcissistic; it was someone else's face. It was a face that she had been given. Not something to be proud of. Then again, she reflected, that we are all given our faces. Beauty was nothing to be proud of. It was good fortune. Pure chance. The permutations of millions of chromosomes had favoured Julia Salomonovich.

There were other vivid reflections. When she stood Mike had towered above her. Even Sarah was taller than her now. And the reception desk at the hotel? Since when did they get so tall?

Wearily she took off the baggy jumper that Julia Salomonovich had always kept in her car in case of emergencies, took down the jeans and made her way to the shower. It was less than two minutes before she re re-entered the bedroom her confidence ebbing once again as she experienced her naked body. She had not washed her hair. How the hell would she be able to deal with that long mane?

She wore a plain primrose silk dressing gown as she sat at the dressing table. She turned noticing the studs in her ears for the first time. They could go too. So could the contents of the makeup bag she had just opened. What the hell was all that about?

She swore and blasphemed as she recognised the first perceived advantage of her present state. Peter had worn reading glasses for several years but had only worn them for regular use for the last three years. They had been the bane of his life. He had lost them regularly and needed them more and more. Clearly Julia Salomonovich had no use for them at all. 'How the hell can I have not noticed that my glasses are redundant?' Her eyes lowered to the large breast she had also inherited and she knew the answer only too well. 'There have been other distractions I imagine.' She noted the breast movement when she had walked. She had anticipated that the bra would have prevented that. She had been wrong. Now, without it on, her breasts bounced around as if they had a will of their own. Christ that was unnerving.

It was no good ignoring her body. It was there. It was a fact of life. She would hide it as best she could but the simple truth was that it would be impossible. She didn't have a disease or an affliction. She was not dying. What she had was natural to fifty per cent of the population. She stroked the back of her hand across her face. She certainly was a natural beauty. Perhaps more than fifty per cent of the population would be delighted to change places with her. No one was going to see her as strange, odd or deformed. Men would look but, hey, she had looked at women for years. All men damn well look. They all ogle for god's sake. It was what men did. She remembered Peter's thoughts.

In the early years of his relationship with Sarah she had felt a pang of jealousy whenever he had looked at another woman. As the relationship grew she recognised the plain and simple fact that men were programmed to assess the female form and to find a mate. What mattered was the fact that he loved her more and more as each day had passed. The one did not sour the other. Indeed Peter had pointed out that a male who did not look at women would be more of a cause for concern. Had Peter Fossard really said that? The prick!

She reached for the band that had kept her hair in place and removed it. Her hair fell down to her shoulders. She took a brush and did the best she could. She stood and removed the dressing gown and stared into the mirror. It was better to do this now than to build up more and more apprehension. She spent several minutes turning in front of the mirror gaining a perspective of who she was. The goddess looked back at her from the mirror and mocked the voyeur with pouting lips. The reflection would have turned Peter Fossard into a pliable plaything. Beautiful women could do that to men. She didn't affect Julia Salomonovich. Alarm bells rang. She whispered to herself. 'Let's not go there', and wrapped the dressing gown around herself once more tying the cord at her tiny waist.

Shaving! That was a plus. No more shaving; that and the glasses. She couldn't see many more advantages. She lay on the bed and tried to sleep but the spectre of Professor George Merrick and Walter Krantz invaded her thoughts and she returned to the dressing table.

She looked at the features of Julia Salomonovich once again. 'You'll never make a lock forward girl, that's for sure.'

She turned once more to the clothes in the suitcase recognising and beginning to understand the reality of her new existence. A new day was dawning

Chapter 80

JOEL RESPONDS

Joel Salomonovich had not been at his imperious best since he had moved from New York after the death of Abraham Goldstein. He had had no need to be.

Falling in love had mellowed the rebellious young man. Family life had moderated his behaviour and dealings with people even after Rachael's death.

He had become less cautious and more tolerant of others. The harmonious village life of Rachael and Vincent had not disarmed him. There would always be edge to his character, Rachael had known that, but he had not been the driven man of his youth. Yes, there was his remorseless quest to find Bühler, the man who had destroyed his family but this had required patience and had proved disappointing on so many occasions. The vehemence of his hatred remained unabated and unrelenting but the longevity of his quest assuaged the daily hostility and the poisonous bile that he had endured for so many years.

Joel's passions had been rekindled. He felt a new inertia. Now was the time for justice and revenge. A new resolve imbued and reinvigorated his spirit. His body bristled with anticipation. The common response by one so blighted and deeply afflicted is to dash pell-mell into the fray. Joel's calculating mind conquered the expedient and anticipated the denouement. He would not skew out of kilter and forewarn his quarry. Perhaps Marta Salomonovich would have been fearful for her angst-ridden son. She need never have feared.

The majestic Joel Salomonovich was back in his pomp, armed with the pragmatism of his mother and an inexorable hatred of his nemesis. Divine retribution there may eventually be but Joel prepared to mete out his own brand of justice before the Lord got hold of either Bühler or Merrick. This would be a dish served white hot. He cried 'Havoc', made several phone calls and 'let loose the dogs of war.'

Joel planned meticulously. He and Rebecca stayed in London for a further four days. He was rarely far from the phone. Bühler's movements were being traced. Fraser Hume, Leroy Gomez, Connor John and Tony Molinaro were as good a team any. They also had the advantage of being American and being unknown to the German underworld.

On the fifth day the phone rang. Joel rose from the luxury of his Dorchester bed and lifted the receiver. Fraser's animated voice spiked his appetite for action. D Day. He listened to Fraser intently and processed the data. Joel drew a deep breath. 'It's time Fraser. I'll be with you in the morning. Be sure that you have one of your guys meet me. He rang the airport, booked a flight to Innsbruck and flew four hours later.

Chapter 81

BÜHLER PLANS HIS OWN METAMORPHOSIS

Reinhart Bühler was quite clear about one thing. Merrick, alias Felix Elder, was not to be trusted. He could smell a double-cross a hundred miles away and the stench was overpowering. The old man considered his position. He had a new goal. If he could use Merrick's damn invention he could kill several birds with one stone. Though there was little evidence to suggest that people make all the right decisions in life when given a second chance Bühler considered the fabulous merger of his wisdom and experience with the body of a young Arian Adonis to be the requisite ingredients of perfection. He recalled the English saying about youth being wasted on the young. Exactly! Fit, strong, young, knowledgeable, intelligent and experienced he would storm to power and live the life that had been denied to him, as he had, by necessity, had to cling to the shadows and the night for so many years. A new persona; a new life; a new beginning. Only one person would know and he wouldn't need to know for long.

What of the two women who had escaped? They had never seen or known of Felix Elder and George Merrick was dead. Finding the women would please the professor, if such a person now existed. But since when did that count? What was in it for him other than an empty hope? He would be paid well and had taken precautions against Merrick's proclivity for 'tying up loose ends.' But what then? What was left in life for him? No, the only way forward was to deal with Merrick. Lure him someplace with his invention. He needed help and knew that it was to hand but in this case it required him, and him alone, to know all of the facts.

There were ways. He picked up the phone. 'Heinrich? Es geht.' He put the wheels in motion

Chapter 82

JULIA, SARAH AND MIKE LEAVE THE GUEST HOUSE

Mike Tyler had hardly slept for seventy two hours but by five-thirty that morning he had already showered and taken a short walk. This wasn't at all his normal way of starting the day. For many years it had been accepted practice for Peter to pick Mike up on his way to the rugby club on Saturday lunchtimes. Peter always gave himself plenty of time. Mike would often be either in his pyjamas or in the shower. The unshaven and bleary-eyed sufferer of excess alcohol from the previous evening would move slowly and generally forget half of the kit he needed. Purposeful working mornings were entirely unknown to the heroically unproductive Mike Tyler.

He sat on a style some hundred yards from the guesthouse and pondered the situation. He was way out of his depth and he knew it. The concepts were complex and the dynamics unfathomable. Mike had struggled to get a third class degree – this was way more challenging and far beyond his comprehension. He was reading a metaphysical treatise bereft of learning. He couldn't concentrate. How many times had he read a page from a novel then had to re-read it wondering what he had been thinking of when he had read it the first time? Distraction affected his thought processes all too easily as he failed to focus, like a schoolboy stuck with an unenlightening teacher. But for all his determination to comprehend he was simply out of his analytical depth.

Sarah showered early too and, seeing Mike from her window had decided to join him at the style.

He smiled as he saw her walking towards him. 'Hi, nice day … is …' he stumbled over his next word before coming up with … 'up yet.'

Sarah took his hands in hers and looked up into his face. 'Let it go Mike. Let it go. You mean Julia. Say it, She. Her. The woman. The beautiful young woman. If I can say it then you so can you. Her name is Julia. I know. It's going to take time.'

'But Lucy and Chloe... they must be going spare. You must contact them soon?'

Sarah grimaced and put her arms around him. 'I know that you always look after the girls Mike and I love you for it, but do you really think that I would abandon them at this time if there was another way? Really? Go on Mike. What would you say to them over the phone? We left a note and assured them that I was attempting a last ditch effort in Germany. Of course they are never out of my mind. Of course I'm frantic. But over the phone? I have left messages for them to meet me at home at three this afternoon. We have much to do before then. We'll have breakfast then leave immediately afterwards. I imagine that we have all slept very little and spent the evening assessing the situation. I know that I have.'

'Me too but I didn't get anywhere. Give Sarah, what the hell are we going to do?'

'Well I haven't heard from Julia as yet and she may well have alternative suggestions but I believe that we should go to Julia's flat in Oxford, take what she needs from there; drive to Bristol; shop for Julia's needs, and they are many, trust me; then wait for the girls. What we say to the girls, and if Julia even thinks it wise for her to meet the girls, is a matter for her. I don't feel that we can make those decisions on her behalf. Yes', she said using Mike as a sounding board. 'It's for her to decide.'

Mike Tyler looked down dispirited by the ghastly alternatives. Sarah continued. 'I have always treated you like a brother Mike and you have always given me your loyal support. I need it now like never before. I'm depending on you Mike...Please don't let me down. You have to be my rock. You do understand that Mike, don't you?'

Mike Tyler discovered a resolve that he didn't know he had. This was a call to arms; a plea for help from Sarah. His sinews stiffened and his chest expanded as they walked back towards the guesthouse. A new resolute Mike was emerging. He didn't understand what the hell was going on but he knew that Sarah needed him and that lent a new purpose to his life.

'Sarah you can depend on me. I won't ever let you down. Not ever. Believe me.' It was almost six o'clock.

Sarah and Mike approached Julia's room and Sarah knocked on the door. Mike continued down the corridor to his room and turned to wait for Julia's door to open. The door was pushed ajar and Julia whispered to Sarah. The communication was short and the door was closed.

Sarah followed Mike to his room. 'Well?' he asked. 'Well what?' She replied. 'Well what did she say?' he prompted.

'About what?' She returned.

'For God's sake, what did Julia, yes Julia, I can say it, what did Julia goddam say?' He sat on the bed and put his head in his hands.

'Sorry. I've lost it again. Already. I know. I know. OK. I'm up for it but tell me how it is. What did she say?'

Sarah sat down next to him. 'She said that she would need another twenty minutes to be ready and that she needed help.'

Mike laughed. 'What's so funny?' Sarah asked puzzled.

'What's funny? I'll tell you what's funny. All these years he has hassled you about the time it takes you to get ready and now ...' Mike didn't know how to complete his rambling philosophical dissertation and meandered into meaningless drivel.

Sarah hugged him. 'Well my friend, at least you have retained your sense of humour. Me? I'm fresh out of punch.'

The two remained hugging each other for some time then Sarah left to join Julia. It was twenty five minutes before there was a knock at the door. Mike answered it. Sarah stood in the doorway. 'We're ready Mike.'

Mike gathered himself for the day ahead. 'OK, if you put your bags in the corridor I'll take them out to the ....'

His last word trailed off as he turned to see Julia standing in the corridor. Her hair was brushed and looked good considering the neglect that it had withstood over recent days. She wore a light blue sweater and navy slacks. Mike was taken aback. This was the woman that didn't want to be looked at? This was one that definitely would be. Oh, she was modestly dressed but oh ... the stunning girl with the equally stunning smile and beautiful body was highly unlikely to remain unscanned by any red-blooded male for more than a nanosecond.

Mike let out a long low sigh. Julia checked him immediately. 'Get stuffed Mike. Now hear this. Both of you. Hear it loud and hear it clear. I'm only going to say it once and that's it. This is me. I've moved on'.

She hesitated as Mike lost control. 'My God! I know it's you but I can't think it's you. I just can't. What are we going to do? What next? I daren't even think about it.'

Julia swore and walked over to him. He towered above her. Mike backed down. 'Sorry. I'm so sorry. I... I just can't think straight sometimes. I know it's hell for you but ...'

'No, you don't know. It has taken just about every goddam thing that I've got to come out of that room looking like this and this is the greeting I get? Get a grip! Look. It's like this. I've been thinking. I'm lumbered with this right?' She gestured to her face and body sweeping a beautiful arm downward more gracefully than she imagined she could have. 'I woke up this morning; that is to say if I ever slept, and I considered my unfortunate position. I began with my condition, before this bizarre in extremis, as a soon to be corpse.' He wove a parenthesis around 'extremis' and 'corpse' by gesture of hand as he accentuated the words. 'I was in pain. There was no hope. No salvation. Only death. I have no belief in the hereafter. I was due for annihilation. In short I should be dead now.' She stood. She had a speech to deliver and, though time was short, she was determined to go through with it.

'So let's look at the case. The mitigation and the aggravation. The mitigation: I am alive and the insidious pain has gone. I am alive, forty years younger and fit as a fiddle. I am educated and have great potential in my present position. I am good looking. Wait. That could be aggravating, yet half the population of the world would probably change places with me if they could. The feminine half that is.' She was still analysing her predicament as she spoke, using Sarah and Mike as sounding boards – a familiar technique, becoming common amongst them. 'Yes that's aggravating.' She was about to be interrupted by Sarah, a capacity now beyond Mike, but she waived her hand almost dismissively towards her and continued. She would finish and be damned.

'The aggravating features: First, yesterday I was defensive. I hid my figure behind a thick sweater and jeans, though, come to think of it the jeans ... well ... what I mean is, I covered myself up. Last night I thought it out. Just how many years am I going to keep on looking like some dyke? Sorry. You know what I mean. Look I've been landed with this. It's not an illness and it's not a disease. At some point or other I have to make a decision. Accept it or... well the alternative is obvious and I don't need to tell you what it is. The way that I have dressed this morning is a statement of intent. Oh, you needn't worry. I'm not going near a man, not in that sense anyway. Not with a barge pole and a gallon of disinfectant. But I, that is we, have to be realistic, I can't continue to be Peter Fossard; I ask you; look at me.' There was a prolonged silence. 'There's an end to it. My old body ceased to function the day before yesterday. Peter Fossard's carcase has... well who knows.' Julia relented a little recognising that she had gone further than she had intended and that she had pained Sarah. She put her arms around her to comfort her in her strange bereavement. After a few tender moments she moved to the centre of the room, lowered her arms and turned full circle. 'This is me. For better or for worse. Whether you like it or not. This is my new reality. Get used to it. If I can I'm sure as hell that you can too. You've got the easy part.'

Julia remained standing, the view of her body unhindered by the arms that had been used so effectively before. 'Are there any questions? If you have any, ask them now. I'm looking to the future and you should be doing so too. I know that there are major problems ahead Chloe and Lucy being prominent among them. What's best for them? Sarah, my great fear is that I will outlive you by years. I don't want to. Oh I know that I can drop dead tomorrow like anyone else. But the odds are that I will live for a further forty years after you go and I can't... I can't... well you know. I'm younger than the girls for god's sake.'

'I don't know what all the problems will be. Merrick warned us that they would see myriad. I have no doubt that he envisaged them all. We will perhaps, not absorb them until we experience them. God he was bright. He foresaw it all. The bastard died too easily and yet it was that same shithouse that gave me life. It's a wonder he didn't use the thing on himself. He probably would have if he had had time. He probably used me as a guinea pig. The sly old...well that's it. I've embraced the gender. Tell me the alternative. No? And Mike... once again, take your eyes from my tits.'

Mike Tyler was indeed assessing the form of one of the opposite sex. He couldn't help it. It was just what he did; twenty-four seven. He choked, as he comprehended his unconscious action. 'Oh, look, I didn't, I mean, Christ what's a bloke to ... you know what I mean ... god.' He left his hopeless defence in the air.

Julia was embarrassed but not offended. 'Mike, that's just it. You fucked your lines up but you couldn't have put it better.' Sarah had never heard Peter say the F word in front of her before but then, she thought; this was not exactly the same Peter and the circumstances justified the sentiment.

Julia continued, 'We are what we are and just now I've accepted it and there is nothing that you or I can do about it. There is nothing that we can ever do. Of course I can shoot myself and that's an end to it but just now that's not top of my list. There is no alternative. *There is no going back.'*

Mike didn't have an ounce of energy left to exert and it was Sarah who broke the silence. 'Julia, that's Peter coming through loud and clear. Pragmatic to the end. Come on. It's time for breakfast. Mike put the bags in the car we'll need to be off soon but we must eat.'

Chapter 83

JOEL'S SEARCH FOR JULIA

Fraser Hume, Leroy Gomez, Connor John and Tony Molinaro watched the Bombardier 45 Lear Jet drop between the Tyrolean peaks, their granite walls amplifying the roar of the two Honeywell engines. As rubber hit runway Fraser led the way along the upper floor to the escalator. Joel's Innsbruck entourage assembled to meet the boss. Little fazed the four. This was different.

The plane taxied to a stop and the door opened. Joel climbed down the steps with purpose. It was less than ten minutes before he sat in the first of two cars making their way to the Innsbruck Hilton. He sat in the back with Fraser and began his business.

'OK, where the hell is Julia?'

Fraser assessed his man. Now he saw what his father had seen in the man. Charismatic, demanding and driven Joel Salomonovich was magnificent in his certainty. 'Joel, things are weird', he began. 'This is not like anything else I ...' He stopped. Joel had raised his hand.

'I don't want excuses Fraser. I want answers and I want them now. Give. What do you have? We can't contact her and I'm pissed off. I need information now.'

Fraser knew the truth of that. 'Joel', he faltered before taking a deep breath and beginning. 'I'm putting two and two together. I hope I'm making four.' Joel looked less than impressed with the overture. 'The thing is ... the thing is it all fits but none of it makes sense.' The first movement wasn't an improvement on the overture. 'OK here is what I have. Someone has been very interested in you ...'

Joel's dormancy ended. His nostrils flared and he vented his pent up rage. 'I don't give a fuck about me and Merrick. I gave you a job. That came first. It was straightforward. Find my granddaughter. Got it now?'

Fraser ran a finger under his collar and loved New York a little more. 'Joel, that's what I'm trying to tell you. Somehow or another it's all connected.'

'Connected? What's connected? What are you goddam talking about?' He stopped abruptly and waived Spencer to continue.

'Here's what we have. As I said someone has been trying to find out about you. Someone who has had access to Sir Nicholas Hansen's set up. I think you need to ring him Joel. This someone has not been looking for your good points Joel. He's out to get you. MI5 are checking you out too as a result. Our man has connections in high places. He began to access information some months ago by the look of things. It must be someone who has known you. Someone with an intimate knowledge of your past.'

Fraser was thinking as fast as he was talking. Even now the facts were being reprocessed meticulously.

'Let's leave that aside for a moment and go on to Julia. She left Frankfurt airport on Tuesday at eleven o'clock and disappeared somewhere on the autobahn to Koblenz before eleven twenty nine. She phoned her German friend at eleven twenty three. At eleven thirty seven a black Porsche exploded nearby. The driver was a private detective called Gunter Ulbricht. Legend has it that he was less than particular about the work he undertook. He worked alone and was based in Koblenz. Tony checked out his place last night. Joel, he recovered these papers.' Fraser pulled out a file from the side pocket of the limousine as they swung into the Innsbruck Hilton Hotel forecourt.

'Keep talking. Why am I here in Innsbruck? What the hell has this to do with Austria?'

The concierge opened the car door as they pulled in to the front entrance of the hotel. Joel pulled it shut took out the papers from the file and began to read. He scanned the pages rapidly, reopened the door and walked into the hotel foyer. Leroy Gomez handed a door pass over as Joel walked to the lift.

'My room. Ten minutes. All of you.' The lift doors closed on four very apprehensive men.

Chapter 84

JOEL READS GUNTER ULBRICHT'S PAPERS

Set in the heart of Innsbruck against background of the Tyrolean Alps the Hilton offers the most fabulous of views. Joel entered his room and pulled the blinds. There would be no distractions. He took the file to the desk and reopened it. It contained four sheets of paper. The first was a report from Fraser. He threw it to one side and began on Gunter Ulbricht's purloined papers.

Fraser knocked on the door and entered. Joel was pacing the room still reading the papers. Fraser remained silent. The first confirmed that Ulbricht had been detailed to do a surveillance job on Julia Salomonovich. The second was an invoice and the third recorded the case's progression. Joel groaned.

Julia had been watched for more than eight months. The surveillance was undertaken by Ulbricht whenever she crossed the water and by a Gordon Foster, of the Foster and Makinson detective agency of Ipswich, when in England. Joel turned to Fraser. Fraser gave an imperceptible nod to confirm that Ipswich was being 'swept.' Information was due. He turned back to the invoice. The fees and expenses listed times and places. Joel considered that they could well be a correct record. He didn't know all of Julia's movements over those months but he knew sufficiently well to suggest that Ulbricht had been thorough.

There was a knock at the door and Fraser opened it. His three men filed in and stood as Joel sat at the desk. No one spoke. Joel continued to read. He picked up Fraser's assessment and blew hard. 'Bühler. You came up with Reinhardt Bühler? He's still out there. My god! How the fuck is he involved with Julia for God's sake?' Fraser nodded at the appropriate junctures but the stage was left for the monologue to continue.

'OK so why would Bühler pay Ulbricht to keep tabs on my granddaughter after so many years? What would be the sense of that? It doesn't add up. What is it that I don't know Fraser? Why am I here in Innsbruck? I'm ready. Give it up. How come Bühler?'

Fraser Hume took the chair proffered. 'Joel, look at the headed sheet and the signature.

Hans Kohler? Importer.' It took Joel a couple of seconds to comprehend the significance of that name. 'Bühler. He had used his alias as an importer in the fifties.'

Fraser had one more card to play. 'This is just in Joel. I picked up the e-mail in my room five minutes ago. It's from Ipswich.' Fraser anticipated the pyrotechnic fall out. Joel gripped by a paroxysm of pain, anger and rage beat the desk with his fists. It was several seconds before he recovered himself sufficiently to speak rationally.

Molinaro shifted his feet nervously. Joel began in measured tones. 'Merrick has paid for Gordon Foster and Bühler has stumped up for Ulbricht; is that right? OK so they're in cahoots. Why? What are they up to? What has Julia to do with it? Why do they want her?'

Joel paced the room. Right now he needed Abraham Goldstein. Abraham had been the best listener ever. Joel had often believed that his ideas had sprung from Abraham. He needed him now. He considered his response.

'First we find Julia. She can't have just disappeared. I guess that this is why we are here in Innsbruck?' He didn't look for Fraser's nod. 'So, is it Bühler or Merrick that's got her?'

Fraser Hume knew Joel well. He had let his rage abate and knew that he had assimilated the facts. It was time to break further news.

'Joel, Merrick's dead. He died of a heart attack at an infirmary in Munich the day before yesterday. Unfortunately one of the bastards is beyond our reach now.'

Fraser could see that it was going to take a little time for Joel to consider the ramifications of George Merrick's demise. Fraser took his time then began slowly.

'Joel, over the last few days Connor, Leroy, Tony and I have done a lot of spadework. We believe that we know of Bühler's whereabouts. We knew that Merrick had flown into Munich a few days ago. He came in from Bristol by private plane. On board that plane was a certain Walter Krantz. Krantz had a private infirmary near Munich. The staff there didn't know much about Merrick. However, it seems that no one works there for long and few have access to all parts of the building. This, in itself, is significant.'

Fraser noted Joel's impatience and decided that this would be his last indirect remark. 'Another thing; a nurse at the place, what's her name', he said, reaching for his notes, 'Yes, a Nurse Gudrun Hackemann. She went back to her home one evening and got blown to smithereens. They found the remains of another body too. Walter Krantz was having an affair with Nurse Hackemann. The affair was widely known in the local village, and, Walter Krantz has not been seen since the house went up in smoke. The Bundespolizei forensics team are on the job but I think we know the outcome of their deliberations. It was Krantz! The device used was similar to the one that took out Ulbricht's black Porsche; just a mite more powerful. It all points to Merrick but it's hard to see the guy's doing it alone. Is it me or is everyone that we need to talk to being systematically eliminated. Did Bühler's mates do for Merrick? 'Who did for Krantz and Hackemann? Who did for Ulbricht?' He left the questions hanging in the tense air.

Joel rose from the chair and went to the window pulling the blind back a little. 'A moment!'

It was a full minutes before he returned to Fraser and his men. He had absorbed the data and recognised the enormous infrastructure, connections, clout and expertise that had gained it. Fraser was Spencer's true heir in more ways than one. To have gained the information that his team had, in the limited time they had, required professional expertise of the highest order. Joel sought more.

Fraser pressed on knowing that Joel would have acknowledged as much were it not for the imperative nature of their meeting.

'There was a car accident. I'm afraid it was Julia's car', he saw Joel's pained expression but carried on. 'The car was empty. The Landespolizei checked the local Krankenhaus. No one fitting Julia's description checked in that night. Our contacts checked all the hospitals in the area. Again, nothing doing. The car was abandoned. Joel, it was definitely Julia's car.' Joel hauled himself to his feet, slowly and deliberately walking from the window to the desk. He needed a further moment to assimilate the information. He engaged Fraser's eyes and nodding for him to carry on. Fraser observed the grave countenance before him and composed himself before continuing. The gravitas of the man was awesome.

'OK, er, then the trail goes cold. Julia disappears. All we have to go on is this. Two guys were supposed to be driving an ambulance from the infirmary to someplace in Austria – they have been questioned but they know very little other than they stopped for a pee in the bushes and the ambulance was high jacked. By whom we don't know. Another ambulance had left with two patients in it the day before. That too was destined for Austria. We have reason to believe that Julia was in one or the other of them. They are certainly not at the infirmary. That has been checked and the staff isolated, if you know what I mean. We don't want someone tipping Bühler off. Our European brothers are coming up trumps when it comes to support.'

Joel returned to the desk taking in the data. Fraser followed. 'These guys', he pointed to Connor John, Leroy Gomez and Tony Molinaro, 'are the best and ....' Joel nodded his approval. He turned back to Fraser. 'I only employ the best Fraser.'

Joel leaned forward cold and emotionless. He gave Fraser to understand that he should continue once more.

'We went back to Bühler. We lost Julia for the time being but we got Bühler. He's here or at least not far from here. To get to Julia we thought that we needed to get on Bühler's back.'

'Fraser', Joel interrupted, 'my first concern is the welfare of my granddaughter. All other matters can wait. Fuck Bühler for the time being. You said that you had lost her 'for the time being.' What the fuck does that mean for God's sake. Find my granddaughter.'

Tony Molinaro's cell phone rang. He moved to the far corner of the room and began mumbling into it.

Fraser thought hard for a moment and decided to continue not deflected by Joel's demand for immediate action. 'Joel, I know this is hard but hear me out. Please.' Joel nodded acquiescence but Fraser wasn't going to have the floor for long. He knew it had better be good.

'Go ahead.'

It is only by going to Bühler that we can get to Julia and find out what this is all about. The truth is, for all our work, we haven't a clue what's driving this. What's going down? What's the motivation?'

Tony Molinaro joined the others. 'Tony?' Fraser asked.

'Bühler's about. We need to move now.' Fraser noted Molinaro's hesitation. He had rarely seen that. 'Go on.' He turned to Joel. 'Mr. Salomonovich your granddaughter has used her passport and has returned to England. She arrived at Birmingham Airport yesterday morning.'

There was silence. Joel traded on his years of sanity and managed, just managed to keep himself together. Anguish and relief in quick succession were difficult emotions to hold on to with any certainty. Drained, he slumped in the chair. 'Where is she? I want to know where she is and I want to know that she is safe.' He slammed his large fist down on the desk punctuating each syllable as he screamed his command. His voice dropped and he now whispered. 'Don't rest until we have her safe.'

The group split and four mobiles flashed open. All favours were being called in. All contacts exploited. Police and business contacts, intelligence and government agencies were pushed and pushed hard. Joel's communication centre went into overdrive but there was no trace of Julia after she had left Birmingham Airport.

After half an hour or so Tony Molinaro approached Fraser Hume. The conversation resulted in Fraser interrupting Joel's call to Rebecca and Laura. He put his hand over the receiver. 'Yes?'

Fraser said. 'It's now Joel. We must go now if we are to get Bühler. We have a window and it's now. It may be a short cut to getting Julia back. At least we know that she was alive yesterday. We have the passenger list for yesterday's flight to Birmingham. The fax is coming through. We'll take that with us. Perhaps there are others we know on the list? Who knows? It's time to go.'

Chapter 85

FELIX PLOTS BÜHLER'S DOWNFALL

Felix Elder had just one loose end to resolve. Only Bühler could put George Merrick and Felix Elder together as one and the same. Felix was young, fit and strong. At his age Bühler could be despatched quite easily. As easily as Merrick had been. There was a certain symmetry to that. Gudrun Hackemann's house had exploded, as had Gunter Ulbricht's black Porsche, there was no need for a third incendiary. Felix had moved to the Kirchdach Hotel in Gschnitz having felt that he had outstayed his time at the Innsbruck infirmary.

He paced his room reassessing his plans. People! It was always stupid people. Why could they not execute his plans as instructed? He had to design the grand strategy. All he asked was for the pawns to play their undemanding little parts properly.

The pawns of life. The stupid, trite, clichéd, imbecilic pawns of life. The parasites whose world would not have changed since the Stone Age were it not for a handful of geniuses. The brainless, banal masses whose contribution and vacuous, sordid little lives held little significance in the grand scheme of things.

When asked to provide the simplest of tasks these minions always fell short and buggered up the works. They lived in their little homes in their little minds, happy in their stupidity and ignorance.

Felix let it go. The general population of Great Britain dismissed, he turned to address his present circumstances, recognising his frustration. He wanted to get on with his life. To move forward. The time was right. There was a whole new exciting world out there. He pulled the curtain to one side and took in the freshness of the Tyrol. The clean white lines of the mountains contrasted sharply with the dark blue cloudless sky; it was a good day to be alive. There would be many of them in the very near future. But for now? The phone hadn't rung. Where the hell was Bühler?

Bühler needed fixing. He had ideas above his station and was now an irritating superfluous fly in a superfluous ointment. Bühler had not returned to the hotel. Had he got wind of Felix's intentions? How could he have? Perhaps the intuition which had served him so well over the years? Perhaps? It was pointless speculating. Bühler needed him and would settle for nothing less than a new life. Felix knew the truth of that. He picked up the phone. Almost twelve hundred miles away a receiver was lifted. A secretary put the call through to her civil servant boss and replaced her receiver. He in turn walked to the window and looked at the grey dismal weather shrouding Trafalgar Square.

'Tisiphone', Felix spoke through a frequency modulator. His voice transformed.

'Who are you?'

The civil servant gave nothing away.

'I have a request from Tisiphone.'

'Tisiphone died.'

'That is true but he left one request and that was that I clear up any link to London.'

'There's a link? A link to us?' There was a short pause before: 'What do you want?'

'A man is missing. He must be found.'

'There are many men.'

'Approximately one twenty sixth of them whose surnames begin with B I shouldn't wonder.'

'Where can I contact you? How do I know that the link is severed?'

'You can't. You don't. I'll contact you. Make it quick.' Felix snapped the phone down. There would be action and very soon. Of that there was no doubt.

It was twenty minutes before he rang the number again. The Greek Fury, Tisiphone the Avenger, alias Felix Elder got the information and assistance he had required and left Austria for Germany.

Bühler would be instructed to meet a comrade at a particular rendezvous in the belief that he would gain information on Merrick. The double cross had required the last favour the posthumous Merrick's 'old school tie' would call upon.

As Felix drove the rented Audi he reassessed his plan. Once Bühler was out of the way he would have to move and move fast. There must be no trail left to lead anyone to Felix Elder. This would be the only crime that could be traced to him. His name would be changed. He liked the name he had given to Astrid. Yes, Michael Mitchell. No. A clean break. No connections. The telephone directory would provide a name. Perhaps he would return to Munich and see Astrid and lie low for a little while before then? Perhaps. He was ready for more of that and time wasn't important anymore. He had all the time in the world. And next time? When Felix Elder, aka telephone directory man, was approaching his forties another specimen would be found. Easy. No sense in growing old. No need to experience that insidious arthritis, no point in being bloody lame again.

Felix considered the longer term. He would return to England. He had transferred money from George Merrick's account in England to a Zurich bank deposit box in good time. Presently he would transfer that money to an account he would open in Cambridge. He had 'bought' his father's cottage from one George Merrick shortly before his demise. The proud 'new' owner would enjoy his walks in the woods and the opportunity to meet his 'new' neighbour Joel Salomonovich. He would revel in seeing the old man suffer from his infirmities and the loss of his granddaughter. His seething pathological hatred of Joel Salomonovich surfaced once more.

Cambridge. In the fullness of time he would apply for a post there. He knew the ropes; indeed he knew how to adjust the ropes. With a little manipulation he would be back at work, full of the energy of youth, astounding the world with his genius once again. He had all the time in the world to establish his qualifications and his credentials.

This time however, there would be other facets to his life. This time around things were going to be considerably different. He considered his feelings. George Merrick would not have wanted that. His work had been paramount. He felt a little unsure of himself – something that he had rarely experienced. This was unexpected. Was Felix Elder influencing his thoughts? Was Felix Elder's personality blurring his judgement? He decided to monitor future responses.

The phone rang. It was Bühler at last. Felix gave instructions, insisted that Bühler repeat them to him and put the phone down. The last connection with George Merrick would be severed as would Bühler's filthy neck.

Chapter 86

JOEL FOLLOWS BÜHLER

It was Connor John's enquiries that had eventually led Fraser's group to Bühler. Connor had worked closely with the West Germans before the wall came down. As a captain in the USA's Special Forces he had worked closely with many of the men who had been taken into German intelligence. The Green Berets lost a top man when Connor John called it a day and moved back into Civvy Street.

Like Fraser Hume, Leroy Gomez and Tony Molinaro, Conner John had a labyrinthine network to pull on. With the help of former 'associates' sitting in the CIA's Langley Virginia headquarters he was able to gain considerable access to the files the Hauptverwaltung Aufklarung, which had been the General Reconnaissance Administration Department of the former East Germany.

Connor had saved Marty Hooson's ass more than once. The least he could do was to stop staring over the damn Potomac. The river would still be there in the morning. Bühler might not be. Hoosen opened the Rosenholz files. These files, which named Nazis and sympathisers, had 'unaccountably' fallen into the hands of the CIA when the wall came down. The CIA set about recruiting many of them, granting immunity from prosecution for former atrocities. Some had connections with the Ministerium Fur Staatssicherheit, commonly referred to as the German Democratic Republic's Stasi, or secret police. Their intelligence network was as extensive as it ever had been and now the microchip had enhanced their operations.

The security and intelligence departments were as thorough as they were ruthless and the passing of time had left Bühler vulnerable. The price wasn't high enough. His time was up. They sold him out.

Joel spotted the bastard immediately. Sixty years on and now Bühler was in his sights. He nodded slowly. 'You sure?' Fraser knew by the look on

Joel's face that he was quite sure that Bühler was the man loading the Audi with groceries 'OK let's go.'

'Bühler has a keen nose. It has served him well for many years. He doesn't let his guard down. Not ever.' Fraser knew his job and Joel watched the operation with admiration.

Fraser lifted his mobile. 'Tony?' Tony Molinaro was parked a block away. He kicked the 500 cc Yamaha into life and rode in Fraser and Joel's direction. Fraser pulled the Ford out and drove in the opposite direction passing the bike no more than a hundred metres from Bühler. Connor John was waiting around the corner and they abandoned the Ford and got into the back seats of Connor's purring Mercedes. On the word from Tony Molinaro he took off towards Bühler's silver Audi. Bühler was just leaving and the Mercedes, keeping a suitable distance, followed. Leroy Gomez moved from a nearby newspaper stand and found the Ford with its keys in the ignition. He waited for his call then set off in the direction given. If Bühler spotted anything he sure as hell wasn't giving any sign of it.

'He's planning something Joel.' Fraser's voice was intense. The man was doing his thing. 'How many people do you know that do a lot of shopping then don't set off home with it? Yeh. Not many.'

Joel was anxious. 'We're losing him', he growled as the Audi disappeared into heavy traffic ahead. 'Not if I know Tony Molinaro we're not. He's lodged the tracker devise alright. Bühler aint going anywhere without us knowing about it.' Fraser produced a hand held devise and switched it on. 'Immer geradeaus mein freund. Keep going straight on, he's half a mile ahead.'

Three cars made their way north past Garmische Partenkirchen. They turned along the Romantische Strasse, which leads to Augsburg a little more than fifty miles beyond.

'He's turned off Fraser.' It was Leroy Gomez. 'He's going to Oberammergau. What the hell is going there for?' Fraser thought for a moment. 'Well it's not for the Passion Plays; you can bet on that. He's going down a one way track. We have his location and if he moves he must come back to the Romantische Strasse. Old habits die hard. He doesn't know anyone's on to him but he's a belt and braces man. He may not know that we are here but he will have a hell of an imagination after all these years. Maybe he's meeting someone. Hell, it doesn't matter. We just need to wait someplace and get him where we want him.

Tony Molinaro parked the Mercedes in a tree lined Rastplatz well back from the road. He got out and hid behind bushes. They had the car tagged but not Bühler. There could be a switch. He waited patiently for the silver Audi and Bühler to pass by.

Joel Salomonovich said nothing. He had said nothing for some time. He nodded and sat back into the black leather appreciating the work of professionals.

Tony Molinaro praised the German motor industry. 'Mercedes, BMW, Porsche, Audi. All great cars', he enthused. He then checked out a particular blue Audi that passed by. It was a hired car, latest model, and driven by a handsome young man with black hair. Little escaped his notice.

Never the less Tony Molinaro couldn't have known that the driver of the blue Audi was if fact an old professor called George Merrick. He had maintained a mean vigil but that fact had slipped well below his radar.

Chapter 87

JOEL AND BÜHLER MEET AT THE POLLAT GORGE.

It was a little less than half an hour before Tony returned to the car. After a further two minutes Fraser made his decision. Connor John, Leroy Gomez and Tony Molinaro concurred. It was time to follow Bühler. 'OK, let's …'

Joel raised his arm. 'Hold it. Wait.' He could feel it in his water. He could always feel it in his water. It was not the intelligent who would inherit the earth. That was the prerogative of the intuitive and the brave. Something. There was something. He could sense it as a sure as a shark could sense blood in the water. He knew. He didn't know what he knew or why he knew. But he knew. Fraser looked quizzically at Joel. Joel held his head high like a bloodhound sniffing the air. Just wait a little longer.'

It was moments later that Bühler's Audi arrived back at the Romantische Strasse. The bug had malfunctioned. Had the posse followed the Sheriff their cover would have been blown. The posse was fortunate to have had the Marshall with them and to have remained under the cover of the snow peppered evergreens of the Rastplatz.

Connor appreciated Joel's intuition. 'Good call sir. Damn good call.' The praise was lost on Joel. He was checking the tracker with Fraser. 'He's a sly old bugger, that's for sure but he hasn't found it', said Fraser with considerable professional respect for his quarry. They noted that the tracker had kicked in again.

'Temperamental little bitch, eh Connor?' The bug had been identified as female.

A little while later Bühler left the main highway and headed west towards Linderhof.

'Let him get further ahead Fraser. I'm guessing and that he'll stop and expect anyone following to pass by. God knows what then.' Joel exuded certainty. The tracker indicated that Bühler had indeed stopped. The surveillance experts were further impressed.

Fraser noted that Bühler had begun to move again. They followed. The road to Linderhof was awe-inspiring. The Alps rose majestically from the deep gorges and the virgin snow brought out an array of sunglasses. The going was slow. The narrow road led back to Austria near the Ammerwald and descended towards the shores of the Heiterwanger Lake. It didn't improve, as it swept north through Muhl and Weisshaus. It turned east towards Alterschrofen where, shimmering in the Bavarian backcloth, the most beautiful of castles came into view.

'He's making for Neuschwanstein castle.' Leroy Gomez had seen most things the world had to offer. The view of the castle still extracted a; 'Now that is something else.'

The majestic medieval imitation stood high in the forest, its white limestone walls, quarried from the nearby Swan Lake at Alterschrofen, shone like ivory in the late evening sun. The lake beyond captured its last rays and offered them back to the edifice in reverence of its splendour.

The erudite Connor John offered, 'The guy who had it built, Ludwig the second? He went insane after it was built. They had him put away for years then they killed him.'

Leroy shot back. I don't blame them, it's one hell of a piece of real estate to get your hands on.'

One glance from Fraser halted talk of the castle being used to film Chitty Chitty Bang Bang and Sleeping Beauty. Tony Molinaro had been to Disneyland and guessed that some bright guy had stolen the blueprints for the place.

Fraser called for Tony to stop the car. The signal on the tracker was strong but it was clear that Bühler had stopped again.

Four men alighted from the car. Fraser and Joel walked towards the castle, Leroy Gomez stayed put at the west exit and Connor John set off to towards the Marienbrucke, the magnificent bridge that spanned the Pollat Gorge high above the waterfall cascading from the mountainside down to the lake. Tony Molinaro drove to the east exit and stood by the castle wall awaiting further instructions. Bühler was going nowhere without Fraser's men knowing about it.

Reinhart Bühler had left his Audi in the car park and it took less than a minute for Fraser and Joel to locate it. It was Connor who came in on the line. 'He's walking to the bridge Fraser. It's late. I don't see anyone else walking that way. There are tourists. One or two stragglers, making their way back to the main drag, if you can call it that. Why the hell is he going out there? Shit. There is someone else there too. A young guy. Blonde hair and I bet he's got blue eyes to go with it. His type, in more than one way, I shouldn't wonder. No, guess again he's making for the exit too. Stereotyped another.'

It was Fraser: 'Just watch him. Don't move in. I'll get Tony and Leroy to make sure that no one else follows the path to the bridge. Joel and I will move in as soon as they get there.

It was less than two minutes later when Fraser and Joel approached the bridge passing and ignoring Conner as they went by. Two men, well able to cordon off a motorway closed the pathway. Leroy Gomez fell in behind Fraser and Joel.

Ex SS Obersturmführer Reinhart had a premonition. He knew he would when it eventually happened. A shiver ricocheted down his spine and he felt a sudden chill in the air. For most of his life he had known that eventually the dreadful moment would arrive. He had seen George Merrick in his new guise at some distance. He had begun to approach him. It seemed that the arrangements were going to plan. Bühler had alternative thoughts. There had been no visible indication of trouble but Felix Elder had suddenly changed direction and headed swiftly towards the undergrowth adjacent to the Pollat Gorge.

He glanced at the men walking behind him looking for an outlet, saw yet another two fit, athletic individuals by the bridge, turned away and spotted yet another, incongruously reading an information leaflet, to the fore.

Bühler's face betrayed him and, from behind the distant undergrowth, Felix could see the terror in his eyes as he saw Bühler reach under his coat for the Luger, his hand shaking, his body sweating despite the chilly evening air. A small black hole appeared at the back of the hand that held the gun. The luger fell to the ground. Connor John rarely missed. Bühler held his bloody hand screaming for the marksman not to shoot again.

Like all cornered bullies he began to bleat when his turn came. The wife beater whose wife's big brother turns up, the paedophile who cries that the police manhandled him and the robbing knife man who suddenly realises that the guy he just hit on was in the SAS. All would suffer the same indignity. Fear struck his vitals as his shit belied his former certainty. He knew. In his very soul he knew. The future held only the terror of the rope after a merciless wait for the hangman to approach.

Oh yes! The death penalty had gone but how long had his fellow travellers lasted in prison? The odds were not good. He would hang as sure as if the Nuremberg lot had got him so many years ago. The macabre portent sobered his mind and rapidly placed a new construction on his thoughts.

Joel Salomonovich stepped forward, the relief of his malign intent etched deep into his face, desperate to gain information before exacting revenge. Still Julia remained his first concern even as his hatred burned like the fiery brimstone that would surely set light to Bühler in Hades.

Joel began, speaking in English, shocking Bühler who had expected to hear German. He had anticipated that his quarry would resist. To be defiant. To gloat and to die like a soldier. The quivering mess in front of him would have gained a reprieve from the liberal elite. There was no one of that ilk present and stripped of the arrogance of power Joel saw Bühler for what he was.

Bühler edged his way towards the side of the bridge that spanned the Pollat Gorge. Joel stopped him. 'You'll never get there. Stay where you are. I want answers and for each one that you don't give me? Part of you goes. Question. Where is Julia Salomonovich?'

Now Bühler thought of many things that the Simon Wiesenthal guys might ask of him. The whereabouts of Julia Salomonovich was not one of them. He was confused and didn't answer. He would never use his right knee again due to his unfortunate delay in answering the question. Joel put a dispassionate bullet into it with clinical detachment as he detonated years of pent up rage unleashing the firestorm of hatred. Disfigured by his malice and damned by his seething hatred, loathing poured from his soul leaving his body aching and void.

Bühler screamed in agony as he fell to the ground. He looked up at Joel Salomonovich uncomprehendingly as he screamed, 'Why? Why? Why?' He turned with his back to the ground using his arms to get nearer to the bridge. Fraser's men made to stop him but Joel stayed them. Another shot pinged from the silencer. It pierced Bühler's left shoe. He screamed again.

Unfettered by any sense of humanity Joel continues with his persecution.

'So, Obersturmführer Reinhardt Bühler, you scream like the pig you are. I can smell your fear. I will ask you once again. No answer means the loss of another leg. Are you ready for that? Here goes.'

Bühler held up a hand and screamed again. 'You're the devil incarnate. What the fuck do you want from me? Who the fuck is Julia Salomonovich? My name is Maier Why are you…?'

The bullet piercing Bühler's left shoulder was not as clean an affair as those which had hit his right hand, right knee or left foot. All three had been clinical hits. Clean shots. The third shot ruptured the entire joint splintering bone shrapnel into a thousand parts. Bühler screamed like scalded cat.

Joel remained resolved, cold and unmoved. After the execution of his father and brothers he had appeared dispassionate in his calculated hatred and shock. He was no more animated now.

Fraser Hume, Connor John, Leroy Gomez and Tony Molinaro had seen a lot. LA, Chicago, Vietnam, The Wall, The Gulf. They had seen plenty. As a silver flash of steel ripped across Bühler's face they knew that they were in for a reprise.

Bühler's hand wiped his face and he looked down at it in disbelief. 'For Christ's sake what do you want? God! Tell me. It's yours. You're crazy. Mad. You're fucking mad. Ferucht. Verstahen?

The blade flashed again. Bühler lost part of his left ear. Joel was warming to the task; his lack of emotion challenging his well-worn associates' composure.

'Listen you piece of shit. It can be easy or it can be hard – even now. I can keep you like this …no I will keep you like this until the morning; using tourniquets to stop you from bleeding to death, if I have to. Tell me where Julia Salomonovich is.'

Joel had thought the question to be straight forward. Bühler didn't know the answer. The delay prompted Joel to lurch forward and deliver a frenzied assault on Bühler's groin. The first sickening kick could have been construed as persuasive. The second, third and fourth were purely gratuitous. Bühler lay on his side grasping his crutch as he fought for air, his head hanging over the long drop to The Pollat Gorge.

'Don't even think about it. You are going nowhere. I ask you again. Where is Julia Salomonovich?'

'She's dead for pity's sake. Merrick killed her. I had nothing to do with it. Why do you persecute me? I know Merrick. I admit that I associated with Merrick. But I swear to you I do not know what you want of me. What have I done? I am an old man. What do I know?'

Joel closed in on his prey as he reached into his pockets and produced a pair of leather gloves. He put them on as he spoke.

'What do you know? What do you know? I'll tell you. You know of a story that happened many years ago. I'll take you back. Do you remember Hamburg? Do you remember?' Joel screamed the words into what remained of Bühler's ear as he slapped his hand across Bühler's face. 'Do', slap, 'you', slap, 'know', slap, 'who', slap, 'I', slap 'am?'

Bühler was losing blood rapidly and Joel knew that his time was limited. Joel changed tack again and asked about Julia.

'What did Merrick do to her?' He ground the butt of his revolver into Bühler's broken shoulder as he spoke. Bühler screamed in agony but all the years of acting paid dividends. Slowly, as if making his last will and testament, he began a false confession.

'I don't know who you are. Mossad yes? But you got the wrong man. I am an associate of Merrick's. That is it. I have heard that he killed a young woman. He, he has killed half a dozen folk this week for all I know. What is one more? The man's crazy. He's a psychopath. And you shoot me? In the name of Christ ... Why?'

The next shot blew Bühler's right ankle away. The shock threw him further to the edge of the bridge and he hovered perilously close to the abyss. Joel saw it all and cautioned Bühler.

'There's no way that you are taking the easy way out Bühler. No way. I'll ask you again. Trust me. You think that you have had it all. I haven't begun yet. This knife will make your arsehole three times as long as it is. You'll be pissing out of your shithole before the night is through.'

Bühler had had enough. One last lurch of his arthritic carcase and he could make the gorge. Five seconds later – oblivion. And about time.

'SS Obersturmführer Reinhart Bühler.' Bühler's contorted face screamed a silent question of Joel. 'Oh yes I know you well. Again I ask you. Do you remember Hamburg? I see that you do. An execution. No, I know there were many. But this one. Yes this one. Simon Salomonovich and his two sons. You took them from the university. Yes? You shot them like, like, like Jews.' Joel's fevered pitch was causing great concern even for his battle hardened associates. 'There was a young boy but we will get back to him. He continued. 'You took away a girl and made her work as a field whore. And as you left you shot an old man who demonstrated with you.'

Bühler's pained eyes opened. He was in agony but could not believe what he was hearing. 'How?'

Joel struck Bühler a sickening blow to his midriff. He threw up into the Pollat. 'Remember this face. Let this face haunt you. Let it haunt you for the remainder of your miserable existence. Do you remember?' Joel plunged the knife into Bühler's crutch. 'I was that boy and I have remembered just as you asked me to. The men you butchered were my father and brothers, the old man was my friend and the girl was my sister. She sends you this. He turned his hand and Bühler lost his manhood. Bühler reached forward in agony and pulled hard on Joel.

An epoch of hatred ended as Joel Salomonovich and Reinhardt Bühler plummeted into the Pollat Gorge. The great adversaries' trials were over as their bodies smashed into the rocks below and were swept away in the foaming river.

Fraser had seen Joel reach down for Bühler and had been about to caution him when he had made his last desperate movement on earth. Fraser had sprung forward but he was too late. Joel had gone.

The four Americans lost their focus, their purpose, and quite possibly their jobs. Despite the febrile atmosphere their professionalism kicked in. Fraser spoke first. 'OK let's go. We'll leave Sleeping Beauty to her castle.'

Connor John broke the silence as they headed back to the Mercedes. 'Just like the movies.'

Leroy opened the door and sat in the rear with Fraser. 'What the hell are you talking about Connor?'

Connor John didn't need an answer or directions. They headed for Fussen. They needed to get to Munich Airport then to London, and fast. Fraser made calls. He considered the purchase of his season ticket for the Giants to be a good buy after all.

A lone figure emerged from the trees not forty yards from the macabre spectacle. Felix Elder was not unappreciative of Joel Salomonovich's night's work, or of the significance of his observation of a seminal moment from such a vantage point.

'Two birds with one stone, Salomonovich does my work and there's no connection with Felix Elder. Perfect. Just perfect!'

Chapter 88

JULIA, SARAH AND MIKE IN OXFORD

Julia, Sarah and Mike arrived at Julia's Oxford flat in the late morning. Julia took the key from the said indispensable handbag and entered with Sarah and Mike. The small immaculately furnished flat was located in the city centre. The A420, less than a hundred yards to the west, led to the M4. Mike observed that they could get to Bristol from there within the hour.

Sarah entered, more sure of her intentions than Julia. 'Come on, there's things to do. Pick up the mail Mike', Sarah asked politely. Mike complied without hesitation. He was all out of questions.

Sarah pushed open the bedroom door and moved towards the wardrobes. The mirrored doors slid easily and she began to take clothes from it laying them on the bed. She groaned as she entered the long overdue shower.

It took a little time. She had accepted that it would. The need to dress femininely devalued incrementally the further from the … She had not accepted that she would dress provocatively. There would be nothing low or short, nothing sheer or split and no footwear that required circus skills to remain upright while attempting to maintain balance.

Sarah asked Mike to lift two suitcases from the top of the wardrobe and suggested that he might like to make a drink

Mike, taking a second or so to assimilate the requested tasks, caught Sarah's eye and noted the nature of the work she was undertaking. 'Oh, er, of course. I'll just er …' He left the women to continue with their packing.

'My God there is so much. We'll not get it in the car if we are not careful. Is it all necessary Sarah?'

Sarah burst into tears and sat on the bed. 'I'm trying. I'm doing my best', she cried. 'It's not easy for me either Peter. Julia. I'm sorry.'

Julia sat at Sarah's side and put her arms around her. Her body heaved with the passions that had been contained for weeks. Julia knew that Sarah was at breaking point and understood that she had been less than helpful in terms of their immediate task. Circumstances had inevitably led her to become too self-centred. She recognised that now. She had shown little empathy with her life's partner.

'I'm sorry Sarah. I know. I just seem to be thinking about me when ...'

Sarah interrupted her. 'No. Please no. It is about you. It is about the new Julia.' She began to dab her eyes with the tissue that Julia had taken from a pack in her handbag.

'This damn thing is becoming surprisingly useful all of a sudden', Julia smiled.

Sarah laughed through her tears. 'I know.'

Julia chided her mildly. 'It's about both of us Sarah. I won't forget it again. I promise. Go ahead. You know what you are doing. What do I know? Go ahead. Anything you say; your field.'

Julia moved away from the bed and sat at the dressing table, something, she observed that she had done a disturbing number of times lately. She watched Sarah, reflecting on their different mentalities. Men! Women! Both had one head, two arms and two legs. That was about it. Nature and nurture wove a magical difference between the genders; the result of several millennia of evolution. Her own evolution had better become a revolution if she was to survive. Nature and nurture; which would have the more dramatic impact over the coming months and years?

Sarah resumed her work selecting clothes, shoes, handbags and jewellery. She then began rummaging through draws for identification and information regarding Julia Salomonovich.

Julia had had enough and decided to join Mike. She had not been alone with him for a little over a week when Sarah had gone to the hairdressers and left him 'in charge' of visiting Peter at the hospital. A week! It could have been a year!

'Hi.' Mike turned towards her sheepishly. 'Don't do it Mike.' He faked puzzlement. 'Don't go funny on me and for God's sake take your goddam eyes off 'em. My face is up here.

Mike Tyler blushed. 'I'm sorry. It's just natural. I don't know that I'm doing it. I probably do it all the time. If you're so conscious of it I suppose I've always been obvious to women. It's a wonder they never mention it.' He returned to the teapot. It wasn't a beautiful teapot but it didn't make him feel uncomfortable.

'Just try to stay with me OK, yeh?' Julia began. 'But before you purge yourself, just to let you know, and to make you feel just that teeny bit better, every goddam man I've come in contact with so far has talked to my tits. You are not, repeat, not alone.'

'It's all so confusing ... Julia ...'

'Well done. That's a start. Julia; that's it. Go on.'

'That's just it; I don't know how to go on,' he replied.

'I'll tell you how Mike. This is the best that I can offer. Listen, OK?'

'I know that you didn't have a brother or a sister so you haven't had a niece. Well you have one now! Think of me that way. In fact that's not a bad idea at all. I'm Julia Tyler; your niece from out of town. We could get away with that, always supposing that folk believe that such an ugly bugger as you could have a beautiful girl like me as his niece.'

Mike and Julia laughed out loud, holding their stomachs and bending double with the pain of full-blown belly laughs. As the laughs subsided there was a new understanding and a new realisation that there was a future; a way forward; a coping strategy.

Sarah put her head around the door and called for Mike to take the suitcases to the car.

'That was good', she said, taking Julia's hand.

'What was?'

'You and Mike laughing. There's been precious little of that lately.'

Julia took Sarah's hands in hers. 'Not bad for a man that should be lying in a mortuary.'

Sarah smiled nervously at that. 'Don't. Please don't. Not even in jest.' She hesitated for a moment.

Julia interrupted her deliberations. 'What is it Sarah?' Sarah hesitated again then said. 'Do you know what? I made the right decision. I just began to believe it when you were talking of death and the mortuary. Despite it all, you are here, thinking, talking, living... being. What do you think? Do you think I made the right decision?'

Julia took Sarah's chin in his hand and lifted her bowed head. 'On the face of if you are asking me which is preferable, the cold grave or your company.... I'll go with the company.

OK, I expect there to be many challenges ahead not least our age difference. But, looking so far ahead so soon isn't going to profit us a great deal. Sarah, you made the right decision for the here and now. Now we have to make it work.'

Sarah crumpled with relief and kissed Julia on the cheek. 'I think that once we've got past Lucy and Chloe, and that's going to be traumatic enough, we will try to start anew. There's little alternative. You got Mike laughing and I heard what you said about being his niece. I think that this is the way forward. You stay with me at home now that Peter has gone and I'll take Mike's niece in as a boarder. You can find a job and I will take Peter's pension and cash in the insurance policies. Let's face it Julia, to all intents and purposes, as no less a person than Professor himself George Merrick callously remarked, Peter Fossard has ceased to function. I feel no guilt.

So, Lucy and Chloe first and then it's time to move on. Come on Mike's waiting.'

Julia picked up her handbag, threw it over her shoulder and made for the door.

The bag wasn't such a burden now and its contents were becoming increasingly important.

Chapter 89

FRASER AT THE MANOR HOUSE

Fraser Hume had inherited Spencer's characteristic thoroughness. Joel Salomonovich may well have, 'done a Sherlock Holmes at the Reichenbach Falls', as Tony Molinari had so graphically put it, but there were many loose ends to tie up. Fraser determined that he would remain working for Joel Salomonovich to the best of his ability until he was satisfied that his family had been served appropriately. He would not relinquish his duty until he was satisfied that the task he had been set had been completed. It was as difficult to determine 'appropriately' as it was 'satisfied.' As always, when dealing with Joel Salomonovich the waters ran deep and were far from clear.

Joel and Bühler's bodies had not been recovered. They probably lay in the deep waters of the Alpen Lake. The odds of them surfacing were slim. Had either Joel or Julia's bodies been found Rebecca and Laura could, perhaps, have accept the loss of their loved ones and moved on but an empty feeling imbued their spirits and there was to be no sense of closure.

Had Joel's businesses, financial affairs and will been less complex, solicitors, who as a breed are disinclined to move with anything resembling urgency, could get to grips with his estate.

Joel's will stated that almost everything was to go to Julia with generous provisions for Rebecca and Laura. The fact that Julia was presumed dead, and that it would take time to establish as much, left the immediate future uncertain. Rebecca and Laura were both eminently sensible and conservative but both were wracked with the pain of their losses and saw little reason to accelerate proceedings.

Fraser's instinct was to keep Connor John, Leroy Gomez and Tony Molinaro on the European side of 'The Pond.' He rang Ian Smith. Ian made an appointment with Rebecca and Laura. The board would next meet at The Manor House shortly.

Ian Smith met Fraser at his club in Mayfair. Smith was well connected. Both nursed a large Armagnac.

Fraser began after a long silent gaze into the flickering flames of the huge hearth. He leaned forward from the high backed Chesterfield, sent the liquor swilling around its bowl and waited for it to settle like a ball in a roulette wheel.

'The thing is… the thing is something…don't ask me what… and it's only because my water tells me so…something, something just doesn't add up. Es riecht nach…. yeh? And to high heaven. I've spent many years keeping ahead of the game. Like Bühler I survived by knowing a stench when I smell one. I know! I saw it with my own eyes. Joel and Bühler are sure as hell have gone to the great beyond but why do I feel that there is something else? Connor smells it too. What the..?

Ian Smith shook his head at the waiter hovering close by. He needed a clear head. 'Well that's your jurisdiction and you're welcome to it. Look Fraser, the new owners of the corporation will be Joel's sister and daughter-in-law unless Julia turns up. I know, I know', he smiled. 'We have to start believing that she is dead too, though god knows who it was that used her passport to come back into the country. Landed in Birmingham? Do me a favour!

Did you know that they took her clothes from her flat and emptied her bank accounts too? If she was alive she would have showed. She would have contacted her mother and aunt.'

Fraser noted Ian Smith's aristocratic profile, his highly brushed white hair, matching eyebrows and colonial moustache, perfect fingernails and shining white teeth. The two thousand-guinea suit didn't detract from his suave urbanity either.

They turned to one another conspiratorially. 'I'm running the show now Fraser and I want you to know that you have the whole weight of the Salomonovich organisation behind you. Do whatever it takes. Don't leave a stone unturned.'

Fraser feigned a hurt grimace and Ian Smith understood.

'I'm sorry Fraser. I know you won't. Whatever it takes, whoever it takes.'

There was a nod of affirmation between the two men. Both knew that they could trust the other. Fraser reflected that the number of such trustees was rapidly declining. Ian Smith was not hard to call.

Ian Smith recognised as much too and decided to confide. 'You are a credit to your father.'

Fraser searched the old man's face. 'I knew him many years ago when he had, shall we say, semi-official duties on behalf of the United States. A fine man Spencer Hume. Joel only took the best. You certainly didn't get the job because of your father.'

He bent forward in a conspiratorial lean. 'As we are to work together there is, perhaps, something that you should know. I have recently visited my doctor. He has confirmed that cancer has spread into my bones and that I should not plan in the long term. I want to see this through Fraser. I thought that you should know.

They shook hands warmly and leaving the drawing room walked towards the front door. 'What will you do first Fraser?'

Both Ian Smith and Fraser Hume donned their coats in the cloakroom. 'We'll start by checking out the disappearance of Julia. And you?'

'I'd better meet with Rebecca and Laura Salomonovich. They need to know what their options are.'

'You going to let on?'

'Oh, it's no secret. Sir Nicholas Hansen and a couple of your countrymen have been keen to get their hands on Joel's operation for half a dozen years or so; ever since Joel started to show less interest in them.'

The doorman opened the highly varnished door and let in the chilly early December night air.

The damp foggy sight that greeted them would have depressed those with a propensity for pessimism. Neither man gave it a second thought.

Chapter 90

LUCY AND CHLOE

Lucy Davenport and Chloe Glendenning were intelligent mature young women. Both were happily married; Lucy to Martin, a banker and Chloe to Edward, a successful stockbroker in the city.

Both women had concentrated on their careers as art dealers. They had heeded their parent's advice well. Peter and Sarah had struggled in the early years of their marriage and the good things of life had come, perhaps a little late. Both girls were resolved to put a tidy sum away before starting a family.

The girls met infrequently but spoke on the phone almost daily, as they did to their parents. The nuclear family may have lived far apart but they would probably have spoken less had they lived in the same house. A common phenomena as Peter had often said to Sarah when she had pined for her daughters company.

It was with some unease that Lucy had rung Chloe on the night that Peter and Sarah had flown to Munich five days earlier. The girls and their husbands had visited Peter in the hospital the night before. They had visited every Wednesday and Sunday since their father had been admitted seven weeks earlier.

In truth the last seven weeks had been easier on Sarah than the previous seven months. Sarah had barely coped when Peter had been at home. The MacMillan nurses had been angels. Looking after him required devotion, endurance, patience and a strong stomach. Lucy and Chloe were pleased that others had the capacities which they lacked.

They loved their father dearly but had struggled to cope with his illness. They hadn't the stomach to nurse him and the poignant guilt this brought into their consciousness left pangs of shame and inadequacy. The dreaded visits left them feeling debased, ashamed and unworthy.

The agonising sight of their father's translucent emaciated body gnawed at their vitals leaving them wracked with unwarranted guilt. They were unable to deal with the trauma of loving without the reciprocal capacity for ministration and the bitter irony of their feelings of neglect and inadequacy.

The numbing daily charade of each and every hollow visit and the absurdity of the banal words spoken with false smiles belied their deep love, affection and concern left them damaged and fragile and rendered them utterly and painfully helpless.

It was Lucy who had taken the call that day. It was the hospital. Peter Fossard was been transferred to Germany. Their mother had signed papers and was taking their father to Munich to seek pioneering treatment. Their mother needed to act quickly if the opportunity afforded to their father was to be taken. Their mother understood the magnitude of the decision and wished them to bear with her until she was able to contact them. The message would have to suffice in the short term.

Suffice in the short term. Neither daughter recognised that expression as one that would be used by their mother; certainly not to them, and most surely not in the present sensitive circumstances. Yet the release papers had been signed and the signature was instantly recognisably their mother's.

The message received was brief though Sarah had, indeed, agreed to a much more detailed synopsis. Professor George Merrick had edited the piece considerably. The less known about the project the better from his point of view. Never the less the girls were not to be alarmed and their mother would be contacting them as soon as she was able.

There was an addendum, which requested that the girls were not to consider their parents missing; they were quite safe but there would be difficulties in contacting them over the next forty-eight hours. On all accounts they were not to panic. Their father was in the best possible hands. Their mother would contact them as soon as she was able.

Both girls discussed the situation with their respective husbands and both advised the same. Their mother may not be stable but she was doing what she thought was right. Hadn't she always? They would be best advised to wait a couple of days until their mother rang. Both husbands, having visited Peter, knew that Sarah was whistling in the wind and played down any rising hopes. Both knew too that their wives would grasp at any straw that the same wind blew their way.

Three days had gone by and still nothing. They were desperate but, as the girls frequently said to one other, without much conviction; 'No news is good news.'

It was on the fourth day that Mike Tyler had rung Lucy and Chloe. He made a simple request. Be at the family home on the following day and come alone. Their mother would be arriving in the afternoon.

The anxious girls arrived early, hugged each other as they met then sitting nervously in the living room waiting for their mother to arrive. They knew what the fate of their father had been. He would surely have died that morning. That was the reason for the timing of their mother's return. Wasn't it?

Chapter 91

FELIX TAKES A BREAK

Felix Elder couldn't believe his good fortune. He had planned to meet Bühler at Neuschwanstein and had also planned to leave alone. He had the luck of the devil himself! He considered that he had already had more luck than George Merrick had had during his entire lifetime.

Karma! What karma? Why? Why did some folk get all the luck? George Merrick had been driven and had strived against obstacle after obstacle after bloody obstacle had been placed in his way. The faster he tried to progress the more impediments obstructed his path. With anything approaching a modicum of luck he would surely have achieved so much more.

Felix Elder? Felix Elder took the low road. He hadn't shouldered responsibilities. The man had eased his way through life and had taken the time to smell the flowers on the way. Oh yes, he had acquired unique skills and had worked hard to develop his body but these outcomes were for the aggrandisement of himself and not for the good of others.

Elder had not filled in the stupid, unnecessary bureaucratic forms, spent late evenings grafting over poorly expressed papers or, completed a myriad of unnecessary trivia to achieve some contrived target set by some illiterate nincompoop whose purpose in life was to stifle individuality and harness originality.

No, Felix Elder had lain back while George Merrick had driven rough shod through life at speed and he had been stopped at every damned traffic light. At each and every light 'drifters' such as Elder, had cruised up alongside, mocked him with sarcastic smiles then moved along sedately.

But who was laughing now? Felix Elder's karma had been transmuted every bit as much as his body. The wheels felt well-oiled and the road smooth. The omens were with him and a new optimism lightened his countenance, brought forward a smile and lifted the darkness which had descended so many years ago. Shortly things would be different. They would be very different indeed.

The chap from the ministry had provided Felix with the information he had requested regarding Bühler's life. The networks had been connected. Bühler had reacted, as Felix believed he would. He had responded by travelling to Neuschwanstein in order to eliminate him, and... and... well, none of that mattered now.

Felix had arrived at The Marienbrucke and found cover. The Nazi's had always been assiduous in their timekeeping. Bühler was to prove no exception. He had approached the bridge within seconds of his appointed time and had seen Felix emerge from the secluded pathway with a briefcase which he believed to contain the transmuting device.

Felix had observed Bühler's reactions as he spotted the Americans. He had remained hidden in the bushes, a point not lost on him when he reflected that this was the second time that he had covertly observed Joel Salomonovich in woodland at close quarters.

Before Bühler had had time to react Joel Salomonovich and his entourage had arrived and the macabre scene had been played out before him.

Joel Salomonovich? Felix had had plans for him too. The Dutch police might like to pay him a visit. Jan Kuyper's killer had never been found. New DNA techniques may well convict the bastard. Oh, what a bonus that would be. However, the Pollat Gorge witnessed an ethereal re-enactment of Sherlock Holmes and Moriarty falling to their deaths over the Reichenbach Falls locked in that well recorded deathly embrace, as one of the Americans had observed.

Now both Salomonovich and Bühler were gone. There was nothing and no one left to connect him with George Merrick. He had won. My god he now had everything. At least almost everything.

He couldn't believe his luck. Now he could return to England secure in the fact that he was safe. He had both the money and the time to work and indulge his passions. He would go to England and discover the whereabouts of Julia Salomonovich and Sarah Fossard. He would then go to his father's cottage for a short time and introduce himself to the mourning Laura and Rebecca Salomonovich.

Perhaps he would press his offer for the Manor House? It would be very large for the two women now and he knew that it would hold bitter memories for both of them. They might just be persuaded.

Then he would take time out. He too would smell the flowers. It was almost Christmas.

Perhaps Astrid would provide a distraction over the festive season? There was time. Actually there was all the time in the world. He picked up the phone and called her.

Chapter 92

SARAH MEETS LUCY AND CHLOE

Mike Tyler's flat was a little over a mile from the Fossards house and it was there that Sarah had left Julia and Mike. The triumvirate had decided that, on balance, Sarah should first meet with Lucy and Chloe alone.

The front door opened and both daughters stood to attention militarily, staring first at each other and then at the living room door, waiting for their mother to appear. Both were desperate to see her; the anticipation tangible. Both approached the moment with a terrible foreboding. Neither spoke. Sarah opened the door and there was a momentary pause before she broke the silence.

'Don't I get a hug?' Both girls ran to her. They didn't know what to expect but it certainly wasn't a well-groomed, sane, familiar, smiling mother. The relief was audible.

The questions flowed thick and fast and it was only when Sarah raised her voice by that familiar authoritative single decibel and semitone that the girls acquiesced and subsided.

Sarah asked them to sit. They did as they were bidden and settled ready to hear of the death of their father. Both girls were quite sure of the outcome of their mother's bizarre visit to Germany. Their husbands had cautioned them against false hope, quack remedies and charlatans. Chloe reached for her mother's hands and Sarah's familiar reassuring smile came forcibly to her lips. Sarah had always given them strength and belief with that smile.

Lucy began tentatively, easing her mother into her explanation. 'Mum, where have you been and where's dad?'

Sarah took a deep breath and almost whispered. 'Come closer. Lucy on the settee with me. Chloe come...on the chair. I am going to need your love and your support. This is going to take some time and a lot of understanding.

I'm not sure that I understand any of it myself but…well… we have talked it over and have decided that we did the right thing no matter what you may think to begin with.'

Lucy and Chloe looked at one another. It might still be, as they feared, that their mother was about to talk gobbledygook. And who was the other - as in we?

Sarah saw their expressions. 'I'm sorry. It's just that…'

Chloe broke in. 'Take your time. Would you like a cup of tea or something stronger? It looks like you need…'

Sarah put her arms around her two daughters and began. 'No. I'm all right. Listen carefully, I'm going to tell you everything but I'm afraid that you just won't believe me.'

Sarah began with her visit to their father at the hospital and her meeting with Professor George Merrick and Walter Krantz. She took out Merrick's card from her handbag and showed it to Lucy and Chloe in turn as if to verify her sanity. She described her return visit to the hospital and her meeting with both men again.

Sarah shivered when mentioning Merrick and Krantz's names and Chloe, concerned at her discomfort, asked if she was warm enough. 'Quite warm enough thank you darling.' Sarah smiled, her buoyancy still at odds with her daughter's expectations.

When the mode of leaving the hospital and the flight in the Lear Jet was related, Lucy and Chloe looked at each other in disbelief. They interrupted periodically and on each occasion Sarah answered briefly and begged to move on.

The next bit was going to be tough and Sarah began with the theme of metamorphosis. Now Lucy and Chloe were beginning to believe that Sarah was indeed in need of psychiatric treatment. Where was she going with all of this?

Sarah stood. She felt an urgent need to walk. It may have been illogical but it eased her tension. 'The professor asked your father and me if we would sanction an attempt to, well to, er, I know how silly this sounds, but I, that is we, or maybe it was just me, I don't know…'

It was Lucy who stopped her. 'Mum, just say it. Whatever it is Chloe and I are here for you. We love you and nothing that you can do or say can change that.' Chloe nodded her assent.

Sarah took the umpteenth deep breath of the week and went on. 'OK, this is it. They coupled your father to someone else and pushed the damn button. He changed into someone else. There you are. Stark raving bonkers yes? Are you here for me now or just hoping that it's not contagious? I know. You love me and nothing can change that but I suppose that you now want to have me certified? Is that what's going around in your minds?' The girl's hesitated a little too long, their eyes lingering on their mother. Sarah laughed. 'There I knew that it was what you were thinking.'

In the silence that followed Chloe and Lucy considered what their mother was asking them to believe. Both were of the opinion that she needed help but both felt their reunion would eventually prove cathartic. The stress had been monumental. A little time with her loved ones would help. In due course she would recover and they would be able to move on. She needed love now more than anything and they would listen to whatever she said without conflict or denial. There would be time enough for healing; time enough for her to confront her demons.

It was Chloe who broke the silence once again. 'If Dad is, as you say, someone else now, where is he and where is his…you know, his, well.... his body?'

Sarah caught the tone. 'Dad is not 'someone else.' He is Dad. He just doesn't look like.....'Listen girls, I'm sane. I know just how far fetched all of this sounds but Uncle Mikey knows all about it too and he will tell you the same story.'

Both girls shouted in unison. 'Uncle Mikey.'

Lucy went to her mother taking her hands in hers. 'What's he got to do with all this? He's been with us, fretting for the past four days. He's not been with you Mum. Don't you remember?' Sarah ignored the question, stroking Chloe's arm, as she went on.

It took a further half an hour for Sarah to relate the remainder of her story. There was the ambulance journey from Munich to Innsbruck and the death of the professor. At each stage Sarah begged her daughters not to believe that she was insane. At each stage they began to believe that she was just that.

Except that.... except that there was a core of validity in her detail and a note of sincerity and reality in her delivery. Her story was as at least as compelling as it was fanciful.

The two young women listened intently knowing that there was a moment at which their mother would have to produce their father if what she had said was to be proved. Talk was good in its own right. Soon she would be confronted with the reality and her case would inevitably fold. Lucy and Chloe hoped that their mother would not fold with it.

Sarah continued relating the story of the escape from Innsbruck and the flight back to Birmingham, the night at Hockley Heath and the decision to leave their father with Mike until she had explained what had happened to them.

She concluded her story, and yet another silence followed. This a little longer. 'So the question is do you want to see your father? Both women were shocked but quick to respond. Sarah cut them short. 'Remember, he is not… well you know what he's not.'

Sarah picked up the phone and made a call. Mike answered. 'Sarah? Now?' Five minutes. OK.'

Sarah had been present at the meeting with Professor Merrick when Peter's fate was discussed and she had doubted her own sanity. Mike had spent a little time with Julia and he now doubted his sanity. How could Lucy and Chloe be expected to believe that their father now inhabited someone else's body? And, as yet, they were not aware of whose body that was. Before that revelation took place she knew that she needed corroboration from elsewhere. 'Uncle Mikey' was her only option.

During the five minutes that elapsed between Sarah calling Mike and his arrival at the house Lucy and Chloe had given each other several meaningful looks. Sarah offered tea and the sisters were quick to accept the opportunity to talk while she went to the kitchen to make it.

Lucy began. 'Soon this nightmare will be over. She's obviously had a breakdown. It will take a little time. Uncle Mickey has been in the dark as much as we have. Reality will hit home soon.' Chloe responded. 'Do you think we ought to have a doctor here when it does?' Both lowered their eyes to the floor and prayed for guidance.

Lucy began. 'Actually she doesn't look bad at all. I expected to find her distressed and bedraggled and to be with 'Uncle Mikey.' She says that she was with him. Why did he leave her alone? Good old irresponsible Uncle Mikey. Now he is past redemption.'

Both paused for a moment trying to make sense of Mike Tyler's part in the macabre play been acted out before them; if he had indeed, played a part at all. Lucy considered her limited knowledge of those suffering post-traumatic stress. 'She may look OK Chloe but grief can cause all kinds of problems. Perhaps they don't all result in people looking gaga. I don't know.'

'So what do we do when this charade is over?'

Sarah appeared in the doorway. 'Well Chloe, it sounds like the two of you just need to select the appropriate sanatorium. A little electric shock treatment should work wonders don't you think?'

Both daughters protested but Sarah raised her hand to stop them. 'Girls, were I in your place I would be thinking and saying exactly the same things. I just wonder when I'm going to wake up.' The doorbell chimed. 'That will be Uncle Mikey.' She went to the front door and Mike Tyler came in shaking the rain from his coat before he did so.

Lucy and Chloe stood and embraced Mike Tyler amazed that he had arrived at all. Both searched for an empathetic or sympathetic expression in his face. They anticipated that he would somehow get them to understand that he knew about their mother's state of mind. He registered no such communication but merely smiled pathetically as he greeted them. Their father would have called him a bozo for looking so feeble. He sat on the settee and motioned for the girls to sit on either side of him. He had always had free rein in the Fossard household with one exception. Peter's armchair by the fire remained sacrosanct. They waited for Sarah's evidence to be called forth not anticipating the main witness's arrival in the dock.

Lucy and Chloe took their drinks from their mother casting glances intermittently between Sarah and Mike. The tension was unbearable and Sarah could hardly bring herself to begin.

Sarah coughed several times, not to clear her throat but to relieve the terrible stress she was under. The strategy failed. She opened with what was, to the girls, a frustrating reprise of events leading up to Mike's arrival.

Sarah opened the palm of her hand upwards indicating to Mike that he had the floor now. The girls turned to him. Surely he wasn't going to corroborate her story?

'OK, er, right. It's like, well, where do I start Sarah?' She knew immediately that she would have to go it alone. Mike, bless his heart, would not be of any use to her. He just didn't have the stomach.

'Hockley Heath. You brought me from Birmingham Airport Mike, remember?' She turned to Lucy and Chloe, 'And your father, for reasons I'll explain presently, followed behind in a taxi.' She turned her attention back to Mike. No luck. She turned from the unhelpful Mike to her daughters once again.

'Uncle Mikey and I booked in to a guesthouse and I left him in his room while your father booked in and took another room. I explained that your father was in the room opposite and Uncle Mickey, like you, decided that I was in need of a psychiatrist.'

The sister's mouths were wide open. Both turned their attention to Mike questioningly once again. Surely both of them hadn't lost it? Surely the charade would end soon?

Mike, seeing Sarah struggling with her burden, felt compelled to relieve her.

'Your mum called, er, the person who was your father, if that makes sense, into the room and I was astonished. Trust me I asked every question I could think of to verify who, er, it was. Lucy, Chloe, there is no doubt. It's not a trick. I thought that it would be. Believe me your father's brain, no not his brain, his mind and memories are in the other person's body. If there is one thing that I am certain of, it is that. Your mother and me are both either sane or insane. You will have to judge. But we know the same to be true.

It's fantastic I know. It's beyond belief, again, I know. Unbelievable but it's true; as God is my witness. Professor George Merrick was the most gifted man in the universe and he died, we believe, taking his invention with him. We cannot give you corroborating medical evidence. That went with him too. But we do have incontrovertible evidence never the less.

The sisters had been transfixed by Mike's confirmation of Sarah's rendition. Their Uncle Mikey's had hardly been less dramatic in his delivery. They fought to make sense of it all. Neither believed either of them but both were afraid to pursue the matter to its inevitable conclusion.

Sarah felt the time was right. 'Shit, there wasn't a right time and that was swearing.' 'The question that you are avoiding is whose body has your father taken.'

Sarah began by explaining the process much as Merrick and Krantz had done to Peter previously omitting the identity of the donor until the last moment. She now understood the wisdom of that strategy as she detailed the last hours of their father's bodily existence and the hopelessness of his insidious illness.

She paraphrased Krantz. 'The only donor they could use would be one in a vegetative state. As he had said, they wouldn't get volunteers. It had to be a fully functioning healthy body. The brain and its patterns, the long term memory blocks, the mind and soul may not function but as long as the rest of the body did they would have an acceptable donor.'

'There is a further problem of course', the professor had said.

'And that is', she had enquired.

'Permission from the donor or a relative,' Krantz had explained. 'We have the one. As you can imagine we have scoured the country for information of others but no luck so far.'

'Why are you still searching for a donor?' Sarah had asked. 'Is there something that you are not telling me about the man you have? Is he a psychopath or something?'

'That would not matter,' the professor had said ready to make a rapid exit. 'The man would have a whole new set of thoughts and memories. No, the fact is that we don't have a man.' He had paused before dropping his bombshell. 'We only have a woman.'

Lucy and Chloe gaped at Sarah in much the same way as Sarah had gaped at Merrick.

Sarah had looked at their father for help. He had been falling away rapidly and the nurse had injected morphine. The decision had had to be hers and hers alone.

The sisters were stunned. Lucy looked first at Mike and then deep into her mother's face. 'Are you telling me that dad's a, a...'

Neither woman was prepared to listen further. Enough was enough. The sheer magnitude of the outrageous suggestion challenged their comprehension and questioned their sanity. Both stood. No more!

'Lucy. Chloe.' The voice came from the doorway. A young woman had appeared there unnoticed. She had arrived with Mike and had remained in the hallway listening to Mike and Sarah relating their fantastic tale. It was time for her to emerge.

Chloe collapsed. Lucy followed.

It took four hours before Lucy and Chloe began to recognise the truth. It would take a lot longer before they would accept it.

Chapter 93

FELIX VISITS ASTRID FOR CHRISTMAS

Felix Elder had never felt so well but perversely that presented a problem. His sculptured physique bore testimony to the extraordinary number of hours pumping iron, his amazing cardiac and lung capacities to his daily extensive running and climbing and his flexibility to his punishing, tortuous stretching regimen.

These dull, monotonous, boring exercises did not excite Felix at first. He knew however, that unless he observed a strict maintenance programme it would take less than a few months for the inevitable decline to begin. He began with, what he considered to be, the mindless exercises. He researched programmes and eventually settled for an hour and a half a day. That, he considered would be all that he would be able to stand. In fact he soon found the pumping, running and stretching to be less of a chore than he had first imagined. The success he had with all three raised his motivation levels even when he considered that he might well spend the time more profitably.

When at the old cottage his five-mile run took him past The Bothey. From there he ran along the riverside to the lake that bordered the land that had belonged to Stanley Mainwaring, Vincent Haan and Joel Salomonovich and was now the home of Rebecca and Laura Salomonovich.

From the lake he entered the woodland road that he had cycled along so many times as a child. Having warmed up he picked up the pace and passed The Pheasantry and then returned to the old cottage. He resolved to do a longer run along the coast when he was mentally attuned to the ordeal. Physically he knew that he would not have a problem with the distance; it was his mentality that would determine his rate of progress.

He called at The Manor House to introduce himself as the new owner of the cottage but the 'Ladies of the House', he was advised by Mr. Manners, a new retainer engaged to run the place, were not presently 'seeing' visitors due to a recent tragedy.

Felix was eager to get back to work at Cambridge but knew too that that particular ambition would take time to achieve. Planting Michael Mitchell's qualifications would be a considerable task. Convincing his second rate former 'colleagues' would present less of a challenge. He would take a research assistants job and drip feed the wonders of science to the undeserving. Little by little they would recognise true greatness if not the originator of it.

The term had ended. There was little point in making contact now. Besides he had much to do, much to learn and all the time in the world to achieve his ambitions. All the time that is except in relation to Julia Salomonovich. He needed a rest before he targeted Julia. A time for reflection. Besides there was fun to be had and Astrid was only a phone call away. Weihnachten in Deutschland. Yes Christmas in Germany would be excellent as long as she didn't want to spend too much time with her tiresome family and friends. He rang.

Astrid was delighted. She was relieved that Felix had rung. She doubted that she would see him again. Yes, she was spending Christmas Day with her folks and New Year's Eve with friends but other than that she didn't have plans for the holiday month. Felix examined the information and rationalised it while exchanging a few minor pleasantries.

'So will you come Michael?' Felix had his answer. 'Of course but I can't come until Boxing Day and I must leave on New Year's Eve in the morning. You will be in Berlin for the rest of the holiday I take it?' She answered in the affirmative. Felix had a warm place to stay over Christmas and excuses for not having to meet Astrid's family and friends.

He arrived in Berlin on Boxing Day as agreed and Astrid picked him up at the Tegel Airport in Reinickendorf to the north of the city in the purple beetle. Within twenty minutes he was sitting in Astrid's rented Dorotheenstrasse fourth floor flat just a short stroll from the University.

As soon as Felix put down his bags she took his hand and took him to the window. She wrapped herself around him and pointed southwest into the city. 'Just there. Just a two minute walk away is 'Unten den Linden.' We shall walk there tomorrow. Very romantic I think. Perhaps we shall take a, what do you call it; you know a short journey on the Spree. The river is beautiful you know.

Felix did know. He had spent many happy moments in the city, more particularly at the university. He didn't enlighten Astrid.

'Trip.' 'What.' 'Trip was the word you were looking for.'

'Ah yes, trip.'

'So that's a walk and a trip. Is there anything else that you would like?' Astrid was as tactile as she had been in Rosenberg. Her hands moved down his chest and beyond. Felix was having fun again.

Chapter 94

JULIA AND SARAH'S NEW LIFE TOGETHER

Sarah Fossard felt the loss of her husband deeply. It was true that Peter was still there but the man she had loved was not. This troubled her. Before the trauma of Peter's metamorphosis she had believed that the strengths of their relationship had been their love, their kindred spirits, their friendship and their shared memories. They were confidants, comfortable and intimate.

Peter had changed but only in the physical sense. Why then had their relationship become so strained? Why had their long easy conversations dwindled to brief exchanges? Why had their affection cooled to the occasional peck on the cheek? Their sexual relationship had ceased. Of course it had. Neither was attracted to the other in the physical sense but there was a chasm growing between them and Sarah felt her loss acutely. The New Year had come and gone. There had been little evidence of festive spirit.

Julia became more confident and less dependent on Sarah as the spring approached. There were tensions in the house that had not been there before. Peter and Sarah had always been comfortable in each other's company. The natural order of things had now changed. Julia had far more energy than Sarah had. Where the two had sat together contentedly on an evening Julia wanted something more. She was still reluctant to go out but felt caged and fettered. Where she had been content to read a book by the fireside there was unease and a restlessness which caused her to go to bed early and to communicate less. Sarah was in her late fifties; Julia in her early twenties. Their differences manifested themselves in a thousand ways. .

It had been mid-February before Julia had left the house by herself for the first time. It had taken a great deal of nerve but she needed tablets for a headache and had decided that there was no reason why she couldn't go to the chemists herself. She had walked the route a thousand times before and knew the area to be quite safe, not something, she realised, that she had ever had to take into consideration before. However there was a new dynamic now and she was acutely aware of it. She felt vulnerable and would need to be cautious when planning to walk.

She survived the trip to the chemists and that increased her confidence and encouraged her to be a little more adventurous. It was February twenty ninth when she caught a bus into Bristol city centre.

Thankful for the cold day she had dressed in a heavy jumper, jeans and overcoat. Perhaps by the time the summer came she would be more comfortable and assured and.... and.... she left her thoughts there.

On the face of it Bristol was pretty much the same place that it had been twelve months earlier; the last time that Peter had been capable of walking around the city centre. Now, however, she saw things from a quite different perspective.

She stopped to look in the clothes shops. They captured her interest. She saw advertising that had gone unnoticed before. Was it really so focussed on women? Her perception of the world was changing and she recognised the fact. Peter was disappearing quickly and she knew that this would be a tragedy for Sarah.

By the end of March Julia walked the city streets with confidence and bought and wore her first dress on the last day of that month. She made an appointment at the hairdressers and had a makeover. The lipstick felt strange but looked good. Her eyes were sensational. Sarah would have to teach her how to do them.

She enjoyed the trappings of her gender, the swish of her hair as she turned quickly and, perhaps, a little too frequently. The swing of her earrings and the seductive movement of her breasts. The negatives were becoming positives as she was subsumed by her gender.

She had been flustered and embarrassed by the chap who had taken her case from the carousel at Innsbruck Airport. She had changed. When a young man opened a door for her at the newsagents, and smiled to let her through, a warm thrill had rushed through her body and she had thanked him with a smile.

The dreaded handbag had become indispensable. She took interest in the myriad types of clothing and noted her preferences with less and less embarrassment. She acquired a feminine walk not knowing how much was nature, how much nurture and how much was from necessity. The shoes alone. The shoes alone. God, women suffered for their shoes. And again the shoes. When stood upright they were not visible. Either she had to lean forward or stick her feet out in front of herself to see them.

She noted and acquired the feminine wrist. Limp but graceful yet natural too. 'Where the hell had that come from?' And again the clothes. Peter Fossard couldn't have told you what Mike Tyler had worn on the previous evening if there was a million dollars resting on it. In fact he couldn't be sure if Mike had worn clothes, and he would have cared even less.

Now she examined each and every woman with a careless scrutiny gaining 'The Knowledge' like a London taxi driver learning the streets.

Peter Fossard had prided himself on the subtlety of his 'scanning' of women. They never knew. Of that he was sure. Julia Salomonovich would beg to differ. She was uncomfortably aware, yet somehow excited, that she had been 'checked out.' Somewhere deep, very deep, there was a twinge of regret but it was suppressed as a greater instinct took precedence and lay subsidiary to her passions and a condescension to her, as yet, unformulated intentions. The impermeable and intransmutable were being eroded by her newfound sensibilities.

She sat in the coffee shops – people watching. Mainly women watching. She inspected their clothes and accessories, their mannerisms and their nuances; discovering what age, figure and type wore what. She sat for an hour at a time, lingering with a cold cup of coffee and a Danish. That was something new too. She hadn't had a sweet tooth before.

It was mid-April and, as a rule Sarah was usually home before seven. It was almost nine. Leaving work she had rung Mike and had arranged to meet him in the city. They had talked at considerable length. Almost exclusively about Julia.

Sarah had drunk three glasses of wine, something that she had rarely done during the day in the past, and was feeling the depression that follows the elation a surfeit of alcohol engenders. She was disintegrating under the pressure of her burden and needed a shoulder to lean on.

She had supported Julia in the early days believing that she would gain strength from familiarity and become more supportive. The opposite had happened. As Julia grew in confidence she had become more adventurous. She was young and her boundless energy emphasised the incongruous nature of their relationship. Peter had been her rock; Julia demanded attention, became unreliable, self-centred and less considerate of her feelings. Sarah knew that they were drifting apart and felt the utter helplessness of her untenable position as she began fall apart before Mike's eyes. Dismantled, she sought comfort in his company.

Mike's had been surprisingly reassuring. He had been there for her when she needed him. She had said to him that Julia seemed distant and in a world of her own. Mike had remarked. 'You know better than I Sarah, she is in a different world; a whole different world. You have to accept that and move on too.'

Mike's frank assessments and surprisingly sure touch reassured Sarah and she began to depend on him. His judgements were sober, his actions surprisingly reliable and his steadfastness unquestionable. He gave the support she so desperately needed.

He had put his arm around her to comfort her and it led to a kiss. Not a passionate kiss. Not a lover's kiss; but a kiss none the less. Then he had whispered in her ear. 'We'll just have to grow old together. We will never forget her, always be there for her when she needs us and remember Sarah; I will always be there for you too. Always. I promise.'

Both were embarrassed and Mike made an excuse to leave but both knew too that they needed the other as Julia became ever more distant to them both.

Sarah walked into the living room and Julia, having heard the door open, turned the TV off and stood waiting for Sarah to enter. She asked Sarah how her day had been. Sarah didn't answer. She was startled at another transformation.

Julia's dress clung tight to her figure, the hemline well above the knee. It was the last straw and the dam burst in Sarah's eyes as she buckled under the strain and the chaotic aftermath of her loss of Peter. She had had no one to grieve for. The time was now. She wept.

Julia's was heart broken at Sarah's distress but the moment was seminal and it was better to be cruel now and to be kind later. She could not abide disabusing her mind further. No longer able to contain her youthful intent and new unapologetic mentality, she began.

'It's me Sarah. It's who I am. I am who I am, and I am Julia Salomonovich or Tyler or whatever else you want to call me. One thing is for sure. I am a woman and there is nothing that you or I can do about it. We keep saying it. Now we have to start living it. At first I accepted the grim reality now I must embrace the living truth. We must draw a definitive line under our perceptions and accept things as they are. Not as we would wish them to be.'

Nothing could have rendered the subject closed more certainly. Sarah's words failed to materialise. Silly! How silly of her to think that her life could remain the same. There dawned a belated understanding of how things really stood. There had been a sad absence of logic before. Where had she been? Her marriage was over. She saw the truth of that now. The Peter that she had known and loved was leaving. Slowly he was being replaced. Julia shared her memories but she knew that she could not share her future. Six months earlier Peter Fossard had died. Now she saw that he was dying again. That was it. The absurdity of the thing! The whole world had been turned upside down. Had Mike really kissed her? Did she imagine that he had kissed her 'differently?' She was going mad. It wasn't surprising.

She smiled the smile of a simpleton unable to comprehend, and, beaten, retired to bed.

Julia pulled out the catalogues and magazines that she had bought in the mall, from her bag at the side of the settee and absorbed herself in them until the early hours of the morning. There was much to learn. Little now remained of the fabric of her former thoughts. There was one direction now and oestrogen was driving the bandwagon.

Later she lay in bed rapidly distilling her thought. There was a new calm. The turmoil had been quelled with her acceptance of the inevitable. She began to dream, ascending from her self-pity and leaving her outpourings of grief behind. That same grief had initially stoked rebellion. It was now well behind her as she embraced her new reality. Now unfettered by convention and transcending boundaries an immutable and indestructible self-belief replaced her initial tacit acceptance as she dismissed her uncertainty.

She was not reconciled to her delicate profile as she stood at the mirror; for there was no need for reconciliation. She stood proud and willing to embrace her new persona. A formidable tub-thumping denunciation of her former self would serve only as a trite confession of guilt in the chaotic aftermath of her transmigration.

This was no masquerade, no uncomfortable lie, no tawdry enactment or delusion. The future was not a dreadful certainty. It was a new beginning to be embraced with vigour. Now she rose unapologetic and unequivocal.

'Enough! What is normality?' She must remain true to her new self. And there was but one self. Thinking otherwise was the road to perdition. There was no further need to steel herself for the public's invective. There would be no further erosion of her self-belief. She refused to nestle in a valley of tranquillity at the cost of her sanity. Her delineations clear, her searing grief and anger vanquished. She tore at the bars of her prison and broke free of her bonds. She did not seek rehabilitation. She had not jettisoned the past. She had merely consigned it to anecdote.

She knew the impact her sparkling eyes, pouting lips and décolletage would have but began to believe that it would not militate against her nature and she revelled in the power that it gave her. There would be no duplicity. She had emerged scathed but unsullied; the nostalgic pining for her former self diminished by her resolve to live again. The fragile relationship and internecine battle with Peter was over. The loss of an intimate relationship with Sarah would be a bitter price to pay but an uneasy accord would not be sustainable and would compound her feelings of inadequacy. The chaos that had engulfed her and corroded the foundations of her new nativity was beaten, baring testimony to her newfound sensibilities.

There could be no more poignant illustration of her transformation than the certainty of her willingness to succumb to her sensitivities. She refused to be possessed by Peter. She was who she was. There was no burden of guilt. Her life was not unpalatable. She remained undiminished. Her proud spirit would not be quelled. She would be uncompromising and embrace her new unquenchable appetite for life. She stiffened slightly at the delicious irony of that.

Her initial isolation had not insulated her from the future. Through the distorted prism of self-loathing she had witnessed the futility of denial. Little now remained of the fabric of her former mentality. The chameleon's guise was now dispensed with as powerful impulses and passionate urges heralded the dénouement of her metamorphosis.

The devil could come for her bloody soul. He wouldn't have it.

Chapter 95

FELIX'S INSPIRATION

Felix always enjoyed his time in Germany. Astrid was about as near and as far away as he wanted her to be. The arrangement worked just fine; the attachment one sided. He visited her for a week in December and for a long weekend in early January too. She wanted him to move in with her but he had other ideas. Mike Mitchell would disappear quite soon when it was convenient for him to do so. The timing would depend on circumstances.

Back in Cambridge Felix found work at the university as a research assistant and was soon amazing everyone with his contributions. It was April when he was asked to attend a meeting. There had been great speculation. It was almost as if the great but unlamented George Merrick had reappeared. He heard George Merrick referred to as a bloke who 'had a face a dog wouldn't lick' by one female ex-colleague. Another joked that he was glued to his chair when the old professor spoke. 'If I hadn't been glued to the chair I'd have left', he said, lacking the timing to go with his supposed witticism. Felix laughed at the joke and marked the chap down for a fall.

He wasn't a professor, he was the hired help, but he was back. He sat in his father's old chair on wet weekend in the old stone cottage. 'Time my boy. Time. That is all it will take and I have plenty of that.'

The rain relented on the Sunday morning and he set out for his daily run by the lake. He came upon two ladies making their way back from the village and stopped to pass the time of day with them.

'Good morning ladies. I hope that you are both quite well?' Laura Salomonovich looked at her elderly companion and smiled warmly. It was splendid to hear a young man with such good manners and one who spoke so well.

'Good morning', they replied in unison.

'I am your new neighbour. I live in the cottage beyond The Pheasantry. Professor Merrick's old place. Bit of a character I've been told. I called upon you a little while ago but the man, er...'

'Manners?' enquired Laura.

'Yes, that was it, Manners. He said that you were unavailable. I'm afraid I use the place sparingly', he said pointing in the general direction of his cottage. I have only returned recently. It is so nice to make your acquaintance. I do so hope that we shall meet again in the near future. Perhaps when I am more soberly dressed. I'll bid you a very good morning ladies.' With that Felix gave a court bow and jogged away not having asked the names of the two women or having given his own. There would be time for that.

He sat at his father's desk reassessing his plans and contemplating his future. He knew what he wanted. He wanted to be young again and to have Rachael Haan as his wife. He had the former. The latter would take further genius; 'But then', he considered, that, in itself, did not present a difficulty. The modus operandi was the debating point.

Suddenly a memory swept in from the deepest recess of his mind. His rescue of the unfortunate shipwrecked adventurers a little over five years ago. Where was it? Off the coast of Madagascar? Mauritius? Or was it ....? No he had not been shipwrecked so how could he...? how could he...? The memory disappeared as quickly as it had formed but the thought had registered.

What was that? What had entered his consciousness? Then climbing. An excruciating pain and dropping into oblivion. That memory was fleeting too but again he remembered the thought and experienced the certainty of it. He left his father's office and lay on the old couch in the sitting room. George Merrick analysed Felix Elder's memory and rapidly comprehended a new reality.

He possessed George Merrick's mind but the convolutions of Felix Elder's brain stored traces of his memories too. The memories of Felix Elder were hidden in the deep recesses. If they proved dominant how long would it be before a bewildered Felix Elder awoke and George Merrick and his fabulous brain died?

He set to work immediately. It was true that his lifestyle had changed. He had believed that his interest in keeping in shape had stemmed from vanity and that his newfound sense of humour had been generated by the situation that he now found himself in and the changed relationships he had with others. Nature and nurture. Again the recurrent theme!

Felix Elder must be stopped.

He worked for more than sixty hours during the following three days aware that his genius had remained substantially intact. 'But for how long?'

It was on the morning of the fourth day, during the early hours, that he found his answer. He would set up his device again. This time the circuit would not connect George Merrick and the device to Felix Elder. 'This time...of course...yes ... this time.... Felix Elder you are a genius. Who needs George Merrick?'

He needed to act and to act immediately. He closed the curtains. Within the hour he was prepared and pressed the remote noting the time on the grandfather clock in the sitting room.

It was a little under seven hours later when he awoke. Refreshed from his sleep he assessed his senses. How would he know if the experiment had been a success? When had he ever failed? The calculations were made. The analysis had been thorough. Success was assured. To Felix Elder the laurels to George Merrick the grave; or was that the other way round? It was of no consequence.

What of Julia? If a mind as robust and agile as Felix Elder's had had his memories affected how much more likely would it be that a far inferior mind like hers would be subjected to Peter Fossard's memories?

It struck him then. He had it all. The answer. The bloody answer to it all. All his problems solved with one solution. Perfect. Absolutely perfection; seamless; faultless. He laughed out loud. Karma; Felix Elder's bloody Karma. Did anyone ever have so much going for them? Better to be born lucky than to be born rich they say. Better to be born a genius like George Merrick and be a lucky bastard like Felix Elder to boot.

He had strengthened George Merrick's grip on Felix Elder's mind. It was time to invite Julia to a little party at his home and to reintroduce her to his device. It was time to weaken Peter Fossard's grip on Julia Salomonovich. He had dispatched Peter Fossard body; it was time to take away his mind and replace it with another's. All very simple really! At least for one such as George Merrick.

Soon she would recall only the thoughts and memories of Julia Salomonovich. He would merely reverse the polarity; then plant thoughts and beliefs in her mind. It was so simple. He would save her life, bring her back to her loved ones, court her and ... there were things to do ... he must not get ahead of himself. There was a need for reflection and further analysis. He needed to get away. He would visit Astrid, in Berlin, walk 'Unten der den Linden', gaze across the Spree and smell the flowers as he finalised his plans.

As always the plans would be meticulous and this time, yes this bloody time, he would work alone. The asinine hoi polloi that masqueraded as the competent would not be engaged. They were not to be trusted. Always they buggered up the works with their incompetence.

He arrived in Berlin just eighteen hours after making his decision to go. Astrid would prove an adequate distraction as he considered the details of his plan.

George Merrick, Felix Elder and Michael Mitchell's emotional detachment left them all indifferent, aloof and unconcerned. The neurosis remained unabated.

Chapter 96

FELIX BIDS ASTRID AUFWIEDERSEHEN

Felix was adapting quickly. He comprehended the changes to his personality, his psyche rapidly absorbing and distilling the feedback of a strange and exciting new world. Trips to Germany had proved an excellent release and Cambridge provided him with the stimulation, if not the rewards and kudos, that ego demanded. They would come later. The physical training was becoming less arduous. He had been right. It was the mental thing. The hardest part was to make the effort to get changed and to make it to the start line. The ancient Chinese proverb was right too: 'A journey of a thousand miles starts with the first step.' Initiating anything was the tough part for many whatever that enterprise may be, he noted. He believed the relevance of that was clearly not evident to a considerable proportion of the student body he taught. Slowly his body was influencing his decisions and changing his attitudes. The phenomena fascinated him.

Felix and Astrid were dining at one of their favourite haunts on the River Spree. The Alte Liebe is the oldest of Berlin's restaurant boats and boasts excellent fare. The two sat side by side in silence, Astrid holding Felix's upper arm and leaning her head into his chest. She had fallen in love with him and knew that she had from the moment that she had first seen him in the Rasthof on the way to Kranebitten. Now Felix was beginning to feel the pressure of her hope.

She had kissed him and told him that she loved him. She had felt the pain of unrequited love when a reciprocal declaration was not forthcoming. Nothing had prepared her for the dull pain at realising that he meant everything to her but that she meant little to him. It was clear to her now that, to him, the relationship was fine as it was. She began to feel distanced and was humiliated by the acceptance of her predicament.

To Felix the situation had been straightforward. He got sex. She got him. Why spoil it? He knew that she was seeking some kind of commitment; that her body clock was ticking. He held all the trumps and saw little reason not to play them dispassionately.

Felix sensed the end was nigh for Michael Mitchell. If she followed there would be no trace. It was time. For a man with all the time in the world a body clock meant nothing. He played with his food, having lost his appetite. This relationship, he now knew, had run its course. Astrid had served her purpose. He lacked the experience, the inter-personal skills and finesse to end the relationship courteously and cleanly. Rarely had he been so far out of his depth. Like an immature teenager, he resolved to inform Astrid of his decision from the other side of the channel at some indeterminate time in the future. That would solve it! At least for him it would.

When he made love to Astrid he had made love to Rachael Haan. Always to Rachael Haan. Astrid was a good-looking girl of that there was no doubt. Oh, she was active in bed, that was true, but she wasn't Rachael Haan. His beloved Rachael. His one and only Rachael. Rachael had died and that was that but Julia's resemblance was so striking that he had momentarily mistaken one for the other. Julia Salomonovich had been Rachael Haan!

Astrid moved her head from his chest and asked him what he was thinking. He stunned her with his response. 'I'm thinking that I must return home immediately. There is much for me to do. I really can't spend another day here.'

Astrid was heartbroken. She had anticipated Felix staying for much longer and she had wanted to arrange a time to visit him in England. She often teased him that she didn't even know the exact whereabouts of his home. She knew of Nottingham but she had never been there. She was keen to visit his family and friends there. Mrs. Astrid Mitchell of Nottingham had sounded so good to her. She sighed heavily and stroked his arm again gazing first at him enquiringly and then, when no response was forthcoming, out across the river.

'Must you go so soon?' There was no reply. 'Is it possible for me to come with you? Again silence. 'Are you mad at me for some reason? Have I done something wrong?' Still she was prepared to dilute controversy rather than face the harsh reality that she was losing him.

Astrid felt an intense sadness. She had spoken to him and he had not replied nor exerting the slightest discernible interest in her. She heaved a despondent sigh. Where he had been engaging he was now sullen and withdrawn. Where he had been articulate, unassuming and warm he was taciturn, brittle and uncommunicative. There was an uneasy strained atmosphere between them and his words and callous indifference lacerated her confidence. She was falling apart.

The dark clouds of suspicion were not a recent manifestation. She knew that he had concealed far more than he had revealed. The stench of duplicity hung heavily in the air. She guessed that his façade hid a secret turmoil and fretted that his charm was a veneer but she was in love and unwilling to admit that it was unwise to permit such an emotion to thrive, holding on to the frail hope of redemption. Now she saw what a vain thought that had been. The passion of her attachment had blinded her and there now dawned a belated understanding. She had the unpleasant impression that he was sadistically playing with her emotions and using her.

He had tired of her need for constant affirmation and the ensuing fracas had reduced her to tears. He knew that a bitter estrangement could provoke retaliation and potentially damaging revelations. He had responded to these unmanifested threats with bitter recriminations.

Astrid felt the chilly air of reality as he responded to her pleading with renascent aggression. 'I'm shouting because you're not hearing. The truth is that you smother me', he said with an exaggerated ennui which cut her to the quick.

The sickening brutality of that remark and the vehemence of his voice caused her to drop her head into her lap, the cruel invective engraved on her heart. Cowered, the hapless victim felt sick to the pit of her stomach. She spiralled deeper into despair. She wouldn't miss him. No. She would miss who she had thought he was.

The torrents of tears and her unassuaged anguish had no discernible effect on the baleful and sinister Felix. He saw Astrid merely as a part of the essential evolution of his being. His ruthlessly manipulative mind observed no cynical indifference to her. She had played her part and played it well, until now, but it was over.

There was a sullen truce as they walked Unten den Linden back to Astrid's flat. He left within the hour taking all his belongings with him. She noted that he had.

During the days that followed Astrid's grief remained undiminished. Emotionally scarred and brought to the brink of a breakdown she tried to understand but could not.

She recognised her supine acquiescence, the tissue of deceit and the impenetrable wall he had erected as a precaution against intrusion into his life and knew that she should have been more cautious. But she had fallen in love. She had been hypnotised by him. She had given him her all and he had thrown it back in her face. She felt innocent, persecuted and humiliated. She could have salvaged a modicum of her integrity if she had only recognised the truth but knew that she had not been brave enough to look hard at that which she wished to ignore. A mind cannot be perverted by innocence, she reflected. She should have known.

Schadenfreude? Yes he took pleasure from other's misfortune. Michael Mitchell personified the word. And when he had spoken to her, his words had often left her confused providing substantial latitude for many layered interpretations. She recognised that she had been duped, used and manipulated.

It would be some time before Astrid Swartz would raise her head above the parapet again. She had drunk wine with the worst of the Borgias.

Having dispensed with Astrid, Felix was concentrating on his immediate future. Astrid had served her purpose and the diversion had been beneficial. Now he was ready to move on. The experience had been necessary. It was time to merge Mike Mitchell and Felix Elder. Julia would not remember Mitchell's name after he had finished with her. Her memories would be confined to Julia Salomonovich the first. It was time for him to become acquainted with Julia Tyler, to take her memory and reacquaint her with Julia Salomonovich of The Manor House.

It was on the flight home that the final piece of the jigsaw fell into place. It would take intricate planning. 'My god you really are a genius', he uttered under his breath. The stewardess thought she had missed his and asked if he had requested a drink. 'Just a glass of water miss. I'm in training.'

Chapter 97

FRASER MEETS SIR NICHOLAS HANSEN

It had been seven months since Joel Salomonovich and Reinhart Bühler had plunged into the Pollat Gorge. It had been a very long seven months for Fraser Hume. He had yet to use his Giants season ticket. He hadn't wanted to. There was something sinister that he had missed. He knew it in his guts.

Something linked Joel Salomonovich with Bühler; Bühler with Merrick; Merrick with Sarah Fossard and Fossard with Elder. And, looming high above the conundrum there was Sir Nicholas Hansen.

His professional pride was wounded. There was some small detail. The Pollat Gorge wasn't the end of the Joel Salomonovich and Reinhart Bühler affair. There was more to it. But what? What had he missed? He sought cognition not through idle curiosity but with a burning professional desire to know and besides, he thought, he owed Joel at least that much.

What did he know that would make sense of it all? What didn't he know? Where would he find it? Who should he talk to?

Fraser retained his team for two months before Leroy Gomez and Tony Molinaro returned to 'The Firm' in Manhattan. They remained there for forty eight hours before taking a flight to Atlanta, another to Paris and the Eurotunnel to London. They took rooms in a small hotel in Hammersmith and got their instructions from Fraser via public telephone.

Fraser and Connor were holed up in a hotel much used by Joel Salomonovich's organisation. It was located on Half Moon Street just off Piccadilly. It was expensive but Ian Smith had sanctioned the transaction without a second thought.

It was Ian Smith who inadvertently provided the breakthrough. The phone rang. 'Fraser, Sir Nicholas Hansen wants to see you. He wants to run a few ideas past you. He wants to take over the firm. He's got the clout and will

344

be hard to resist. If he can prove that Julia Salomonovich is dead the road is clear for him. Rebecca and Laura Salomonovich would have little alternative but to sell. The long and short of it is that they are looking to retain me and I wanted you to know that. He's a crafty bugger for sure. With me onside he hopes to increase his bargaining power.

Ian paused with some gravitas. 'Fraser, there are other developments. He has a team tracking you and another searching for Julia Salomonovich. I don't know whether she is dead or alive but if she is alive and he gets to her....well, he's a ruthless bastard Fraser. He paid a lot for his knighthood. There were plenty against it. One thing's for certain; He's been lucky or, at least, those who have stood in his way have tended to get unlucky. In some cases so unlucky that they frequently expire shortly after crossing him. Funny thing that.'

Fraser Hume could have offered Ian Smith a list of 'funny things' in connection with Sir Nicholas Hansen. He remained silent for a few moments before asking. 'How do I get to Hansen?'

'You got something Fraser?'

'Nothing solid but I need to shake a few trees and rattle a few cages and see what happens. A leitmotif; there is one somewhere. A piece of the jigsaw is missing and until I get sight of it we're going nowhere.'

'And Hansen's men?'

Fraser smiled. 'They might just as well as walk about with cowbells around their necks. I've got 'em covered Ian. Thanks all the same.'

Fraser arranged to meet Connor John in a little Italian place on Piccadilly.

'Looks like we are in for the long haul Connor.'

Connor rationed his words at the best of times. The tanned finely chiselled face gave little away. The finely honed body did. He nodded. Connors verbal reticence could appear surly to the unacquainted. He was deeply intelligent and not given to idle gossip. Focussed and professional. That was Connor John.

'Pack your bags were off in the morning. Pack for the sun, I'm told it's hot on the Amalfi Coast at this time of year.' The Italian restaurant had been appropriate.

Two hours after the Chianti had swilled down their spaghetti bolognaise a chauffeur arrived at their Half Moon Street hotel. Fraser Hume and Connor John were whisked away downtown and taken to Heathrow. The Lear Jet left within half an hour. They landed at Leonardo da Vinci Airport, Rome two hours later and were transferred by helicopter to Sir Nicholas's yacht, 'The Miranda', moored at Ostia a few miles from where they had landed. It headed south towards the Amalfi coast immediately they were on board.

A valet appeared on deck as they boarded and they were shown to their quarters. It took a further twenty minutes for Fraser and Connor to shower and change. They were summonsed soon after. Sir Nicholas didn't waste time.

The white hull of 'The Miranda' cut through the azure sea in the late afternoon heading south; the breeze fresh and warm. Neither man spoke. They were shown to a laid table on the aft deck and sat inspecting the opulence of their surroundings.

It was several minutes before the yellow-cravated, white-jacketed magnate appeared. He smiled as he approached the table and bid the men to remain seated. 'No formalities here my friends', he said, the polished accent traceably aristocratic.

'To business. Henry', he looked at the waiter, 'pour the aperitif and leave us.' Henry did as instructed. 'Mr. Hume and Mr. John, may I call you Fraser and Connor?' The question was rhetorical; then laden with meaning. 'Your reputations precede you gentlemen and I am quite confident that I can confide in you.'

There was no discernible communication between Fraser Hume and Connor John. There was no need. Both knew the other had just listened to what they knew to be a 'sounder' put out to gauge the response more than to elicit a reply.

Hansen continued disappointed that there had been no discernible response.

'Fraser, I have taken much care in formulating my bid for the Salomonovich organisation but I have a major difficulty and I feel that you can resolve my problem.' Fraser smiled acknowledgement. Connor was unmoved. Sir Nicholas didn't miss either's response.

'Ian Smith has indicated to you that I wish to retain you. If you agree to that I have a contract here on board. I will leave that for your consideration after our little tête-à-tête. The terms are generous but I imagine that you will be the judges of that. As such I wish you to consider the fact that you now work for me. I trust that your allegiances will then be to me?'

Again he had elicited no responses. They were good.

'Following on from that, and I know that I press ahead with demanding alacrity, there are certain recent events that have raised questions and I would like to have answers to them. I take it that you understand the precise nature of my inquiries?'

Fraser nodded. 'Joel Salomonovich and Reinhart Bühler perhaps?'

Sir Nicholas paused before cagily prompting further. 'Is there anyone else in on this little escapade?'

Fraser thought hard. The contract wouldn't be signed. What did Hansen want? Who was the other person or people he was interested in? He answered.

'There are others. If there's one individual that you want the low down on, and I have the information you want, you can have it for sure.'

'Professional. That's what they said about you. Professional. You offer me carte blanche without giving me anything. Cute. OK, I'll initiate proceedings. What do you know of Professor George Merrick?'

Fraser gave a comprehensive account of all the details of Merrick's life. That is, all the detail he knew that Hansen would already know. He threw in a little spanner in the works for good measure.

Fraser began: 'Professor George Merrick. I take it that you knew him.' He smiled at a theatrically offended Sir Nicholas. 'Of course you did. We know that you gave him access to your mainframe. An old student perhaps? You are a Cambridge man are you not Sir Nicholas?' Sir Nicholas was not amused that his security had been breached so easily and was not used to having his feathers ruffled so easily.

'I want a full report by the time we arrive at Amalfi but for now we'll cut to the chase. What was Merrick up to? What had Merrick to do with Joel Salomonovich? Oh, I know they grew up in the same neighbourhood. What I want to know is why Merrick took so much interest in him in later years. 'He wanted to know about a chap called Reinhart Bühler. I know who the bastard was but what the hell did Merrick want with a bloody aging Nazi?'

Connor's face remained unmoved. He was thinking fast. Fraser nodded a couple of times mentally applauding Sir Nicholas's dexterity in handling his considerable frustration. Connor reckoned that Hansen and Fraser were well matched.

Hansen reached into a box on the table and took out a Cuban and lit it. Fraser lifted his eyes to Connor John. There was an imperceptible response and both knew that the signatures on the contract would remain unsigned. Sir Nicholas knew it too, all parties reserving more than a measure of scepticism.

Fraser moved his queen to king's rook four. Hansen hovered above his bishop caressing the thought of taking it. It was too obvious. Surely. He walked to the hand rail looking towards the setting sun.

'We are both gentlemen', he said to Fraser, ignoring Connor John. 'Here is what I want. I will provide you with men and with the wherewithal. I won't broach the subject of a contract again. No pack drills. You will find me very generous my friend.'

Fraser caught Connor's eye again then nodded as he took Hansen's proffered hand. Hansen tuned to go. 'Please', he opened his arms wide, 'you are my guests. My home is your home.'

Sir Nicholas hesitated at the threshold. 'Just one other small matter. The whereabouts of Julia Salomonovich? Is she dead or alive?' If she is dead there have been no reports to indicate as much. If she is alive then where is she? Did you know that?....I'm so very sorry my friend, I will rephrase that. Of course you know that someone used her passport and flew into Birmingham airport with it.' Hansen did not seek confirmation. Fraser knew that he hadn't and that both had made that point well. 'We have searched the Birmingham area and found nothing. We did find a taxi driver at the airport who says that he was asked to follow a car to a guesthouse on her arrival day. No one by the name of Salomonovich signed in but the landlady's recollection of the young woman who did register offered a resemblance to Miss Salomonovich. The file on the table is all we have. Good night gentlemen.'

He left. Neither Fraser Hume nor Connor John spoke a further word of business that evening. Had they done so they would have been picked up by the micro mic integrated into the table decoration. As it was Sir Nicholas Hansen was unsurprised by the unproductive report he received the following morning. Apparently the two Americans had little appetite for discussing their immediate plans after Sir Nicholas had left.

If Fraser and Connor had spoken on the subject that evening one or the other might well have pointed out that the information in the file was incomplete and that it was not all that Hansen had. It was also hard to avoid the conclusion that the main purpose of meeting had not been to employ them to find Julia Salomonovich but to bring them on side.

Two gentlemen located in the borough of Hammersmith had been very thorough in their investigations. And, when it came to bugging, two could play the same game.

Chapter 98

FRASER MEETS SIR NICHOLAS IN LONDON

Seven days later Fraser arranged to meet Sir Nicholas Hansen in order to update him on developments. Tony Molinaro and Leroy Gomez had reported Hansen's men's progress and it had seemed inevitable that they would soon be up to speed. Fraser would hand Hansen what he would inevitably discover in the coming days plus an intriguing fraction more. As Leroy Gomez had observed; 'Always keep 'em wanting more.'

Fraser and Connor left the hotel on Half Moon Street and walked the two hundred yards or so to Piccadilly. They turned left and within a couple of minutes were entering the Ritz.

Hansen's men were waiting in the foyer and, after the inevitable frisking in the lift, escorted them to his suite. Sir Nicholas, sitting at a large desk, greeted them warmly and, as ever, proceeded immediately.

'So Fraser you have made progress?' He smiled realising his error. 'Old habits die hard. Of course you have.'

Fraser gave Connor a nod and he rose. He walked deliberately to the end of the desk. The move surprised Sir Nicholas and he noted his misjudgement. He believed that there was far more to Connor John. He wasn't Fraser Hume's yes man after all.

Connor began. 'Here's what we have. Merrick died suddenly in Munich. Heart attack or so we are told. No history of that though. Joel Salomonovich and Reinhardt Bühler find a spectacular spot to jump into a gorge together within days of Merrick's heart attack. The gorge thing? It happened. We were there. Meanwhile Salomonovich's daughter is missing presumed killed. By whom? Why? Before Merrick went to Munich he chartered a jet. He took a cancer patient by the name of Peter Fossard and his wife Sarah with him. According to the Bristol Infirmary they let him go home to die at the request of his wife. Why the hell did she change her mind and take him off on a jaunt across Europe? Who knows?

OK, so he arrives at some kind of sanatorium between Munich and Augsburg. In a couple of days the director of the place and his lover, a nurse, are blasted to kingdom come by some sophisticated electronic gadgetry. Coincidence again? Oh no, I think not.'

'Near the sanatorium there is a further mystery. A young woman drove a car into a granite mountainside. The injuries sustained left her brain dead by all accounts. Some old guy, resembling Merrick, brings her to the sanatorium. The police told us the registration number of the car being driven by the young woman. It was registered to Julia Salomonovich, Joel's granddaughter. She disappears in Germany, somewhere just north of Koblenz. The widow of the cancer patient, a Mrs. Sarah Fossard, goes AWOL too.

You want answers Sir Nicholas? Trust me! So do we!

Julia Salomonovich was killed. Fact or conjecture? Well how about this? She and Sarah Fossard flew back to Birmingham airport within days of leaving England. Where did they fly from? Munich? No, it was Innsbruck for god's sake.' Connor resumed his seat. 'You see Sir Nicholas we haven't been idle these past three months. We know that there is something that binds all this together and that all this mumbo jumbo is intended to blind us. There has to be something but, as yet...' Connor left it in the air and resumed his seat.

Fraser took over. 'We have been busy as you can see but all we have right now are questions. I thought that Fossard was a rare name. Do you know how many Fossards there are in England? We can place Julia Salomonovich and Sarah Fossard at Birmingham Airport in December. But remember we are informed that Julia Salomonovich is dead. Is this really Julia Salomonovich or a look alike? If it's a look alike, for what purpose?'

Sir Nicholas had sat listening in contented that his own men had discovered as much as Fraser's. It was the last part of Fraser's piece that was new to him. He fumed. 'You have worked for me for a week and now you tell me things that you have known for a month?! You do all this fantastic work and then tell me that you can't even find two women? Why?'

Fraser gave Hansen as steely an eye as he had ever received. 'Before I work for any man I make sure that he is dealing with me on the square. Now I know the score. I'm in. But we do things my way or no way.'

Ultimatums were what Sir Nicholas gave to others. This was as disturbing as it was unexpected.

He rose. 'Give me a few moments.' He left the room.

Fraser reckoned, rightly, that Sir Nicholas was checking out his team's progress. His feedback was confirming their investigations, providing short cuts and dotting the Is and crossing the Ts. Still Fraser had provided nothing more than Sir Nicholas would have within days. He returned to the room.

'The hospital, that this, er, what was his name, er, Peter Fossard was in..... it was Bristol General was it not? Surely a simple look in the Bristol telephone directory...'

Fraser cut him off. 'We got the last piece of information late last night Sir Nicholas. Since then you have had our attention.' He noted Hansen's contempt, disdain, and condescension, and lack of genuine data, then, with considerable alacrity, saw him absorb the impact, pull on his mentor, Machiavelli, and regain his composure.

Fraser resumed. 'Of course we have now found her. Sarah Fossard that is. It seems that her husband's body was cremated in Germany. She has a friend staying with her.' He looked at his notes. 'Yes, Michael Tyler. He's an old family friend. But there's no sign of Julia Salomonovich. We've had Joel's place watched but no show so far.'

'Yes, it's covered', Fraser said, answering Hansen's question before it was asked, 'I now have the Fossard's house monitored.'

'As I said her husband was cremated in Germany. It's crazy, I know, but she didn't stay there for the ceremony and the ashes were scattered on the lawns of the crematorium. Strange for her to have so little regard for a man she so clearly loved, don't you think?'

'But.' Sir Nicholas sensed that there would be a but. He poured the soda into his whiskey. 'Go on', he urged.

'That's it, except to say that the thing that fascinates me is the sheer thoughtlessness of Miss Julia Salomonovich. She has a grieving mother and aunt in Suffolk and by all accounts this family's loving sweet daughter hasn't rung them to let her know that she is alive as yet. Or has she? Or is she? See? Always second guessing!' He noted Hansen's animation and calibrated his intensity. 'And, she appears to be pretty active for one declared to be in a vegetative state after so recent an accident.'

Sir Nicholas sank deeper into the divan, the tips of the finger of his hands playing allegretto on its opposite number.

'No the girl's alive, I know it. She is the heir to Joel Salomonovich's fortune as you know. The deal must now resume with her.'

Sir Nicholas went for a short saunter around the suite to deliberate. When he returned to the table Fraser Hume and Connor John had gone.

The Ritz would not send Sir Nicholas Hansen a bill for the broken mirror and chair.

Fraser Hume and Connor John were beholden to no man.

Chapter 99

FELIX MEETS JULIA

Felix had returned to England his vigour replenished and his purpose focussed and directed. He parked at the far side of the road a hundred yards or so from the Fossard's residence. The Edwardian detached red brick house would be visible through the large oak dominating the frontage of their extensive property for a several weeks to come. The cold unrelenting winter still held sway though the calendar indicated that spring should have arrived.

Surveillance has thrilling, exciting and dangerous connotations. The reality is more prosaic. Felix Elder had spent the best part of three days with little to reward his patience. The lady at number 19 was getting suspicious he believed. During the previous day she had walked her dog past the car on three occasions. By eight-thirty on the third day she had already past a further twice. Her net curtains twitched hourly and Felix began to plan another strategy.

'People! Always bloody interfering people! For every well planned action there was at least one equal and opposite need for someone to bugger up the works.'

His progress so far? The chap that had accompanied Sarah Fossard appeared to have taken up residence in the Fossard's place. Clearly he had been delegated shopping responsibilities. Little else to report.

It appeared that Julia Salomonovich had either not returned to the family home or had decided to move on. This was not at all what he had anticipated. No! She would be close by. He considered the psychological basis for his hypothesis. His evaluation substantiated his deduction. He had no doubt that it would.

In Germany Felix had asked Sarah Fossard to consider the implications of accepting his amazing proposition. Now she would begin to understand the labyrinthine consequences of her seminal decision. He, however, was irritated by the fact that he had miscalculated the speed of deterioration of the foundations of her matrimonial relationship. Such a strong bond! Yet it had taken three months, perhaps a little less, for the couple to separate. The dynamics of their relationship had changed as patently and transparently as Peter Fossard had changed.

Relationships! The relative position of one person to another. One of the positions had now changed. By definition the former relationship had surely ceased to exist?

He sat in his brand new bright red BMW 3 series, a car suited to his newly generated personality but incongruous to his core, waiting for Julia to arrive. Surely the split couldn't have been so acrimonious after such a short time? Surely she would visit? He calculated that he was not likely to be in for the long haul but reclined the seat a tad.

He gave developments further thought. The two sciences neurology and psychology. The former ostensibly pertaining to the brain and the later to the mind. But where were the boundaries? Where were the divisions? When nervous we sweat and our hearts beat faster. Nervousness is a psychological phenomenon. Sweating and heart beat are physical manifestations. Why does one cause the other?

What of the memory? Where is the store? The brain? Then how does a memory enter the brain? Where and how does a chemical become a thought? And again, if chemicals can change our thoughts, what of our hormones? How do they form our opinions and create our thoughts? How fiercely are we driven by our hormones? The senses inform our thoughts. They are similarly perceived but how differently are they conceived and construed?

Perception! What of the role of perception on the psyche? With transmutation comes the destruction of self-perception. It would take time to erect the new building blocks.

During a normal lifetime self-perception mutates slowly does it not? The dashing Casanova changes incrementally into the venerable grandee of the golf club. Yet as the person remains constant, his self-perception does not. The beautiful woman who turned young men's heads accepts her role as a matriarch with relish and pride. The same brain makes decisions but the chemicals are diluted or changed and the mind offers a different, and given time, a more acceptable perspective.

And, more particularly, in the immediate aftermath of Peter Fossard's metamorphosis, how had his mind changed? Awash with a torrent of new chemicals surging through her body Julia Salomonovich would be unpredictable, capricious and volatile. Imagine the extent of the physical, chemical and biological mayhem.

He had given Julia time to find her equilibrium. Time for her to rationalise and experience her new relationship with her new world and time for her to gain a new self-perception. We are what we are because of our bodies as much as our minds. He of all people now knew the truth of that!

He had believed that the time he had allowed for Julia's stabilisation should have been sufficient. Irritatingly it had taken a little longer than he had anticipated but he now conceived that it had not been quantifiable.

He had anticipated his own mind's reaction to his new body and brain. It was clear that he could transfer his mind into the body of another but would there be a residue, a trace, or remnant of the former's mind in the convoluted recesses of his new brain?

When given a different perspective of the world the 'self' would unquestionably change beliefs and attitudes to life. So much was clear. It was the extent to which these phenomena affected the individual that would be the great unknown.

He considered his own position and then calculated Julia's in relation to it, accepting the variable probabilities.

Firstly he considered George Merrick and Felix Elder. He acknowledged that George had become taciturn as a result of Joel's clandestine trysts with Rachael. He considered that to be a valid position but now he was free of the inevitability of his self-inflicted isolation and the world offered new possibilities. The encumbrance and loathing of his physical being had reduced his cynicism commensurately. He had not been subsumed; rather he felt almost semi-detached from his former being.

Merrick had not been interested in women. A woman, yes. He hadn't hidden from his obsession. But before and after Rachael there had been nothing. He had not mixed with others. Certainly not the opposite sex. The pain of losing Rachael had been too great and he had recoiled from further contact with women. They had caused him great anguish and were not to be trusted. The whole damn lot of them had laughed at him and he had cursed their fickle minds. They were damned as a gender.

Now, as Felix, women were attracted to him he had begun to reciprocate willingly. Now the laughing had stopped. He knew that they were interested in him and felt the considerable power of that. When he smiled they returned it. Not with a giggle or a snigger but with the raising of an eyebrow, a demure half smile or coquettish swish of hair.

Now he looked in the mirror not to only to check that his collar was down or that his tie was fastened correctly but to admire his reflection; proud of his stature, physique and fine features. Clothes, which had previously been of little relevance to him, had now gained a new prominence. Presentation wasn't so shallow after all.

The body had changed the mind; the surging testosterone his personality. It was a natural consequence. His vanity had been his work. Now it took on other facets.

Secondly: Peter Fossard and Julia Salomonovich. What of them? What would she be experiencing now? Her transition would have been even more traumatic than his. The repercussions would have been too.

Julia would begin by rejecting her new being. Her own body would repulse her. This experience would be in complete contrast to his. She would

354

fight against her very existence. Fight her demons. Mourn her loss. She would be grateful too. She should have died a painful death. Now that the physical pain had ended the mental anguish would begin. But even so....

She would rebel. She would become a recluse, dress as androgynously as possible to assuage attention. There would be tension with others. Men for sure. Women too. And his wife? She would surely suffer as much as her husband. It would not take long for them to realise that there was little left of their physical relationship. True they had shared memories and family but to share their lives would be impossible. Even after thirty loving years it would surely prove insurmountable. There would be a crack and the fissures would widen slowly but surely.

As soon as she gained confidence in her new persona Julia would take a pride in her appearance; as surely as night follows day. She would be subject to her hormones. Her newly acquired self-perception would drive her down the one-way road that would lead her to her destiny.

Her diminutive figure would shape her character as surely as it would attract the attention of men. This would prove pivotal. If the bond with her former self remained strong the trauma could repel her and cause her to repress her feelings, resulting in her spiralling descent into withdrawal and likely paranoia.

If the bond was weak she would accept her new role in full and move on with it. If, as he considered was most likely, she considered her options rationally and then took command of her own destiny, her mind would accept the inevitability of attracting men but decline their advances leaving her mind unsullied, chaste, pure and unblemished and her sanity intact.

The truth was that these categories helped Felix to formulate his thoughts. He recognised the reality that Julia's mind could not be so readily classified. Only the strength of the stimuli she would be exposed to, the confidence that she had in her own ability to cope, coupled with any residual pragmatism and resolve, could determine her future.

Felix decided to get back to work as soon as he was able. There was much to do and he was excited at the new perspectives that offered so many more opportunities to develop his new science.

The damn curtains twitched once again. The interfering old hag was forcing his hand. He would have to change strategy.

As he reached for the ignition key there was movement. The chap from the hospital was leaving the Fossard's house. He passed Felix's car and continued walking. Felix allowed him the fifty yards or so the bend in the road then turned the car around and followed. He passed Mike Tyler and parking in a side road, began to follow on foot.

They had walked through the suburbs for a little more than ten minutes before Felix noted Mike Tyler feeling in his coat pockets. He pulled out a bunch of keys then entered a three-storey block of flats. Felix assumed that this was his own place. He also rationalised that if Mike Tyler was living at the Fossard's house it might well be the case that Julia Salomonovich was staying at his flat as a reciprocate and convenient arrangement. It made sense.

He collected his car, parked and settled in for another lengthy stay. A light came on in a second floor window as darkness fell and Mike Tyler appeared at the window. He drew the curtains and the lights went out.

Mike Tyler emerged from the block of flats holding several envelopes. That too made sense. He had picked up his mail. Felix decided to follow him on foot. It soon became apparent that he was returning to the Fossards home. Considering the interfering dog walker and curtain switcher and the likelihood that Julia was staying at Mike Tyler's flat, he decided to return to his car.

When he returned the light had been switched on again. Mike Tyler was at the Fossard's residence. Betting on Julia Salomonovich being in the flat was suspended.

It was on the following morning that an unshaven and uncomfortable Felix spotted Julia leaving the building. He watched her get into her car and took a note of its number. The silver Fiesta disappeared into the heavy traffic.

On the following afternoon Felix parked his car in an adjacent street to the flat. He walked around the corner towards her car and bent to tie his shoe lace next to it. He reached under the chassis and attached a magnetic tracker. Now he had her tagged. He walked on a little before returning to his car.

Julia appeared almost immediately. She pulled away slowly and Felix slipped into the traffic following her to the M32. She got off at the next junctions and made for the Broadmead Shopping Centre, parking amongst a thousand other cars. Thursday afternoons appeared to be busy to Felix but, in truth, he had rarely visited shopping malls in the past and had little to compare Thursdays with.

Julia wore a black cotton top and a dogtooth black and white skirt with the hemline just above the knee, dark tights and black high-heeled boots. All her clothing was clearly of high quality. She now spent much more on clothes than she had previously believed necessary. A pair of small gold rings swung from her ears and a black bag hung on her left shoulder. She clicked along the ceramic tiled floors pushing her curled hair from her face every few paces.

She had been amazed at the variety of clothing available to women; not having noticed that before. For Peter it had been a suit, jacket and trousers, jeans, shirts or jumpers. The colours were conservative and the fabrics generally consistent. Julia's choices were incredible. Dresses, skirts and tops in a myriad of types, colours, designs and fabrics; and the shoes! Peter had had two black pairs, a brown pair, a suede pair and a pair of trainers. Julia had 'inherited' the dozen or so pairs selected by Sarah from Julia Salomonovich's Oxford flat wardrobe. The collection had increased considerably over the past few weeks. Again the types and colours available increased the importance of careful selection. Yes; she could see why men were easily bored with shopping and women were so fascinated. It stood to reason. It just depended which gender was doing the reasoning.

Felix followed her as she made her way through Marks and Spencer's, briefly stopping to look at the clothes but it was clear this was not her central purpose. She sashayed through the busy lanes to a café on the perimeter of a huge auditorium given the underwhelming and unimaginative title of 'The Food Hall' and ordered an 'espresso and Danish'. She took her tray to a seat near the perimeter wall looking into the huge auditorium. She picked up her cup in both hands and set about observing her fellow man – and woman.

Felix entered the café. There was a table free next to Julia's and he made for it smiling at her as he sat, hoping that she hadn't spotted him earlier. Julia returned his smile coyly and turned to the hall once more conscious of the unnerving possibility of being observed. Julia was in learning mode. Felix guessed as much.

It took half a cup of coffee before he plucked up the courage to talk. She had turned to him when he had coughed and was about to turn away when he decided to engage her.

'Excuse me. I'm not much of a shopper. You look like you are.' Julia froze wondering what was coming next acutely conscious of her body once more.

The handsome tanned young man continued. 'I wonder if you could possibly help me. I need a cash dispenser. An ATM? Could you tell me where I might find one?'

Julia had become increasingly familiar with the layout of the mall over recent months but as the ATM was directly opposite them and not more than twenty-five yards distant, the directions she gave were simple. Felix laughed at his apparent stupidity. Julia turned back to the hall but Felix pressed her further.

'You must think me an absolute idiot. I must be going around with my eyes closed. I do apologise.'

Julia laughed. The guy seemed alright but it was time to go. She turned away feeling a little less uncomfortable then smiled at him, reached down for the bag at her feet and bid him goodbye.

He surprised himself. 'Goodbye. Next time I see you I'll ask you if you've seen my nose. I know that I put it somewhere.'

Julia laughed out loud. 'Next time perhaps I'll give you even simpler directions.'

He declined the opportunity to enquire, 'Next time?' which had been on the tip of his tongue. He left it at that. It was plenty for the time being.

She eased out of her chair and, leaving a small tip on the table, smiled politely at Felix once again before leaving. She felt his eyes on her back as she walked into the busy shopping lanes of the mall. Surprisingly it was not an entirely unpleasant sensation.

Felix waited for ten minutes before leaving. He didn't want to bump into Julia again. That would look bad. And he would wait at least a week before making further contact. That would be soon enough.

He considered Julia's development. How strong was the bond with her former self? Had she been repelled by his presence? Clearly not. Had she been uncomfortable? Maybe. Had she accepted her new role and moved on? To some extent. Would she consider her options rationally and take command of her own destiny if push came to shove? Insufficient data. Would her mind accept the inevitability of attracting men but decline their advances leaving her mind, unsullied, chaste, pure and unblemished with her sanity intact as formerly debated? Perhaps. Was there hope? He believed that there just might be. It would be a long week.

Chapter 100

LAURA'S DEATH

Vincent Haan wasn't the first or last occupant of The Manor House to die of a broken heart. It was true to say that Stanley Mainwaring's death certificate gave the cause of death as a heart attack. Dr. Henry Owen had written similar dispatch notices for both Mrs. Mainwaring and Vincent Haan. Now Laura Salomonovich suffered the same fate. Dying as result of a heart attack and dying of a broken heart seemed much the same thing to Rebecca. She had never been superstitious but had begun to believe that The Manor House was cursed. She would leave as soon as the coroner confirmed what she already knew to be true; that Julia was dead too.

Now she sat in the huge house empty but for the cleaner who called daily and the gardener who called in at the kitchen each morning for his 'elevenses.' Even Manners, the faithful retainer, had tendered his notice and retired to his native Cornwall. She had an offer for the place before she had been granted probate but held back hoping against hope that some miracle would return Julia to her. She had not felt so utterly lonely and desolate since Amsterdam so very long ago.

She and Laura had met the 'handsome young jogger', as Rebecca had described him, several times. On one occasion he had stared across the lake and had said, in a very serious tone, that the ladies must never sell the place without letting him make the first bid. They had accepted his petition and promised him that, though a sale was not foreseeable at that time, he would certainly be the first to know when it was.

A weary Rebecca contemplated her lot. 'How quickly life changes. I was a girl. Happy with my parents and my home. Suddenly I was a slave of the Third Reich; then a wife living in Canada. As a widow I lived in New York. Then as a sister and aunt I retired in comfort to England; a place I had never been before. Now I am alone again. I was the one who was lost, yet fate has determined that I shall spend my remaining years alone. Father,

Mama, Reuben, Benjamin, Joel, Simon, Julia and now Laura. Vincent Haan and Henry Owen too. I found my family and my friends and now they have left me. All are gone.'

Sir Nicholas Hansen had been most careful in his dealings with Rebecca and Ian Smith had advised her well but the complexities of any future proposed sale of Joel's assets was not of the least interest to her. She was an intelligent woman of that there was no doubt, but she had never had the simplest grounding in the field of business. Besides, the truth was that she didn't really care. She was now worth millions of pounds and every single one of them was of no importance to her. Her needs were few and her zest for life diminished and meaningless. One million, a hundred million, a thousand thousand million; it was all the same. The deal, when it came, would be met with disinterest.

Chapter 101

JULIA AND FELIX

It was the following week and Julia had gone to the supermarket. A voice came from behind her. 'Have you seen my nose miss?' She turned to face a smiling Felix. Stupidly and coyly she pointed to his nose, instantly regretting that she had. She spoke demurely. 'Are you following me?' She immediately wished that she hadn't.

Felix put his hand on his heart and replied melodramatically. 'I am a fool but I am ashamed to say that I am not.' He smiled. 'Unfortunately, Fair Rosamund, Sweet Helen, my Dearest Josephine I have come shopping for vegetables and a decent fillet steak but if you wish me to follow you around you only have to ask and I shall obey your command.' He bowed deeply. 'Your servant ma'am.'

Julia thought the man to be quite humorous, engaging and polite if a little eccentric. He had obvious intelligence and wit and, she believed, that he would be attractive to women. 'Damn it, he was handsome and she found him attractive. Damn it again, he was and she did.'

Felix set off down the aisle and disappeared from view leaving Julia in disarray. It was good that he had gone. What was she thinking? 'Good. That's over.' But then... she had enjoyed their little exchange and it hadn't been unpleasant. Now he had gone and...

Felix poked his head out from behind the shelves. 'I just realised my utter impoliteness. My name is Michael Mitchell and you are...'

Julia felt that she should have known. Men don't just walk away from beautiful women. Swift to discourage any expectations she responded curtly. 'Julia and I really must...'

Felix cut her short putting his hands to his lips. 'Julia. Perfect. Goodbye Julia. I will treasure the moment always.' He smiled and made his way to the cash tills. She watched him leave by the revolving doors pushing a trolley full of bags as he went.

Felix was pleased with his rapidly improving sense of humour. He valued its useful application and was exhilarated by its energy. There were facets to life, previously dismissed as trivialities that, though not vital or necessary, never the less were life enhancing. A strange phenomenon! Utterly inconsequential in the grand scheme of things but, never the less, interesting.

He knew that Julia had watched him leave the supermarket. How could she not? He also had a clearer insight into her emotional development. It had been written all over her beautiful face.

Chapter 102

FRASER'S TEAM MEET IN LONDON

Fraser recalled Leroy Gomez and Tony Molinaro from Hammersmith. They sat in the hotel on Half Moon Street listening attentively as Fraser Hume's progress report became evermore complex. He closed with; 'So, that's it gentlemen. Are there any further questions?'

Leroy Gomez had plenty but settled for; 'Yeh, who killed Kennedy? And, while you're at it where did they stash Elvis? Don't you ever get the easy ones Fraser?'

Tony Molinaro's question betrayed his southern Italian ancestry every bit as much as Leroy Gomez's Las Vegas background had betrayed his. 'Who do we hit first Fraser?'

Fraser called Connor John over. 'The floor is yours Con.'

Connor John took a deep breath and began. 'If you think Fraser's bit was complex get ready for this. No lesser man than Sir Nicholas Hansen is pulling the strings.' Tony Molinaro was about to erupt when Fraser caught his eye and shook his head. He subsided. Connor continued. 'No Tony, we have not sold out. Ian Smith is playing the biggest game of his life and we're at quarterback. We continue to work for Joel.'

'How the hell does that work Con?' It was Leroy Gomez who asked the question.

'Hansen believes that we are working for him but it is unlikely that he will trust us. He knows that he needs us and he wants us 'on side.' He wants us to find Julia Salomonovich, if she's still alive that is. He also believes that we could be useful when it comes to facilitating negotiations for the Salomonovich interests. If Julia is dead then we turn to Joel's sister Rebecca. Both trust us. We are on the inside. My father found Rebecca in New York many years ago and brought her to England. Both Julia and

Rebecca Salomonovich have reason to be grateful to Spencer Hume. Hansen believes that we could swing the deal if push comes to shove.'

Connor John gave them a brief moment for reflection. He knew Leroy and Tony well. There would be questions. It was Leroy. 'OK so who do we report to and how much are we telling.' Both looked to Connor.

'Very good Leroy. It didn't take long did it? This is what's goin' down.'

Fraser poured coffees all round as Connor resumed.

'Hansen has given us nine of his best men. We will begin with surveillance duties working in three teams of three of his men. They will be led by Leroy, Tony and me. Hansen's guys will report to us. Fraser has a team too. They are winging their way from The States as I speak. It's not difficult to guess that Hansen's men will report to their master before reporting to us. The three guys in the air won't. They'll be keeping an overall eye on the other teams and will be reporting to Fraser. Quis custodiat ipsos custodes?'

Leroy's response was inevitable. 'Like shit. What you talking about man?'

Fraser translated. 'Who guards the guards Leroy? That's what the man said.'

Leroy whistled. 'Tight. No one trusts no one, right Con? Who'd I get?'

Connor continued. 'Leroy you got Sword.'

Leroy was, as ever, quick to pass comment. 'Say what?'

'Listen up Leroy your team's code named 'Sword.' Your three guys will be checking out Sarah Fossard and the friend who lets Julia Salomonovich use his place. Mark Shatner is the man keeping an eye on your team.' Leroy was happy with Shatner and nodded his approval.

Tony, you're 'Juno' and will be tracking the enigmatic Miss Salomonovich. You got Vince Colletti.' Tony Molinaro had known Vincent Colletti since their days on the East Side of New York, first as unruly youths and later as rookie cops. He too nodded his approval.

'I'm off to the Salomonovich's place in Suffolk. Al Curtis is my man.'

'Let me guess Con, you're pure 'Gold', laughed Leroy.

'Pure genius Leroy. Pure genius.'

Fraser took over. 'We don't know if we are going to learn anything by staking out these guys but we sure as hell don't know where else to go. Let's see if they can bring something to us.'

Tony broke in. 'Question. Why do we not just confront Julia Salomonovich?'

Fraser explained. 'Firstly Hansen doesn't know exactly where she is as yet and, until I know what's going on, I'm not keen for the bastard to find out. Vince Colletti will double as her minder. Secondly, Connor and I reckon she's safe for the moment. If Miss Salomonovich wishes to play dead Hansen would be only too happy to keep things that way. We don't want to scare her away or send her running home.'

Leroy had a question too. 'I'm confused Fraser. Whose side did you say we're on?'

Fraser thought for a moment. 'That's a difficult one Leroy. Let's just say for the moment that we are on our side.' Leroy nodded accepting the answer. Looking around at the company it was a good side to be on.

Fraser and Connor began to fill in the fine details of their plan of action. It was almost four hours before Leroy and Tony had digested the dossier.

Connor was the first to leave the Hotel. He picked his tail as soon as he turned into Piccadilly from Half Moon Street. He loitered outside The Ritz, and then turned round abruptly walking back towards the Green Park Underground Station. He 'clocked' his man. He hadn't seen him before. He wouldn't see him again. By the time his tail had descended the underground steps Connor had evaporated into thin air. The tail stood bemused scratching his head. Connor had clearly done this spying thing before. Leroy and Tony were also tailed. They had been to the same finishing school.

Chapter 103

FELIX AND JULIA

Felix wasn't prepared to wait a further week before re-engaging Julia. He calculated that once a person's pattern of movement had been established staging further 'unexpected' meetings wouldn't prove too difficult. It was a question of probabilities. It would be easy to follow Julia but to get her to come to him was preferable. If she was to walk in on him then she could hardly suspect that it was he that had sought her company.

He discovered that Julia had joined a health club and joined immediately as Michael Mitchell. He found that she went to the club each Saturday morning and so contrived to be there before she arrived.

It was nine-thirty when Julia looked along the row of treadmills and spotted Felix. He was hot and sweaty and had clearly been running for some considerable time. She took a machine half a dozen stations apart from him and began to jog. Five minutes into her run Felix passed her by, said a quick 'hi', and left. Julia was disappointed that he had not stopped to talk but she reckoned that as she was exercising, Michael had merely been considerate. It was clear too though that he wasn't interested. 'Thank god for that', she thought, unconvincingly.

She was there the following day too but Michael was not. The skilled fisherman understood his prey. His extensive study of psychoanalysis, psychiatry and psychology had not been wasted. Little that the young George Merrick had studied had ever been wasted. As no lesser person that the former President of the Royal Ornithological Society, the redoubtable Sir William Wyatt had remarked, George Merrick was a remarkable person.

It was a further three days later, long days to Julia, that she followed Felix into the health club car park. The tracker had remained in place and intact. Felix was still getting a signal. He sat in the car park waiting for her car to appear then got out, taking his time to take his kit out of the boot. He walked slowly to the entrance aware that she was catching him.

'Hello Michael.' He turned and smiled with mock surprise. 'Ah Ah. Judith right.' Julia was a little hurt and Felix saw it cross her face. 'Julia', she said disappointedly. He opened the door to let her through. 'Ladies first.' She anticipated that he would follow her towards the locker rooms but he smiled and offered. 'See you later' and walked towards two young women who were seated in the café area in the foyer of the building. She turned to see him laughing with them. 'Of course, he would be...' She entered the locker room.

Felix asked the women if they had change for a five-pound note. They hadn't but the encounter had elicited the desired response from Julia and it had served its purpose.

He rushed to change, beating Julia to the treadmills. It was a busy morning and there were few available. Julia came down the aisle and stood next to Felix feeling very self-conscious. He couldn't resist it. 'Are you sure that you're not following me Julie?'

Julia blushed. 'Julia', she corrected him.

He didn't let go. 'I see that you blush with guilt. Tell you what; if you are a good girl I'll buy you a coffee after your workout. I can't say fairer than that if you won't leave me alone.'

Julia began to protest her innocence but he smiled and put his hand on her arm. His eyes opened wide as he laughed. 'Come on, I'm only joking.' Julia first protested her innocence again then insisted that she had known that he was teasing. She then made it quite clear that she would only have coffee with him if she was buying. The buying of the coffee seemed to neutralise things a little and made her feel a little more secure. 'God knows why', she thought. But it did.

She trained for a shorter period than she had previously and made to leave the gym. The sweating Felix, panting between breaths asked, 'Are you swimming first.' Julia had come a long way in accepting her fate. Putting on a swimming costume was to be several steps down the line yet. 'No, I'll wait.' She instantly regretted having made it clear that she would wait an indefinite amount of time for a stranger.

The clothes she had brought were carefully chosen. 'What the hell was up with her?' she thought. 'This won't and can't go anywhere.' But she waited in the cafe all the same. As with Dr. Jekyll the drug took a little more of Mr. Hyde's character away and replaced it with his own every passing day. Peter Fossard was losing his battle hands down.

Julia had been sitting in the café for almost twenty minutes before Felix strolled to the table. She had spent some time in making herself look good but it had seemed like an eternity before he had arrived. He clearly wasn't desperate to have a coffee with her at all. Julia was both relieved that he had eventually emerged and anxious too, hoping that conversation would not prove awkward between them. She stood and went to the counter to buy his coffee ignoring his protestations.

'So', she offered waiting for Felix to speak and take the terrible strain from her shoulders.

Felix knew her precise thoughts. He reached forward and brought her face towards him catching her off guard. 'Stay there a moment', he placed his finger just below her left eye and removed an imaginary dot. 'There that's better. I couldn't possibly talk to you with your make-up all over the place. It'd put me off my coffee.' They both laughed; Felix with the contentment that sitting with the beautiful Rachael Haan gave him and Julia from relief, her heart thumping.

The touch on her face had been gentle and a tingle ran through her vitals. She had felt this before. Just once. But that was in a different world and long ago. Felix drank his coffee and stood to leave. 'Well Julia we'll have to do this again sometime but I've got to make tracks. See you soon I hope?'

Julia couldn't believe it. She had waited twenty five minutes and gone to the trouble of changing her clothes three times before leaving Mike's flat before so that she would look her best. He had sat with her for five minutes at best.

It would be some time before she reconciled herself to her obvious attraction. 'Michael I...' He turned. 'Nothing, just...well I'll see you soon.' Again she blushed. Felix had her where he wanted her, and he knew it.

He produced his mobile. 'You can see me tonight if you wish;' he played with the phone, 'Looks like I'm going to be free after all. Eight o'clock alright?' She nodded. It was all so fast. 'Put your address here', he said offering her an open diary and a pen. She began to scribble and he pressed near to her as he looked over her shoulder. He smiled at her as he reclaimed the diary and put it into the pocket of his jeans. 'See you tonight', he said rolling his eyes to the sky. 'Ciao.' He strolled out at the same sedate pace he had entered.

Julia wondered what the hell she had just done. The guy had been hard to get so she had gone after him. She had chased him until he had caught her. What was that? Now she had him – did she want him? It was eleven o'clock when she pulled out of the health club car park. Nine hours. Nine hours and... my god how had it happened?

She stood at the wardrobe wondering what to wear. Again she marvelled at the different approach to clothes that the genders had. The extent of her choices had multiplied exponentially over recent week. Before then it had been barely been worthwhile contemplating. Now it was of paramount importance. It hadn't taken long for that trait to develop. Clothes were exciting now. The choice was vast. Tops, skirts and dresses with hemlines from knickers to ankles and necklines from roll neck to daring, trousers and jeans; all in a myriad of colours and fabrics. A million pairs of shoes. All unique.

She hadn't got his phone number. She didn't have his address. There was no way that she could let him know that she couldn't possibly go out for the evening with him. Still she went through the wardrobe. By seven she had showered. She wouldn't go. That was for sure. A seven thirty she was dressed in a navy dress, white sling backs and had checked out her handbag for the fifth time. There was no way that she was stepping out of the house. At eight o'clock she was checking herself in the mirror rehearsing her 'It was all a big mistake speech.' He arrived late and she had panicked that he wouldn't come. 'Where had all her insecurity come from?' The doorbell rang. She would get it over with and tell him to go to hell and that would be an end to it.

She opened the door and was greeted by a handsome man in an expensive suit holding a beautiful bouquet of orchids. He smiled. 'For Julia. A beautiful Lady.' He bowed. At eight-fifteen the couple drove away heading towards the city centre. He had even remembered her name.

Julia was relieved that Michael Mitchell was so easy to talk to. He talked to her face, unlike many of the men that she had encountered so far. He seemed genuinely interested in her without being intrusive and was almost old fashioned in the way that he spoke and held the car and restaurant doors open for her. She had expected the brashness of youth but had found a fellow traveller.

When they parted he took her key and placed it in the lock, he pushed the door open and she looked at him nervously, ready to repel any advance. He took her right hand in his, put her key in it and thanked her for a 'lovely evening.' He paused for a few moments, and then turned away wishing her a 'gute nacht und schöne träume.'

He didn't call her or go to the health club for three days. Julia was frantic. 'What had she done? Why hadn't he called?' She had no means of contacting him.

As the days dragged by she began to believe that she had indicated her reticence to engage with him by her demeanour or some gesture during their evening together. Perhaps it was a biological thing? She hadn't acquired some pheromone perhaps? Yet he had seemed happy and relaxed in her company. Besides they could just be friends. That was all that she wanted. Or was it? God knows. She didn't.

Felix knew Julia's routes well. He offered to take one of the health club receptionists for a drink as she finished work. He saw Julia across the road before laughing out loud and placing his arm around the surprised young woman. She laughed too as they entered the pub. Julia saw what Felix had wanted her to see. He was sure that she would be at the health club on the following morning. She was.

He smiled as she made her way to the treadmill, reassured that his manipulative skills were intact. He made a short detour over to her.

'Hi.'

Julia was trapped. She wanted so much to be with him, but was afraid to be.

She was hurt by his neglect but safe with the distance between them; distraught by his indifference but smitten with his engagement. There was no answer to her unasked question. Wisdom comes from experience. And she had no previous experiences to learn from. She stood alone, abandoned to the fates.

Professor George Merrick had learned a great deal since subsuming Felix Elder. Now he was learning to conduct and extemporise as Michael Mitchell.

He asked Julia out and took her to the cinema. As he parked the car outside her flat she felt him seductive and dangerous. He leaned forward and felt his soft lips against hers. She tried hard to resist but her every movement betrayed her emotions. Slowly she surrendered to his will while anticipating the appalling danger of her predicament. He spoke with a touching softness, noted her trembling voice and gentle responses as he massaged her graceful neck and fragile mind.

Sufficient evidence emerged to substantiate Felix's theory and that alone would have sustained him in a previous existence. His eyes flickered with amusement as he smiled at his prize reassuringly. It was not enough!

He rang her on the following day confident that his quarry was trapped. He called for her in the afternoon. She opened the door and fell into his arm. He caught her eye and anticipated her move towards her coat. He held it like a matador's cape, charming and solicitous she turned her back to him and slipped it on smiling a grateful 'thanks' then, swinging her bag over her shoulder, she moved to the door. He held it for her and she past under his arm and into the warm evening air. 'Death in the afternoon.' The matador had won.

With a frisson of pride she recognised the sensual potency of her swaying long hair as she walked to his car. With a sense of foreboding she understood the seductive quality of her swaying hips and discovered that she was unable to modify her movements. His dark penetrating eyes undermined her confidence yet drew her ever nearer to him. Her nascent passion and new found sensibilities challenged her nurture and gnawed at her mentality. The conflict found a sharper focus as she began to surrender to nature incrementally.

They walked to Felix's Mercedes and he opened the door for her. She sat swinging her nyloned legs elegantly under the well. She knew that he would not have missed that. They were silent. Both content for them to be so. Felix analysing and interpreting Julia's actions and reactions; Julia absorbed by the startling reality of her situation.

Then a flashing vision surfaced from the depths of her mind. A memory. But whose memory? How could she remember such a memory? Gunter Ulbricht. Who was Gunter Ulbricht? A friend. Such a dear friend. Oh but she had felt like this before. She had been cautious in Gunter's company both in England and in Germany. Why?

Koblenz! But she had never been to Koblenz. How could it be so? Yet she remembered the Alt Stadt clearly. Montabaur. Her good friend Gunter lived in Montabaur. The Schloss Montabaur, high on the mountain overlooking the beautiful River Lahn. The Zigeurner Schnitzels that Gunter ate were huge. She had often wondered how he had maintained his athletic build and teased him that he would be a fat old man one day. And the Mosel. The beautiful trip down the Mosel from Koblenz to Cochem. The picturesque market place at Bernkastel-Kues and the ever present red ivy leaved geraniums cladding the fronts of the half-timbered buildings. Traben-Trarbach and fruity white Riesling. The Reichsburg Castle towering over Cochem's pastel-coloured buildings and Baroque towers. Above all the firework displays reflected in the river and the illusion of castles in the air.

Then it had gone. Julia was clearly shaking and Felix had not anticipated such a strong reaction. Something had happened. Something new. He needed to know. 'Hey, you look a little shaky.' It was almost a question.

'I just, kind of, had a déjà vu moment. But it can't have been. I'm sorry. I'm not making sense. It's not making sense. No I...... forget it ... please.'

It was little to go on, but it was enough. Felix had experienced traces of George Merrick's memories but he had not suffered such a serious flashback. On the other hand his old work ethic had diminished; his dedication to physical training astonished him; his sense of humour fascinated him; and, his libido confounded him. Yes of course. Felix Elder lived within him. How else could his new reality be accounted for?

The shell was the obvious manifestation; but the mind ...My god the convolutions of Felix Elder's brain had retained his memories and had begun to change George Merrick's personality just as Julia Salomonovich was influencing Peter Fossard. What would be the extent of this invasion? Was it aggressive? Could it be contained? Could it be encouraged? He believed that he had the answer.

Felix had known that he had had to act before his supreme capacities deserted him. He observed Julia acutely and planned to return to his laboratory on the following morning. He must move quickly.

In a previous life Julia would have taken time to recover from the shock that she had just had but the recent weeks had strengthened her resilience and she recovered sufficiently to continue with the evening.

Was the evening a huge mistake? Would there be recriminations and regrets? Would she be denounced as a fake? The unpalatable truth was that Felix was not at all repugnant to her. Indeed, she was attracted to him. No. She steeled herself once more. This was just a meal and a drink. No more! 'Calm yourself.' But her self-doubt was not so easily assuaged. The full impact of her situation struck her emotional fragility and a knot tightened in her stomach. She sought refuge in a reciprocal smile as he drove on into the night. Her eyes stared ahead unseeing; engulfed by a wave of desperation.

Noting her huge sigh Felix smiled to himself. He looked through the transparent window into her intimate soul. He alone had an insight into her psyche and was ready to manipulate her feelings further.

'My word! That was a big sigh. I do hope that you are not tiring of my company already.'

She smiled weakly. 'No not at all.' The modulation and inflections in her voice betraying her emotions to the informed recipient. He did not wish to dismantle her defences fully. At least not yet. No, allaying her anxieties would suffice for the present.

He knew that she would not trust her instincts. Did they belong to her? That would compound the belief in her inadequacy. It was too soon. He should have known that. It would take more time to weave her newfound being into the fabric of her new life. Too soon. It would take time for the emotional struggle in her mind to become reconciled to her body. It was premature for her to have spread her wings so soon. She had surrendered to her emotions. He had beguiled and deceived her and she had permitted him to do so without commensurate comprehension. He had understood his quarry well.

He pulled in to the kerb side, stopped the engine and leaned towards her raising his hand to her cheek. Her identity hung by a thread as in breathless anticipation she surrendered herself to the inevitable. 'I have wanted to do this since I first laid eyes on you' he whispered, in a voice of touching softness as he put his arm around her and drew her to him.

She ached with longing yet still her body refused to confirm or refute his approach such was her confusion and turmoil. She felt alone, bewildered and possessed; excited but used.

Now their noses touched and still he delayed. She lowered her eyes to his lips and swallowed. Still she waited. She suspended rational thought as her soft lips met his and a cocktail of emotions engulfed her.

The kiss was long and passionate and perversely cathartic. It stemmed the torrent that had threatened to sweep her away. Her intense vulnerability eased as they parted but still she could not do other than avert her eyes.

He saw that and lifted her chin tenderly. She raised her watery eyes; a nervous smile playing on her lips. It seemed that little remained of the fabric of her former self. Her lips quivered as she tried to speak. He placed a finger on them and continued his seductive manipulation.

'Badoura.'

She raised her eyes to his, questioningly, recognising how attracted to him she really was.

'Badoura? She was the most beautiful woman to have ever lived. You must read Tales of the Arabian Nights my dear.' (Again that anachronistic and unexpected idiom destabilised her).

She blushed unable to respond to his compliment. Strangely now that she had surrendered to the inevitable she felt her situation less stressful; as if the confession had really cathartically diminished her guilt too.

She had committed herself and that had temporarily relieved the burden. Her defences may have been dismantled but she felt safe in this man's arms and she had not felt such security for a very long time. She banked her emotional insecurities on his wide shouldered and lodged her inner chaos on his charity. She nestled into her lover holding him tightly to her. Professor George Merrick had made her a female. Michael Mitchell had made her a woman.

They remained in that embrace for some time Julia's breasts rising and falling as the subtle yet profound formative influences internalised her feelings. The tacit admission of her frail reality had led to a nervous acquiescence. The Rubicon had been crossed.

And Felix knew it!

He looked down at the woman in his arms. At last he had his one true love; for there in the guise of Julia Salomonovich was Rachael Haan. His Rachael Haan. He whispered to himself. 'Soon my dear. Very soon we shall have everything and I shall have all the time in the world.'

She felt his powerful arms as he raised her to him once again. Felix Elder engaged George Merrick's ferocious intellect and recalibrated his manoeuvres. He assessed Julia's development once again. She had resisted well but the inevitable was manifest. His calculations, as always, had proved accurate. The woman had been vanquished; her fate decided.

He recognised that he too had adapted. He had acquired a sense of fun, a willingness to undertake physical exercise and the result had been to offer less to the world of science. Everyone had to make sacrifices. Was that not so? Now it was Julia's turn to adapt. This embrace must underline the finality of his conquest.

Julia wanted the moment to last forever as Felix kissed her softly one more time. They smiled at each other as he started the engine. He grinned mischievously. 'Put me down woman. Leave me alone.' he demanded, behind a mask of feigned innocence. She smiled at him coquettishly as he swept the car back onto the lane.

They sat in silence each taking the occasional sideways glance to confirm the reality.

Julia studied his face. She was shocked. She had kissed him and wanted to do so again. Yet there was no revulsion. No chaotic aftermath; no recriminations or regrets; no uncomfortable truths to be revealed, indeed, nothing had militated against her nature. True there was an accompanying anxiety, which so often prefaces love, but rebellion there was not.

Felix saw the vivacious Julia's proud and delicate profile and smiled at her reassuringly as she caught his glance. He had dismantled her defences with precision but there was more.

Now he viewed Julia with a new perspective. He had stopped the car to 'test the water' and found her 'conducive.' That was the word – conducive. But then, more. Yes, much more. He had kissed this woman and had felt something new rising within him.

The car stopped at The Old Oak, an ancient coach inn known as the Half Way House to locals. Felix had been informed by a quickly grown circle of acquaintances that it provided excellent cuisine. He got out and walked around the car opening the door for Julia. She had waited nervously wondering if that was what he would do. She had been right to take a little time to gather her bag from the well. She swung her legs out demurely and took a couple of paces from the car. She trembled with excitement and anticipation hoping that he would remain warm to her. He smiled at her as he pocketed the keys and took her hand in his, as she had hoped he would. He opened the door for her and they entered the pub. They chose a seat; he took her order for a drink and went to the bar.

Julia sat to the side of the huge red brick hearth and contemplated her immediate future. She was terrified. However the evening went she had already determined that Michael Mitchell would not be coming into Mike Tyler's flat that evening. Rational thoughts were best considered now! He had been nothing, if not a gentleman so far but she knew what men were like and would not trust him. My god - trust him? Could she trust herself? Was she really having these thoughts? No. No. Not even ...

Felix returned with two glasses of an overpriced Flourie. They sat closely both holding on to their drinks. To strangers their gestures and animations marked them out as lovers. They spoke and smiled a great deal. He held her hand affectionately and twice brushed her long hair from her face with recognisable affection.

Julia dreaded being asked about her past and was therefore reluctant to ask about Michael as this would be most likely precipitate reciprocal enquiries. That was strange, she thought, he hadn't enquired at all. Why not?

George Merrick's intellect had not been blunted by his ardour. Felix remained resolute and observed all. He knew that she would expect him to ask her about her family, her history and her experiences. The problem had been analysed.

He began: 'I expect that a pretty girl like you ...' (Pretty girl – again that strange use of language for one so young) '... is always asked about herself. I won't intrude ...' (again) ... 'upon your past. Tell me what you are doing now and what your plans are for the near future. Me? I'm taking a year out. It's time that I did. It seems like I have been working for years without a break. Perhaps I will travel. I don't know. What about you?'

Neatly done. Julia did not have to reveal her past or make up a false history. Neither had she to make up mythical parents or siblings. At least not yet. Perhaps a time would come when she could reveal ... but then that would be much later and may not be necessary at all. Her spirits had plunged as he suggested that he may travel abroad during the forthcoming year. This seemed to preclude her from his plans.

Again there was the strange push and pull that Michael exerted on her psyche. She wanted to be close. When he approached her she was afraid. She wanted to be with him but he was going away. She wanted to stay the night in his arms but knew that he must go. She wished to be with him but knew he could not share her thoughts. She tried to reconcile the irreconcilable as the hours drifted by. What had she seen in his eyes? A flickering amusement? It had disappeared as quickly as it had appeared but it had left her uncomfortable. Was he playing with her? She prayed not.

They left the pub and were outside Mike's flat soon after. Felix opened the door and brought her to him. He pecked her on the cheek and was gone before she could catch her breath. Oh how she had wanted him to stay. And oh, how relieved she had been that he had left.

Three hours later she was still turning restlessly in her bed. She examined her emotional insecurities. Was there a twinge of regret in her heart? Had she surrendered herself too easily? Angst ridden she sought solace in her innocence, vulnerability and helplessness. Defenceless she recognised the deadening isolation of being single for the first time in many years and the aching and longing of unrequited love. Oh, Michael had not dumped her but then again, he was going away. Filled with dread that he would leave her or, for that matter, that he would stay, she had little to hang on to. She could see that exorcising her demons to gain a semblance of normality would not resolve her inner conflict. She didn't feel the need to revolt against her nature and recognised the heart piercing truth of that. Perhaps she should surrender to the fates. Abdicate responsibility? Confused and tormented she descended into turmoil. Her mind parted from reality and she dropped into a deep sleep crying with resignation.

She awoke the following morning feeling the same reflective melancholy that descends on a drunk the day after the night before. There had been no affirmation of a chosen route. Nothing had confirmed or refuted her deliberations. Only the intense vulnerability had remained compounding the belief that she had neither control, nor the will to determine her future. No, there would be no humiliating caprices or condescension masquerading as direction. She would face the future and go with her instincts; if indeed those instincts were hers to go with.

She lacked conviction but was resolved. An essential evolution had taken place; a second metamorphosis.

She stood by the window watching the rain. She recalled a day just a few months earlier in another dimension. What was this? It had been December. She had lain in a hospital bed dying. Like then the drizzle had run down the windowpanes. Morning had dawned and she had wondered what the day would bring. At least now there would be a day.

She dressed and left the flat for the gym hoping to meet Michael. She had accused him of following her. Now she felt that the boot was on the other foot. Never the less, this day was not a day for dying. It was a day for living to the full.

But what of Michael? She had noticed that she smiled attractively at the mention of his name. His smile had reassured her and nourished her confidence. Her body quivered at the thought of not seeing him again and her eyes watered.

She could not guarantee that she would not betray her emotions if, or when next, they met. She felt a quiet desperation at recognising that uncomfortable truth. The impenetrable wall had been breached and, stunned and incredulous she understood the truth.

Julia Salomonovich imbued her spirit and would not be denied. Peter Fossard had accepted defeat and died.

Chapter 104

FELIX AND JULIA, SARAH AND MIKE

Julia didn't hear from Felix for a further six days. He considered that to be a suitable period for her to reflect on her predicament. Had he known it six hours would quite likely have sufficed.

He left Bristol for his father's house in Suffolk; a house he had described to Julia as his 'house in the country.' His planning had been meticulous but there was always time for adjustments and refinements. He revisited his intricate master plan a thousand times. Nothing must go wrong.

The last phase of his opus was nigh. All was well, despite the bungling asinine personnel he had employed. Within a few months he would begin further research and stretch the boundaries of science still further. He would live in the Manor House, smile at his sweetheart and toast the demise of Joel Salomonovich with the fine wines of his cellar. The dish for the evening would be, appropriately, best served cold.

George Merrick had always had solutions. In the comfort of an old stone cottage he presented them to Felix Elder.

Julia was ready. He was sure of it. All the signs were there. She was a classic case. She had mirrored his predictions. The patterns had been uniform the correlations impossibly high.

It was time. He changed into his running kit and breezed through a lap of Lord Allenby's ancient estate stopping only to take a look at the Manor House across the lake.

'Soon', was all that he said.

Felix returned to Bristol to terminate Michael Mitchell's existence. He had served his purpose. He had used the sobriquet well always carrying cash taken from ATS machines in Cambridge under the name of Felix Elder. He used cash when in Bristol at all times. The rent for his flat had been paid for in the name of Michael Mitchell. He had not joined the health club but had paid for each session individually thus avoiding having his photograph transferred to a plastic membership card.

When Michael Mitchell left Bristol there would be nothing to link him with Felix Elder of Cambridge. Perhaps someone would remember the man. Perhaps someone would remember seeing him with Julia Salomonovich but who could possibly connect the two and find them in a sleepy Suffolk village. The balance of probability weighed heavily in his favour.

What of Julia's disappearance? Wouldn't Sarah Fossard, her daughters and Mike Tyler inform the police of her disappearance? If the national press or television were to publish her name or show her photograph the Manor House would soon be swamped by them.

Eliminating them was out of the question. Where would it end? The husbands of the daughters would be next. There would be others no doubt too. No, the only way ahead was to take Julia to the Fossard's home, confront Sarah Fossard and make a clean break. Julia must make it clear that she needed time and that Peter Fossard had died. They would hold out hope for the future but the break would be clean and never mended. Felix would see to that.

Julia's heart beat quickened as she drove into the health club car park. Felix's red BMW gleamed in the summer sun. She saw him taking a drink from the fountain by the weights room.

Having jettisoned considerable baggage and having found a new resolve she felt a little more confident than she had been previously. Felix saw it in her eyes and gait as she walked towards him.

'Hi.' They greeted each other in unison; that unfortunate occurrence leaving the floor for the next contributor. The awkwardness of incipient love strained the atmosphere and her newfound confidence withered.

Floundering in self-doubt and paralysed by fear Julia played a card that she had not known she had. She flashed her eyes at Felix demurely then lowered them sensuously tantamount to leaving the cue to speak with him. He synthesised the impact of her thoughts on her demeanour and behaviour. Not wishing to undermine her confidence further he responded immediately.

'I've been meaning to contact you. There's something I wanted to ask you. I do hope that you don't think me too forward.'

Had Julia not been lost in Felix's eyes she might have noted the quaint old terminology that had attracted her attention on previous occasions. She had noted that other boys appeared brash and shallow, their language stilted and lazy by comparison. Perhaps it was her age?

'Please, what is it Michael?' Julia had not begun her warm-up exercises as yet but her heart was racing.'

'Could I see you for a little while after you have finished here?'

Was that it? She was disappointed. 'Of course. I won't be long. Can you wait for me?'

He could.

Julia took the least amount of time she considered to be respectable before leaving for the locker room. She also limited her activities to walking and lifting very few light weights in order not to appear ruddy faced.

She spent a careful but short time grooming her hair before making for the cafe. She had once waited for him there, now he had waited for her and this boosted her confidence further.

Julia had expected them to stay in the cafe but Michael had been quite anxious for them to leave.

'Come on, we're going. The club's not the best place for coffee.' As they crossed the car park he asked her to follow him. They drove in convoy for a couple of miles before stopping at a roadside country pub. They met in the car park and he put his arm around her slender waist.

He took her through the building and out to the rear garden. Several tables sprouting huge parasols were laid out on the lawn. Julia sat in the shade and went to her handbag.

Felix saw the familiarity of that movement and smiled. 'My shout', offering her a drink. He had heard the term used by others on the previous evening and was pleased that he had employed it appropriately.

Julia ordered a coffee and waited anxiously for him to return wandering what he was it was that was so important for him to say.

'My shout', Ciao.' She wondered. What a strange combination of words Michael used. Sometime he sounded like the young man he was but occasionally he lapsed into ... well, he sounded anciently proper.

He appeared at the doorway with drinks in hand and smiled at her as he walked to the table. She returned his smile. He was grateful that they were alone.

'Julia I've been thinking. I'm leaving Bristol. I've sold my flat and I leave on Saturday.'

Julia was heartbroken. She couldn't believe it. 'But it's Thursday Michael. that's just two days away. It seems all so very sudden? Is there a problem?' He saw her watery eyes once again and knew that he had won.

'The thing is. The thing is Julia.' Felix was finding the going far tougher than he had thought it would be. Astrid had been dispensable; a plaything. He had been callous and calculating. It had been easy to dismiss her. Julia was his prize and the stakes were high. His throat was dry and he took the top off his highly irregular glass of lager.

Julia sensed that he was going to ask her to go with him. Why else would she be there. She begged the fates that he would ask and prayed that she would have an answer.

Felix caught the sentiment of his first night in Rosenheim. There was a wraithlike parallel; the unexpected, the girl, the unasked question and the obvious mutual attraction.

'Julia. It was only when I decided that I was leaving Bristol that I realised how much I would miss you.' She took his hand in hers. 'I don't want to sound arrogant but most folk (again that anachronistic language) see me as a hugely confident chap. (Again). I am, except, that is, when I'm around you.'

Felix translated the text in his mind. 'You excite me and are special to me.'

'I have never let anyone get this close to me before; at least not for a very long time.'

Felix's translation: 'I was hurt very badly in the past and you are my salvation. It took a very long time for the very special person that is you to come along.'

Julia felt his pain and stroked his troubled brow.

'Julia I want you to know that I care for you and that I will always be there for you.'

Felix's translation: 'At last you are not alone and you will be safe and have the security that you crave.'

He sat by her side and took her in his arms. 'Julia I love you. I love everything about you. You are so very very beautiful but above all I love to be with you and miss you when I leave you. That is why I have been so reticent in the past. I couldn't trust myself to be with you.'

Further translation was unnecessary. Felix had disarmed her with what had passed for candour.

They held on to each other as they kissed. It was several minutes before Felix held her at arm's length and asked her: 'Please will you come with me on Saturday.'

There would be people to see, things to arrange and.... she checked her racing mind. 'Yes Michael. I will.'

Felix took her in his arms once again. Four other couples and half a dozen men came out of the pub, nodded 'good day' and took seats around adjacent tables. Felix smiled again reflecting on their timing.

George Merrick had never had luck. Felix Elder was as jammy a bastard as ever graced the face of the earth. Perhaps not! Perhaps it had been that George Merrick had always had a negative approach to life outside his research. Felix was always so bloody positive. Perhaps he was making his own luck by being so positive. He consigned that dismal philosophy to the dustbin. Felix was just such a fucking lucky sod.

The mood was sombre in the Fossard household. Julia had a difficult story to relate to Sarah and Mike and recognised that there would be recriminations a plenty.

She had dressed conservatively in a navy suit and had decided to begin with a speech about her new self and the reality of what that meant. It was she that would have to live her life. Yes that was it. She would point out that the house was Sarah's. She was leaving and thought that that would be the best thing for Sarah and quite possibly for herself. Of course they would meet – occasionally. She would not mention Michael. That would be too much. If Sarah suspected as much she would surely not mention it. She would take the few remaining belongings from the house and return to Mike's flat.

The planned oration was wasted. Julia let herself into the house and, by habit, called out in the same fashion that Peter Fossard had for years.' It's only me Sarah.'

It was a little time before a shaken, dishevelled and guilty looking Sarah descended the stairs. Mike Tyler followed her sheepishly.

There was no anger; just a stunned numbness. Julia had considered her own relationships and found them to be acceptable. But this? Was this any different?

The three sat in the in silence. How could there be recriminations? Who would have the recriminations? How could any of the three of them justify their actions or accuse another? Did they need to?

Still there was silence. Not reflection. Just silence.

It was more than a minute after sitting down that Sarah began. She sniffled into a tissue. 'I'm so very sorry ...'

Julia waived her words away. 'No Sarah it's me that should be sorry.' He took her hands in his. 'Neither of us wanted this. If things had remained the same we would have remained the same. I know that you have always been faithful, as I have. You have still been faithful.' Sarah began to sob again. 'Sarah I told you;' He turned to a bewildered Mike, 'and I told you too Mike, that Peter Fossard is dead. I hadn't expected you two to get together I must admit', (both reddened with acute embarrassment, their heads bowed), 'but on reflection it is perhaps ... well ... at least you have each other and I know that you are in safe hands Sarah. I truly wish you both well.'

Julia swallowed, the lump in her throat choking her as she emitted each word. She had meant what she had said but the situation had been surreal and the dreadful final acceptance of the dénouement of her marriage was unbearable. She felt tears rolling down her cheeks and wiped them away.

Mike riddled with guilt, had been unable to look either of them. What had he done! It would be futile to attempt to mitigate his actions. He continued to stare at the carpet, guilt ridden.

Sarah, tears streaming down her cheeks too, had sought forgiveness in Julia's eyes. Yet Peter Fossard, the wounded husband, was dead and he would have borne her no malice had he viewed the very scene from heaven itself.

Julia had no alternative. One could not travel to the past. The time continuum moved in one direction only. What was it that L P Hartley had said? The past was a different place. They did things differently there. Precisely! Just so! She lived in a different world now. How could she carry the burdens of the old world on her shoulders? What right did she have to demand from those she would soon distance herself from?

And now? Now she was free. The equation had been squared. There could be no recriminations. There was no turning back.

She began: 'I came to say that I am going away for a time Sarah. Please don't believe that I am going away because of today. I have met someone.'

Both looked at Julia with some incredulity. He caught the depth of astonishment of the already bewildered pair. 'Sarah, Mike, as I have so often repeated, Peter is dead and I too have a new life to live.'

Julia slumped into the armchair. Perhaps the effort had been too great for her, perhaps the cocktails of emotion had been too heady. She feinted.

She remembered the Manor House and the lake. Her mother. Her mother and Aunt Rebecca. They really must be missing her. She must get in contact soon. She really must ... then ... Sarah was fussing over her; Mike with a glass of water in his hand was urging her to take a sip. She recovered slowly confused by her strange memories. The air was close and the room warm. She took a further sip and then breathed deeply frantically trying to interpret her thoughts and contain her emotions.

Sarah and Mike had a different perspective and both felt the burden of guilt. They had comforted each other on many evenings and that had gradually led to a more tactile relationship. They had sought comfort in each other's arms and solace from their friendship. The pair had become dependent on one another and soon they had become lovers; the desperate need for companionship and the cataclysmic effect of Peter's fate driving them together.

It was half an hour later and after several dozen reassurances from both parties that all was well that Julia left her home for the last time.

The final curtain, which had been due to be drawn between them a few months earlier, had been rent asunder. It was time to go. It was time to move on.

Chapter 105

Fraser's First Report to Hansen

Sword had little to do. Sarah Fossard and Mike Tyler got up on a morning and rarely left the house. They read the papers which were delivered, made meals and when the sun shone, sat on the patio at the rear of the house. They could quite easily have been mistaken for man and wife and, judging by the evening lighting sequences, it was clear that the pair slept in the same bedroom.

Sir Nicholas Hansen's surveillance team had been active for ten days and their daily routine had varied little. At the weekend the upstairs curtains of one of the two front bedrooms remained closed until late morning and apart from a shopping trip to the supermarket and a short Sunday afternoon walk in the park there had been little to report.

Sarah Fossard and Mike Tyler appeared to have called a halt to their social lives and retreated to the safety of 'Chez Nous'. Mark Shatner was well aware that Sir Nicholas Hansen now knew of the whereabouts of Sarah Fossard. His team would file a duplicate report as Fraser had said they would.

Juno had been given Julia Salomonovich's address at Mike Tyler's. No show. The team also reported to their two masters and neither was amused. Vincent Colletti spoke with Tony Molinaro. 'The team's thorough; I'll give that to the Brits. They have a room opposite and surveillance is good. Shame that they don't know Colletti has bugged 'em. The buggers bugged eh! There's a fire escape at the back but there'd be no reason for her to use it. We let one of Hansen's guys into the place. The girl's not there. He's bugged the room too but he left that part out when he reported back to me. He seemed happy with his evening's work.' Tony smiled, 'I hadn't the heart to tell him that I bugged it within an hour of her leaving. How do I know that? The iron was still warm and there were no suitcases around. She hasn't returned.'

Fraser added 'Ergo ...'

Tony looked disappointed. 'Don't tell me you started with Connor's fucking Latin crap too.' Fraser smiled and motioned for him to continue.

'Juno has no reason to believe that their room is bugged. They're coming over loud and clear. Hansen's wasn't a happy bunny when he was told that the girl had left and had taken her suitcases with her. He comes over all suave and sophisticated in public Fraser but when he's pissed he loses it. Mostly others shit themselves, believe me.'

Fraser felt reassured that he could rely on Tony Molinaro's continence.

'Looks like she's gone away for a while Tony. Juno's on it and they're keeping Hansen informed.'

Gold had drawn a blank too. They had been tasked with the surveillance job on The Manor House. Rebecca Salomonovich was old, unexciting and unadventurous. There was little to report. The Bothey and the Pheasantry stood empty and according to the gossipy old woman who ran the post office, the young man who now owned the white cottage at the end of the wood visited 'only on the occasional weekend.'

Connor's extensive network had anticipated a little more. Hansen expected a great deal more.

Gold got back to Connor. 'Nothing Con. The sky's blue, the trees are green the sun is shining and, unless I miss my guess the lake here is wet. That's about it.' Al Curtis reported to Connor too. Nothing much Con 'cept there's a guy living at the white cottage. He brought plenty with him. I'd say he's staying for a while. Checks out that he works at Cambridge University. Bright kid. He bought the place from a George Merrick who died recently. They must have known each other at the university. Perhaps that's why. He works in the same department that Merrick did.'

Connor reported to Fraser. 'Is Al checking this guy out?' Connor looked at Fraser. It was enough. 'Sorry Con, I guess I'm just getting edgy. I know we've put a good team together. Let me know.'

Fraser's nose was twitching again. He felt something in his water yet again. His intuition had rarely failed him. It was almost tangible. It didn't add up but it was there. Something. What the hell was it? The ether was so damn thick with it he could smell it. He opened his mobile and called Sir Nicholas Hansen. He had nothing to report. Whether he had or not.

Chapter 106

FELIX AND JULIA AT THE COTTAGE

'What the …' Al Curtis saw her before Connor or Gold had. The guy Mitchell had opened the cottage door and had stepped out. He was talking to someone lingering in the threshold as he began his callisthenics regimen. He was dressed in running vest and shorts. Curtis was curious; he hadn't seen anyone other than Mitchell arrive at the place. True he hadn't staked it out continuously, that would have been impossible, but he hadn't neglected it either. He decided to wait for the runner to leave before checking the cottage and reporting on Gold.

A young woman emerged from the cottage also dressed to take a morning run. Al Curtis had seen many photographs of Julia Salomonovich. He had not expected to see her there in person. This didn't make sense. No sense at all. He watched the couple jog out of sight before ringing Connor John.

'Con, Al.' Connor came in. 'OK Al what you got?' Al drew a deep breath and said. 'The Salomonovich girl, yeh? She just turned up at the cottage near Joel Salomonovich's place. What the hell she doin' here? Have I missed something?'

Connor had no more idea than Al Curtis. 'Stay at the cottage. If they're just going out running, they're coming back soon. Keep Gold out of it for now. No sense in Hansen knowing more than he needs to. You do the legwork. Stay there.'

Connor got on to Fraser and relayed the news. It was greeted with some scepticism. 'Is he sure Con? Like Al said, what the hell would she be doing there? I knew there was something. God knows I've always known that there was something. But, shit, it beats the hell out of me what it is even though the obvious link is Merrick and Julia Salomonovich lives across the lake from there. You take over from Al. Send him back to babysit Gold. I'll get back to you later.'

Fraser reprised the situation. Julia had returned to her homeland but she hadn't gone to see her much loved aunt who believed her to be dead. Instead she hung out with a young guy who recently bought a house nearby and guess whose house that had formally been? No lesser person than the deceased Professor George Merrick. How recently had he bought the property? Who the hell was he?

There was no need for Juno to continue looking for Julia. She was in Gold's area now. Tony Molinaro could be brought in. And Juno? Let them sit on their asses. Keep them out of the goddam way.

Fraser rang Tony and asked him to get across country fast. 'OK Fraser, I got this. Julia Salomonovich has been seeing one Michael Mitchell, you might want to check the guy out, no one has heard of him. He's a big guy, fit and strong. The girls at the local health club went soft when I enquired about him.

'Seems to be a real ladies man.'

Fraser caught on. 'What's his thing at the health club Tony? Run?'

'Yeh he runs but he pumps too.'

'And he just dropped out of sight yeh? No one knows where the hell he is. That's what you're going to tell me Tony. Right?'

'What you got Fraser? Your guessing's way too good for guessing – what gives?'

'What we've got is our guy and your gal and I'm beginning to see the Turner's Fighting Temeraire emerging from the fucking mist. Tony went silent at the end of the sentence waiting for an explanation. He didn't get one; art had not been his strong suit. It went with the Latin.

Fraser considered his options. 'Leave Vince Colletti to keep an eye on Juno and get here quick. And Tony; keep the Brits out of this verstanden?'

Tony Molinari had a last thought. 'I got some of it Fraser but tell me; what's Hansen up to and who's pulling the dead man's strings?

Fraser smiled. 'Cute Tony. Keep singing the same melody. It makes me feel that I got company. Perhaps I'm not going gaga after all.

Chapter 107

REVELATIONS

'Well?' Fraser sat at Joel Salomonovich's desk at The Manor House, a privilege accorded by Rebecca Salomonovich the instant that Fraser Hume had invoked Spencer Hume's name. He looked at his three summoned generals accusingly. He yawned; he hadn't slept much lately and didn't consider it likely that things were about to change in the near future. He reached for the dossier he had requested from Ian Smith and looked for mathematical equations.

Salomonovich and Merrick, geniuses. OK? Equals yeh? A dead and alive Julia Salomonovich; a dead Joel Salomonovich; a dead George Merrick; a dead Reinhardt Bühler; a dead Walter Krantz; a dead Gudrun Hackemann, and a dead Gunter Ulbricht. A dead Peter Fossard and a wife who now lived with a man called Tyler. Julia Salomonovich calls herself Tyler and lives near the Fossards. A man called Mike Mitchell who lived near the Fossards, works in Cambridge and has bought the said dead George Merrick's home near Joel Salomonovich's Manor House in Suffolk. A loving niece who does not inform her aunt that there is no need to mourn the loss of her last relation. Put 'em together – what you got?

When Fraser put his mind to the problem he drew big blanks, but what was it that his father, Spencer, had said so many years ago when they had played the 18th hole at the Rochester? He was ten at the time and was looking for his ball on the edge of the fairway and semi. 'I know that it's here. That's where it landed. I watched it all the way.' Spencer had replied. 'Can you see it?' Fraser replied that he could not. 'Then go and look elsewhere. You can see a ball when it is where it should be. The reason you can't see it is because it's someplace else. Go look in the rough even if you don't think it's over there. It sure as hell ain't on the fairway; and sure enough he had found the ball in the rough.

He thought he saw an answer but that would mean... and that could not... because if that ... then ... no that was quite impossible ... but supposing ... that would be ... What if Merrick?' The ball was quite clearly nowhere near the fairway.

Fraser knew there was something. He could taste it. Damn it he could smell it. Damn it he had said that very thing to himself a thousand times lately. All he lacked was the data to interpret what his subconscious already knew; that which he must already have. He had knowledge in need of interpretation so that it could emerge and illuminate. The pieces of the jigsaw were there in front of him. He just needed a glimpse of the picture; something to ignite his enlightenment.

'What, in the name of crap are we missing?' He recalled Joel's invectives at his last meeting in the same room. The menace was incomparable but the message rang with the same clarity and intent.

He paced the room. 'All evidence is interpreted with reference to characters and their relationships. I guess we have all the information we need to solve problems long before we use what we have. What are the relationships between our characters? It's clear they are all interconnected.'

'OK. Let's start with Joel and Merrick.' Fraser took this one on himself. 'Both were highly intelligent. Both were driven men. They knew each other in their youth; grew up in the same village; fancied the same girl. They didn't get on. It seems that Joel got the girl. Merrick resented it. Both left the girl though. There must have been something there? We know Joel came to the States. My dad worked for him but, according to Merrick's research on Hansen's mainframe, he originally spent time building up his business in Amsterdam. The death of one Jan Kuyper interested Merrick. But Merrick doesn't have what it takes to patrol the streets of Amsterdam to follow up his research. He needs someone. How come he lights on Joel Salomonovich's nemesis, Reinhardt Bühler? He got to Bühler and Bühler had contacts. They discovered the connections. So what of Bühler's part in all this?' He nodded at Connor John. 'Connor's got this.'

Connor John sat on the corner of Joel Salomonovich's desk, a posture he would not have considered had the owner been present. 'You will recall guys that I worked with the West Germans before the wall came down? I spoke with Marty Hooson at the CIA yeh? Hooson got me what I wanted from the Hauptverwaltung Aufklarung and the Rozenholz files. The Stasi had a whole lot on Bühler and his tribe. One thing's for sure; Bühler was a maniac. A psychotic given unlimited power to wield his hatred on the Jews. He was bright alright but he lost his father in the first war and his mother committed suicide. I guess the words Bühler and stable were never going to be buddies. As I say somehow Merrick got to Bühler. Walter Krantz comes in here. Don't ask me how. One thing is for sure Krantz made a lot of money and there is little paper work to establish how. Let's take a leap of faith. Let's say that he was bound up with the Stasi, I have Hooson on it as we speak. What if he had access to Bühler? Merrick gets to Bühler through Krantz.

What does he sell him? He wants to get revenge on Joel Salomonovich. Why would he want to use Bühler? Why is Bühler unique?'

Fraser took on the narrative. 'To understand what's been going down here you have to understand George Merrick's psyche and his genius; if we are capable of that.

Connor John moved slowly still distilling the flood of information he had received from around the world during the previous twenty four hours and warmed to his task.

'Merrick was a cold fish. In his early years he had not welcomed intrusion from the less gifted. He had a really strange upbringing having had little contact with others. He had met Rachael Haan in his early teens and, according to Joel's sister, he had been unable to express his love for her. He was an 'awkward suitor' she said but, of course, this must have come from Joel. This suppressed passion tormented him. He drew a curtain down over his past but would not embrace the new reality. Rachael died in childbirth and Merrick saw Joel as her killer. Driven by his hatred for Joel he planned retribution. But over how long a period? My god it took him years to get on to Hansen's mainframe. What did he have then that he didn't have before? What gave him the impetus to make his move?'

In essence Connor had his man. 'George Merrick's road to perdition was paved with hatred forged in the crucible of torment, fomented by suppressed hurt and anger. He had been a dormant volcano waiting to explode for years. Why erupt now? The extent of his implacable hatred for Joel Salomonovich was nigh on incomprehensible. Over the years it was clear that he spiralled deeper and deeper into despair and that his grief had burned undiminished. Disfigured by his malice, blighted and damned by his hatred he had retreated into his personal hell. Fuelled with the bitterness and a sulphurous sense of betrayal hatred poured from his soul leaving his body aching and void and this nourished his malignant neurosis further. Nothing would quell his anger and seething bitterness.'

'Powerful impulses and irrational urges pervaded his relationships with others. His neurosis stemmed from twisted facts, brooding hatred and the end of reason. His invectives were delivered to enquiring innocents and to the pontificating learned with equal contempt. Disproportionate responses of Herodian proportions were meted out with clinical dismissals. He scythed down his imaginary adversaries with his arrogance and certainty, contemptuously brushing aside the views of others, grotesquely blowing their shortcoming out of proportion and unaware of the need to refer to a moral compass, he haughtily dismissed his fellow man which left him empty and melancholic. Unfettered by compassion, the significance of which eluded him, he presented his views as incontrovertible. Thus transfigured he stood resplendent in his menace brooding with a seething hatred of mankind. All of mankind.'

'The blemished genius George Merrick's did not grieve for his tarnished reputation. Others were not worthy of his condescension let alone his considered opinion. His life was impossible to reconcile and his venomous feud with Joel Salomonovich, which had continued unabated for years, heralded a dénouement of apocalyptic magnitude.'

'Taciturn and humourless in his grief his ferocious blitzes brought him into conflict with administration and management at regular intervals but his genius withstood criticism. He noted that others sought to burnish their reputations through memoirs and deferred disbursements of thirty pieces of silver paid for his silence. In such circumstances he would refrain from criticism adding only that 'one should forgive him if he retained a measure of scepticism;' unable to yield completely to his welling tide of contempt for their pathetic contributions.'

'In his youth he always endeavoured to deal with the high principle, now he was prepared to dirty his hands with low pragmatism. He had read Machiavelli well and knew the politics of power. He also knew the power of money and had made himself indispensable to several members of the aristocracy and aspiring magnates. A young Nicholas Hansen had been such a student. Others had entered the civil service and all had been grateful to engage Professor George Merrick's genius. He had not made friends rather he had acquired influential contacts. When required they inured him from the criticism that he would surely have endured and the sackings that would just as surely have followed.'

Connor concluded his piece. 'Such was the man. Bitter, twisted, cold and indifferent he had sought vengeance on and the humiliation of Joel Salomonovich.'

Fraser thanked Connor for his astute assessment. 'So that's about it. Merrick hated Joel and this dossier certainly gives us an insight into Merrick's twisted mind. Question. What more does this tell us?'

Connor John broke in. 'Given that Merrick contacted Sir Nicholas Hansen and subsequently Bühler and Krantz. Given that Julia Salomonovich went missing and that Bühler had obviously gone to Neuschwanstein Castle to meet someone ....' he hesitated for a second. Something. Yes something.

It was Tony Molinaro. 'What do you have Connor?'

Connor John was transfixed; a fragmented recollections suddenly rearranged themselves and settled slowly into position.

'No ho ho ho. Woha woha. Waho. No way' Connor resisted Leroy Gomez's irritation as he synthesised his thoughts.

He began deliberately. 'The handsome young man with black hair in the blue Audi that passed us when we lay in wait for Bühler at the Rastplatz; the description of the guy Michael Mitchell in Bristol; the description of Felix Elder, the guy whose life hung, literally by a thread, in the Cheddar Gorge and who miraculously recovered; the description of the guy taken into the Munich clinic along with Julia Salomonovich on the day when Merrick turned up there; the guy who was kidnapped in an ambulance and has not been seen since. This on the same day that the professor had unexpectedly died.'

Connor John's eyes stared ahead unseeing. His mind raced ahead, the soft focus sharpening frustratingly slowly.

There was a certain ... not a logic ... a ... a ... not a theorem... in fact a wild... something. Something. 'What if? What if? What the bloody well if..?'

Fraser caught his line. 'You're not suggesting? Surely you're ... Surely not!'

'No! But then ... give me another explanation. Fine!' It made little sense. Certainly there would be a huge leap of faith not to mention a huge leap in ... but what if? What if, for god's sake, what if?

Fraser spoke in whispers to Connor. 'Con, tell Mark and Al to keep watch on their targets and on Hansen's men and we need Vince to keep a watch on Mitchell and the girl.

It was later that evening that the four met at the Rose and Crown in Fraser's room, less than half a mile from the Manor House. 'Anything?' Fraser asked Tony. 'Not so far Fraser. They came back from their jog but no show since. Vince has taken over and the bad guys have been sent home. Hansen won't like it.' Fraser dismissed the last part of Tony's report.

Fraser found difficulty in beginning proceedings. How had he arrived at his ridiculous postulation? Through conjecture, speculation, presumption and suspicion? Where was the rigour of deduction? Exactly! Better to feed the facts to the guys and to see what they came up with.

He began and the men dropped silent. 'OK the purpose of this meeting is to brainstorm our ideas about what the hell is going on. I want you to think out of the box, suspend rational thought and to start thinking the unthinkable. Go with the flow, don't inhibit any thought.'

The three men looked at each other. Leroy offered, 'I've been thinking out of my box all my life Fraser. What's new?'

Fraser doubted that anyone had thought out of the box as much as he was asking for but continued.

'We know that Julia Salomonovich, the dead Julia Salomonovich, the one who had the car accident near Munich when she should have been hundreds of miles away near Koblenz, is in the cottage that once belonged to George Merrick.' He waited for that huge sentence to sink in. 'She is in there with a guy called Michael Mitchell but this Mitchell guy, is, according to Tony, using an alias. His real name, and I hesitate to say that, is Felix Elder. I asked Al Curtis to work on this guy. He works at the same University, in the same department that Merrick worked in. Strange thing about Elder; he showed no interest in research until earlier this year. Been climbing mostly. An adventurer. He had a major accident then disappeared from the face of the earth a few months ago at about the same time that Julia Salomonovich had her accident. That, by the way, would be the same time that a Sarah Fossard and her dying husband left a Bristol hospital and disappeared into the ether; the same Sarah Fossard who took Julia Tyler, alias Julia Salomonovich, in as a lodger. I hope that you are following me 'cos I'm not sure that I am following myself.'

Fraser paused again. 'OK, make sense of this bit. Julia Tyler or whatever her name is leaves the Fossard's home and moves into Peter Fossard's best pal's flat. According to neighbours Julia Tyler is Mike Tyler's niece. A neat family connection if you are an only one and single, as Mike Tyler is, wouldn't you say? Especially when Julia Tyler is almost certainly Julia Salomonovich. Mike Tyler moves in with Sarah Fossard. Let me know when you make any semblance of sense out of any of this. Feel free to jump in.'

Connor raised an eyebrow. Fraser knew they were tapping into a positive line. Tony Molinaro registered something distant. It refused to come into focus. 'Go ahead Fraser.' He needed more. Leroy nodded in agreement.

'Merrick contacts Hansen; yet another Cambridge man. He researches Joel and a Nazi called Bühler. They meet at a place near Munich and the director of the place and a nurse are blown to kingdom come. What is this place near Munich? A private infirmary owned by Walter Krantz.'

'Mark Shatner used contacts; he tells me that the place is replete with an experimental lab far in excess of the needs of a few elderly psychosomatics. So we have Merrick, the Fossards, Elder and Julia Salomonovich all in the same place at the same time. And we have a laboratory for a mad scientist. Scotch the last comment I don't want to lead you on. Next up, according to Mark Shatner's contacts, Peter Fossard dies but his wife leaves the clinic with a surprisingly healthy Julia Salomonovich; the same Julia Salomonovich who was in a coma days earlier when brought into the infirmary by no less a character than George Merrick.'

All four were already aware of ninety percent of the facts but the intensity of delivery and the deluge of data began to distil their thoughts.

'Questions. Why would Sarah Fossard leave Munich before her husband's funeral? Would she do it? Why would she have him cremated in Germany after she had left for Austria? Why would she not have had the body flown home? Stranger still, why did she travel to Innsbruck at all and what was her connection with her fellow traveller? Oh yeh, and I missed out a car blowing up near where Julia Salomonovich disappeared near Koblenz and the fact that we now know this is a guy who had tailed Julia for many months. Who the hell blew him up?'

The team were shifting uneasily in their chairs. Fraser poured a glass of water for himself and passed the pitcher along. All were lost in thought.

'Then we have the case of the missing ladies. They were delivered to Innsbruck and then? They arrive at Birmingham airport. Just like that. Elder? Elder also appears and, though living in Suffolk at Merrick's old place decides to take a flat in Bristol and changes his name. Next thing he's invited Julia to chez nous. Discuss.'

It was Leroy who broke the silence, his nonchalant Las Vegas air easing the tension. 'Merrick dies yeah? Elder appears. Peter Fossard dies; Julia Salomonovich takes his place by Sarah Fossard's side.'

Conner continued the thought. 'Symmetry. Always symmetry. Loose ends. Always cleaned up.'

Tony Molinaro jolted to his feet. 'One replaces another. You did say think out of the box Fraser.' Fraser nodded affirmation knowing Tony was following the same track that he had travelled a few hours earlier. 'Go on Tony, give us some science fiction.'

A shocked Tony Molinaro stared hard into Fraser Hume's face.

'You've got there ahead of me Fraser?' Fraser nodded once again.

'Keep going Tony.'

Encouraged by the fact that if he had gone mad then Fraser had gone mad before him Tony continued. 'OK, this is mad right? Leroy? Con? Don't laugh; science fiction; remember? Serious. Capice? Just pure science fiction. OK.

Once upon a time a mad scientist invented a machine that, what shall we say, er changed people and ... Fraser I don't have more. At least I can't even think straight anymore.'

All four spent the following moments scrutinising the other three's faces.

Fraser patted Tony on the back as he passed to get to the pitcher of water.

'Yes Tony I followed the same path. Mad isn't it? But as you say, science fiction. OK, give me another explanation. The madness fits. Reality doesn't. If the ball ain't on the fairway it must be ...'

Connor finished the sentence'... in the semi?

Fraser smiled, 'I think it's in the jungle Connor.'

A stunned Leroy looked at Connor. 'Are you saying Merrick is Elder or Mitchell or whoever the asshole is?'

Fraser nodded slowly. 'Only in the land of science fiction Leroy – remember? But if that is the case who is Julia Salomonovich?'

It took a little time; then Leroy's eyes became wider and wider. 'Shit Fraser, you can't be saying ...'

'As I said, it's just science fiction Leroy.'

The ever pragmatic Connor John leaned into the group. 'Keep thinking out of the box gentlemen. What has Hansen to do with this? OK, yeh, Merrick brought him in to start with but somehow it's become personal. Why would that be guys? He's up to his neck in it. Why did he want us onside? He can't know what we have but he knew Merrick was onto something big. Merrick was a phlegmatic guy but Hansen would pick up the vibes. He's like a shark – only with him, it's the money. He can smell it across an ocean and is as ruthless as a great white. It's hard not to believe that he wouldn't keep a close eye on Merrick. He'd monitor his every goddam movement. Trust me! Like you said Fraser, I'm just thinking out of the box.'

Fraser was keen to keep the momentum going. 'Hansen knew that we couldn't be kept out of it for long so he brought us along.'

Connor sensed danger. 'As soon as his guys realise that they are treading water they will be over us like a rash.'

Fraser smiled. 'That's why I have Al, Mark and Vince with them. They're doing a little shepherding at the moment. We need to get them off the scent. I'm going to ring Hansen with my report. Julia Salomonovich has returned to Mitchell's place. I need a word with Miss Salomonovich.'

Connor John, Tony Molinaro and Leroy Gomez saw Fraser's hesitation as he reflected on that meeting. He gathered himself. 'So our priorities are to get hold of whatever miracle Merrick invented; confront Mitchell; play happy families until Hansen loses interest then Mitchell takes a jump without a parachute. We play the long game with Ian Smith running the firm.'

'And the old dame?' The question came from Leroy.

'The old dame, as you call her Leroy, has had one hell of a life. I'll tell you this; I'm going to play it straight down the line with her. Straight down the line.'

Tony Molinaro beamed. 'I just can't wait to see Mitchell's smug fucking face turn sour when we pull the plug.'

'Patience Tony. It will be take patience.'

Chapter 108

JULIA AND JULIA

When Julia left Sarah and Mike it was with mixed feelings; indeed, those of three distinctive personalities. Peter Fossard may well have died but he still loved Sarah. Julia Tyler cared for Sarah too but the bonds had become chains and the urge for release and liberation irrepressible. Julia Salomonovich was emerging too. Deep within her psyche a preternatural history disturbed her thoughts penetrating her memory through a semi-permeable psychological membrane. Feelings, memories, traits and reminiscences filtered through her consciousness. Julia Salomonovich battled for her very existence however tenuous her attachment.

Felix knew that he had to ascertain the extent of the invasion of Julia Salomonovich's memory into Julia Tyler's mind. It was not in his nature to leave things to chance. Deciding to run through the woods with Julia had been a difficult decision. He needed her to see the Manor House, the lake, the Bothey and the Pheasantry. He did not want her to meet the locals nor and more especially, Rebecca Salomonovich. He calculated that an early morning run was as probably the safest time to expose her to her past. He suggested a run within an hour of arriving at the cottage. He needed to act quickly.

He had left the cottage to do a little stretching before the run as he waited for Julia to change. It was then that Al Curtis had seen her leave the cottage. The two set off towards the Pheasantry. The pace was a little sedate for the immensely fit Felix but exercise was not the purpose of this particular jog through the woods.

Julia Tyler slowed then stopped as they approached the Pheasantry. Joel Salomonovich had taken his granddaughter to the building so many times in the past. The place had been indelibly printed on her mind. Felix saw her hesitate and stop.

'What is it Julia?' he enquired, seeking further information.

'I don't know. It feels odd.' Julia looked confused. Felix analysed her response.

'Come on. I'll race you to the lake.'

The lake flickered in the early morning summer sun as they jogged between the oak, birch, sycamore and ash wood that led to the pastures. Soon the Manor House came into view and they slowed to a walk.

It was clear that Julia was perplexed. She apologised for her confusion, then immediately wondered why she had felt that necessary. Disorientated she asked to sit but Felix surprised her with his firmness.

He took her by the arm. 'Just a little further and we can rest.'

Felix took her to a copse of trees where the drive met the road. It was a specific copse. A copse that had been there for many years. A copse that had witnessed his greatest pain. He took Julia in his arms and kissed her. This time he that had the girl.

Julia was a little more confused. The copse had been off the beaten track and Felix appeared to have taken her there specifically for the kiss. She had waited for further tenderness but after a few seconds he had urged her to push on with their jog.

They ran back to the lake then took the path that led to the Rose and Crown. Felix was careful to scan the way ahead.

Julia stopped again. 'Déjà vu.'

Felix understood. This was the exact spot that George Merrick had come across Julia Salomonovich and Gerhardt Severin. 'Genesis!' The germ of an idea had sprung from there as he had looked into Rachael Haan's face. Felix knew paramnesia when he saw it. What startled him was the dramatic effect it had had on Julia. She faltered and he held her tight.

'I need to sit. I feel a little faint; a little strange. Perhaps we shouldn't have set off for a run so soon after our journey.' She sought the experience of ... of ...Whose experience had she relied on in recent weeks? There was someone ...who? She was afraid. She hadn't seen Aunt Rebecca for such a long time. Who was Aunt Rebecca? The Manor House! Aunt Rebecca was in the Manor House. How did she know that? Sarah. Sarah who? Her grandfather had warned her many times not to walk in the woods. Ah, her grandfather. Chloroform! She panicked.

'Please Michael take me back I ... I ... My god the old man!' She looked at Felix. 'The old man was here. My grandfather warned me about.... oh, the last place ...my grandfather and grandmother lived there ... I ... I ... What is happening to me?'

Felix had part of the answer he was looking for but was Julia Tyler's mind being sublimated or vanquished? Julia Salomonovich memory was emerging as he hoped that it would but the intensity of her experience gave rise for concern.

Felix put his arm around her and shepherded her to the woodland path leading back to the cottage; the cottage Al Curtis had just bugged.

Chapter 109

JULIA TYLER LOSES HER MIND

Aided by a concerned Felix Elder what remained of Julia Tyler stumbled towards the old cottage, flashbacks intensifying her paranoia. Al Curtis could see that she was trembling through his field glasses some two hundred yards distant.

Felix took little time in fixing Julia with a 'nice cup of tea' and 'something to calm her down.' She was asleep within seconds.

He lifted her easily into his arms and placed her on the bed dispassionately. He took a small box from under the bed and relieved it of its contents. He uncoiled several lengths of wire and attached electrodes to her head. It took no more than thirty seconds.

Al Curtis listened in. Nothing. He rang Fraser. 'Hi, the girl's tripped or something. At least she's badly shaken. Do you want ...?'

Fraser jumped to one more conclusion. 'Al just sit tight. We're in for the long haul. Unless I miss my guess they're not going far. Not for some time anyways. Keep tabs.' Al Curtis surveyed the surrounding woods. No sign of Hansen's men.

Felix engaged George Merrick's fierce intellect. Julia's Salomonovich's mind had triumphed over Julia Tyler's. Now a subliminal memory would be implanted. It would take several hours to have her forget him but respond to him.

Al Curtis listened in to the tapes being played over and over again.

'Fraser?' 'Al. Sounds like a brain washing session's going on in the cottage and you know what? The science fiction thing you mentioned; sounds more and more like science fact to me. Where do we go from here?'

Fraser was rolling; it took no time at all for his response.

'Sit tight Al. I'm sending Tony. If they split I want Tony with the girl and you with Merrick. Forget Mitchell and Elder; that's Merrick you got in there. God knows how but the bugger's made science fiction a fantastic reality but he did it all right.

Fraser snapped the mobile shut and Tony Molinaro left immediately not requiring direction. Fraser turned to Connor John and Leroy Gomez.

'Now ask yourselves one more question. Why would Merrick brainwash Julia Tyler or Julia Salomonovich? Why would he want Julia to be the girl she used to be? As I see it there would be no purpose unless...' Fraser was thinking out of the box again, trying to make sense of it all; using the other two as sounding boards. 'Unless. Unless he intends sending her back home. OK so she's back home; then what?'

Connor John continued in the same vein. 'He's planting things in her mind. Why would he do that? When ... when ... when he's going to send her back to the Manor House. Meet her later. Yes, that's it; he's going to meet her at the Manor House; like it's the first time.

Fraser shot out of his chair. 'Genius; pure genius. He wants it all and he's bloody well going to damn well get it. He gets the girl and Joel's millions. The bloody genius. The cunning bastard.' Fraser sprang into action. 'Leroy get over to Joel's place. Tell Rebecca Kinnear that you want a room for the night and stay tight. And Leroy, get a photo of Joel's wife; one of her, say, in her early twenties.' Leroy Gomez shrugged his shoulders questioningly. Fraser smiled. 'Let's just say that I have one hell of a hunch Leroy.'

Leroy nodded and made for the door. 'Just another day at the office Fraser. Let me know if the Titanic resurfaces with Elvis on board. Ciao.'

Chapter 110

JULIA SALOMONOVICH RETURNS

Tony Molinaro and Al Curtis remained unoccupied for the best part of six hours. It was evening when the cottage door opened casting a shaft of light that split the warm night air. The illuminated corridor almost reached them. Tony kept low in the undergrowth and gave the sleeping Al a nudge.

Felix Elder emerged from the cottage with a bundle on his shoulder. He took great care in placing his burden on the rear seat of his BMW before fastening a seat belt around it. Tony Molinaro's imagination was not stretched. Fraser's instructions were that Tony should follow Julia and Al was to follow Merrick, Elder, Mitchell or whatever name the guy went by these days. It looked like Tony and Al would be able to keep each other company, at least for the first part of the evening.

'Wait, let them go Connor', said Al, viewing a small hand held screen. He touched the screen and a pulsating throb vibrated in his hand as he watched the GPS tracking device locate the red BMW's position.

Tony and Al pushed their sleeping bags into the boot of the Mercedes, checked the homing device once again and made a sedate rate of knots pursuing the BMW at a comfortable distance. Tony smiled. 'Game on. They're not going anywhere without us.'

It was less than three minutes later. 'He's stopped Al', Tony considered the situation for a moment and made a decision. 'He's taking the wrapping off Al. He covered the girl remember? Now he's driving along with the girl in the backseat as casual as you like. Tell you what. We don't need the homer; I know where he's going. Time to talk to Fraser; he got it right again.

Chapter 111

JULIA RETURNS TO THE MANOR

Tony Molinaro was wrong! At least in the short term. The red BMW made for the road and headed towards Ipswich. He just hadn't anticipated Merrick's ability to conjure up the impossible. He called Fraser. 'What's the conniving bastard up to now?' Perplexed he cautioned Tony. 'Keep your distance. Don't spook him just yet.'

'He's stopped Fraser; someplace five hundred metres ahead. We're out in the sticks. Something's going down. I'm leaving Al and walking on to get a closer look. Talk to Al'

Tony jogged down the B1083 hugging the tree line as he spotted the red BMW up ahead. It was parked off the road on dirt track leading to an abandoned farmhouse. It too had been abandoned.

'Al. Tony here. Get to me quick. The bastard's switched cars.'

Al Curtis drew up within seconds. 'Go.' Tony Molinaro was seething. Never, but, never did he lose his man. But how the hell had the guy managed to park another car on a road to Ipswich for god's sake?

'Trouble is Tony; now we don't know what the hell we're looking for.'

'Yeh well it's a smaller car. The tracks were real small; and that all we got.'

Fraser was not amused.

Felix drove the hired navy Fiesta along the A1152 meeting the A12 near Woodbridge. He looked in the rear view mirror. Nothing. He turned. Julia was still out. He drove on.

George Merrick had always planned meticulously. Felix's reconnaissance had been thorough. The Ipswich Hospital forecourt was well lit and was served by CCTV. He found his spot in the cover of an old oak.

Checking the car park he took Julia from the rear of the car to the driver's seat, opened the mobile he had taken from her handbag and made a quick call. He put the phone in her hand closed the door and walked away taking care to avoid the cameras. The operation took less than a minute. The dawn would break in less than an hour.

Felix hid nearby waiting for a response to his call. In less than a minute two paramedics approached the car. Satisfied, Felix set off on his five mile cross country run. He approached his BMW cautiously taking the tree line. He observed the car for over ten minutes before making a short dash to it. The engine fired, he smiled as drove off towards his 'cottage in the country.' All was well.

Tony Molinaro observed Felix from the undergrowth. He flicked his phone open. 'OK Al, he's back in the Beamer. He's alone.' Immediately Tony saw the headlights coming around the bed. 'Take it easy Al. No sense in rushing.'

The transmitter was functioning well. He called Fraser Hume hoping for redemption.

Chapter 112

REBECCA IS REUNITED
WITH JULIA

Rebecca Kinnear took the call in the early hours of the following morning. A young woman answering to the name of Julia Salomonovich had been found in a car in a hospital car park in Ipswich. Her delirium had rendered her barely audible or coherent but her driving license and further ID, discovered in her handbag, had revealed who to contact in case of emergency. Felix had seen to that.

Rebecca replaced the receiver and sat on her bed. Shocked she took a tissue and wiped the tears from her eyes. Almost immediately her mother's pragmatism came to the fore and putting on her dressing gown she walked along the hallway. She stopped to knock at a door.

'Mr. Gomez? Are you awake?'

Leroy Gomez was indeed awake. In fact he was dressed, at the door and listening to the creaking floorboard he had previously noted to be four paces short of the door to the left. He knew that it was Rebecca who was at the other side of the door before she knocked. His reconnaissance had confirmed that there was just the one telephone on the upper floor of the house and the call was taken there. It was her bedroom door that gave a mournful groan when opened. He opened his door a little.

'Hi, I heard the phone. News?'

Leroy caught the trembling Rebecca and saw her to a chaise longue situated in the recess of the bay window of the landing.

'Take your time Lady. We have all the time in the world. Who rang?'

Rebecca related the phone call from the hospital.

'I must go to see her immediately. She will need me. My god, she doesn't know about her mother. Mein Gott!'

Leroy comforted the old woman and agreed to her request. He closed the door, picked up the photo of Rachael Salomonovich that he had procured from Rebecca earlier in the evening and took a good look at it. 'Fraser Hume my old buddy you guessed right again. The girl's the goddam spitting image of her grandmother.'

Within forty minutes they were making enquiries at the Ipswich hospital's reception desk. Julia lay on her back, a saline drip attached to her left arm. Rebecca took a deep breath and entered the room. She let out the air in a deep sigh as when she saw Julia laying there. She smiled lovingly and moved towards her cautiously. Julia's eyes trembled then opened slowly; her vacant eyes searching for cognition.

A second reawakening; A second reincarnation: A second metamorphosis: Another episode of angst and confusion.

Rebecca perceived her great niece's vulnerability and the dam burst. She bent towards Julia kissing her cheek with great care and tenderness.

She rose slowly raising her head to the ceiling like a rabbit smelling the air for danger. She faltered. Something!

'Aunt Rebecca is that you. I ... I don't know what happened. I was driving to...' she sought for a specific memory. A montage of recollections flooded into her memory banks once again. A pastiche here; a cameo there. A mosaic of hopes and aspirations came to the fore then tantalisingly disappeared. The softly focussed anthology lengthened and broadened unrelentingly. It was all too much.

'Please.' The sister smiled at Rebecca then nodded to the policewoman standing by the door. She bent forward again and kissed Julia's hand. Hesitatingly she said. 'Welcome home Julia. Welcome home.' Rebecca turned to the sister questioningly.

'She must rest. There are no serious injuries. Please come with me; she is in good hands. The doctor and the police would like to see you if you are up to it?'

Rebecca affirmed as much and shuffled along the corridor to a small office knowing that only she could break the news of Laura's death. So many times fate had dealt her a cruel hand. Trembling she reached for a tissue from her handbag and, as ever, straightened her back. Marta Salomonovich had a worthy daughter. Even so, why had her instinct left her apprehensive when her relief should have been unqualified?

Chapter 113

FRASER HUME MOVES

Fraser Hume was incandescent. His men were the best; they had done their thing. No! The fault was not to be found with them. That wasn't it! It was he that had underestimated the genius that was George Merrick. He would not do so again. Thank god the girl had resurfaced. Merrick wouldn't be far away. Tony's call had come as a huge relief. Leroy's call hadn't had a dissimilar effect.

Fraser called Ian Smith. 'The girl's back Ian. Hansen will be sniffing around soon. I left his entire invasion fleet kicking its heels in Bristol, London and out in the sticks by Merrick's cottage. My guess is that Hansen will soon light the blue touch paper. It's time for me to ring him. He'll get wind soon anyhow. Ian? Ian?'

'Yes, I'm here Fraser. I'm just considering our options. How is the girl? Who is the girl? Is it Fossard, Tyler or Salomonovich?'

'Tough one Ian. Technically it's Fossard and, let's get this right, there never was a Tyler; that was pure invention; like Michael Mitchell come to that. It looks like Salomonovich, it talks like Salomonovich but it absolutely ain't Salomonovich, except in Merrick's warped imagination. We need to talk to Joel's sister.'

Ian Smith sensed that Fraser had something. 'Fraser?'

'Just a germ of an idea Ian. We need to talk too. Can you keep Hansen in the cold for just a little while longer? Tell him to be patient. A couple of days would do it. Best you don't know where I'm going with this. There's a whole lot that we don't want to let out of here. Trust me if we foul up now the world and his mother are going to be circling. What we have we keep, capice? My boys are good. The less people know about Merrick and his experiments the better. You are going to have to trust me on this one Ian.'

'Two days tops Fraser. You know what Hansen's like. You'd better get the show on the road 'cos I've got a whole lot of persuading to do. Go to it and good luck.'

Fraser turned to Connor John. 'The bastard thinks he's safe tucked away in his little cottage. Gold has reported in. So Hansen knows where Michael Mitchell alias Felix Elder is but he doesn't know that he's Merrick. He doesn't know that Julia has returned either. Yes, he's had Rebecca Salomonovich's place bugged but we buggered it up. We have to believe that he's in the dark. Leroy had a tail but switched cars with Tony on the way to Ipswich and he took 'em to London, lost 'em and ...' He tailed off with a gesture that signified the inevitable. Job done!

'Connor, check with Leroy. We need an update. I want the girl home, Gold fucked, Merrick's place raided and a long hard talk with Rebecca Kinnear, and, oh yeh, get me Hansen on the blower; it's time I fed him some more shit.'

Connor John sensed the gathering storm. Fraser was a dispassionate operator but he sensed the increasing crescendo, raising tempo, mounting energy, rhythmic pulse and lengthening cadence of his actions. The portents lay heavy.

Chapter 114

Hansen

Sir Nicholas Hansen was not at all amused. His three units had been completely outgunned and he could hardly complain to Fraser Hume that his subterfuge had not yielded results. Fraser had controlled his men and had limited their feedback; of that he was sure.

He rarely lost and was determined that he could salvage this one. He had wanted to buy Rebecca Salomonovich out but four people had stood in his way. He had ingratiated himself with Ian Smith: or had he? The jury was out on that one. He'd tried to buy Fraser Hume's loyalty and had discovered that it wasn't for sale, and, as yet, he hadn't found Julia Salomonovich. Rebecca Kinnear now came into the frame.

Smith was smart. He posed as a facilitator but was subtly obstructive. Fraser Hume was Joel Salomonovich's man through and through. He and his team were ruthlessly professional and he admired them for that, but if they got in the way... well!

The old woman? She wanted out. That was clear. The sticking point? The law requiring five years to pass before she could sell if the body of the girl wasn't found. Solution? Find the girl and somehow - anyhow - get Smith and Hume onside. Be nice. Nasty could come later if nice failed. The option was on red alert.

It was a merciful relief to him when Fraser apprised him of the reappearance of Julia Salomonovich. He moved quickly. Fraser had anticipated that he would and he was more than one step ahead of the game.

Chapter 115

FRASER AND REBECCA

There was something in the ether; a tangible expectation. Over the years Fraser's dispassionate disposition had proved a considerable weapon in his dealings with his enemies. His deadpan unemotional detachment had branded him a serious poker player; even so, as he sat at Joel Salomonovich's desk his face betrayed him.

Connor John, Tony Molinaro and Leroy Gomez sensed a dénouement. They would be Stateside soon.

Leroy sat in the bay window tapping an annoying beat on the sill to some tune playing on his mind. Tony shook his head at Connor and Leroy's fingers fell silent.

The door opened and a weary Rebecca Kinnear shuffled into the room; the soft light not concealing the wretched pain etched into her face.

It was just two hours earlier, after the strain of attempting to make sense of her missing days to her 'Aunt Rebecca', that Julia had felt feint and collapsed onto the bed. The incident had gone unwitnessed by hospital staff.

Fraser had acted quickly insisting that Julia leave the hospital immediately. Rebecca had begun to remonstrate with him but he had taken her by the arm and guided her purposefully out of the ward room. It had been the tone of his voice rather than his missive that had convinced Rebecca that she should accede to his urgent petition.

Rebecca then signed the appropriate release forms while Fraser fended off medical opinion that Julia should remain for observation. Hippocrates failed to impress. Julia was wheeled through the sliding glass doors at the front of the hospital where Al Curtis carried her to the waiting Mercedes. Now they were in Julia's room in The Manor. She lay sedated in the bed.

'Mrs. Kinnear. It's many years since my father reunited you with your brother', Fraser began. 'I hope that you and I can be frank with one another and that you feel that you can trust me to act in your best interests at all times?'

Rebecca sensed the importance of the coming missive. 'I always have Mr. Hume. You may take it that I trust you implicitly.'

Fraser had keen antennae. He had noted the Rebecca's recent emotional detachment from Julia. He had witnessed Rebecca and Julia's interactions in the past consequently, over the past few hours he became intrigued and perplexed in equal measure.

The attachment had been strong, warm and unconditional. Now the aunt certainly showed concern for the niece but there was little emotional input; no holding of hands, touching of fevered brow or sighs of hope.

Hope! That was it. There was no seeking of spiritual aide or pleading for divine intervention. No prayers of self-sacrifice if the loved one could just be saved. Only a forlorn resignation resided. Was it defeat perhaps? This from a woman of such strength of character? The redoubtable Rebecca Kinnear? The daughter of Marta Salomonovich? The sister of the mighty Joel? Hardly!

Fraser hadn't had the time to address Rebecca as tactfully as he would have wished. He steeled himself.

'What I am about to tell you will make you question my sanity let alone your own. I cannot soften the impact of what I say. Perhaps I should present you with a brutal truth. There is no other...'

Rebecca turned her watery eyes towards him, her aura of serene acquiescence and acceptance permeating his being. She surprised Fraser by taking his hand and guided him to the hallway.

'I am an old woman Fraser Hume; suddenly a very old woman.' She smiled resignedly. 'Please sit.' She sat beside him and took both his hands in hers as if to reassure him. Anxiously he waited for her to begin.

Rebecca smiled the reassuring smile which prefaced so many of her conversations. 'If you are going to tell me the Julia Salomonovich that was my brother's granddaughter is not the woman currently in Julia Salomonovich's bed I will not disabuse you of your opinion.'

Fraser glimpsed the sharp intellect of Joel Salomonovich. He lowered his eyes and whispered. 'You know?'

'Know? Oh no, I know so very little about so very much but I do know that you have much to tell. I have learned, often by necessity, to be patient. You will recall that you sent Mr. Gomez to me? I did not ask why. I know that there is danger afoot and that you are looking out for my best interests.' She clasped his hands tighter still. 'I want you to know that I have put my trust in you completely. I know too that you work out of respect for my brother. He told me that if anything should happen to him that I should put my faith in you and Mr. Smith. I am not blind. I have seen a great deal in my life.' Fraser saw that she had. 'I also see a great deal of your father in you. I do not have the presumption of intelligence but I am not witless.' She smiled a tired smile. 'At least not yet for a little while.'

Fraser began to object but the gentle pressure on his hand and the curiously reassuring nod halted his protestations.

'Come now; it is time for you to tell your story. The time for action is nigh, am I right? Now we are both ready.'

Fraser had underestimated the old woman as his father had once done. He wouldn't make the same mistake again. That was the second time he had had to swallow that sentence within twenty four hours, he reflected. He still sought further understanding.

'But you've see the girl. She looks identical to Julia Salomonovich. How can you be so sure?'

Rebecca smiled weakly, warmly and, thought Fraser, surprisingly encouragingly. 'Inside... inside I know. How does a mother recognise which of her identical twins is which? She knows. The bodies may be the same but it is the eyes that expose the soul. There are no two identical souls. No Mr. Hume; that is not my brother's grandchild. She looks like her, she speaks like her and she has a collection of reminiscences that are similar to hers...but the young woman is not Julia Salomonovich.

Now, you must tell me what has happened. I believe that you know much more. Why would you ask Mr. Gomez to stay in this house? Why were you not satisfied when the girl that you were seeking had already returned? You knew that the girl was not Julia but expressed surprise that I, who have known her from her birth, recognised the same. It is clear there is much that I do not know. Now I ask you please to tell me what you know.'

Fraser understood now. Simon Salomonovich and his sons Benjamin, Reuben and Joel were all academics; all immensely bright. The daughter had been the same. Only her wretched incarceration had curtailed her education and deprived her of her calling.

He began. 'We have very little time.' He saw her protestations, recanted and started from the beginning. It was forty minutes before he had given a brief account of what he knew.

Rebecca had sensed that the content of Fraser's missive would be dramatic. She could scarcely have anticipated how fabulous it would be. She nodded comprehension, encouraging Fraser to continue, but the unbelievably fantastic became prosaic as his sensational account habituated her psyche and inured her senses.

Reciprocating Fraser took Rebecca's hands in his and lowered his head. 'I am so sorry Mrs. Kinnear. So very sorry.'

Fraser continued to hold her hands. It was, perhaps a minute of silence later that, though she had not moved, he felt a surge of energy emanating from her.

Rebecca Salomonovich stood tall, proud and indomitable; her mother's resolve and pragmatism triumphant. Fraser saw Joel's steely eyes one last time as she rose and walked to the window.

Fraser eased Julia's bedroom door open and looked in. The capsule he had placed in her drink would put her out for long enough. He turned back to Rebecca. 'So, the question is what do we do now?'

Again the smile. 'Mr. Hume, please tell me. A man of your undoubted ability does not come empty handed. Your plan is?'

It was Fraser's turn to smile. He was brief. He looked at his wrist. 'OK we have a few more minutes before we can expect a visitor.' He raised his arm to waive aside her concerns. 'All is well Mrs. Kinnear. All is well. This, with your permission, is what we are going to do.'

Rebecca Kinnear had experienced a great deal in her long and painful life. Fraser's plan rendered her opened mouthed and speechless.

Chapter 116

TO CATCH A FIEND

Fraser Hume took the call from Connor John. 'Fraser? Con here. Tony and I have him in our sights. Ian's with us. Elder has just turned into the Manor House drive. He's got it with him. He'll be knocking on the door anytime. It's time for you to disappear.'

Felix Elder strode confidently across the gravel path, took the two steps to the Manor House portico in one stride, then pushed a hand through his thick black hair before taking the last three steps with the consummate ease of an athlete. He rang the bell. The small heavy case swinging from his right hand came to rest as he rehearsed the role he was to play.

It was, he considered, more than time to claim his prize. Rachael Haan lived on in Julia Salomonovich. Now he would be rewarded for his devotion.

Rebecca Kinnear opened the door and looked questioningly at the handsome young man in the portico. He was tall which caused her to lean arthritically backwards awkwardly to meet his eyes. The man before her was responsible for the death of her remaining loved ones. Her role would have to transcend her feelings.

Felix Elder smiled at the old lady. 'Mrs. Kinnear. I don't suppose that you remember me? I met you with the other lady... by the lake ... I live in the old cottage ...perhaps you recall?'

Rebecca remembered him alright but she allowed a few seconds to pass before simulating recognition. 'Oh yes. Of course. I'm afraid that the house is not for sale. At least not yet. We did promise to let you know and...'

Felix interrupted her. 'No, no, no. I haven't come about that. No, I was speaking to folk in the village the other day and they mentioned Julia Salomonovich lived here. I must say that I was really shocked. I knew her when she was at Oxford.'

Rebecca. Pushed the door too, slipped the latch and opened the door she had held half closed and bade him enter. They stood in the vestibule as he took his coat off and hung it on the hall rack.

'Please come this way.' Rebecca led him to Joel's office. She smiled. 'Would you like a cup of tea? Coffee? Perhaps something stronger?' He declined. 'I'll just tell Julia that you are here.' She left leaving the door wide open.

Felix sat in the Chesterfield behind Joel's mahogany desk; a broad smile swept across his face as he contemplated the future. His pleasure was short lived.

The co-ordinated assault was swift and precise. Tony Molinaro shot through the doorway from the left of the hall and stood braced to the right. Leroy Gomez came from the right and stood to the left. Both pointed semi-automatics. Connor John flashed between them and had the bewildered Felix's case in his hands within a second. Fraser Hume walked through the doorway and made his way towards the protesting Felix.

'What's happening? What is this all about? Are you mad? You must have got the wrong ...' Fraser cut him short with a crack across the face. The protesting stopped immediately.

'OK, let's see exactly how much I've got wrong professor.' Alarmed Felix lifted questioning eyes.

'Yes as all of these gentlemen know only too well you are the late Professor George Merrick Mr. Felix Elder; or should that be Mr. Michael Mitchell.' Fraser allowed a few silent dramatic seconds before: 'You see George I know it all. The game is up.'

'Ah ha! I see you glance at your case. I know of that too. And the motive behind your presence here today? Getting in with the family eh? The previous brain washing at your father's old cottage ought to pave most of the way wouldn't you say?'

George Merrick's mind was recalculating and recalibrating rapidly, his eyes not leaving the case. A score of options were scanned within seconds. Escape, reason, barter, denial, all seemed hopeless. Another man now blocked the doorway. Al Curtis entered whispering something to Fraser Hume. Still there was silence. Al gave his gun to Connor John and approached Felix. He moved cautiously before handcuffing his wrists behind him and placing him on a chair in the centre of the room. Another entered. Felix wondered how many more. Where the hell were they all coming from?

Ian Smith, stick in hand, ambled into the room, his straight backed brigadier like posture unyielding to his infirmity. He took the chair proffered by Connor John. Fraser looked into Felix Elder's eyes, sighed, shook his head slowly and began.

'I know what you did; I just don't understand why or how?' he caught the responding sneer. 'Oh I know that I am not worthy but then again, given your reputation professor, who is?' Felix's nostrils flared with contempt; seething malice leaching from his pores.

'What are you going to do now? Call the police? How pathetic. I am worth a hundred of any one of you. Your ignorance hinders my discourse and your limited perception my willingness to engage with you.'

Fraser had heard of the vanity, conceit and arrogance of George Merrick, his colossal self-belief in his pre-eminence, his utter supercilious condescension and disdain for the rest of humanity. Still, although the force of the fiend's ascendant invective made him uneasy, his magnetism and charisma drew him in. He knew that he must act quickly.

He took the case and placed it on his lap. Felix Elder's eyes followed it like a magnet. 'Ah, I see that I have your attention now.'

Fraser thought that the man would explode if he became any more animated.

'Do not meddle with things that are far beyond your feeble understanding. Do not presume...'

Leroy Gomez took a pace forward threateningly. Fraser was quick to admonish him. 'No Leroy. The guy's ... well ... he's history. It's well and truly over.'

Connor John approached with a syringe in hand. 'Now, if I have anything to do with this, this is going to hurt.' He plunged the needle and thumbed the liquid into Felix's left arm. His eyes glazed over and the incredible ego that was George Merrick slumped in the chair.

It took no more than twenty minutes before Fraser had a working knowledge of the machine. Felix Elder told him all he had wanted to know. Connor John had used all the pharmaceutical contacts the CIA could offer.

Adjustments to the device could be made. If the machine was to be used again the chances were that memory pervasion could be halted now that greater stability had been finessed.

Fraser looked towards Rebecca. The old woman took a deep breath and nodded. She and Fraser left the room.

A further twenty minutes later Felix Elder was coming round and making demands of those around him. Tony Molinaro placed his hands on either side of his head. 'Listen, I don't give a fuck who you think you are, if you bleat one more word I'll ...'

He was interrupted by Julia Salomonovich. 'Mr. Molinaro, I have seen too much violence in my long and tragic life; I do not wish to witness any more. Certainly not in my own home.'

The voice was that of Julia Salomonovich but the idiom and vernacular pre-dated one so young. Felix Elder's eyes narrowed as he hurled his invective at Fraser Hume. 'You imbecile. You do not know what or who you are dealing with. What gives you the right to..?'

Fraser screamed back. 'What gives me the right? What gives me the right? What, in god's name gives you the right you fucking egocentric maniac?'

Fraser, shaking from his furious onslaught, caught Ian Smith's nod and glanced towards Julia Salomonovich. 'I'm sorry.'

'Rebecca Kinnear looked out from behind Julia Salomonovich's eyes. 'I imagine that, as a modern woman, I will be subjected to much worse language over the coming years Mr. Hume but I thank you for your concern.'

'Over the coming years!' Fraser Hume reflected on the opportunity the vivacious young woman before her had at last; an opportunity previously denied to her by Bühler and the Third Reich. Ian Smith considered the phrase too. For him there would be no 'coming years.'

'Al, Tony, let Sword, Gold and Juno know where we are. Hansen is in London. It won't take long for him to get here. When he does I want you to entertain his guys for a little while. Get 'em to clear up the cottage business, have 'em check the grounds. Anything, but get them out of the way. I need him to be alone.'

Felix Elder had begun another tirade. 'And gag that bastard before I strangle him. Listen, Vince Colletti and Mark Shatner are baby-sitting the Z team at the moment. I'm sure that you can keep them occupied. Ian, Connor and I can handle our end. When Connor gives the word, it's time for you to disappear. I'll see you at the next Giant's game with a bit of luck.'

Fraser took a chair, turned it towards him and sat with his arms on the backrest. 'There's going to be some changes around here Merrick and I do mean changes.'

Felix Elder struggled with the cuffs as Tony Molino unfastened him and led him from the room. 'The cellar for him. Don't make it too cosy and keep him quiet.' Tony led Felix away.

He turned to Julia Salomonovich. 'I guess the old arthritis has gone?' Julia, still assessing her new feelings, capacities and structure, answered weakly.

'Mr. Hume I cannot express my feelings in words. I ... I ... I'm not at all sure that there are words to... but most of all I suddenly lost that dreadful tiredness and I could breathe once again. I mean breathe as I once could. I had forgotten what it was like to take a huge deep breath. I imagine that it will take time before I feel free to move more expansively. For so many years my fragility has warranted caution and ...'

Fraser interrupted her; something he found to be strangely less discourteous to do to the younger manifestation of Rebecca Kinnear. 'I am sorry to be so abrupt', he began, subconsciously re-correlating and recalibrating his consideration and respect for the aged yet beautiful young woman. He had to push on.

'Madam'; he felt easier with this address, 'I need you to be as active as you can be. You are young and agile and must act as such. Our plans depend upon it. It won't be long before Sir Nicholas arrives. Please familiarise yourself with your capacities. It is essential if we are to succeed.'

Julia Salomonovich left the room.

Fraser took a deep breath and looked at Leroy Gomez. 'Keep close by Leroy. I'll call you when I need her.' He turned back to Connor John. 'Time to make another phone call Con. 'It's time for the last piece of the puzzle to be put in place. But before that ...' Fraser walked towards Ian Smith, put his arm around his shoulders and offered the dying man a bright new future.

Chapter 117

THE POLICE STATION

The facade of the old stone police station would still have been recognisable to PC Hollingsworth some forty years after his demise though the interior would have left that unfortunate gentleman as bemused and befuddled as ever.

A young constable sat at a computer punching the keyboard with some alacrity and not a little dexterity. The phone rang and he reached forward his attention still being given to the screen before him.

With the calm and practiced assurance bequeathed to him by past generations of the constabulary he offered his place of work, rank and name to the caller.

The officer's eyes widened as he scribbled the details of the disturbing communiqué. 'Sir, may I ask your name and how you came by this information?'

The line had gone dead before he was half way through his first request.

'Curious. Could be a hoax I suppose.' It took all sorts and that was a fact but ...well ... how could he respond? How should he respond? Would he respond at all? Of course - he must.

He turned to the desk sergeant.

Chapter 118

DÉNOUEMENT

Cecil B. DeMille. That's who he was: Cecil B De fucking Mille. Fraser sat in Joel's chair. His director's chair. He had chosen the film set, the actors and actresses; written the screenplay and determined the plot. Soon the central characters would take to the stage and the cameras could record a Poirot style dénouement. If only the cast could remember their parts.

Timing. As always. Timing. Hansen would be a further ten minutes. His progress monitored by Al Curtis. The affable constable who left the police station with his sergeant would be ably directed by Tony Molinaro and would enter stage left in accordance with Fraser's direction.

The Manor House was dimly lit. All he needed now was Norma Desmond to demand her bloody close up. He paced Joel Salomonovich's office honing his own lines.

The headlights of Sir Nicholas Hansen's Rolls Royce flashed a warning and the noise of the grinding gravel ceased abruptly with a crunch. Sir Nicholas was in a hurry.

He walked briskly to the steps of the Manor House, flanked by the two ever present burly bodyguards. The door opened before he reached it.

'You?'

Fraser Hume stood in the doorway.

'But, but ... I got a message from ...'

Fraser ushered the rarely confused magnate and his entourage into the hall.

'Ah, Sir Nicholas, you seem surprised to see me. Did we not agree that I should keep you informed of developments with regard to Joel Salomonovich's estate?'

Sir Nicholas Hansen raged within at Fraser's impertinence but maintained a dignified silence.

'Go on Mr. Hume. I had rather thought that you had forgotten our agreement but I am pleased to see now that you have been most conscientious in that regard.'

Fraser caught the barb, dismissing it with a mild rebuke. 'Well I take my work very seriously. I'm hurt that you would think otherwise.' The repost, he considered, was as pointed and as civil as the barb.

When the cool but civil exchanges were competed Fraser bade them follow him and they made their way along the hall to the reception room.

Sir Nicholas was offered a chair but refused it standing between the hired help. 'I am a busy man Mr. Hume. We have played our game for long enough and I have found you to be most resourceful but I am through with these shenanigans. I had a call from Miss Salomonovich this afternoon. She has indicated that a takeover is in the offing. I am here to offer terms. I have my proposals with me. The principles and sums involved will be decided shortly. The detailed contract will take our legal teams a little longer. I had not considered the fact that you would be involved in proceedings. Perhaps you will enlighten me as to your role in this matter?'

Fraser drew his quarry in further. 'To be quite frank, as you English are so fond of saying, this takeover leaves me in your employ;' he caught the triumph in Hansen's sneer; 'so I guess I don't have a role from here on in unless you want me to... but no, I guess not. Still, as my last farewell I'll take you to Miss Salomonovich and Ian Smith; they are waiting for you in Joel's office. I'll be back in the States before...' Fraser anticipated the movement of the two big guys. He put his hand up in repost. 'Sorry, the details may be dealt with by the experts but Miss Salomonovich is most insistent that this meeting is limited to the three of us. She was very clear on that matter. I could go see if she will change her mind if ...'

Sir Nicholas Hansen was steaming. 'I'm not being held up another second. Without turning he shouted. 'You two stay here.' With that Fraser opened the door and the two walked in silence down the hallway to the office. Fraser opened the door for Sir Nicholas.

'What the ...'

The scene greeting Sir Nicholas was not at all what he had expected. He walked into the office and saw Ian Smith lying prostrate on a bed with a number of electrodes attached to his head. Julia Salomonovich sat at the desk opposite.

As he began to turn to Fraser to demand an explanation a thick band of insulation tape was placed over his mouth by Leroy Gomez. Connor John and Fraser pulled his arms behind him and he was handcuffed instantly. There had been no sound.

Immediately Fraser and Connor John placed a struggling Sir Nicholas on a second bed and connected electrodes to his head too. The 'operation' took less than thirty seconds.

Sir Nicholas' wide eyes appealed for an explanation. The unpitying magnate was to find that the world reciprocated on this occasion and gave none. An electrical charge hit him and he lost consciousness.

Fraser didn't waste time. In contact with the whole operation he confirmed status. All was well.

The two recumbents began to stir. One was assisted, the other sedated and taken to the cellar. The cast was on cue; the prompter redundant.

Sir Nicholas Hansen stood tall. He walked gingerly towards Julia Salomonovich. !'My god twenty five years younger is good; I can't imagine what being sixty years younger would be like my dear.'

Julia Salomonovich nodded understanding. 'You have a tough task ahead of you Mr. Smith; I mean Sir Nicholas; and not much time to acclimatise yourself to your metamorphosis. Metamorphosis! Yes that is truly what it is.'

Fraser Hume's voice didn't betray the stress he was under. 'We have little time. The two Neanderthals next door will be getting impatient if they don't see their trainer soon. Sir Nicholas, I hope that you can make it next door and that you are able to convince Ug and his pal to come back tomorrow to fetch you. The ball's in your court now.'

A more generously spirited Sir Nicholas Hansen paced the room, getting his bearings as he did so. 'Good eyesight, no arthritis, no cancer, no pain. Good. At six foot I am now three inches closer to the ground. Perhaps that is good too. Further compensation? A few more quid in the bank I'd say.'

Fraser was impatient. 'Are you ready? I know it's asking a lot but can you manage it? Can you carry it off?' Sir Nicholas nodded. A relieved Fraser continued. 'OK, let's go.'

Fraser, Julia and Sir Nicholas walked down the hall to the reception room. It was clear that Connor and Leroy had had little report of Hansen's men.

They turned enquiringly towards their boss.

Sir Nicholas was ready for his close up. 'Danny, Brett I want you to go to Sword, Juno and Gold. Tell them that it's all over. I expect them to return to London. I'll have further instructions for all of you in the morning. I'm going to 'The Miranda' later tomorrow. The Italian lads will take over. I won't need you until further notice.'

The two guards looked at one another. There was a strained silence in the room.

It was Danny. 'Are you alright boss you sound strange and you said...'

Sir Nicholas Hansen was rarely questioned or contradicted. Ian Smith knew the truth of that. He glowered at his underling. There were no more questions. The big guys made for the door.

There was audible relief as the Rolls Royce turned from the gravel path onto the road. The actors dared to believe.

'Right, there's still plenty to do this evening. Don't take your eyes off the ball.'

Julia began. 'Ian I hope ...'

Fraser was abrupt. 'There is no Ian present. Please understand this right now. Who you see is who they are. You are Julia. He is Sir Nicholas. If we are going to get away with this you must stick with it. Is that absolutely clear to everyone?'

Rebecca Kinnear's tender sensitivity was etched in Julia Salomonovich's beautiful face. George Merrick, Julia Tyler and Sir Nicholas Hansen. The first she loathed; the second was lost to the real world and the third a duplicitous rogue who would have harmed her family without a second thought or regret.

None of them had been found guilty, condemned or sentenced by a court. All had been damned by the cabal now gathered in the office. She had suffered a great deal in her life but had never before sought recompense nor believed salvation to be her entitlement. It was with some unease and disquiet that she followed Fraser's instructions.

Connor, Leroy, Julia and Sir Nicholas nodded ascent. 'Only we here present plus Leroy Gomez, Tony Molinaro and Al Curtis know what we are about. Only this circle knows of the machine and its capacity. Only us. OK, next. We have Ian Smith and Felix Elder to get rid of. Smith, with due respect, Sir Nicholas, will be easy to account for; Elder less so.'

Sir Nicholas analysed his predicament too. Fraser's plan was perfect. A masterpiece. He got to live on. Sir Nicholas had neither wife nor child. He had the financial background to undertake the role of a magnate. The takeover would not take place; a merger would. Salomonovich and Hansen or Hansen and Salomonovich. Bigger than both of its parts.

Soon he would back off; put the business in the hands of his board and live a new life. He had loved the day to day cut and thrust of business which he had immersed himself in since the early death of his own wife. Perhaps he would go back and smell the roses. Yes, he felt well enough and young enough. A second chance. He wasn't young but, then again, forty two wasn't old either. With his money all things were possible. All he had to do was see Fraser's plan to completion.

Fraser Hume had another consideration which pragmatism and the need to focus on the immediate had temporarily diminished in importance. The machine. The device. Funny, that's what it was called. The machine or the device. Funny! No scientific name. Strange too that something without a name could become such a powerful weapon. It's possible uses were not lost on him.

Disposing of Elder was a necessity but Fraser had only a working knowledge of how to operate the machine not the capacity to understand its complex technology. If the boffins by the Potomac couldn't break it... well it would be lost forever. Perhaps he should keep it. Perhaps there would be a time when ... when ... It was time ... but not for that.

Fraser gathered himself. 'Right, Al and Tony get Elder and meet me by the folly. I'll be with you soon. Connor, help me with the other two.'

Time past quickly. Fraser had anticipated that it would take a little more than ten minutes for the troop to rendezvous at the folly. It had taken twelve.

'Leroy, it's time to attract the attention of the cops. The two of them are currently booking the 'Manor Poacher', three hundred, maybe three fifty yards down river from the lake. I hope the fine's not too big for your guy Sir Nicholas. Ian Smith's face shone in the moonlight. He rubbed the noble knight's finely chiselled chin. God he felt well.

Eton and Oxford had spawned many a fine actor. Rupert Carrington-Brooke was such a one. An unlikely rural poacher of no fixed abode and lacking any form of identification, he readily admitted to being the elusive rascal responsible to the crime Sergeant Dawkins himself had admitted to having done as a young lad.

The Sergeant had his pocket book out having caught Rupert, alias Samuel Beckett 'red handed.' The irony of the actor's second sobriquet being completely lost on the good sergeant. Perhaps, thought Rupert, he should have given the reason for his presence as 'Waiting for Godot', but thought better of it. It would only have confused matters.

Constable Marlow tried to put a face to the name. He had heard of Samuel Beckett but was unsure whether it was in his present patch or nearer Ipswich where he had served his time as a cadet.

Proceedings were interrupted by distant shouting. The two officers looked at one another. There were several voices and the volatility of the altercation placed the officers of the law in a difficult position. Difficult that is until the first shot was fired and a piercing scream pierced the night air.

The sergeant took three steps before turning to the sullen poacher. 'You stay right there; do you hear? Rupert gave a nonplussed gaze and opened his arms. 'Governor, would I?'

It was the last that the world would see of the infamous Samuel Beckett. 'The Manor Poacher.'

The two officers ran through the long grass making their way to the lake, torches in hand. Three hundred yards down the river they came to the dam and made their way along the bank. There on the far side, silhouetted against the lights of the Manor House and lit by the moon, were the central characters of Fraser Hume's play.

Act two was in progress. The principles were shouting at one another.

Chapter 119

AN INSPECTOR CALLS

It was the following morning and Sergeant Dawkins was rendering an account of events to the Sussex County Police Homicide Squad's chief inspector. Later Constable Marlow would confirm the sergeant's account.

Sergeant Dawkins began: 'A man now known to me as Felix Elder had his arm around an old woman's neck. 'If you don't back off I'll shoot her', he yelled.'

The chief inspector, more from habit than doubt asked, 'You're quite sure it was Elder who shouted?'

'Quite sure', was the slightly offended sergeant's reply.

'Please carry on.'

'Well sir', the sergeant offered with even greater certainty, 'the old chap says, 'You're going nowhere. Let her go and you can take the money. Just leave her alone.' But he made a fatal mistake sir. I shouted across the lake sir. I shouted, 'Stay where you are all of you.' Perhaps it was my fault sir. You see Elder turned towards me. Seeing his chance the old fella rushed him. But he was too slow sir. Elder shot him. There was a tussle as the old woman went for 'im. He shot her too sir. Just like that. As cool as you like.'

The sergeant stared into his pot of tea shaking his head. The chief inspector was not at all convinced. 'So you saw Elder shoot both Rebecca Kinnear and Ian Smith?'

'That's right sir and Constable Marlow saw the same. Sorry Sir. I'm sure he can speak for 'imself sir.' He grimaced at his error and stared harder at his tea.

'I decided that we had to get to the other side of the lake as soon as possible sir. It's a couple of hundred yards I should say to the far end of the lake where the river runs over the weir. There's a bridge there you see sir. Fastest way over. Another shot went off as we crossed the bridge. Mrs. Kinnear, god bless her, weren't dead, she picked up the gun that he must

421

'ave dropped.' The sergeant's brow furrowed. 'Funny thing that. Why did he drop the gun?' Momentarily reflecting he examined his teacup even further. 'Anyway he did and it did for 'im so to speak.'

'She picked up the gun you see sir. Mrs. Kinnear I mean. She shot him as he made off. Then she, sort of, well er, she died.

The chief inspector remained perplexed. 'So, what are we to make of it all? There are so many questions left unanswered. It's clear that you saw the incident and I don't doubt your account, or the corroboration of PC Marlow. Yes his account was remarkably similar when we caught up with him earlier. You certainly seem to have had an unhindered view, but it beggars belief that a theft or burglary gone wrong could escalate to such a degree. Then there is the location. Did the old woman and the infirm man jog after the super fit Elder when he legged it? Why didn't they ring us? What did they hope to achieve by confronting Elder? Did they know him? Was he a guest at the house? Sure he had three thousand in his wallet but who has three thousand sitting on the sideboard? Why did Elder throw the gun down next to Mrs. Kinnear? How did a dying old woman pick up the gun and shoot Elder from ten yards, killing him instantly? What of the shots you heard when you were with the poacher? Where the hell is the poacher? You see sergeant I know that you saw what you saw, and I don't doubt you for a moment, but how crazy is all this? It just doesn't make sense at all. None of it!'

The chief inspector paced the interview room confused and irritated. It was like a melodramatic Victorian Savoy opera except that three copses had littered the stage before the curtain had gone down. Still, the evidence was overwhelming. Two of the counties officers had witnessed the bizarre event. How did the characters get there? Who knows? The fact is that they had.

Another fly in the ointment! Documents recovered from the cottage suggested that Felix Elder had also previously gone by the name of Michael Mitchell and that the previous occupant, the late Professor George Merrick's papers had not been removed after his death. Facts were facts but there were so many loose ends. So many that little made sense at all.

The following evening's dew was suitably repelled by the wellington boots worn by all those present by the lake. Chief Inspector Sam Dexter stood at the far side of the lake with Sergeant Dawkins and PC Marlow shouting instructions to his officers on the Manor House side. He had asked the grieving Julia Salomonovich to light the building as it had been lit on the previous evening after offering her his condolences on the death of her aunt.

The view had been unhindered and clear. Yes, those on the other side of the lake had been fifty yards away and in silhouette, but if three people were shot, witnessed by two reliable police officers who had arrived on the scene within a couple of minutes of the incident... and then finding the said shot folk... OK there was a weird feeling to the case but ... well ... When Julia Salomonovich was up to it he would interview her. The chances were that she would have no idea what had really happened either.

Chapter 120

APRES DÉNOUEMENT

Fraser Hume, Connor John, Tony Molinaro and Leroy Gomez were offered drinks by the stewardess in the Club Class compartment. All accepted. All took their large Jack Daniels straight, slotted it home in one and ordered another.

At twenty nine thousand feet the 747 was making 481 knots.

The four had been silent for some time. Leroy Gomez swilled the second glass of amber liquid around his glass and took a shot. 'Penny for 'em Fraser.'

Fraser Hume smiled. 'I was just thinking that this case must be killing the guy in charge. How come he ended up with three bodies? Where the hell was the poacher? How were Merrick, Mitchell and Elder connected? He had two witnesses; two of his own officers. The question was: Why were they there? An anonymous call to the police station that evening had caused them to apprehend a poacher. The officers had been on hand. Luck? Any senior officer worth his salt would smell a rat. But would he put the rest of the story together? I think not.'

'Tell me this. If you had seen what Clouseau and his pal had seen would you come to the conclusion that those you saw shot were already dead? That the shots they heard when charging the poacher were the lethal ones? That when you got to the weir those responsible were making their way through the woods in the opposite direction? That the whole thing was a con? That the folks shot were not who they appeared to be? That Rebecca Kinnear was alive and well and not grieving for ... well herself?'

Fraser threw the rest of the second shot down and ordered a third.

'He knows there's more alright but he's shafted.'

Tony Molinaro smiled. 'Talking of being shafted...'

Fraser saw what was coming. '... and Merrick still got the last word. Good job the machine self-destructed before we attempted to board the plane.

I'm not sure that we could have explained that one away while on board. He was a crafty bastard to the end.'

Connor John turned off his reading light. 'Time for a well-deserved sleep. I guess Sir Nicholas Hansen and Julia Salomonovich will have plenty for us in the not too distant future.'

'Ain't that the truth?' Leroy Gomez rarely missed the opportunity to offer a coda.

Chapter 121

LOOSE ENDS

Sir Nicholas Hansen surveyed the Amalfi coast from 'The Miranda.' Was it so long ago and in Rhodesia? Yes it was Rhodesia when he last noted such an abundance of bougainvillea. He had travelled a long way since those heady days of independence in the new Zimbabwe.

He politely declined a whiskey and soda despite the seven p.m. ritual previously so rigorously observed by his predecessor. His valet had raised an eyebrow, either the boss was off colour or he had turned over a new leaf. Still, he would have one prepared on the following evening at the same time. On the dot as usual.

That was strange too. The boss had rarely thanked him for his services when not with guests or clients. Perhaps he had had some life changing experience. A metamorphosis or something? Still, just as long as he didn't decide to spend more time on 'The Miranda.' Life was pretty cushy when Sir Nicholas wasn't around and he had rarely had his services called on away from the yacht.

The villa came into view and Sir Nicholas recognised it immediately. It was exactly as the photograph had shown it. The photographs he was delighted to have found in his attaché case. Fraser Hume was certainly thorough.

There was much to assimilate. Here on 'The Miranda', left to his own devices, he felt comfortable. The villa could prove likewise. The contents of the safes would be most revealing, as would the contents of his bank accounts and financial affairs. But HQ? There he would be under the microscope. True he could lose his temper with an inquisitor and see him off but there was much work to be done.

Friends? The bastard had few of those. Colleagues? It was unlikely that he had considered anyone as such. Family? None. At least none of which he was on speaking terms. Lady friends? Who knew? Perhaps all kinds of folk would come out of the woodwork when he took up the reins. Business? His lieutenants may find themselves more trusted than they had previously imagined possible. Whatever happened he could feign illness. No one could possible suspect the truth.

He noted the launch being lowered and made his way to the aft deck wondering what mysteries the villa would reveal. He was not a youth but he appreciated his new found health and, taking a huge breath of Mediterranean air, vowed to keep off the whiskey and soda.

Sergeant Kathryn Ellis of the Avon and Somerset Constabulary stood at the door and enquired if Mr. Michael Tyler was at home. Mrs. Sarah Fossard replied that he was not but that if there was anything she could assist the police with she would be pleased so to do.

The fast-tracking young sergeant thought for a moment mentally checking her protocol before replying. 'Mrs?'

'Mrs. Fossard. Sarah Fossard.' Sarah smiled at the young officer and felt a little older.

'I'm afraid I have bad news for your ... I mean ... Mr. Tyler.'

Sarah ignored the faux pas and sought clarification with an enquiring turn of the head.

'May I come in for a moment madam?' Sarah opened the door and showed the sergeant into the lounge. 'I'm afraid that I have bad news for Mr. Tyler. His niece Julia Tyler was knocked down and killed in London yesterday and...'

Sarah Fossard slumped forward in her chair. The sergeant, trained for such occurrences, was immediately at hand.

'You were close?'

Sarah had lost Peter for the third and last time. Numbed by the finality she stared into the distance unseeing. Belatedly she took in the sergeant's question.

'Close?' She whispered breathlessly, 'Close? Yes I suppose you could say that we were. Yes, oh dear yes.' She dropped her head for a few moments before ... 'Would you care for a cup of tea?'

The sergeant accepted the tea as a duty rather than a need for refreshment. 'Oh I thought you'd never ask', she chirped. 'Come on, I think we could both do with a cuppa.'

She didn't leave Sarah until Mike Tyler returned an hour or so later.

The wedding plans for the following month would have to be delayed. Their four guests would understand. Lucy and Chloe would see to it.

Connor John's contact at MI5 had repaid a debt. Sarah Fossard had closure and Peter Fossard no searching relatives.

Fraser Hume stood amongst the thousands, hands aloft, in praise of a hero. The last minute touchdown at the Giant's Stadium had been blessed with genius, a commodity he had dealt with in large measure during recent months.

Walking out of the stadium he made his way to the hot dog stall. It was American and that was good. He had been away too long. Anything American would be just fine. He found his Mustang in the parking lot and checked his wallet for the barrier activating ticket. He thumbed the plastic card next to it pensively. The shiny new HSBC bank deposit card caused him to take a deep breath. The Bryant Park, Fifth Avenue Branch held a certain device and sundry other items. Banks, as always, provided useful insurance.

He took the New Jersey Turnpike north then headed across the George Washington Bridge. Soon he would be at the apartment he called home. Fifth Avenue never looked so good.

In the short term he would work for Joel's organisation and ensure that the merger went through smoothly. In the long term? Well he had never... no matter, there was probably all the time in the world.

Julia Salomonovich had heard the English saying that 'youth was wasted on the young.' Her resurgent spirit and new found energy beckoned a bright new future. Her brother's granddaughter had had so much to live for. Her life must not be wasted. Marta Salomonovich would have considered such a waste to be a sin. No, she would live the life that she had been so cruelly denied.

It was difficult for her to reconcile her belief system with some of the idioms of the young and their music, language and culture left her cold but, for the first time in more than sixty years, the optimism of youth propelled her into the modern world. The opportunity that she had been afforded would be used productively. She would go to the ball!

The Manor House and the village remained dear to her. She hoped that they always would. She would apply to university. True she had 'inherited' graduate status but now she wanted to learn more. She wanted to understand what her brother had built over up the years. She would study business.

When the merger had been completed she would take an interest in the business and subsequently learn from the very capable, and now caring, Sir Nicholas Hansen.

The last three months had passed by quickly. She was assimilating her situation rapidly, conferring respect to the aged and infirm previously afforded to her and accepting the patronising cant of the elderly with respect her perceived inexperience. She smiled at the accepted culture, understanding now that it was just that; accepted.

Accepted? Yes. Just that! Accepted into a society which took her for what they saw, not for who she was. Accepted into a clique of young folk without reservation where the elderly would be disdained. Sharing secrets reserved for her new generation. Hoping, dreaming and believing in a bright future rather than reflecting on a mellow past and all without the naïveté of youth but powered by its unflagging enthusiasm.

She walked past the village hall as she made her way to the post office when a gust of wind blew her beret off. A young man rescued it from the gutter wiping it clean on his jacket sleeve. Doctor Henry Owen's grandson, Lawrence, presented her with it gallantly. She found the young doctor's smile to be most agreeable.